Vladimir Ilyich Ulyanov (1870-1924), better known as V.I. Lenin, was the foremost leader of the October 1917 Revolution in Russia. He was a communist revolutionary and theorist. He served as head of the government of the Russian Republic from 1917 to 1918, of the Russian Soviet Federative Socialist Republic from 1918 to 1924, and of the Soviet Union from 1922 to 1924. His important books include, among many others, *What is to be Done*, *Imperialism, the Highest Stage of Capitalism* and *The State and Revolution*.

Prakash Karat is a member of the Polit Bureau of the Communist Party of India (Marxist) and its former General Secretary. He is the author of *Language, Nationality and Politics in India* (1972) and *Subordinate Ally: The Nuclear Deal and Indo-US Strategic Relations* (LeftWord, 2008), and has edited *A World to Win: Essays on The Communist Manifesto* (LeftWord 1999) and *Across Time and Continents: A Tribute to Victor Kiernan* (LeftWord 2003).

Revolution!

Revolution!

Lenin in 1917

Edited by Prakash Karat

LeftWord

Offset edition published in November 2017
Digital print edition, January 2020

LeftWord Books
2254/2A Shadi Khampur
New Ranjit Nagar
New Delhi 110008
INDIA

LeftWord Books is the publishing division of
Naya Rasta Publishers Pvt. Ltd.

leftword.com

ISBN 978-93-80118-65-9

CONTENTS

INTRODUCTION

Prakash Karat

V. I. Lenin's role in 1917 captures a unique revolutionary moment. Lenin's writings and speeches, between the February and the October Revolutions, embody what Georg Lukács called the "actuality of the revolution".[1] Lenin's entire corpus of writings in the eight months between the two revolutions offers a concrete lesson on the theory and practice of revolution. There are hundreds of pages published that record the theses, tracts, resolutions, articles, letters and speeches from Lenin. Some of the articles and speeches are written with a cool analytical mind, and some are written in feverish haste. Together they provide a unique view of how the revolution unfolded.

These writings—only a selection of which are available here—reveal the workings of Lenin's mind, which was able—by his close connection to the Bolshevik rank and file and to the masses—to grasp all the events as a whole with all their contradictions. Lenin was able to analyse the nature of inter-imperialist contradictions, coolly assess the correlation of class forces in Russia, see how the peasant masses were moving towards the revolutionary movement and set the "line of march" for the proletariat which had to lead the revolution. This was possible, no doubt, because even in exile and even underground Lenin kept in close contact with his party workers and the mass leaders. Their views and their tempo informed his writings at each turn.[2]

These writings of Lenin represent the culmination of theoretical and practical work which marks out Lenin as the only creative Marxist of his time who took the theory of Marx forward—as a revolutionary strategist, audacious planner of the socialist revolution and one who could set out the contours of a new State and society after the revolution. It is an astonishing fact that Lenin could complete his important work

[1] Georg Lukács, *Lenin: A Study of the Unity of his Thought*, London: New Left Books, 1970 (originally published in 1924).

[2] For a window into Lenin's relationship with the rank-and-file, see Cecilia Bobrovskaya, *Rank-and-File Bolshevik. A Memoir*, New Delhi: LeftWord Books, 2017.

State and Revolution in August-September, while being underground, just weeks away from the revolution. Here is the example of a dialectical genius who could theorise from a revolutionary movement in progress and by that provide the blueprint for a revolutionary state.

"Lenin in 1917" was not a sudden phenomenon. It was a product of an accumulation of revolutionary theory which combusted with the gathering mass discontent of the working class, the peasantry and the army of peasant soldiers on the war front.

Lenin developed this theory over a period of nearly two decades in mainly four areas, which had a direct bearing on the October Revolution. First, Lenin analysed the nature of capitalist development in Russia, understood the role of the peasantry in Russia and studied carefully the differentiation of the peasantry and its potential for revolutionary struggles. This was done in *The Development of Capitalism in Russia* (1898). Second, Lenin looked carefully at the Russian bourgeoisie and concluded that it was not capable of carrying out a bourgeois-democratic revolution. The task had to be taken up by the workers and the revolutionary sections of the peasantry. He worked out these ideas in *Two Tactics for a Social Democratic Revolution* (1906). Third, Lenin precisely studied the international situation, looking at the question of finance capital and the growth of monopolies, at the emergence of inter-capitalist and inter-imperialist conflict and at the places where revolutionary change—the "weakest link"—might be possible. This was accomplished in his *Imperialism, the Highest Stage of Capitalism* (1916). Finally, in two texts—*What is to be done?* (1902) and *One Step Forward, Two Steps Back* (1906)—Lenin worked out the role of the revolutionary party and the nature of its organisation as well as disassociated this kind of party from the revisionism that would make it unprepared for revolutionary times. Between the two revolutions, Lenin produced *State and Revolution*, which was—in a sense—the culmination of his theoretical endeavour. In other words, his analysis of capitalism and imperialism, of the national and colonial questions, his theory of revolution, and the role of the Communist Party in making the revolution, are not discrete ideas that Lenin came up with responding to contingent matters. His entire body of writings is part of a unified theoretical framework.

II

When the February revolution occurred, Lenin was in exile living in Zürich. For his first comments on the revolutionary upheaval in Petrograd, Lenin had to rely on newspaper reports.

Lenin's "Letters from Afar", were quite literally so, given the distance between Petrograd and Zürich. But in these five letters written in quick succession, Lenin sets out an audacious plan for a proletarian revolution. All the elements of the revolutionary theory, which would mark the full flowering of Leninism, are present in the letters.

The February Revolution and the overthrow of tsarism, he wrote in the first letter in March 1917, required an "all powerful stage-manager". This "all powerful stage-manager", Lenin wrote, "this mighty accelerator was the imperialist world war". Lenin had anticipated this in the text that he wrote between January and June 1916, *Imperialism, the Highest Stage of Capitalism*. The thesis of that book provided the impetus for Lenin's breakthrough in theory and practice. Stunned by the betrayal of most of the European social democratic parties at the outset of the First World War in 1914, Lenin sought to uncover the true nature of the war and the forces that fuelled it. What he found was important: that modern imperialism was the outcome of the development of monopoly capitalism, that rival imperialist nations were fighting for control over territories and over the division of the spoils, that workers of one nation were being set up to fight against workers of another nation in an imperialist war. This was Lenin's analysis of the war, one that set him against the "social chauvinists" of the Second International.

Lenin's assessment of the imperialist war led to his break with the German Social Democratic Party leader Karl Kautsky—his ideological mentor—and most of the other Social Democratic leaders such as Georgi Plekhanov (a leader of Russian Social Democratic Labour Party) and Emile Vandervelde (the leader of the Belgian Labour Party). Lenin and the Bolsheviks participated in the Zimmerwald conference in September 1915, where Lenin said that the socialists must "turn the imperialist war between the peoples into a civil war".[3] It was this

[3] *LCW*, Vol. 21, 1977, p. 348.

stance against the war that moved Lenin into his studies that produced *Imperialism* the next year.

Tsarist Russia was an active participant in the imperialist war, being part of the Anglo-French entente. The Russian social democrats were divided over the war. Led by Lenin, the Bolsheviks opposed the war. But their allies in the social democratic camp—the Mensheviks—and the Socialist Revolutionaries did not oppose the war. A section of Mensheviks supported the war on the grounds of "national defence". In 1915, Lenin wrote about the Bolshevik Party's clear attitude towards the war:

> In each country, the struggle against a government that is waging an imperialist war should not falter at the possibility of that country's defeat as a result of revolutionary propaganda. The defeat of the Government's army weakens the Government, promotes the liberation of the nationalities it oppresses and facilitates civil war against the ruling classes. This holds particularly true in respect of Russia.[4]

Here is Lenin's clear assessment—developed by his party—that "national defence" was a weak attitude towards the war, that the Russian socialists must try to convert the imperialist war into a civil war and that this warfare might sufficiently weaken the government and produce revolutionary conditions. This is precisely what occurred less than two years later.

Lenin characterised the February 1917 revolution as a "bourgeois revolution" and the provisional government formed by Alexander Kerensky as a government of capitalists and landlords. The situation had changed. Tsarist autocracy had crumbled—weakened by war and by the uprising of the workers and the peasants. In Kerensky's government, Alexander Guchkov was the new Minister of War, while Pavel Milyukov was the Foreign Minister. Neither wanted to take Russia out of the war. Lenin saw the changed situation clearly. In his third "Letter from Afar" (March 1917), he wrote, "Now we are in

[4] "The Conference of the R.S.D.L.P. Groups Abroad" (March 1915), *Lenin Collected Works* (henceforth *LCW*), Vol. 21, p. 163.

transition from the first stage of the revolution to the second, from *coming to grips* with tsarism to *coming to grips* with the Guchkov-Milyukov landlord and capitalist imperialism". Lenin had no illusions about the "capitalist landlord government" and its lack of will to end the predatory, imperialist war. In the fourth letter (March 1917), Lenin caustically remarked, "To urge the government to conclude a democratic peace is like preaching virtue to brothel-keepers". The bourgeois revolution was not capable of being revolutionary, as Lenin had noted in *Two Tactics for a Social Democratic Revolution*. This was now positive proof.

It was this revolutionary failure of the bourgeoisie that drew from Lenin his audacious leap. "The proletariat", he wrote in the third letter, "if it wants to uphold the gains of the present revolution and proceed further to win peace, bread and freedom must *smash*—to use Marx's expression—this ready-made state machine and substitute a new one". Here we get from Lenin an intimation of the necessity of smashing the existing state, which he develops later that year in *State and Revolution*. What was necessary was not to support the Provisional Government of Kerensky and to preach revolutionary defeatism, but to prepare the workers, peasants and soldiers to set up a revolutionary dictatorship of the proletariat and the peasantry. This could happen, Lenin argued, if the Soviets—the vehicle of the people's aspirations—supplanted the Duma (the bourgeois parliament) and took power.

With this revolutionary goal for a second, socialist revolution in view, Lenin called in his third letter for proletarian organisation. "You will not achieve durable victory in the next 'real' revolution if you do not perform miracles of proletarian organisation!", he wrote. The Soviets and the people's militia had to replace the old state.

III

Lenin arrived at the Finland Station at Petrograd on the night of April 3. The next day, at two meetings, Lenin read out his April Theses. These took the Bolshevik leaders and other revolutionaries by surprise. Astonishment, stupefaction and plain confusion were the reactions to the political programme Lenin set out.

The April Theses called for no concession to "revolutionary defencism", which meant the continuation of the imperialist war in defence of Russia. Lenin called instead for the revolutionaries to oppose the war and to end the rule of the "bourgeois-landlord government". He rallied the workers, peasants and soldiers to make the Soviets the real seat of power. This was the essence of the April Theses that Lenin expounded first to the Bolsheviks and then to a meeting of the Bolsheviks and the Mensheviks.

It was in these April Theses, which were published as "The Tasks of the Proletariat in the Present Revolution", that Lenin gave specific call for a second revolution. As he put it, "The specific feature of the present situation in Russia is that the country is passing from the first stage of the revolution—which placed power in the hands of the bourgeoisie—to its second stage, which must place power in the hands of the proletariat and the poorest sections of the peasantry".

Lenin recognised that the Bolsheviks—his party—were in the minority in the Soviet of Workers' Deputies. The task for the proletariat was to convince the other socialist parties that they must come over to the side of the Bolsheviks. "It is necessary with particular thoroughness, persistence and patience to explain their error to them", that is, to the broad sections of the masses who believe in revolutionary defencism. If the masses shift their view, then their representatives would be forced to follow. Patient work was required so that the masses could see that the Soviets of Workers Deputies are the only possible form of revolutionary government.

What is of note here is that neither the Mensheviks nor the Socialist Revolutionaries nor any of the other socialist parties produced the kind of precise theory developed by Lenin and the Bolsheviks. None of the Menshevik leaders—neither Plekhanov nor Vera Zasulich, nor Fyodor Dan nor Julius Martov nor Alexander Potresov produced a coherent revolutionary theory. It is a sign of the confusion that prevailed amongst the other socialist parties, who put their faith in the provisional government and could not see the power of imperialism. None of these party leaders developed the kind of theoretical armour that Lenin had prepared since 1898 and that the Bolsheviks had developed in their struggles since the split with the

Mensheviks in 1903. It was, therefore, possible for Lenin to call upon the proletariat to offer the Bolshevik theory to their class and to push the Mensheviks from below; no other socialist party had the theory to offer the proletariat at that time.

The second part of the April Theses set out the new forms of State power, with Lenin indicating various policies that would need to be enacted by the second revolution's state. The new state would not be a "parliamentary republic . . . but a republic of Soviets, Agricultural Labourers, Peasants", with their deputies from throughout the country. It would be a state that would confiscate all landed estates, nationalise all lands and end predatory landlordism. There would be no need for a police force and an army, nor for a bureaucracy. The Soviets would set up a "Commune State".

The direction of the new politics broke the link between social democracy and the Bolsheviks. It was time to change the name of the party and call it a Communist Party. As Lenin put it, "you must take off your dirty shirt and put on a clean one". He also called for the creation of a new International, not one that had been ground down by social democracy's vacillation.

The essential elements of Lenin's new revolutionary strategy had been contained in his "Letters from Afar". But these had not had a direct impact on the Bolshevik ranks. Only the first letter was published in the party paper, *Pravda*. The editorial board did not print the rest. They would only be published after the October Revolution.

The April Theses, therefore, became the catalyst and the initiator of the second stage of the revolution, which would succeed in October. Lenin had to struggle to convince the Bolshevik Old Guard and party committees about the efficacy of the new theses. The inner-party struggle lasted just three weeks. On April 24, at the National Conference convened by the party, Lenin's resolution was adopted.

Here was a rare historical moment, when the sheer intellectual power of Lenin's theory and practice set in motion a revolutionary vanguard to lead the revolutionary movement.

IV

Lenin had developed an agrarian programme for the Russian Social Democratic Labour Party (R.S.D.L.P.) based on his exhaustive study of how capitalism developed in agriculture, which appeared as *The Development of Capitalism in Russia* (1898). Lenin refuted the Narodnik (or populist) idea of a homogeneous peasant mass. He produced a class analysis of the Russian countryside, which analysed the main contradiction as between landlordism and the mass of the peasantry. He further identified the poor peasants and agricultural workers as the rural proletariat who would be the firm allies of the working class.

Lenin's distinctive contribution to the programme of the R.S.D.L.P. was his concept of a worker-peasant alliance to take on the tsarist regime and to isolate the bourgeoisie. The slogan of the revolutionary dictatorship of the workers and peasants was a concrete manifestation of the worker-peasant alliance.

The programme of the R.S.D.L.P. (1906) recognised the path of the peasant agrarian revolution. After the February Revolution, Lenin reiterated the programmatic demand of the nationalisation of all the lands of the landlords and landed estates. However, in the April Theses, the emphasis shifted to the disposal of the land by the local Soviets of the Agricultural Labourers' and Peasants' Deputies and the organisation of separate Soviets of Deputies of Poor Peasants.

The necessity of forging the worker-peasant alliance for a successful revolution dominated the revolutionary strategy of Lenin after February. The "crucial point of revolution" had arrived, as far as Lenin was concerned, in September, when "in a peasant country . . . a peasant revolt was developing". Lenin's keen eye on the countryside enabled him to see the direction of the revolution. To allow the capitalists and the landlords to crush the peasant revolt—as they planned to do—would be treachery. That is when Lenin called for the people of Russia to strike—the Bolsheviks had to set it off with an insurrection.

The imperative of maintaining worker-peasant unity continued after the October Revolution. Lenin called for the land confiscated from the landlords and estates to be redistributed to the peasantry.

The new State had to respond to the demand voiced by the congress of peasants in this regard.

The other crucial contribution by Lenin was on the national question, which was also directly related to the colonial question.

Tsarist Russia was a prison house of nationalities. Lenin advocated the right of nations to self-determination as the basis for an end to national and colonial oppression. He also articulated the class position that the working class of the oppressor nation should champion the cause of the oppressed people, while the workers of the oppressed nation should strive for unity with the workers of the oppressor nation.

Lenin wrote "The Right of Nations to Self-Determination" in 1914. He was the first Marxist to spell out the consistent working class position on the national question. In doing so, he countered the stand of Rosa Luxembourg and other Marxists who felt that the right to self-determination was a bourgeois category, which should be superseded by the unity of the working class.

Along with the peasant revolts, there was a growing ferment among the people of the nationalities under the White Russian yoke—in Ukraine, Georgia, the Caucasus and Central Asia. The Bolsheviks, by advocating the end of the tsarist empire and the right of self-determination, succeeded in harnessing support of the working people of these oppressed nations to the new Soviet project.

Lenin noted in October 1917 in "The Crisis Has Matured" that, "Next to the agrarian question, the most important question in Russia's state affairs is the national question, particularly for the petty-bourgeois masses of the population".

By September, the revolutionary unrest had affected the people of the oppressed nationalities. Lenin noted that next to the trade union curia, the most radical was the "national" curia in the Democratic Conference convened by the Central Executive Committee of the Soviets.

Lenin, unlike most European Marxists, was able to grasp the true significance of the national and colonial question. In formulating the Marxist stand on the national question in tsarist Russia, he also established the connection between the working class movements in the advanced capitalist countries and the anti-colonial struggles and national liberation movements in the colonies. Both were linked by their common struggle against imperialism and capitalism.

At one stroke, the Russian Revolution was integrally linked to the national liberation movements as Lenin had, in his revolutionary strategy, included the liberation of the oppressed peoples from Russia's "internal colonialism".

Thus the agrarian question, the national question and the national liberation struggles of the colonies were brought into the overarching class struggle. The struggles of the peasantry, the struggles of the oppressed peoples of the colonies and the working class of the imperialist countries were all bound together in the worldwide fight against imperialism, the centralised and highest stage of capitalism.

Lenin's revolutionary strategy had thus a worldwide significance. It is this strategy in the era of imperialism that launched the twentieth century as a century of revolutions and national liberation struggles.

V

How did Lenin steer the course for the party and the revolutionary movement in the succeeding months? The Lenin of 1917 was not a monochromatic one—the intrepid revolutionary who advanced step-by-step to the holy grail of revolution. The tactical genius of Lenin was in full display in these stormy months. There were many ups and downs in the period leading to October. At one time, Lenin envisaged a peaceful transition to the second stage of the revolution. This would have been possible if the Mensheviks and the majority could have been won over to challenge the Provisional Government and establish the power of the Soviets. The April Theses had emphasised the importance of patient work among the masses to win them over to the slogan of "All power to the Soviets".

By July, this work had yielded results in a situation of deepening crisis precipitated by the disastrous continuation of the war. "Down with the Provisional Government" was the slogan heard in mass demonstrations in Petrograd.

In the first week of July a million people demonstrated in the streets of Petrograd which shook the Provisional Government. The Mensheviks and the Socialist Revolutionaries in the Government sided with the rightwing in launching repression against the Bolsheviks who were held responsible for the near spontaneous mass protests. Hundreds of Bolsheviks were arrested and Lenin had to take refuge in Finland. It is at this point that Lenin, underground again, signalled a change in tactics.

In the second week of July, Lenin wrote in "The Political Situation", "All hopes for a peaceful development of the Russian revolution have vanished for good. This is the objective situation: either complete victory for the military dictatorship, or victory for the workers' armed uprising; the latter victory is only possible when the insurrection coincides with a deep mass upheaval against the government and the bourgeoisie caused by economic disruption and the prolongation of the war".

Lenin explained why the slogan "All power to the Soviets", which had been raised consistently since the April Theses, was no longer relevant. "The slogan *All Power to the Soviets!* was a slogan for peaceful development of the revolution which was possible in April, May, June, and up to July 5-9, i.e., up to the time when actual power passed into the hands of the military dictatorship. This slogan is no longer correct". Since the conditions had now changed and the other socialists seemed unwilling to go beyond the confines of the Provisional Government, Lenin began to push his party to prepare for insurrection.

By the end of August, the attempted *coup d'ĕtat* by General Kornilov had been defeated in which the Bolsheviks played a key role. By the beginning of September the Bolsheviks had won a majority in the Soviets of Petrograd and Moscow.

Lenin sent two letters to the Central Committee between September 12 and 14. In these he argued for immediate preparations for an armed insurrection. First, he differentiated between the Marxist and Blanquist conception of insurrection. "To be successful, insurrection must rely not upon conspiracy and not upon a party, but upon the advanced class".[5] He went on to point out the difference between July

[5] "Marxism and Insurrection", *LCW*, Vol. 26, p. 22.

and September. In July, the majority of the class and a majority of the masses were not with the Bolsheviks, so it would have been wrong to take power. But in September, the situation had changed. "We have the following of the majority of a *class*, the vanguard of the revolution, the vanguard of the people, which is capable of carrying the masses with them".[6] Further, the unrest among the peasant masses had reached a peak.

Lenin, who had stressed the importance of patient, sustained and planned work among the masses to win them over to the slogans of *All Power to the Soviets* and against the imperialist war, now urged the Bolsheviks to prepare for armed insurrection.

For Lenin, the end of September had "undoubtedly marked a great turning point" in the history of the Russian Revolution. The "crucial point of the revolution" had arrived. With the spreading peasant revolts, the nationwide crisis had matured.

In a note meant only for the leading committees of the party, Lenin warned that, "For to miss such a movement and to 'wait' for the Congress of Soviets would be *utter idiocy*, or *sheer treachery*". He concluded the note by tending his resignation from the Central Committee, so that he could freely campaign among the rank and file of the party and at the party Congress.

The final letter to the Central Committee members was dated October 24, just the day before the insurrection. "To delay the uprising would be fatal", he wrote. "With all my might I urge comrades to realise that everything now hangs by a thread". He concluded with this verdict: "History will not forgive revolutionaries for procrastinating when they could be victorious today (and they will certainly be victorious today), while they will lose much tomorrow, in fact, they risk losing everything".

Today did finally happen. The very moment when Lenin was dispatching the letter, the Bolshevik Military Revolutionary Committee decided to act, to pre-empt the decision of the Provisional Government to move against the party and close down their papers. The Bolshevik party led the insurrection and the October Revolution got underway.

6 "Marxism and Insurrection", *LCW*, Vol. 26, p. 24.

VI

Lenin does not, throughout the period between February and October, dwell much on organisation and the party as such. That is because Lenin in 1917 had already in hand a revolutionary organisation, the Bolshevik party. Such a party was shaped after an intense struggle within the Russian Social Democratic Labour Party (R.S.D.L.P.). The Leninist concept of a party of the working class emerged out of this struggle.

The biggest working class party in Europe, adhering to Marxism, was the German Social Democratic Party. It was a party with a mass membership that grew from 385,000 in 1906 to over one million by 1914. It was a model for other socialist parties to follow.

In Russia, Lenin argued for a different type of party. Under tsarist autocracy, there were no bourgeois-democratic liberties. A Marxist party had to organise clandestinely while utilising whatever legal opportunities existed. But this was not a model for a party working in conditions of harsh repression alone. In 1902, Lenin published his powerful book *What is to be Done?*—a tract which set out the concept of a revolutionary party and a revolutionary ethic. Lenin argued that the working class could not develop "consciousness" by itself in order to play a revolutionary role. Trade union activity would provide only an "embryonic" consciousness which is essentially economic. It would require a revolutionary organisation from without to inject the political consciousness into the culture of the working class. The party would thus be distinct from the class and would be constituted of the workers with an advanced consciousness—a vanguard. It would be through the network of trade unions, workers' societies and cooperatives that the party would establish live links with the workers and the masses.

Such a party would have to be a centralised one to take on the modern centralised state under capitalism. It would be buried by a discipline that would be like a "military" one, but which would be voluntarily accepted. Those who join the party would work like professional revolutionaries.

To create such a party, Lenin had to fight hard within the R.S.D.L.P.. At the Second Congress of the party in 1903, there was a dispute over the party rules regarding the discipline to be applicable to party members. Lenin happened to lose the vote on his version of Party rules. But he did not give up. In May 1904, Lenin published *One Step Forward, Two Steps Back*, which set out the main organisational principles of a party of the working class and effectively rebutted the Menshevik idea of a party. Lenin persevered and at the reunited R.S.D.L.P. Congress held at Stockholm in 1906, the principle of democratic centralism was incorporated in the Party rules.

Democratic centralism meant "Freedom of discussion, unity of action—this is what we must strive to achieve". Further, Lenin clarified this concept, "In the heat of the battle, when the proletarian army is straining every nerve, *no* criticism *whatsoever* can be permitted. But, before the call for action is issued, there should be the broadest and freest discussion and appraisal of the resolution, of its arguments and its various propositions".[7]

The organisation that Lenin set up went through various twists and turns as the Russian situation evolved. The 1905 revolution and the period between 1905 and 1907 saw the advance of the movement. It swelled the ranks of the Bolshevik group. Lenin had to fight to ensure that the more class-conscious workers entered the party.

It is during the 1905-06 period that the Bolshevik organisation became predominantly working class and the presence of workers in the party committees increased significantly. In 1906, 62 per cent of the party membership came from the working class. This was in contrast to the Menshevik membership, which in the leading bodies was dominated by intellectuals and middle class elements.

The period of reaction that followed from 1907 saw the party having to work illegally and much of the organisation had to go underground till the upswing of the movement which began in 1912. The Bolsheviks constituted themselves into a separate party breaking finally with the Mensheviks.

The Bolshevik organisation that existed in 1917 was thus one that had been steeled through clandestine work and the conditions of harsh repression. At the same time, the party organisations had utilised all legal and semi-legal opportunities to run newspapers, conduct

[7] "Report on the Unity Congress of the R.S.D.L.P.", *LCW*, Vol. 10, p. 381.

extensive political and agitational work among the workers and the mass of the population. The February revolution produced a military organisation committee which did political work amongst the armed forces and also raised the armed militias of workers. This was the party that Lenin helped produce. Its preparation before 1917 meant that Lenin did not have to write extensively about party organisation and party discipline during the revolutionary situation. The party came to 1917 prepared for action.

VII

Lenin emerged from 1917 as the potent symbol of how a social revolution can be achieved through revolutionary theory and practice. It is this message which has been sought to be negated and vilified ever since Red October.

The most obvious and persistent way has been to reduce Lenin to a Russian phenomenon. This was necessary to negate the universal significance of October. With the end of the Soviet Union, Lenin and his work, is to be seen as a historical relic—a failure in his own country. Even sections of the Left and radical circles have signed off on such an epitaph.

In these times of globalised finance capital, even the bourgeois ideologues, occasionally give a thought to Marx, especially when crisis engulfs the capitalist world as it happened in 1998 and more recently in 2008. Some have even hailed Marx as the "prophet of globalisation". But Lenin remains anathema, beyond the pale. Lenin can never be forgiven for putting into practice what Marx thought.

Lenin is thus portrayed as a conspiratorial figure, the progenitor of a revolution, which led to terrorism and violence, as well as the pioneer of a totalitarian state.

A powerful antidote to this toxic propaganda against Lenin and the Soviet Union is the writings and speeches of Lenin from 1917. What do we learn from a study of these writings? A radically different picture emerges than that put forward by those who would bury Lenin's ideas and contribution. Lenin is not the conspirator who succeeded in staging a putsch. Nor is Lenin the dogmatic ideologue who wielded absolute power. And certainly, neither does Lenin come off as a caricature of a dictatorial leader of a "vanguard" party that seized power and built a state that had no relation whatsoever to an emancipatory project.

The truth of Lenin in 1917 was something else, not these falsifications and vulgar distortions. Lenin's praxis occurred at a time when there was a global crisis of capitalism in the form of a world war waged by rival imperialist blocs. Lenin could see the link between the international crisis and the burgeoning crisis within Russia. He could grasp the contradictions which were sharpening and discern the forces which would be unleashed to bring about a revolutionary transformation.

If anything, Lenin's thought and action, between the two revolutions, reveals how the October Revolution was not set on a pre-ordained trajectory. Step by step, Lenin had to fashion the revolutionary strategy based on his theoretical breakthroughs. What brought about the revolution was Lenin's firm grasp of theory and his strong-willed application of that theory based on the ground-level realities of the revolutionary experiences of the workers, peasants and soldiers.

Lenin had understood what imperialism meant as a new stage of capitalism and identified tsarist Russia, embroiled in the crisis engendered by the world war, as the weakest link in the chain of imperialism. He had by the 1905 revolutionary upheaval concluded that the bourgeoisie was, against the conventional Marxist view, incapable of undertaking the bourgeois-democratic revolution. It required a working class-led revolution to carry it forward. According to Lenin, "The bourgeois revolution cannot be separated from the proletarian revolution by a Chinese wall". Again breaking with the conventional Marxist idea of the role of the peasantry, Lenin called for a worker-peasant alliance to end the tsarist autocracy and to aim for a far more revolutionary goal than a bourgeois republic. These were Lenin's creative application of Marxism.

By the time the February Revolution occurred, Lenin's theoretical armoury was ready having taken Marxism to new frontiers. All the elements of the Leninist strategy were in place. But it required a superhuman effort by Lenin to rally his party leadership around this strategy. From the April Theses onwards, Lenin began the arduous task of persuasion—to clinch the tactics to be adopted and put into practice. At every turn in the months of July, August and September, tactics and slogans were changed and recalibrated.

Contrary to the stereotype of a monolithic party with a supreme leader, Lenin's role in the Central Committee and the leading bodies of the party during this period bring out the intense and democratic character of the discussions. Here was a leader who set the pace by his sheer intellectual power and political acumen. Time and again, when he was in the minority, he had to struggle hard to win support.

So is the Lenin of 1917, merely a historical event, devoid of any contemporary relevance? A hundred years after the October Revolution, the world has changed vastly. Capitalism in the twenty-first century is not what it was at the beginning of the imperialist era. Imperialism today is fuelled by a globalised finance capital which is highly centralised and of huge proportions. The period ushered in by the October Revolution of the rise of revolutions and social progress ended with the fall of the Soviet Union and the advent of the neo-liberal age. It brought in its wake a host of sectarian, reactionary and backward looking ideologies. Though neo-liberalism has exhausted itself and has reached a dead-end, the turn towards a progressive alternative is yet to take place.

In such times, Lenin and his work, have great relevance. Lenin was faced with a bleak situation in 1914. The bulk of the leaders and parties of the Second International had abandoned proletarian internationalism and lined up behind their own bourgeois governments in support of the war. Confronted with such a setback, Lenin worked out a theory which enabled the Bolsheviks to exploit the crisis and mobilise the forces to make a revolution.

For this, Lenin had to develop Marxist theory by breaking out of the conventional mould. Lenin in 1917 showed how—armed with a revolutionary theory—it is possible to overcome all odds and make revolutionary advances. He established what he had declared earlier, in *What is to be Done?*: "Without a revolutionary theory, there can be no revolutionary movement".

It would be a truism to state that a revolution like October 1917 with Lenin as the navigator will not repeat again. But a century later, given the experience of the subsequent revolutions in the twentieth century, it would be equally true to say that future revolutions will have to be built on the essential elements that Lenin developed in 1917: utilising the social contradictions to develop the class struggle, strategy and tactics to widen the mobilisation of the people to isolate the ruling classes and a core organisation which provides the leadership and continuity. How new forms of revolution will take shape will depend on the theoretical advances made and the revolutionary praxis that will emerge.

What is required today is the rearming and renovation of Marxist theory just as Lenin did during his time. Equipped with such a theory, a revolutionary organisation and movement can be built which can bring together the millions of working people for a revolutionary transformation of society.

* * *

The texts included in this volume have been matched against the Progress Publishers, Moscow editions of *Lenin Collected Works* (1972, 1977, 1980). Lenin's own notes are marked as such (—*Au.*). All other notes are by the Editors of *LCW*.

LETTERS FROM AFAR[1]

First Letter

The First Stage of the First Revolution[2]

The first revolution engendered by the imperialist world war has

[1] The first four "Letters from Afar" were written between March 7 and 12 (20 and 25), the fifth, unfinished letter was written on the eve of Lenin's departure from Switzerland, on March 26 (April 8), 1917.

As soon as the first news reached him of the revolutionary events in Russia and the composition of the bourgeois Provisional Government and the Executive Committee of the Petrograd Soviet, Lenin began work on an article for *Pravda*—he regarded the press as an important vehicle of propaganda and organisation. "The press is now the main thing," he wrote to Alexandra Kollontai on March 3 (16). "I cannot deliver lectures or attend meetings, for I must write daily for *Pravda*," he wrote to V. A. Karpinsky on March 8 (21), in reply to the latter's invitation to deliver a lecture on the tasks of the Party in the revolution to Russian émigrés and Swiss socialists in Geneva.

The first and second "Letters from Afar" were sent to Alexandra Kollontai in Oslo on March 9 (22) for forwarding to Petrograd. On March 17 (30) Lenin asked J. S. Hanecki whether the first four letters had reached *Pravda* in Petrograd, adding that if they had not, he would send copies. The letters were brought to Petrograd by Alexandra Kollontai, who handed them over to *Pravda* on March 19 (April 1).

The first letter appeared in Nos. 14 and 15 of *Pravda*, March 21 and 22 (April 3 and 4), with considerable abridgements and certain changes by the editorial board, which, beginning with mid-March, included L. B. Kamenev and J. V. Stalin. The full text of the letter was first published in 1949, in the fourth Russian edition of Lenin's *Collected Works.*

The second, third and fourth letters were not published in 1917. The basic ideas of the unfinished fifth letter were developed by Lenin in his "Letters on Tactics" and "The Tasks of the Proletariat in Our Revolution".

Before leaving for Russia, Lenin took measures to circulate the first and second letters among Bolsheviks living in France and Switzerland.

[2] The *Pravda* editors deleted about one fifth of the first letter. The cuts concern chiefly Lenin's characterisation of the Menshevik and Socialist-Revolutionary leaders as conciliators and flunkeys of the bourgeoisie, their attempts to hide from the people the fact that representatives of the British and French governments helped the Cadets and Octobrists secure the abdication of Nicholas II, and also Lenin's exposure of the monarchist and imperialist proclivities of the Provisional Government, which was determined to continue the predatory war.

broken out. The first revolution but certainly not the last.

Judging by the scanty information available in Switzerland, the first stage of this first revolution, namely, of the *Russian* revolution of March 1, 1917, has ended. This first stage of our revolution will certainly not be the last.

How could such a "miracle" have happened, that in only eight days—the period indicated by Mr. Milyukov in his boastful telegram to all Russia's representatives abroad—a monarchy collapsed that had maintained itself for centuries, and that in spite of everything had managed to maintain itself throughout the three years of the tremendous, nation-wide class battles of 1905-07?

There are no miracles in nature or history, but every abrupt turn in history, and this applies to every revolution, presents such a wealth of content, unfolds such unexpected and specific combinations of forms of struggle and alignment of forces of the contestants, that to the lay mind there is much that must appear miraculous.

The combination of a number of factors of world-historic importance was required for the tsarist monarchy to have collapsed in a few days. We shall mention the chief of them.

Without the tremendous class battles and the revolutionary energy displayed by the Russian proletariat during the three years 1905-07, the second revolution could not possibly have been so rapid in the sense that its *initial stage* was completed in a few days. The first revolution (1905) deeply ploughed the soil, uprooted age-old prejudices, awakened millions of workers and tens of millions of peasants to political life and political struggle and revealed to each other—and to the world—*all* classes (and all the principal parties) of Russian society in their true character and in the true alignment of their interests, their forces, their modes of action, and their immediate and ultimate aims. This first revolution, and the succeeding period of counter-revolution (1907-14), laid bare the very essence of the tsarist monarchy, brought it to the "utmost limit", exposed all the rottenness and infamy, the cynicism and corruption of the tsar's clique, dominated by that monster, Rasputin. It exposed all the bestiality of the Romanov family—those pogrom-mongers who drenched Russia in the blood of Jews, workers and revolutionaries, those *landlords*, "first among peers", *who own millions* of dessiatines of land and are prepared to stoop to any brutality, to any crime, to ruin and strangle any number of citizens in order to preserve the "sacred right of property" for themselves *and their class.*

Without the Revolution of 1905-07 and the counter-revolution of 1907-14, there could not have been that clear "self-determination" of all classes of the Russian people and of the nations inhabiting Russia, that determination of the relation of these classes to each other and to the tsarist monarchy, which manifested itself during the eight days of the February-March Revolution of 1917. This eight-day revolution was "performed", if we may use a metaphorical expression, as though after a dozen major and minor rehearsals; the "actors" knew each other, their parts, their places and their setting in every detail, through and through, down to every more or less important shade of political trend and mode of action.

For the first great Revolution of 1905, which the Guchkovs and Milyukovs and their hangers-on denounced as a "great rebellion", led, after the lapse of twelve years, to the "brilliant", the "glorious" Revolution of 1917—the Guchkovs and Milyukovs have proclaimed it "glorious" because it has put them in power (*for the time being*). But this required a great, mighty and all-powerful "stage manager", capable, on the one hand, of vastly accelerating the course of world history, and, on the other, of engendering world-wide crises of unparalleled intensity—economic, political, national and international. Apart from an extraordinary acceleration of world history, it was also necessary that history make particularly abrupt turns, in order that at one such turn the filthy and blood-stained cart of the Romanov monarchy should be overturned at *one stroke.*

This all-powerful "stage manager", this mighty accelerator was the imperialist world war.

That it is a world war is now indisputable, for the United States and China are already half-involved today, and will be fully involved tomorrow.

That it is an imperialist war on *both* sides is now likewise indisputable. Only the capitalists and their hangers-on, the social-patriots and social-chauvinists, or—if instead of general critical definitions we use political names familiar in Russia—only the Guchkovs and Lvovs, Milyukovs and Shingaryovs on the one hand, and only the Gvozdyovs, Potresovs, Chkhenkelis, Kerenskys and Chkheidzes on the other, can deny or gloss over this fact. *Both* the German and the Anglo- French bourgeoisie are waging the war for the plunder of foreign countries and the strangling of small nations, for financial world supremacy and the division and redivision of colonies, and in order to save the tottering capitalist regime by misleading and dividing the workers of the various countries.

The imperialist war was bound, with objective inevitability, immensely to accelerate and intensify to an unprecedented degree the class struggle of the proletariat against the bourgeoisie; it was bound to turn into a civil war between the hostile classes.

This *transformation has been started* by the February-March Revolution of 1917, the first stage of which has been marked, firstly, by a joint blow at tsarism struck by two forces: one, the whole of bourgeois and landlord Russia, with all her unconscious hangers-on and all her conscious leaders, the British and French ambassadors and capitalists, and the other, the *Soviet of Workers' Deputies*, which has begun to win over the soldiers' and peasants' deputies.[3]

[3] Lenin here refers to the *Petrograd Soviet of Workers' Deputies*, which emerged in the very early days of the February Revolution. Elections to the Soviet began spontaneously at individual factories and within a few days spread to all the factories in the capital. On February 27 (March 12), before the Soviet had assembled for its first meeting, the Menshevik liquidators K. A. Gvozdyov and B. O. Bogdanov, and Duma members N. S. Chkheidze, M. I. Skobelev and others proclaimed themselves the Provisional Executive Committee of the Soviet in an attempt to bring it under their complete control. At its first meeting, in the evening of the same day, the Soviet formed a Presidium composed of Chkheidze, Kerensky and Skobelev who, together with A. G. Shlyapnikov, N. N. Sukhanov and Y. M. Steklov, made up the Executive Committee. Provision was made for inclusion of representatives of the central and Petrograd committees of the socialist parties. The Socialist-Revolutionaries were at first opposed to the organisation of the Soviet, but subsequently delegated their representatives, V. A. Alexandrovich, V. M. Zenzinov and others.

The Soviet proclaimed itself the organ of the workers and soldiers, and up to the first Congress of Soviets (June 1917) was factually an all-Russian centre. On March 1 (14) the Executive Committee was extended to include soldiers' deputies, among them F. F. Linde, A. I. Paderin and A. D. Sadovsky.

These three political camps, these three fundamental political forces—(1) the tsarist monarchy, the head of the feudal landlords, of the old bureaucracy and the military caste; (2) bourgeois and landlord-Octobrist-Cadet Russia, behind which trailed the petty bourgeoisie (of which Kerensky and Chkheidze are the principal representatives); (3) the Soviet of Workers' Deputies, which is seeking to make the entire proletariat and the entire mass of the poorest part of the population

....

The Bureau of the Executive Committee was composed, among others, of N. S. Chkheidze, Y. M. Steklov, B. O. Bogdanov, P. I. Stučka, P. A. Krasikov, K. A. Gvozdyov. N. S. Chkheidze and A. F. Kerensky were delegated to represent the Soviet on the Duma Committee.

On February 28 (March 13), the Soviet issued its Manifesto to the Population of Petrograd and Russia. It called on the people to rally around the Soviet and take over the administration of local affairs. On March 3 (14), the Soviet appointed several commissions—on food, military affairs, public order and the press. The latter commission provided the first editorial board of *Izvestia*, composed of N. D. Sokolov, Y. M. Steklov, N. N. Sukhanov and K. S. Grinevich; V. A. Bazarov and B. V. Avilov were added somewhat later.

Meetings of the Executive Committee were attended, in a consultative capacity, by the Social-Democratic members of all the four State Dumas, five representatives of the Soldiers' Commission, two representatives of the Central Trade Union Bureau, representatives of the district Soviets, the *Izvestia* editorial board, and other organisations.

The Soviet appointed special delegates to organise district Soviets and began the formation of a militia (100 volunteers for every 1,000 workers).

Though leadership of the Soviet was in the hands of compromising elements, the pressure of the militant workers and soldiers compelled it to take a number of revolutionary measures—the arrest of tsarist officials, release of political prisoners, etc.

On March 1 (14), the Soviet issued its "Order No. 1 to the Petrograd Garrison". It played a very big part in revolutionising the army. Henceforth all military units were to be guided in their political actions solely by the Soviet, all weapons were to be placed at the disposal and under the control of company and battalion soldiers' committees, orders issued by the Provisional Committee of the State Duma were to be obeyed only if they did not conflict with the orders of the Soviet, etc.

But at the crucial moment, on the night following March 1 (14), the compromising leaders of the Soviet Executive voluntarily turned over power to the bourgeoisie: they endorsed the Provisional Government composed of representatives of the bourgeoisie and landlords. This was not known abroad, since papers standing to the left of the Cadets were not allowed out of the country. Lenin learned of the surrender of power only when he returned to Russia.

its allies—these three *fundamental* political forces fully and clearly revealed themselves even in the eight days of the "first stage" and even to an observer so remote from the scene of events as the present writer, who is obliged to content himself with the meagre foreign press dispatches.

But before dealing with this in greater detail, I must return to the part of my letter devoted to a factor of prime importance, namely, the imperialist world war.

The war shackled the belligerent powers, the belligerent groups of capitalists, the "bosses" of the capitalist system, the slave-owners of the capitalist slave system, to each other with *chains of iron. One bloody clot*—such is the social and political life of the present moment in history.

The socialists who deserted to the bourgeoisie on the outbreak of the war—all these Davids and Scheidemanns in Germany and the Plekhanovs, Potresovs, Gvozdyovs and Co. in Russia—clamoured loud and long against the "illusions" of the revolutionaries, against the "illusions" of the Basle Manifesto, against the "farcical dream" of turning the imperialist war into a civil war. They sang praises in every key to the strength, tenacity and adaptability allegedly revealed by capitalism—*they*, who had aided the capitalists to "adapt", tame, mislead and divide the working classes of the various countries!

But "he who laughs last laughs best". The bourgeoisie has been unable to delay for long the revolutionary crisis engendered by the war. That crisis is growing with irresistible force in all countries, beginning with Germany, which, according to an observer who recently visited that country, is suffering "brilliantly organised famine", and ending with England and France, where *famine is also* looming, but where organisation is far less "brilliant".

It was natural that the revolutionary crisis should have broken out *first of all* in tsarist Russia, where the disorganisation was most appalling and the proletariat most revolutionary (not by virtue of any special qualities, but because of the living traditions of 1905). This crisis was precipitated by the series of extremely severe defeats sustained by Russia and her allies. They shook up the old machinery of government and the old order and roused the anger of *all* classes of the population against them; they embittered the army, wiped out a very large part of the old commanding personnel, composed of die-hard aristocrats and exceptionally corrupt bureaucratic elements, and replaced it by a young, fresh, mainly bourgeois, commoner, petty-bourgeois personnel. Those who, grovelling to the bourgeoisie or simply lacking backbone, howled and wailed about "defeatism", are now faced by the fact of the historical connection between the defeat of the most backward and barbarous tsarist monarchy and the *beginning* of the revolutionary conflagration.

But while the defeats early in the war were a negative factor that precipitated the upheaval, the *connection* between Anglo-French finance capital, Anglo-French imperialism, and Russian Octobrist-Cadet capital was a factor that hastened this crisis by the direct *organisation of a plot* against Nicholas Romanov.

This highly important aspect of the situation is, for obvious reasons, hushed up by the Anglo-French press and maliciously emphasised by the German. We Marxists must soberly face the truth and not allow ourselves to be confused either by the lies, the official sugary diplomatic and ministerial lies, of the first group of imperialist belligerents, or by the sniggering and smirking of their financial and military rivals of the other belligerent group. The whole course of events in the February-March Revolution clearly shows that the British and French embassies, with their agents and "connections", who had long been making the most desperate efforts to prevent "separate" agreements and a separate peace between Nicholas II (and last, we hope, and we will endeavour to make him that) and Wilhelm II, directly organised a plot in conjunction with the Octobrists and Cadets, in conjunction with a section of the generals and army and St. Petersburg garrison officers, with the express object of *deposing* Nicholas Romanov.

Let us not harbour any illusions. Let us not make the mistake of those who—like certain O.C. supporters or Mensheviks who are oscillating between Gvozdyov-Potresov policy and internationalism and only too often slip into petty-bourgeois pacifism—are now ready to extol "agreement" between the workers' party and the Cadets, "support" of the latter by the former, etc. In conformity with the old (and by no means Marxist) doctrine that they have learned by rote, they are trying to veil the plot of the Anglo-French imperialists and the Guchkovs and Milyukovs aimed at deposing the "chief warrior", Nicholas Romanov, and putting more energetic, fresh and more capable *warriors* in his place.

That the revolution succeeded so quickly and—seemingly, at the first superficial glance—so radically, is only due to the fact that, as a result of an extremely unique historical situation, *absolutely dissimilar currents, absolutely heterogeneous* class interests, *absolutely contrary* political and social strivings have *merged*, and in a strikingly "harmonious" manner. Namely, the conspiracy of the Anglo-French imperialists, who impelled Milyukov, Guchkov and Co. to seize power *for the purpose of continuing the imperialist war*, for the purpose of conducting the war still more ferociously and obstinately, for the purpose of *slaughtering fresh millions* of Russian workers and peasants in order that the Guchkovs might obtain Constantinople, the French capitalists Syria, the British capitalists Mesopotamia, and so on. This on the one hand. On the other, there was a profound proletarian and mass popular movement of a revolutionary character (a movement of the entire poorest section of the population of town and country) for *bread*, for *peace*, for *real freedom*.

It would simply be foolish to speak of the revolutionary proletariat of Russia "supporting" the Cadet-Octobrist imperialism, which has been "patched up" with English money and is as abominable as tsarist imperialism. The revolutionary workers were destroying, have already destroyed to a considerable degree and will destroy to its foundations the infamous tsarist *monarchy*. They are neither elated nor dismayed by the fact that at certain brief and exceptional historical conjunctures *they were aided* by the struggle of Buchanan, Guchkov, Milyukov and Co. to *replace* one monarch by *another monarch*, also preferably a Romanov!

Such, and only such, is the way the situation developed. Such, and only such, is the view that can be taken by a politician who does not fear the truth, who soberly weighs the balance of social forces in the revolution, who appraises every "current situation" not only from the standpoint of all its present, current peculiarities, but also from the standpoint of the more fundamental motivations, the deeper interest-relationship of the proletariat and the bourgeoisie, both in Russia and throughout the world.

The workers of Petrograd, like the workers of the whole of Russia, self-sacrificingly fought the tsarist monarchy—fought for freedom, land for the peasants, and *for peace*, against the imperialist slaughter. To continue and intensify that slaughter, Anglo-French imperialist capital hatched Court intrigues, conspired with the officers of the Guards, incited and encouraged the Guchkovs and Milyukovs, and fixed up a *complete new government*, which in fact *did seize power* immediately the proletarian struggle had struck the first blows at tsarism.

This new government, in which Lvov and Guchkov of the Octobrists and Peaceful Renovation Party,[4] yesterday's abettors of Stolypin the Hangman, control *really important* posts, vital posts, decisive posts, the army and the bureaucracy—this government, in which Milyukov and the other Cadets[5] are more than anything decorations, a signboard—

[4] *Octobrists*—members of the Union of October Seventeen, a counterrevolutionary party formed after promulgation of the tsar's Manifesto of October 17 (30) 1905. It represented and upheld the interests of the big bourgeoisie and of the landlords who ran their estates on capitalist lines. Its leaders were A. I. Guchkov, a big Moscow manufacturer and real estate owner, and M. V. Rodzyanko, a rich landlord. The Octobrists gave their full support to the tsar's home and foreign policy and in the First World War joined the "Progressist bloc", a sham opposition group demanding responsible government, in other words, a government that would enjoy the confidence of the bourgeoisie and landlords. The Octobrists became the ruling party after the February Revolution and did everything they could to ward off socialist revolution. Their leader, Guchkov, was War Minister in the First Provisional Government. Following the Great October Socialist Revolution, the party became one of the main forces in the battle against Soviet power.

The party of *Peaceful Renovation* was a constitutional-monarchist organisation of the big bourgeoisie and landlords. It took final shape in 1906 following the dissolution of the First Duma. It united the "Left" Octobrists and "Right" Cadets and its chief leaders were P. A. Heiden, N. N. Lvov, P. P. Ryabushinsky, M. A. Stakhovich, Y. N. and G. N. Trubetskoi, D. N. Shipov. Like the Octobrists, it sought to safeguard and promote the interests of the industrial and commercial bourgeoisie and of the landlords who ran their estates along capitalist lines. In the Third Duma the party joined with the so-called Party of Democratic Reforms to form the Progressist group.

[5] *Cadets*—the name derives from the Constitutional-Democratic Party, the chief party of the Russian liberal-monarchist bourgeoisie. Founded in October 1905, it was composed chiefly of capitalists, Zemstvo leaders,

they are there to deliver sentimental professorial speeches—and in which the Trudovik[6] Kerensky is a balalaika on which they play to deceive the workers and peasants—this government is not a fortuitous assemblage of persons.

They are representatives of the new class that has risen to political power in Russia, the class of capitalist landlords and bourgeoisie which has long been *ruling* our country economically, and which during the Revolution of 1905-07, the counter-revolutionary period of 1907-14, and finally—and with especial rapidity—the war period of 1914-17, was quick to organise itself politically, taking over control of the local government bodies, public education, congresses of various types, the Duma, the war industries committees, etc. This new class was already "almost completely" *in* power by 1917, and therefore it needed only the first blows to bring tsarism to the ground and clear the way for the bourgeoisie. The imperialist war, which required an incredible exertion of effort, so accelerated the course of backward Russia's development that we have "at one blow" (*seemingly* at one blow) *caught up* with Italy,

....

landlords and bourgeois intellectuals. Prominent in the leadership were P. N. Milyukov, S. A. Muromtsev, V. A. Maklakov, A. I. Shingaryov, P. B. Struve and F. I. Rodichev. The Cadets became the party of the imperialist bourgeoisie and in the First World War actively supported the tsarist government's predatory policies and in the February Revolution tried to save the monarchy. The dominant force in the Provisional Government, they followed a counter-revolutionary policy inimical to the people but advantageous to U.S., British and French imperialism. Implacable enemies of Soviet power, the Cadets had an active part in all the armed counter-revolutionary actions and foreign intervention campaigns. Most of their leaders emigrated after the defeat of the counter-revolutionary forces and continued their anti-Soviet and counter-revolutionary work abroad.

[6] *Trudovik*—member of the Trudovik group in the State Dumas, formed in April 1906 by petty-bourgeois democrats—peasants and intellectuals of the Narodnik persuasion. The group wavered between the Cadets and the revolutionary Social-Democrats, and in the First World War most of its members adopted a social-chauvinist position.

The Trudoviks spoke for the rich peasants, the kulaks, and after the February Revolution actively supported the Provisional Government. One of their representatives, Zarudny, became Minister of Justice following the July events and directed the police campaign against the Bolsheviks. After the October Revolution the Trudoviks sided with the counter-revolutionary forces.

England, and almost with France. We have obtained a "coalition", a "national" (i.e., adapted for carrying on the imperialist slaughter and for fooling the people) "parliamentary" government.

Side by side with this government—which as regards the *present* war is but the agent of the billion-dollar "firm" "England and France"—there has arisen the chief, unofficial, as yet undeveloped and comparatively weak *workers' government*, which expresses the interests of the proletariat and of the entire poor section of the urban and rural population. This is the *Soviet of Workers' Deputies* in Petrograd, which is seeking connections with the soldiers and peasants, and also with the agricultural workers, with the latter particularly and primarily, of course, more than with the peasants.

Such is the *actual* political situation, which we must first endeavour to define with the greatest possible objective precision, in order that Marxist tactics may be based upon the only possible solid foundation—the foundation of *facts*.

The tsarist monarchy has been smashed, but not finally destroyed.

The Octobrist-Cadet bourgeois government, which wants to fight the imperialist war "to a finish", and which in reality is the agent of the financial firm "England and France", is *obliged to promise* the people the maximum of liberties and sops compatible with the maintenance of its power over the people and the possibility of continuing the imperialist slaughter.

The Soviet of Workers' Deputies is an organisation of the workers, the embryo of a workers' government, the representative of the interests of the entire mass of the *poor* section of the population, i.e., of nine-tenths of the population, which is striving for *peace, bread* and *freedom*.

The conflict of these three forces determines the situation that has now arisen, a situation that is *transitional* from the first stage of the revolution to the second.

The antagonism between the first and second force is *not* profound, it is temporary, the result *solely* of the present conjuncture of circumstances, of the abrupt turn of events in the imperialist war. The *whole* of the new government is monarchist, for Kerensky's *verbal* republicanism simply cannot be taken seriously, is not worthy of a statesman and, *objectively*, is political chicanery. The new government, which has not dealt the tsarist monarchy the final blow, has already *begun to strike a bargain* with the landlord Romanov dynasty. The bourgeoisie of the Octobrist-Cadet type *needs* a monarchy to serve as the head of the bureaucracy and the army in order to protect the privileges of capital against the working people.

He who says that the workers must *support* the new government in the interests of the struggle against tsarist reaction (and apparently this is being said by the Potresovs, Gvozdyovs, Chkhenkelis and also, all *evasiveness* notwithstanding, by *Chkheidze*) is a traitor to the workers, a traitor to the cause of the proletariat, to the cause of peace and freedom. For actually, *precisely* this new government is *already* bound hand and foot by imperialist capital, by the imperialist policy of *war* and plunder, has *already* begun to strike a bargain (without consulting the people!) with the dynasty, *is already working to restore the tsarist monarchy*, is already soliciting the candidature of Mikhail Romanov as the new kinglet, is already taking measures to prop up the throne, to substitute for the legitimate (lawful, ruling by virtue of the old law) monarchy a Bonapartist, plebiscite monarchy (ruling by virtue of a fraudulent plebiscite).

No, if there is to be a real struggle against the tsarist monarchy, if freedom is to be guaranteed in fact and not merely in words, in the glib promises of Milyukov and Kerensky, the workers must *not* support the new government; the government must "support" the workers! For the only *guarantee* of freedom and of the complete destruction of tsarism lies in *arming the proletariat*, in strengthening, extending and developing the role, significance and power of the Soviet of Workers' Deputies.

All the rest is mere phrase-mongering and lies, self-deception on the part of the politicians of the liberal and radical camp, fraudulent trickery.

Help, or at least do not hinder, the arming of the workers, and freedom in Russia will be invincible, the monarchy irrestorable, the republic secure.

Otherwise the Guchkovs and Milyukovs will restore the monarchy and grant *none*, absolutely none of the "liberties" they promised. All bourgeois politicians in *all* bourgeois revolutions "fed" the people and fooled the workers with promises.

Ours is a bourgeois revolution, *therefore*, the workers must support the bourgeoisie, say the Potresovs, Gvozdyovs and Chkheidzes, as Plekhanov said yesterday.

Ours is a bourgeois revolution, we Marxists say, *therefore* the workers must open the eyes of the people to the deception practised by the bourgeois politicians, teach them to put no faith in words, to depend entirely on their *own* strength, their *own* organisation, their *own* unity, and their own *weapons*.

The government of the Octobrists and Cadets, of the Guchkovs and Milyukovs, *cannot*, even if it sincerely wanted to (only infants can think that Guchkov and Lvov are sincere), *cannot* give the people *either peace, bread, or freedom*.

It cannot give peace because it is a war government, a government for the continuation of the imperialist slaughter, a government of *plunder*, out to plunder Armenia, Galicia and Turkey, annex Constantinople, reconquer Poland, Courland, Lithuania, etc. It is a government bound hand and foot by Anglo-French imperialist capital. Russian capital is merely a branch of the world-wide "firm" which manipulates *hundreds of billions* of rubles and is called "England and France".

It cannot give bread because it is a bourgeois government. *At best*, it can give the people "brilliantly organised famine", as Germany has done. But the people will not accept famine. They will learn, and probably very soon, that there is bread and that it can be obtained, but only by methods that *do not respect the sanctity of capital and landownership*.

It cannot give freedom because it is a landlord and capitalist government which *fears* the people and has already begun to strike a bargain with the Romanov dynasty.

The tactical problems of our immediate attitude towards this government will be dealt with in another article. In it, we shall explain the peculiarity of the present situation, which is a *transition* from the first stage of the revolution to the second, and why the slogan, the "task of the day", at *this* moment must be: *Workers, you have performed miracles of proletarian heroism, the heroism of the people, in the civil war against tsarism. You must perform miracles of organisation, organisation of the proletariat and of the whole people, to prepare the way for your victory in the second stage of the revolution.*

Confining ourselves for the *present* to an analysis of the class struggle and the alignment of class forces at this stage of the revolution, we have still to put the question: who are the proletariat's *allies* in *this* revolution?

It has *two* allies: first, the broad mass of the semi-proletarian and partly also of the small-peasant population, who number scores of millions and constitute the overwhelming majority of the population of Russia. For this mass peace, bread, freedom and land are *essential*. It is inevitable that to a certain extent this mass will be under the influence of the bourgeoisie, particularly of the petty bourgeoisie, to which it is most akin in its conditions of life, vacillating between the bourgeoisie and the proletariat. The cruel lessons of war, and they will be *the more* cruel the more vigorously the war is prosecuted by Guchkov, Lvov, Milyukov and Co., will *inevitably* push this mass towards the proletariat, compel it to follow the proletariat. We must now take advantage of the relative freedom of the new order and of the Soviets of Workers' Deputies to *enlighten* and *organise* this mass first of all and above all. Soviets of Peasants' Deputies and Soviets of Agricultural Workers—that is one of our most urgent tasks. In this connection we shall strive not only for the agricultural workers to establish their own separate Soviets, but also for the propertyless and poorest peasants to organise *separately* from the well-to-do peasants. The special tasks and special forms of organisation urgently needed at the present time will be dealt with in the next letter.

Second, the ally of the Russian proletariat is the proletariat of all the belligerent countries and of all countries in general. At present this ally is to a large degree repressed by the war, and all too often the European social-chauvinists speak in its name—men who, like Plekhanov, Gvozdyov and Potresov in Russia, have deserted to the bourgeoisie. But the liberation of the proletariat from their influence has progressed with every month of the imperialist war, and the Russian revolution will *inevitably* immensely hasten this process.

With these two allies, the proletariat, *utilising the peculiarities* of the present transition situation, can and will proceed, first, to the achievement of a democratic republic and complete victory of the peasantry over the landlords, instead of the Guchkov-Milyukov semi-monarchy, and then to *socialism*, which alone can give the war-weary people *peace*, *bread* and *freedom*.

N. Lenin
Written on March 1 (20), 1917

Published in *Pravda*, Nos. 14 and 15, March 21 and 22, 1917
Published according to a typewritten copy
verified with the *Pravda* text

SECOND LETTER

The New Government and the Proletariat

The principal document I have at my disposal at today's date (March 8/21) is a copy of that most conservative and bourgeois English newspaper *The Times* of March 16, containing a batch of reports about the revolution in Russia. Clearly, a source more favourably inclined—to put it mildly—towards the Guchkov and Milyukov government it would not be easy to find.

This newspaper's correspondent reports from St. Petersburg on Wednesday, March 1 (14), when the first Provisional Government still existed, i.e., the thirteen-member Duma Executive Committee,[1] headed by Rodzyanko and including two "socialists", as the newspaper puts it, Kerensky and Chkheidze:

"A group of 22 elected members of the Upper House [State Council] including M. Guchkov, M. Stakhovich, Prince Trubetskoi, and Professor Vassiliev, Grimm, and Vernadsky, yesterday addressed a telegram to the Tsar imploring him in order to save the "dynasty", etc., etc., to convoke the Duma and to name as the head of the government some one who enjoys the "confidence of the nation". "What the

[1] The *first Provisional Government*, or the Provisional Committee of the State Duma, was formed on February 27 (March 12), 1917. On that day the Duma Council of Doyens sent a telegram to the tsar drawing his attention to the critical situation in the capital and urging immediate measures "to save the fatherland and the dynasty". The tsar replied by sending the Duma President, M. V. Rodzyanko, a decree dissolving the Duma. By this time the insurgent people had surrounded the Duma building, the Taurida Palace, where Duma members were meeting in private conference, and blocked all the streets leading to it. Soldiers and armed workers were in occupation of the building. In this situation the Duma hastened to elect a Provisional Committee to "maintain order in Petrograd and for communication with various institutions and individuals".

The Provisional Committee was composed of V. V. Shulgin and V. N. Lvov, both of the extreme Right, Octobrists S. I. Shidlovsky, I. I. Dmitryukov, M. V. Rodzyanko (chairman), Progressists V. A. Rzhevsky and A. I. Konovalov, Cadets P. N. Milyukov and N. V. Nekrasov, the Trudovik A. F. Kerensky, and the Menshevik N. S. Chkheidze.

Emperor may decide to do on his arrival today is unknown at the hour of telegraphing," writes the correspondent, "but one thing is quite certain. Unless His Majesty immediately complies with the wishes of the most moderate elements among his loyal subjects, the influence at present exercised by the Provisional Committee of the Imperial Duma will pass wholesale into the hands of the socialists, who want to see a republic established, but who are unable to institute any kind of orderly government and would inevitably precipitate the country into anarchy within and disaster without . . . ."

What political sagacity and clarity this reveals. How well this Englishman, who thinks like (if he does not guide) the Guchkovs and Milyukovs, understands the alignment of class forces and interests! "The most moderate elements among his loyal subjects", i.e., the monarchist landlords and capitalists, want to take power into their hands, fully realising that otherwise "influence" will pass into the hands of the "socialists". Why the "socialists" and not somebody else? Because the English Guchkovite is fully aware that there is *no* other social force in the political arena, *nor can there be*. The revolution was made by the proletariat. It displayed heroism; it shed its blood; it swept along with it the broadest masses of the toilers and the poor, it is demanding bread, peace and freedom; it is demanding a republic; it sympathises with socialism. But the handful of landlords and capitalists headed by the Guchkovs and Milyukovs want to betray the will, or strivings, of the vast majority and conclude *a deal with the tottering monarchy*, bolster it up, save it: appoint Lvov and Guchkov, Your Majesty, and we will be with the monarchy against the people. Such is the entire meaning, the sum and substance of the new government's policy!

But how to justify the deception, the fooling of the people, the violation of the will of the overwhelming majority of the population?

By slandering the people—the old but eternally new method of the bourgeoisie. And the English Guchkovite slanders, scolds, spits and splutters: "anarchy within and disaster without", no "orderly government"!!

That is not true, Mr. Guchkovite! The workers want a republic; and a republic represents far more "orderly" government than monarchy does. What guarantee have the people that the second Romanov will not get himself a second Rasputin? Disaster will be brought on precisely by continuation of the war, i.e., precisely by the new government. Only a proletarian republic, backed by the rural workers and the poorest section of the peasants and town dwellers, can secure peace, provide bread, order and freedom.

All the shouts about anarchy are merely a screen to conceal the selfish interests of the capitalists, who want to make profit out of the war, out of war loans, who want to restore the monarchy *against* the people.

". . . Yesterday," continues the correspondent, "the Social-Democratic Party issued a proclamation of a most seditious character, which was spread broadcast throughout the city. They [i.e., the Social-Democratic Party] are mere doctrinaires, but their power for mischief is enormous at a time like the present. M. Kerensky and M. Chkheidze, who realise that without the support of the officers and the more moderate elements of the people they cannot hope to avoid anarchy, have to reckon with their less prudent associates, and are insensibly driven to take up an attitude which complicates the task of the Provisional Committee . . . ."

O great English, Guchkovite diplomat! How "imprudently" you have blurted out the truth!

"The Social-Democratic Party" and their "less prudent associates" with whom "Kerensky and Chkheidze have to reckon", evidently mean the Central or the St. Petersburg Committee of our Party, which was restored at the January 1912 Conference,[2] those very same "Bolsheviks"

[2] The composition of the C.C. Bureau in Russia on March 9 (22), 1917 was as follows: A. I. Yelizarova, K. S. Yeremeyev, V. N. Zalezhsky, P. A. Zalutsky, M. I. Kalinin, V. M. Molotov, M. S. Olminsky, A. M. Smirnov, Y. D. Stasova, M. I. Ulyanova, M. I. Khakharev, K. M. Shvedchikov, A. G. Shlyapnikov and K. I. Shutko. On March 12 (25). G. I. Bokii and M. K. Muranov were added, also J. V. Stalin, with voice but no vote.

The *Petrograd Committee of the R.S.D.L.P.* was formed at a meeting on March 2 (15), 1917, and was composed of all those who had served on the illegal committees and newly co-opted members. The composition was: B. V. Avilov, N. K. Antipov, B. A. Zhemchuzhin, V. N. Zalezhsky, M. I. Kalinin, N. P. Komarov, L. M. Mikhailov, V. M. Molotov, K. Orlov, N. I. Podvoisky, P. I. Stučka, V. V. Schmidt, K. I. Shutko and A. G. Shlyapnikov, representing the Central Committee Bureau.

On the January (Prague) Conference, to which Lenin refers: In January at whom the bourgeoisie always hurl the abusive term "doctrinaires", because of their faithfulness to the "doctrine", i.e., the fundamentals, the principles, teachings, aims of *socialism*. Obviously, the English Guchkovite hurls the abusive terms seditious and doctrinaire at the manifesto[3] and at the conduct of our Party in urging a fight for a

....

1912 the Mensheviks were expelled from the Party by decision of the Sixth (Prague) Conference of the R.S.D.L.P.

The Sixth All-Russia Conference of the R.S.D.L.P. met from January 5 to January 17 (18-30), 1912 in Prague and actually assumed the character of a Party congress.

Lenin was the leading figure at the Conference. He delivered the reports on the current situation and the tasks of the Party, the work of the International Socialist Bureau, and took part in the discussions. He also drafted the resolutions on all major agenda items.

The Conference resolutions on "Liquidationism and the Group of Liquidators" and on "The Party Organisation Abroad" were of tremendous theoretical and practical significance. The Conference declared that by their conduct the liquidators had definitely placed themselves outside the Party and expelled them from the R.S.D.L.P. The Conference condemned the activities of the anti-Party groups abroad—the Menshevik *Golos* group, the *Vperyod* and Trotsky groups, and recognised the absolute necessity for a single Party organisation abroad, conducting its work under the supervision and guidance of the C.C., and pointed out that Party groups abroad "which refuse to submit to the Russian centre of Social-Democratic activity, i.e., to the Central Committee, and which cause disorganisation by communicating with Russia independently and ignoring the Central Committee, have no right to use the name of the R.S.D.L.P." The Conference adopted a resolution on "The Character and Organisational Forms of Party Work", approved Lenin's draft Organisational Rules, made the newspaper *Sotsial-Demokrat* the Party Central Organ, elected a Party Central Committee and set up the Bureau of the C.C. in Russia.

The Prague Conference played an outstanding part in building the Bolshevik Party, a party of a new type, and in strengthening its unity. It summed up a whole historical period of struggle against the Mensheviks, consolidated the victory of the Bolsheviks and expelled the Menshevik liquidators from the Party. Local Party organisations rallied still closer round the Party on the basis of the Conference decisions. The Conference strengthened the Party as an all-Russian organisation and defined its political line and tactics in the conditions of the new revolutionary upsurge. The Prague Conference was of great international significance. It showed the revolutionary elements of the parties of the Second International how to conduct a decisive struggle against opportunism by carrying the fight to a complete organisational break with the opportunists.

3 This refers to the *Manifesto of the Russian Social-Democratic Labour Party*

republic, peace, complete destruction of the tsarist monarchy, bread for the people.

Bread for the people and peace—that's sedition, but ministerial posts for Guchkov and Milyukov—that's "order". Old and familiar talk!

What, then, are the tactics of Kerensky and Chkheidze as characterised by the English Guchkovite?

Vacillation: on the one hand, the Guchkovite praises them: they "realise" (Good boys! Clever boys!) that without the "support" of the army officers and the more moderate elements, anarchy cannot be avoided (we, however, have always thought, in keeping with our doctrine, with our socialist teachings, that it is the capitalists who introduce anarchy and war into human society, that only the transfer of *all* political power to the proletariat and the poorest people can rid us of war, of anarchy and starvation!). On the other hand, they "have to reckon with their less prudent associates", i.e., the Bolsheviks, the Russian Social-Democratic Labour Party, restored and united by the Central Committee.

What is the force that compels Kerensky and Chkheidze to "reckon" with the Bolshevik Party to which they have *never* belonged, which they, or their literary representatives (Socialist-Revolutionaries, Popular Socialists,[4] the Menshevik O.C. supporters, and so forth), have always abused, condemned, denounced as an insignificant underground circle, a sect of doctrinaires, and so forth? Where and when has it ever happened that in time of revolution, at a time of predominantly *mass* action, sane-minded politicians should "reckon" with "doctrinaires"??

He is all mixed up, our poor English Guchkovite; he has failed to produce a logical argument, has failed to tell either a whole lie or the whole truth, he has merely given himself away.

....

to All the Citizens of Russia, issued by the Central Committee and published as a supplement to *Izvestia* of February 28 (March 13), 1917 (No. 1). Lenin learned of the Manifesto from an abridged version in the morning edition of the *Frankfurter Zeitung*, March 9 (22), 1917. On the following day he wired *Pravda* in Petrograd via Oslo: "Have just read excerpts from the Central Committee Manifesto. Best wishes. Long live the proletarian militia, harbinger of peace and socialism!"

[4] See Note No. 2, p. 78 of this volume.

Kerensky and Chkheidze are compelled to reckon with the Social-Democratic Party of the Central Committee by the influence it exerts on the proletariat, on the masses. Our Party was found to be with the masses, with the revolutionary proletariat, *in spite* of the arrest and deportation of our Duma deputies to Siberia, as far back as 1914, in spite of the fierce persecution and arrests to which the St. Petersburg Committee was subjected for its underground activities during the war, *against* the war and against tsarism.

"Facts are stubborn things," as the English proverb has it. Let me remind you of it, most esteemed English Guchkovite! That our Party guided, or at least rendered devoted assistance to, the St. Petersburg workers in the great days of revolution is a fact the English Guchkovite "*himself*" was *obliged* to admit. And he was equally obliged to admit the fact that Kerensky and Chkheidze are oscillating *between* the bourgeoisie and the proletariat. The Gvozdyovites, the "defencists", i.e., the social-chauvinists, i.e., the defenders of the imperialist, predatory war, are now completely following the bourgeoisie; Kerensky, by entering the ministry, i.e., the second Provisional Government, has also completely deserted to the bourgeoisie; Chkheidze has not; he continues to *oscillate* between the Provisional Government of the bourgeoisie, the Guchkovs and Milyukovs, and the "provisional government" of the proletariat and the poorest masses of the people, the Soviet of Workers' Deputies and the Russian Social-Democratic Labour Party united by the Central Committee.

Consequently, the revolution has confirmed what we especially insisted on when we urged the workers clearly to realise the class difference between the principal parties and principal trends in the working-class movement and among the petty bourgeoisie—what we wrote, for example, in the Geneva *Sotsial-Demokrat* No. 47, nearly eighteen months ago, on October 13, 1915.

"As hitherto, we consider it admissible for Social-Democrats to join a provisional revolutionary government together with the democratic petty bourgeoisie, but *not* with the revolutionary chauvinists. By revolutionary chauvinists we mean those who want a victory over tsarism so as to achieve victory over Germany—plunder other countries—consolidate Great-Russian rule over the other peoples of Russia, etc. Revolutionary chauvinism is based on the class position of the petty bourgeoisie. The latter always vacillates between the bourgeoisie and the proletariat. At present it is vacillating between chauvinism (which prevents it from being consistently revolutionary, even in the meaning of a democratic revolution) and proletarian internationalism. At the moment the Trudoviks, the Socialist-Revolutionaries, *Nasha Zarya* (now *Dyelo*), Chkheidze's Duma group, the Organising Committee, Mr. Plekhanov and the like are political spokesmen for this petty bourgeoisie in Russia. If the revolutionary chauvinists won in Russia, we would be opposed to a defence of *their* 'fatherland' in the present war. Our slogan is: against the chauvinists, even if they are revolutionary and republican—*against* them and *for* an alliance of the international proletariat for the socialist revolution."[5]

But let us return to the English Guchkovite.

". . . The Provisional Committee of the Imperial Duma," he continues, "appreciating the dangers ahead, have purposely refrained from carrying out the original intention of arresting Ministers, although they could have done so yesterday without the slightest difficulty. The door is thus left open for negotiations, thanks to which we ["we"=British finance capital and imperialism] may obtain all the benefits of the new regime without passing through the dread ordeal of the Commune and the anarchy of civil war . . . ."

The Guchkovites were *for* a civil war from which *they* would benefit, but they are *against* a civil war from which the people, i.e., the actual majority of the working people, would benefit.

". . . The relations between the Provisional Committee of the Duma, which represents the whole nation [imagine saying this about the committee of the landlord and capitalist Fourth Duma!], and the Council of Labour Deputies, representing purely class interests [this is the language of a diplomat who has heard learned words with one ear and wants to conceal the fact that the Soviet of Workers' Deputies represents the proletariat and the poor, i.e., nine-tenths of the population], but in a crisis like the present wielding enormous power, have aroused no small misgivings among reasonable men regarding

[5] See *LCW*, Vol. 21, 1977, p. 403.

the possibility of a conflict between them—the results of which might be too terrible to describe.

"Happily this danger has been averted, at least for the present [note the "at least"!], thanks to the influence of M. Kerensky, a young lawyer of much oratorical ability, who clearly realises [unlike Chkheidze, who also "realised", but evidently less clearly in the opinion of the Guchkovite?] the necessity of working with the Committee in the interests of his Labour constituents [i.e., to catch the workers' votes, to flirt with them]. A satisfactory Agreement[6] was concluded today [Wednesday, March 1/14], whereby all unnecessary friction will be avoided."

What this agreement was, whether it was concluded with the *whole* of the Soviet of Workers' Deputies and on what terms, we do not know. On this *chief* point, the English Guchkovite says nothing at all this time. And no wonder! It is not to the advantage of the bourgeoisie to have these terms made clear, precise and known to all, for it would then be more difficult for it to violate them!

The preceding lines were already written when I read two very important communications. First, in that most conservative and bourgeois Paris newspaper *Le Temps*[7] of March 20, the text of the Soviet of Workers' Deputies manifesto appealing for "support" of the new government[8]; second, excerpts from Skobelev's speech in

[6] Reference is to the agreement concluded on the night following March 1 (14), 1917 between the Duma Provisional Committee and the Socialist-Revolutionary and Menshevik leaders of the Petrograd Soviet Executive Committee. The latter voluntarily surrendered power to the bourgeoisie and authorised the Duma Provisional Committee to form a Provisional Government of its own choice.

[7] *Le Temps*—a daily paper published in Paris from 1861 to 1942. Spoke for the ruling element and was the factual organ of the French Foreign Ministry.

[8] The Manifesto of the Executive Committee of the Soviet of Workers' and Soldiers' Deputies was published in *Izvestia* on March 3 (16), 1917 (No. 4), simultaneously with the announcement of the formation of a Provisional Government under Prince Lvov. Drawn up by the Socialist-Revolutionary and Menshevik members of the Executive

Committee, it declared that the democratic forces would support the new government "to the extent that it carries out its undertakings and wages a determined struggle against the old regime".

The Manifesto did not mention the fact that the Soviet had

the State Duma on March 1 (14), reproduced in a Zürich newspaper (*Neue Zürcher Zeitung*, 1 Mit.-bl., March 21) from a Berlin newspaper (*National-Zeitung*[9]).

The manifesto of the Soviet of Workers' Deputies, if the text has not been distorted by the French imperialists, is a most remarkable document. It shows that the St. Petersburg proletariat, at least at the time the manifesto was issued, was under the predominating influence of petty-bourgeois politicians. You will recall that in this category of politicians I include, as has been already mentioned above, people of the type of Kerensky and Chkheidze.

In the manifesto we find two political ideas, and two slogans corresponding to them:

Firstly. The manifesto says that the government (the new one) consists of "moderate elements". A strange description, by no means complete, of a purely liberal, not of a Marxist character. I too am prepared to agree that in a certain sense—in my next letter I will show in precisely what sense—now, with the first stage of the revolution completed, every government must be "moderate". But it is absolutely impermissible to conceal from ourselves and from the people that this government wants to continue the imperialist war, that it is an agent of British capital, that it wants to restore the monarchy and strengthen the rule of the landlords and capitalists.

The manifesto declares that all democrats must "support" the new government and that the Soviet of Workers' Deputies requests and authorises Kerensky to enter the Provisional Government. The conditions—implementation of the promised reforms already during

....

authorised Kerensky to join the new government, inasmuch as on March 1 (14) the Executive Committee had decided "not to delegate democratic representatives to the government". *Le Temps* reported this in a despatch from its correspondent. On March 2 (15) the Soviet, "defying the protest of the minority", approved Kerensky's entry into the government as Minister of Justice.

9 *Neue Zürcher Zeitung*—a bourgeois newspaper, founded in Zürich in 1780 and until 1821 published under the name *Zürcher Zeitung*, now the most influential paper in Switzerland.

National-Zeitung—a capitalist newspaper published in Berlin from 1848 to 1938; beginning with 1914 appeared under the name *Acht-Uhr Abendsblatt. National-Zeitung.*

the war, guarantees for the "free cultural" (only??) development of the nationalities (a purely Cadet, wretchedly liberal programme), and the establishment of a special committee consisting of members of the Soviet of Workers' Deputies and of "military men"[10] to supervise the activities of the Provisional Government.

This Supervising Committee, which comes within the second category of ideas and slogans, we will discuss separately further on.

The appointment of the Russian Louis Blanc, Kerensky, and the appeal to support the new government is, one may say, a classical example of betrayal of the cause of the revolution and the cause of the proletariat, a betrayal which doomed a number of nineteenth-century revolutions, irrespective of how sincere and devoted to socialism the leaders and supporters of such a policy may have been.

The proletariat cannot and must not support a war government, a restoration government. To fight reaction, to rebuff all possible and probable attempts by the Romanovs and their friends to restore the monarchy and muster a counter-revolutionary army, it is necessary not to support Guchkov and Co., but to *organise*, expand and strengthen a *proletarian* militia, to arm the people under the leadership of the workers. Without this principal, fundamental, radical measure, there can be no question either of offering serious resistance to the restoration of the monarchy and attempts to rescind or curtail the promised freedoms, or of firmly taking the road that will give the people bread, *peace* and freedom.

If it is true that Chkheidze, who, with Kerensky, was a member of

[10] The foreign press reported the appointment by the Petrograd Soviet of a special body to keep check on the Provisional Government. On the basis of this report, Lenin at first welcomed the organisation of this control body, pointing out, however, that only experience would show whether it would live up to expectations. Actually, this so-called Contact Committee, appointed by the Executive on March 8 (21) to "influence" and "control" the work of the Provisional Government, only helped the latter exploit the prestige of the Soviet as a cover for its counter-revolutionary policy. The Contact Committee consisted of M. I. Skobelev, Y. M. Steklov, N. N. Sukhanov, V. N. Filippovsky, N. S. Chkheidze and, later, V. M. Chernov and I. G. Tsereteli. It helped keep the masses from active revolutionary struggle for the transfer of power to the Soviets. The committee was dissolved in April 1917, when its functions were taken over by the Petrograd Soviet Executive Committee Bureau.

the first Provisional Government (the Duma committee of thirteen), refrained from entering the second Provisional Government out of principled considerations of the above-mentioned or similar character, then that does him credit. That must be said frankly. Unfortunately, such an interpretation is contradicted by the facts, and primarily by the speech delivered by Skobelev, who has always gone hand in hand with Chkheidze.

Skobelev said, if the above-mentioned source is to be trusted, that "the social [? evidently the Social-Democratic] group and the workers are only slightly in touch (have little contact) with the aims of the Provisional Government", that the workers are demanding peace, and that if the war is continued there will be disaster in the spring anyhow, that "the workers have concluded with society [liberal society] a temporary agreement [*eine vorläufige Waffenfreundschaft*], although their political aims are as far removed from the aims of society as heaven is from earth", that "the liberals must abandon the senseless [*unsinnige*] aims of the war", etc.

This speech is a sample of what we called above, in the excerpt from *Sotsial-Demokrat*, "oscillation" between the bourgeoisie and the proletariat. The liberals, while remaining liberals, *cannot* "abandon" the "senseless" aims of the war, which, incidently, are not determined by them alone, but by Anglo-French finance capital, a world-mighty force measured by hundreds of billions. The task is not to "coax" the liberals, but to *explain* to the workers why the liberals find themselves in a blind alley, why *they* are bound hand and foot, why they *conceal* both the treaties tsarism concluded with England and other countries and the deals between Russian and Anglo-French capital, and so forth.

If Skobelev says that the workers have concluded an agreement with liberal society, no matter of what character, and since he does not protest against it, does not explain from the Duma rostrum how harmful it is for the workers, he thereby *approves* of the agreement. And that is exactly what he should not do.

Skobelev's direct or indirect, clearly expressed or tacit, approval of the agreement between the Soviet of Workers' Deputies and the Provisional Government is Skobelev's swing towards the bourgeoisie. Skobelev's statement that the workers are demanding peace, that their aims are as far removed from the liberals' aims as heaven is from earth, is Skobelev's swing towards the proletariat.

Purely proletarian, truly revolutionary and profoundly correct in design is the second political idea in the manifesto of the Soviet of Workers' Deputies that we are studying, namely, the idea of establishing a "Supervising Committee" (I do not know whether this is what it is called in Russian; I am translating freely from the French), of proletarian-soldier supervision over the Provisional Government.

Now, that's something real! It is worthy of the workers who have shed their blood for freedom, peace, bread for the people! It is a *real step* towards *real guarantees* against tsarism, against a monarchy and against the monarchists Guchkov, Lvov and Co.! It is a sign that the Russian proletariat, in spite of everything, has made progress compared with the French proletariat in 1848, when it "authorised" Louis Blanc! It is proof that the instinct and mind of the proletarian masses are not satisfied with declamations, exclamations, promises of reforms and freedoms, with the title of "minister authorised by the workers", and similar tinsel, but are seeking support *only* where it is to be found, in the *armed* masses of the people organised and led by the proletariat, the class-conscious workers.

It is a step along the right road, but *only* the first step.

If this "Supervising Committee" remains a purely political type parliamentary institution, a committee that will "put questions" to the Provisional Government and receive answers from it, then it will remain a plaything, will amount to nothing.

If, on the other hand, it leads, immediately and despite all obstacles, to the formation of a *workers' militia*, or *workers' home guard*, extending to the whole people, to all men and women, which would not only replace the exterminated and dissolved police force, not only make the latter's restoration *impossible* by *any* government, constitutional-monarchist or democratic-republican, *either* in St. Petersburg *or* anywhere else in Russia—then the advanced workers of Russia will really take the road towards new and great victories, the road to victory over war, to the realisation of the slogan which, as the newspapers report, adorned the colours of the cavalry troops that demonstrated in St. Petersburg, in the square outside the State Duma:

"Long Live Socialist Republics in All Countries!"

I will set out my ideas about this workers' militia in my next letter.

In it I will try to show, on the one hand, that the formation of a militia embracing the entire people and led by the workers is the correct slogan of the day, one that corresponds to the tactical tasks of the peculiar transitional moment through which the Russian revolution (and the world revolution) is passing; and, on the other hand, that to be successful, this workers' militia must, firstly, embrace the entire people, must be a mass organisation to the degree of being *universal*, must really embrace the *entire* able-bodied population of both sexes; secondly, it must proceed to combine not only purely police, but general state functions with military functions and with the control of social production and distribution.

N. Lenin
Zürich, March 22 (9), 1917
P.S. I forgot to date my previous letter March 20 (7).

First published in 1924 in the magazine *Bolshevik* No. 3-4
Published according to the manuscript

THIRD LETTER

Concerning a Proletarian Militia

The conclusion I drew yesterday about Chkheidze's vacillating tactics has been fully confirmed today. March 10 (23), by two documents. First—a telegraphic report from Stockholm in the *Frankfurter Zeitung*[1] containing excerpts from the manifesto of the Central Committee of our Party, the Russian Social-Democratic Labour Party, in St. Petersburg. In this document there is not a word about either supporting the Guchkov government or overthrowing it; the workers and soldiers are called upon to organise around the Soviet of Workers' Deputies, to elect representatives to it for the fight against tsarism and for a republic, for an eight-hour day, for the confiscation of the landed estates and grain stocks, and chiefly, for an end to the predatory war. Particularly important and particularly urgent in this connection is our Central Committee's absolutely correct idea that to obtain peace relations must be established with *the proletarians of all the belligerent countries.*

To expect peace from negotiations and relations between the bourgeois governments would be self-deception and deception of the people.

The second document is a Stockholm report, also by telegraph, to another German newspaper (*Vossische Zeitung*[2]) about a conference between the Chkheidze group in the Duma, the workers' group (? Arbeiterfraction) and representatives of fifteen workers' unions on March 2 (15) and a manifesto published next day. Of the eleven points of this manifesto, the telegram reports only three; the first, the demand for a republic; the seventh, the demand for peace and immediate peace negotiations; and the third, the demand for "adequate participation in

[1] *Frankfurter Zeitung*—an influential German capitalist daily paper, published in Frankfurt-on-Main, from 1856 to 1943. Resumed publication in 1949 under the name *Frankfurter Allgemeine Zeitung*; speaks for West German monopoly interests.

[2] *Vossische Zeitung*—a moderate liberal newspaper published in Berlin from 1704 to 1934.

the government of representatives of the Russian working class".

If this point is correctly reported, I can understand why the bourgeoisie is praising Chkheidze. I can understand why the praise of the English Guchkovites in *The Times* which I quoted elsewhere has been supplemented by the praise of the French Guchkovites in *Le Temps*. This newspaper of the French millionaires and imperialists writes on March 22: "The leaders of the workers' parties, particularly M. Chkheidze, are exercising all their influence to moderate the wishes of the working classes."

Indeed, to demand workers' "participation" in the Guchkov-Milyukov government is a theoretical and political absurdity: to participate as a minority would mean serving as a pawn; to participate on an "equal footing" is impossible, because the demand to continue the war cannot be reconciled with the demand to conclude an armistice and start peace negotiations; to "participate" as a majority requires the strength to *overthrow* the Guchkov-Milyukov government. In practice, the demand for "participation" is the worst sort of Louis Blanc-ism, i.e., oblivion to the class struggle and the actual conditions under which it is being waged, infatuation with a most hollow-sounding phrase, spreading illusions among the workers, loss, in negotiations with Milyukov or Kerensky, of *precious* time which must be used to create a *real* class and revolutionary force, a proletarian militia that will *enjoy the confidence of all* the poor strata of the population, and they constitute the vast majority, and will *help them to organise*, help *them* to fight for bread, peace, freedom.

This mistake in the manifesto issued by Chkheidze and his group (I am not speaking of the O.C., Organising Committee, *party*, because in the sources available to me there is not a word about the O.C.)—this mistake is all the more strange considering that at the March 2 (15) conference, Chkheidze's closest collaborator, Skobelev, said, according to the newspapers: "Russia is on the eve of a second, real [*wirklich*] revolution."

Now that is the truth, from which Skobelev and Chkheidze have forgotten to draw the practical conclusions. I cannot judge from here, from my accursed afar, how near this second revolution is. Being on the spot, Skobelev can see things better. Therefore, I am not raising for myself problems, for the solution of which I have not and cannot have the necessary concrete data. I am merely emphasising the confirmation by Skobelev, an "outside witness", i.e., one who does not belong to our Party, of the *factual* conclusion I drew in my first letter, namely: that the February-March Revolution was merely the *first stage* of the revolution. Russia is passing through a peculiar historical moment of *transition* to the next stage of the revolution, or, to use Skobelev's expression, to a "second revolution".

If we want to be Marxists and learn from the experience of revolution in the whole world, we must strive to understand in what, precisely, lies the *peculiarity* of this *transitional* moment, and what tactics follow from its objective specific features.

The peculiarity of the situation lies in that the Guchkov-Milyukov government gained the first victory with extraordinary ease due to the following three major circumstances: (1) assistance from Anglo-French finance capital and its agents; (2) assistance from part of the top ranks of the army; (3) the already existing organisation of the entire Russian bourgeoisie in the shape of the rural and urban local government institutions, the State Duma, the war industries committees, and so forth.

The Guchkov government is held in a vise: bound by the interests of capital, it is compelled to strive to continue the predatory, robber war, to protect the monstrous profits of capital and the landlords, to restore the monarchy. Bound by its revolutionary origin and by the need for an abrupt change from tsarism to democracy, pressed by the bread-hungry and peace-hungry masses, the government is compelled to lie, to wriggle, to play for time, to "proclaim" and promise (promises are the only things that are very cheap even at a time of madly rocketing prices) as much as possible and do as little as possible, to make concessions with one hand and to withdraw them with the other.

Under certain circumstances, the new government can at best postpone its collapse somewhat by leaning on all the organising ability of the entire Russian bourgeoisie and bourgeois intelligentsia. But even in that case it is *unable* to avoid collapse, because it is *impossible* to escape from the claws of the terrible monster of imperialist war and famine nurtured by world capitalism unless one renounces bourgeois relationships, passes to revolutionary measures, appeals to the supreme historic heroism of both the Russian and world proletariat.

Hence the conclusion: we cannot overthrow the new government at one stroke, or, if we can (in revolutionary times the limits of what is possible expand a thousandfold), we will not be able to maintain power *unless we counter* the magnificent organisation of the entire Russian bourgeoisie and the entire bourgeois intelligentsia with an equally magnificent *organisation of the proletariat*, which must lead the entire vast mass of urban and rural poor, the semi-proletariat and small proprietors.

Irrespective of whether the "second revolution" has already broken out in St. Petersburg (I have said that it would be absolutely absurd to think that it is possible from abroad to assess the actual tempo at which it is maturing), whether it has been postponed for some time, or whether it has already begun in individual areas (of which some signs are evident)—in *any* case, the slogan of the moment on the eve of the new revolution, during it, and on the morrow of it, must be *proletarian organisation*.

Comrade workers! You performed miracles of proletarian heroism yesterday in overthrowing the tsarist monarchy. In the more or less near future (perhaps even now, as these lines are being written) you will again have to perform the same miracles of heroism to overthrow the rule of the landlords and capitalists, who are waging the imperialist war. You will not achieve *durable victory* in this next "real" revolution if you do not perform *miracles of proletarian organisation!*

Organisation is the slogan of the moment. But to confine oneself to that is to say nothing, for, on the one hand, organisation is *always* needed; hence, mere reference to the necessity of "organising the masses" explains absolutely nothing. On the other hand, he who confines himself solely to this becomes an abettor of the liberals, for the *very thing* the *liberals* want in order to strengthen their rule is that the workers *should not go beyond their ordinary* "legal" (from the standpoint of "normal" bourgeois society) organisations, i.e., that they should *only* join their party, their trade union, their co-operative society, etc., etc.

Guided by their class instinct, the workers have realised that in revolutionary times they need *not only* ordinary, but an entirely different organisation. They have rightly taken the path indicated by the experience of our 1905 Revolution and of the 1871 Paris Commune; they have set up a *Soviet of Workers' Deputies*: they have begun to develop, expand and strengthen it by drawing in *soldiers*' deputies, and, undoubtedly, deputies from rural *wage*-workers, and then (in one form or another) from the entire peasant poor.

The prime and most important task, and one that brooks no delay, is to set up organisations of this kind in all parts of Russia without exception, for all trades and strata of the proletarian and semi-proletarian population without exception, i.e., for all the working and exploited people, to use a less economically exact but more popular term. Running ahead somewhat, I shall mention that for the entire mass of the peasantry our Party (its *special* role in the new type of proletarian organisations I hope to discuss in one of my next letters) should especially recommend Soviets of wage-workers and Soviets of small tillers who do not sell grain, to be formed *separately from* the well-to-do peasants. Without this, it will be impossible either to conduct a truly proletarian policy in general,[3] or correctly to approach the extremely important practical question which is a matter of life and death for millions of people: the proper distribution of *grain*, increasing its production, etc.

It might be asked: What should be the function of the Soviets of Workers' Deputies? They "must be regarded as organs of insurrection, of revolutionary rule", we wrote in No. 47 of the Geneva *Sotsial-Demokrat*, of October 13, 1915.[4]

This theoretical proposition, deduced from the experience of the Commune of 1871 and of the Russian Revolution of 1905, must be explained and concretely developed on the basis of the practical

[3] In the rural districts a struggle will now develop for the small and, partly, middle peasants. The landlords, leaning on the well-to-do peasants, will try to lead them into subordination to the bourgeoisie. Leaning on the rural wage-workers and rural poor, we must lead them into the closet alliance with the urban proletariat.—*Au.*

[4] See *LCW*, Vol. 21, 1977, p. 402.

experience of precisely the present stage of the present revolution in Russia.

We need revolutionary *government*, we need (for a certain transitional period) a *state*. This is what distinguishes us from the anarchists. The difference between the revolutionary Marxists and the anarchists is not only that the former stand for centralised, large-scale communist production, while the latter stand for disconnected small production. The difference between us precisely on the question of government, of the state, is that we are *for*, and the anarchists *against*, utilising revolutionary forms of the state in a revolutionary way for the struggle for socialism.

We need a state. But *not the kind* of state the bourgeoisie has created everywhere, from constitutional monarchies to the most democratic republics. And in this we differ from the opportunists and Kautskyites of the old, and decaying, socialist parties, who have distorted, or have forgotten, the lessons of the Paris Commune and the analysis of these lessons made by Marx and Engels.[5]

We need a state, but *not* the kind the bourgeoisie needs, with organs of government in the shape of a police force, an army and a bureaucracy (officialdom) separate from and opposed to the people. All bourgeois revolutions merely perfected *this* state machine, merely transferred *it* from the hands of one party to those of another.

The proletariat, on the other hand, if it wants to uphold the gains of the present revolution and proceed further, to win peace, bread and freedom, must "*smash*", to use Marx's expression, this "ready-made" state machine and substitute a new one for it by *merging* the police force, the army and the bureaucracy with *the entire armed people*. Following the path indicated by the experience of the Paris Commune of 1871 and the Russian Revolution of 1905, the proletariat must organise and arm *all* the poor, exploited sections of the population

[5] In one of my next letters, or in a special article, I will deal in detail with this analysis, given in particular in Marx's *The Civil War in France*, in Engels's preface to the third edition of that work, in the letters: Marx's of April 12, 1871, and Engels's of March 18-28, 1875, and also with the utter distortion of Marxism by Kautsky in his controversy with Pannekoek in 1912 on the question of the so-called "destruction of the state".—*Au.* [See Lenin's *State and Revolution*, *LCW*, Vol. 25, 1980, p. 385.]

in order that they *themselves* should take the organs of state power directly into their own hands, in order that *they themselves should constitute* these organs of state power.

And the workers of Russia have already *taken* this path in the first stage of the first revolution, in February-March 1917. The whole task now is clearly to understand what this new path is, to proceed along it further, boldly, firmly and perseveringly.

The Anglo-French and Russian capitalists wanted "only" to remove, or only to "frighten", Nicholas II and to leave intact the old state machine, the police force, the army and the bureaucracy.

The workers went further and smashed it. And now, not only the Anglo-French, but also the German capitalists are *howling* with rage and horror as they see, for example, Russian soldiers shooting their officers, as in the case of Admiral Nepenin, that supporter of Guchkov and Milyukov.

I said that the workers have smashed the old state machine. It will be more correct to say: *have begun* to smash it.

Let us take a concrete example.

In St. Petersburg and in many other places the police force has been partly wiped out and partly dissolved. The Guchkov-Milyukov government *cannot* either restore the monarchy or, in general, maintain power *without restoring* the police force as a special organisation of armed men under the command of the bourgeoisie, separate from and opposed to the people. That is as clear as daylight.

On the other hand, the new government must reckon with the revolutionary people, must feed them with half-concessions and promises, must play for time. That is why it resorts to half measures: it establishes a "people's militia" with elected officials (this sounds awfully respectable, awfully democratic, revolutionary and beautiful!)—*but* . . . *but*, firstly, it places this militia under the control of the rural and urban local government bodies, i.e., under the command of landlords and capitalists who have been elected in conformity with laws passed by Nicholas the Bloody and Stolypin the Hangman!! Secondly, although calling it a "people's militia" in order to throw dust in the eyes of the "people", it does *not* call upon the *entire* people to join this militia, *and does not compel* the employers and capitalists to *pay* workers and office employees their ordinary wages *for the hours and days* they spend in the *public service*, i.e., in the militia.

That's their trick. That is how the landlord and capitalist government of the Guchkovs and Milyukovs manages to have a "people's militia" on paper, while in reality, it is restoring, gradually and on the quiet, the *bourgeois*, antipeople's militia. At first it is to consist of "eight thousand students and professors" (as foreign newspapers describe the present St. Petersburg militia)—an obvious plaything!—and will gradually be built up of the old and new *police force.*

Prevent restoration of the police force! Do not let the local government bodies slip out of your hands! Set up a militia that will really embrace the entire people, be really universal, and be led by the proletariat!—such is the task of the day, such is the slogan of the moment which equally conforms with the properly understood interests of furthering the class struggle, furthering the revolutionary movement, and the democratic instinct of every worker, of every peasant, of every exploited toiler who cannot help hating the policemen, the rural police patrols, the village constables, the command of landlords and capitalists over armed men with power over the people.

What kind of police force do *they* need, the Guchkovs and Milyukovs, the landlords and capitalists? The same kind as existed under the tsarist monarchy. After the briefest revolutionary periods *all* the bourgeois and bourgeois-democratic republics in the world set up or restored *precisely such* a police force, a special organisation of armed men subordinate to the bourgeoisie in one way or another, separate from and opposed to the people.

What kind of militia do we need, the proletariat, all the toiling people? A genuine *people*'s militia, i.e., one that, first, consists of the *entire* population, of all adult citizens of *both* sexes; and, second, one that combines the functions of a people's army with police functions, with the functions of the chief and fundamental organ of public order and public administration.

To make these propositions more comprehensible I will take a purely schematic example. Needless to say, it would be absurd to think of drawing up any kind of a "plan" for a proletarian militia: when the workers and the entire people set about it practically, on a truly mass scale, they will work it out and organise it a hundred times better than any theoretician. I am not offering a "plan", I only want to illustrate my idea.

St. Petersburg has a population of about two million. Of these, more than half are between the ages of 15 and 65. Take half—one million. Let us even subtract an entire fourth as physically unfit, etc., taking no part in public service at the present moment for justifiable reasons. There remain 750,000 who, serving in the militia, say one day in fifteen (and receiving their pay for this time from their employers), would form an army of 50,000.

That's the type of "state" we need!

That's the kind of militia that would be a "people's militia" in deed and not only in words.

That is how we must proceed in order to *prevent* the restoration either of a special police force, or of a special army separate from the people.

Such a militia, 95 hundredths of which would consist of workers and peasants, would express the *real* mind and will, the strength and power of the vast majority of the people. Such a militia would really arm, and provide military training for, the entire people, would be a safeguard, but *not* of the Guchkov or Milyukov type, against all attempts to restore reaction, against all the designs of tsarist agents. Such a militia would be the executive organ of the Soviets of Workers' and Soldiers' Deputies, it would enjoy the *boundless* respect and confidence of the people, for it itself would be an organisation of the entire people. Such a militia would transform democracy from a beautiful signboard, which covers up the enslavement and torment of the people by the capitalists, into a means of actually *training the masses* for participation in *all* affairs of state. Such a militia would draw the young people into political life and teach them not only by words, but also by action, by *work*. Such a militia would develop those functions which, speaking in scientific language, come within the purview of the "welfare police", sanitary inspection, and so forth, and would enlist for such work all adult women. If women are not drawn into public service, into the militia, into political life, if women are not torn out of their stupefying house and kitchen environment, it will be *impossible* to guarantee real freedom, it will be *impossible* to build even democracy, let alone socialism.

Such a militia would be a proletarian militia, for the industrial and urban workers would exert a guiding influence on the masses of the poor as naturally and inevitably as they came to hold the leading place in the people's revolutionary struggle both in 1905-07 and in 1917.

Such a militia would ensure absolute order and devotedly observed comradely discipline. At the same time, in the severe crisis that all the belligerent countries are experiencing, it would make it possible to combat this crisis in a really democratic way, properly and rapidly to distribute grain and other supplies, introduce "universal labour service", which the French now call "civilian mobilisation" and the Germans "civilian service", and without which *it is impossible—it has proved to be impossible*—to heal the wounds that have been and are being inflicted by the predatory and horrible war.

Has the proletariat of Russia shed its blood only in order to receive fine promises of political democratic reforms and nothing more? Can it be that it will not demand, and secure, that *every* toiler should *forthwith* see and feel some improvement in his life? That every family should have bread? That every child should have a bottle of good milk and that not a single adult in a rich family should dare take extra milk until children are provided for? That the palaces and rich apartments abandoned by the tsar and the aristocracy should not remain vacant, but provide shelter for the homeless and the destitute? Who can carry out these measures except a people's militia, to which women must belong equally with men?

These measures do *not yet* constitute socialism. They concern the distribution of consumption, not the reorganisation of production. They would not yet constitute the "dictatorship of the proletariat", only the "revolutionary-democratic dictatorship of the proletariat and the poor peasantry". It is not a matter of finding a theoretical classification. We would be committing a great mistake if we attempted to force the complex, urgent, rapidly developing practical tasks of the revolution into the Procrustean bed of narrowly conceived "theory" instead of regarding theory primarily and predominantly as a *guide to action.*

Do the masses of the Russian workers possess sufficient class-consciousness, fortitude and heroism to perform "miracles of proletarian organisation" after they have performed miracles of daring, initiative and self-sacrifice in the direct revolutionary struggle? That we do not know, and it would be idle to indulge in guessing, for practice *alone* furnishes the answers to such questions.

What we do know definitely, and what we, as a party, must explain to the masses is, on the one hand, the immense power of the locomotive of history that is engendering an unprecedented crisis, starvation and incalculable hardship. That locomotive is the war, waged for predatory aims by the capitalists of *both* belligerent camps. This "locomotive" has brought a number of the richest, freest and most enlightened nations to the brink of doom. It is *forcing* the peoples to strain to the utmost all their energies, placing them in unbearable conditions, putting on the order of the day not the application of certain "theories" (an illusion against which Marx always warned socialists), but implementation of the most extreme practical measures; for *without* extreme measures, death—immediate and certain death from starvation—awaits millions of people.

That the revolutionary enthusiasm of the advanced class can do a *great deal* when the objective situation *demands* extreme measures from the entire people, needs no proof. *This* aspect is clearly seen and *felt* by everybody in Russia.

It is important to realise that in revolutionary times the objective situation changes with the same swiftness and abruptness as the current of life in general. And we must *be able to adapt* our tactics and immediate tasks to the *specific features* of every given situation. Before February 1917, the immediate task was to conduct bold revolutionary internationalist propaganda, summon the masses to fight, rouse them. The February-March days required the heroism of devoted struggle to crush the immediate enemy—tsarism. Now we are in *transition* from that first stage of the revolution to the second, from "coming to grips" with tsarism to "coming to grips" with Guchkov-Milyukov landlord and capitalist imperialism. The immediate task is *organisation*, not only in the stereotyped sense of working to form stereotyped organisations, but in the sense of drawing unprecedentedly broad masses of the oppressed classes into an organisation that would take over the military, political and economic functions of the state.

The proletariat has approached, and will approach, this singular task in different ways. In some parts of Russia the February-March Revolution puts nearly complete power in its hands. In others the proletariat may, perhaps, in a "usurpatory" manner, begin to form and develop a proletarian militia. In still others, it will probably strive for immediate elections of urban and rural local government bodies on the basis of universal, etc., suffrage, in order to turn them into revolutionary centres, etc., until the growth of proletarian organisation, the coming together of the soldiers with the workers, the movement among the peasantry and the disillusionment of very many in the war-imperialist government of Guchkov and Milyukov bring near the hour when this government will be replaced by the "government" of the Soviet of Workers' Deputies.

Nor ought we to forget that close to St. Petersburg we have one of the most advanced, factually republican, countries, namely, Finland, which, from 1905 to 1917, shielded by the revolutionary battles of Russia, has in a relatively peaceful way developed democracy and has won the *majority* of the people for socialism. The Russian proletariat will guarantee the Finnish Republic complete freedom, including freedom to secede (it is doubtful now whether a single Social-Democrat will waver on this point when the Cadet Rodichev is so meanly haggling in Helsingfors for bits of privileges for the Great Russians[6])—and

[6] Soon after its formation, the Provisional Government appointed the Octobrist M. A. Stakhovich Governor-General of Finland and the Cadet F. I. Rodichev Minister (or Commissioner) for Finnish Affairs. On March 8 (21), the Provisional Government issued its Manifesto "On Approval and Enforcement of the Constitution of the Grand Duchy of Finland". Under this Finland was allowed autonomy with the proviso that laws promulgated by the Finnish Diet would be subject to confirmation by the Russian Government. Laws that ran counter to Finnish legislation were to remain in force for the duration of the war.

The Provisional Government wanted the Finnish Diet to amend the Constitution to give "Russian citizens equal rights with Finnish citizens in commerce and industry", for under the tsarist government such equality was imposed in defiance of Finnish laws. At the same time, the Provisional Government refused to discuss self-determination for Finland "pending convocation of the constituent assembly". This led to a sharp conflict, resolved only after the Great October Socialist Revolution when, on December 18

precisely in this way will win the *complete* confidence and comradely assistance of the Finnish workers for the all-Russian proletarian cause. In a difficult and big undertaking mistakes are inevitable, nor will we avoid them. The Finnish workers are better organisers, they will help us in this sphere, they will, *in their own way*, push forward the establishment of the socialist republic.

Revolutionary victories in Russia proper—peaceful organisational successes in Finland shielded by these victories—the Russian workers' transition to revolutionary organisational tasks on a new scale—capture of power by the proletariat and poorest strata of the population—encouragement and development of the socialist revolution in the West—this is the road that will lead us to *peace* and *socialism.*

N. Lenin
Zürich, March 11 (24), 1917

First published in the magazine
The Communist International No. 3-4, 1924
Published according to the manuscript

....
(31), 1917, the Soviet Government granted Finland full independence.

FOURTH LETTER

How to Achieve Peace

I have just (March 12/25) read in the *Neue Zürcher Zeitung* (No. 517 of March 24) the following telegraphic dispatch from Berlin:

"It is reported from Sweden that Maxim Gorky has sent the government and the Executive Committee greetings couched in enthusiastic terms. He greets the people's victory over the lords of reaction and calls upon all Russia's sons to help erect the edifice of the new Russian state. At the same time he urges the government to crown the cause of emancipation by concluding peace. It must not, he says, be peace at any price; Russia now has less reason than ever to strive for peace at any price. It must be a peace that will enable Russia to live in honour among the other nations of the earth. Mankind has shed much blood; the new government would render not only Russia, but all mankind, the greatest service if it succeeded in concluding an early peace."

That is how Maxim Gorky's letter is reported.

It is with deep chagrin that one reads this letter, impregnated through and through with stock philistine prejudices. The author of these lines has had many occasions, in meetings with Gorky in Capri, to warn and reproach him for his political mistakes. Gorky parried these reproaches with his inimitable charming smile and with the ingenuous remark: "I know I am a bad Marxist. And besides, we artists are all somewhat irresponsible." It is not easy to argue against that.

There can be no doubt that Gorky's is an enormous artistic talent which has been, and will be, of great benefit to the world proletarian movement.

But why should Gorky meddle in politics?

In my opinion, Gorky's letter expresses prejudices that are exceedingly widespread not only among the petty bourgeoisie, but also among a section of the workers under its influence. *All* the energies of our Party, all the efforts of the class-conscious workers, must be concentrated on a persistent, persevering, all-round struggle against these prejudices.

The tsarist government began and waged the present war as an *imperialist,* predatory war to rob and strangle weak nations. The government of the Guchkovs and Milyukovs, which is a landlord and capitalist government, is forced to continue, and wants to continue, *this very same kind* of war. To urge that government to conclude a democratic peace is like preaching virtue to brothel keepers.

Let me explain what is meant.

What is imperialism?

In my *Imperialism, the Highest Stage of Capitalism*, the manuscript of which was delivered to the Parus Publishers some time before the revolution, was accepted by them and announced in the magazine *Letopis*,[1] I answered this question as follows:

"Imperialism is capitalism at that stage of development at which the dominance of monopolies and finance capital is established; in which the export of capital has acquired pronounced importance; in

[1] *Imperialism, the Highest Stage of Capitalism* was written in the first half of 1916, and on June 19 (July 2) was sent to Petrograd via Paris. It was to have been published by the Parus publishing house which, on Maxim Gorky's initiative, was putting out a series of popular surveys of West-European countries involved in the war. Lenin maintained contact with the publishers through the editor of the series, M. N. Pokrovsky. On September 29, 1916, Gorky wrote Pokrovsky in Paris that Lenin's book was "really excellent" and would be put out in addition to the regular series. However, the Parus editors strongly objected to Lenin's criticism of Kautsky's renegade position and substantially altered the text, deleting all criticism of Kautsky's theory of ultra-imperialism and distorting a number of Lenin's formulations. The book was finally published in mid-1917 with a preface by Lenin, dated April 26.

Parus (Sail) and *Letopis* (Annals)—the names of the publishing house and magazine founded by Gorky in Petrograd.

Letopis—a magazine of literature, science and politics whose contributors included former Bolsheviks (the Machists V. A. Bazarov and A. A. Bogdanov) and Mensheviks. Gorky was literary editor, and among the other prominent writers contributing to *Letopis* were Alexander Blok, Valeri Bryusov, Fyodor Gladkov, Sergei Yesenin. A. V. Lunacharsky, Vladimir Mayakovsky, Vyacheslav Shishkov and A. Chaplygin. *Letopis* appeared from December 1915 to December 1917. The Parus publishing house existed from 1915 through 1918.

which the division of the world among the international trusts has begun; in which the division of all territories of the globe among the biggest capitalist powers has been completed" (Chapter VII of the above-mentioned book, the publication of which was announced in *Letopis*, when the censorship still existed, under the title: "Modern Capitalism", by V. Ilyin).[2]

The whole thing hinges on the fact that capital has grown to huge dimensions. Associations of a small number of the biggest capitalists (cartels, syndicates, trusts) manipulate *billions* and divide the whole world among themselves. The world has been *completely* divided up. The war was brought on by the clash of the two most powerful groups of multimillionaires, Anglo-French and German, for the *redivision* of the world.

The Anglo-French group of capitalists wants first to rob Germany, deprive her of her colonies (nearly all of which have already been seized), and then to rob Turkey.

The German group of capitalists wants to seize Turkey for *itself* and to compensate itself for the loss of its colonies by seizing neighbouring small states (Belgium, Serbia, Rumania).

This is the real truth; it is being concealed by all sorts of bourgeois lies about a "liberating", "national" war, a "war for right and justice", and similar jingle with which the capitalists always fool the common people.

Russia is waging this war with foreign money. Russian capital is a *partner* of Anglo-French capital. Russia is waging the war in order to rob Armenia, Turkey, Galicia.

Guchkov, Lvov and Milyukov, our present ministers, are not chance comers. They are the representatives and leaders of the entire landlord and capitalist class. They are *bound* by the interests of capital. The capitalists can no more renounce their interests than a man can lift himself by his bootstraps.

Secondly, Guchkov-Milyukov and Co. are *bound* by Anglo-French capital. They have waged, and are still waging, the war with foreign money. They have borrowed billions, promising to pay *hundreds of*

[2] See *LCW*, Vol. 22, 1977, pp. 266-67.

millions in interest *every year*, and to squeeze this *tribute* out of the Russian workers and Russian peasants.

Thirdly, Guchkov-Milyukov and Co. are *bound* to England, France, Italy, Japan and other groups of robber capitalists by direct *treaties* concerning the predatory aims of this war. These treaties were concluded by *Tsar Nicholas II*. Guchkov-Milyukov and Co. took advantage of the workers' struggle against the tsarist monarchy to seize power, and *they have confirmed the treaties* concluded by the tsar.

This was done by the whole of the Guchkov-Milyukov government in a manifesto which the St. Petersburg Telegraph Agency circulated on March 7(20): "The government [of Guchkov and Milyukov] will faithfully abide by all the treaties that bind us with other powers," says the manifesto. Milyukov, the new Minister for Foreign Affairs, said the *same thing* in his telegram of March 5 (18), 1917 to all Russian representatives abroad.

These are all *secret* treaties, and Milyukov and Co. *refuse* to make them public for two reasons: (1) they fear the people, who are opposed to the predatory war; (2) they are bound by Anglo-French capital which insists that the treaties remain secret. But every newspaper reader who has followed events knows that these treaties envisage the robbery of China by Japan; of Persia, Armenia, Turkey (especially Constantinople) and Galicia by Russia; of Albania by Italy; of Turkey and the German colonies by France and England, etc.

This is how things stand.

Hence, to urge the Guchkov-Milyukov government to conclude a speedy, honest, democratic and good-neighbourly peace is like the good village priest urging the landlords and the merchants to "walk in the way of God", to love their neighbours and to turn the other cheek. The landlords and merchants listen to these sermons, continue to oppress and rob the people and praise the priest for his ability to console and pacify the "muzhiks".

Exactly the same role is played—consciously or unconciously—by all those who in the present imperialist war address pious peace appeals to the bourgeois governments. The bourgeois governments either refuse to listen to such appeals and even prohibit them, or they allow them to be made and assure all and sundry that they are only fighting to conclude the speediest and "justest" peace, and that all the blame lies with the enemy. Actually, talking peace *to bourgeois* governments turns out to be *deception of the people.*

The groups of capitalists who have drenched the world in blood for the sake of dividing territories, markets and concessions *cannot* conclude an "honourable" peace. They can conclude only a *shameful* peace, a peace based *on the division of the spoils, on the partition of Turkey and the colonies.*

Moreover, the Guchkov-Milyukov government is in general opposed to peace at the present moment, because the "*only*" "loot" it would get *now* would be Armenia and part of Galicia, whereas it *also* wants to get Constantinople *and* regain from the Germans Poland, which tsarism has always so inhumanly and shamelessly oppressed. Further, the Guchkov-Milyukov government is, in essence, only the agent of Anglo-French capital, which wants to retain the colonies it has wrested from Germany and, *on top of that,* compel Germany hand back Belgium and part of France. Anglo-French capital helped the Guchkovs and Milyukovs remove Nicholas II in order that they might help it to "vanquish" Germany.

What, then, is to be done?

To achieve peace (and still more to achieve a really democratic, a really honourable peace), it is necessary that political power be in the hands of *the workers and poorest peasants,* not the landlords and capitalists. The latter represent an insignificant minority of the population, and the capitalists, as everybody knows, are making fantastic profits out of the war.

The workers and poorest peasants are the *vast* majority of the population. They are not making profit out of the war; on the contrary, they are being reduced to ruin and starvation. They are bound neither by capital nor by the treaties between the predatory groups of capitalists; they *can* and sincerely want to end the war.

If political power in Russia were in the hands of the *Soviets* of Workers', Soldiers' and Peasants' Deputies, these Soviets, and the *All-Russia Soviet* elected by them, could, and no doubt would, agree to carry out the peace programme which our Party (the Russian Social-

Democratic Labour Party) outlined as early as October 13, 1915, in No. 47 of its Central Organ, *Sotsial-Demokrat*[3] (then published in Geneva because of the Draconic tsarist censorship).

This programme would probably be the following:

1) The All-Russia Soviet of Workers', Soldiers' and Peasants' Deputies (or the St. Petersburg Soviet temporarily acting for it) would forthwith declare that it is *not* bound by *any* treaties concluded *either* by the tsarist monarchy *or* by the bourgeois governments.

2) It would forthwith publish *all* these treaties in order to hold up to public shame the predatory aims of the tsarist monarchy and of *all* the bourgeois governments without exception.

3) It would forthwith publicly call upon *all* the belligerent powers to conclude an *immediate armistice.*

4) It would immediately bring to the knowledge of all the people our, the workers' and peasants' *peace terms:*

liberation of *all* colonies;

liberation of *all* dependent, oppressed and unequal nations.

5) It would declare that it expects nothing good from the bourgeois governments and calls upon the workers of all countries to overthrow them and to transfer all political power to Soviets of Workers' Deputies.

6) It would declare that the *capitalist gentry themselves* can repay the billions of debts contracted by the bourgeois governments to wage this criminal, predatory war, and that the workers and peasants *refuse to recognise* these debts. To pay the interest on these loans would mean paying the capitalists *tribute* for many years for having graciously allowed the workers to kill one another in order that the capitalists might divide the spoils.

Workers and peasants!—the Soviet of Workers' Deputies would say—are you willing to pay these gentry, the capitalists, *hundreds of millions* of rubles *every year* for a war waged for the division of the African colonies, Turkey, etc.?

For *these* peace terms the Soviet of Workers' Deputies would, in my opinion, agree to *wage war* against *any* bourgeois government and against *all* the bourgeois governments of the world, because this would

[3] See *LCW*, Vol. 21, 1977, pp. 401-04.

really be a just war, because *all* the workers and toilers in *all* countries would *work for its success.*

The German worker now sees that the bellicose monarchy in Russia is being replaced by a *bellicose* republic, a republic of capitalists who want to continue the imperialist war, and who have confirmed the predatory treaties of the tsarist monarchy.

Judge for yourselves, can the German worker trust *such* a republic?

Judge for yourselves, can the war continue, can the capitalist domination continue on earth, if the Russian people, always sustained by the living memories of the great Revolution of 1905, win complete freedom and transfer all political power to the Soviets of Workers' and Peasants' Deputies?

N. Lenin
Zürich, March 12 (25), 1917

First published in the magazine
The Communist International No. 3-4, 1924
Published according to the manuscript

FIFTH LETTER

The Tasks Involved in the Building of the Revolutionary Proletarian State

In the preceding letters, the immediate tasks of the revolutionary proletariat in Russia were formulated as follows: (1) to find the surest road to the next stage of the revolution, or to the second revolution, which (2) must transfer political power from the government of the landlords and capitalists (the Guchkovs, Lvovs, Milyukovs, Kerenskys) to a government of the workers and poorest peasants. (3) This latter government must be organised on the model of the Soviets of Workers' and Peasants' Deputies, namely, (4) it must smash, completely eliminate, the old state machine, the army, the police force and bureaucracy (officialdom), that is common to *all* bourgeois states, and substitute for this machine (5) not only a mass organisation, but a universal organisation of the entire armed people. (6) *Only* such a government, of "such" a class composition ("revolutionary-democratic dictatorship of the proletariat and peasantry") and such organs of government ("proletarian militia") *will be capable* of successfully carrying out the extremely difficult and absolutely urgent *chief* task of the moment, namely: to achieve *peace*, not an imperialist peace, not a deal between the imperialist powers concerning the division of the booty by the capitalists and their governments, but a really lasting and democratic peace, which cannot be achieved without a proletarian revolution in a number of countries. (7) In Russia the victory of the proletariat can be achieved in the very near future *only* if, from the very first step, the workers are supported by the vast majority of the peasants fighting for the confiscation of the landed estates (and for the nationalisation of all the land, if we assume that the agrarian programme of the "104" is still essentially the agrarian programme of the *peasantry*[1]). (8) In connection with such a peasant revolution,

[1] The *agrarian programme of the "104"*—the land reform bill the Trudovik members submitted to the 13th meeting of the First State Duma on May 23 (June 5) 1906. Its purpose was to "establish a system under which all the land,

and on its basis, the proletariat can and must, in alliance with the *poorest* section of the peasantry, take further steps towards *control* of the production and distribution of the basic products, towards the introduction of "universal labour service", etc. These steps are dictated, with absolute inevitability, by the conditions created by the war, which in many respects will become still more acute in the post-war period. In their entirety and in their development these steps will mark the *transition to socialism*, which cannot be achieved in Russia directly, at one stroke, without transitional measures, but is quite achievable and urgently necessary as a result of such transitional measures. (9) In this connection, the task of immediately organising special Soviets of Workers' Deputies in the *rural districts*, i.e., Soviets of agricultural *wage*-workers *separate* from the Soviets of the other peasant deputies, comes to the forefront with extreme urgency.

Such, briefly, is the programme we have outlined, based on an appraisal of the class forces in the Russian and world revolution, and also on the experience of 1871 and 1905.

Let us now attempt a general survey of this programme as a whole and, in passing, deal with the way the subject was approached by K. Kautsky, the chief theoretician of the "Second" (1889-1914) International and most prominent representative of the "Centre", "marsh" trend that is now to be observed in all countries, the trend that oscillates between the social-chauvinists and the revolutionary internationalists. Kautsky discussed this subject in his magazine *Die Neue Zeit* of April 6, 1917 (new style) in an article entitled, "The Prospects of the Russian Revolution".

....

with its deposits and waters, would belong to the entire people, and farmlands would be allowed only those tilling them by their own labour" (*Documents and Materials of the State Duma*, Moscow, 1957, p. 172). The Trudoviks advocated organisation of a "national land fund" that would include all state, crown, monastery and church lands, also part of privately owned lands, which were to be alienated if the size of the holding exceeded the labour norm fixed for the given area. Partial compensation was to be paid for such alienated land. Small holdings were to remain the property of the owner, but would eventually be brought into the national fund. Implementation of the reform was to be supervised by local committees elected by universal, direct and equal suffrage and by secret ballot.

"First of all," writes Kautsky, "we must ascertain what tasks confront the revolutionary proletarian regime" (state system).

"Two things," continues the author, "are urgently needed by the proletariat: democracy and socialism."

Unfortunately, Kautsky advances this absolutely incontestable thesis in an exceedingly general form, so that in essence he says nothing and explains nothing. Milyukov and Kerensky, members of a bourgeois and imperialist government, would readily subscribe to this general thesis, one to the first part, and the other to the second . . .[2]

Written on March 26 (April 8), 1917
First published in the magazine *Bolshevik* No. 3-4, 1924
Published according to the manuscript

[2] The manuscript breaks off here.

[APRIL THESES]

The Tasks of the Proletariat in the Present Revolution[1]

I did not arrive in Petrograd until the night of April 3, and therefore at the meeting on April 4 I could, of course, deliver the report on the tasks of the revolutionary proletariat only on my own behalf, and with reservations as to insufficient preparation.

The only thing I could do to make things easier for myself—and for *honest* opponents—was to prepare the theses *in writing.* I read them out, and gave the text to Comrade Tsereteli. I read them *twice* very slowly: first at a meeting of Bolsheviks and then at a meeting of both Bolsheviks and Mensheviks.

I publish these personal theses of mine with only the briefest explanatory notes, which were developed in far greater detail in the report.

THESES

1) In our attitude towards the war, which under the new government of Lvov and Co. unquestionably remains on Russia's part a predatory imperialist war owing to the capitalist nature of that government, not the slightest concession to "revolutionary defencism" is permissible.

The class-conscious proletariat can give its consent to a revolutionary war, which would really justify revolutionary defencism, only on condition: (a) that the power pass to the proletariat and the poorest sections of the peasants aligned with the proletariat; (b) that all

[1] Published in *Pravda* No. 26, for April 7, 1917, over the signature *N. Lenin*, this article contains Lenin's famous April Theses read by him at two meetings held at the Taurida Palace on April 4 (17), 1917 (at a meeting of Bolsheviks and at a joint meeting of Bolshevik and Menshevik delegates to the All-Russia Conference of Soviets of Workers' and Soldiers' Deputies). The article was reprinted in the Bolshevik newspapers *Sotsial-Demokrat* (Moscow), *Proletary* (Kharkov), *Krasnoyarsky Rabochy* (Krasnoyarsk), *Vperyod* (Ufa), *Bakinsky Rabochy* (Baku), *Kavkazsky Rabochy* (Tiflis) and others.

annexations be renounced in deed and not in word; (c) that a complete break be effected in actual fact with all capitalist interests.

In view of the undoubted honesty of those broad sections of the mass believers in revolutionary defencism who accept the war only as a necessity, and not as a means of conquest, in view of the fact that they are being deceived by the bourgeoisie, it is necessary with particular thoroughness, persistence and patience to explain their error to them, to explain the inseparable connection existing between capital and the imperialist war, and to prove that without overthrowing capital *it is impossible* to end the war by a truly democratic peace, a peace not imposed by violence.

The most widespread campaign for this view must be organised in the army at the front.

Fraternisation.

2) The specific feature of the present situation in Russia is that the country is *passing* from the first stage of the revolution—which, owing to the insufficient class-consciousness and organisation of the proletariat, placed power in the hands of the bourgeoisie—to its *second* stage, which must place power in the hands of the proletariat and the poorest sections of the peasants.

This transition is characterised, on the one hand, by a maximum of legally recognised rights (Russia is *now* the freest of all the belligerent countries in the world); on the other, by the absence of violence towards the masses, and, finally, by their unreasoning trust in the government of capitalists, those worst enemies of peace and socialism.

This peculiar situation demands of us an ability to adapt ourselves to the *special* conditions of Party work among unprecedentedly large masses of proletarians who have just awakened to political life.

3) No support for the Provisional Government; the utter falsity of all its promises should be made clear, particularly of those relating to the renunciation of annexations. Exposure in place of the impermissible, illusion-breeding "demand" that *this* government, a government of capitalists, should *cease* to be an imperialist government.

4) Recognition of the fact that in most of the Soviets of Workers' Deputies our Party is in a minority, so far a small minority, as against *a bloc of all* the petty-bourgeois opportunist elements, from the Popular

Socialists and the Socialist-Revolutionaries down to the Organising Committee[2] (Chkheidze, Tsereteli, etc.), Steklov, etc., etc., who have

[2] *Socialist-Revolutionaries* (S.R.s)—a petty-bourgeois party formed in Russia at the end of 1901 and beginning of 1902 through the amalgamation of various Narodnik groups and circles (the Union of Socialist-Revolutionaries, the Party of Socialist-Revolutionaries, and others). The views of the S.R.s were an eclectic medley of Narodism and revisionism; they tried, as Lenin put it, to "patch up the rents in the Narodnik ideas with bits of fashionable opportunist 'criticism' of Marxism" (see *LCW*, Vol. 9, 1972, p. 310). The First World War found most of the S.R.s taking a social-chauvinist stand.

After the victory of the bourgeois-democratic revolution of February 1917, the S.R.s, together with the Mensheviks and Cadets, were the mainstay of the counter-revolutionary Provisional Government of the bourgeoisie and landowners, and the leaders of the party (Kerensky, Avksentyev, Chernov) were members of that government. The S.R. Party refused to support the peasants' demand for the abolition of the landed estates and in effect stood for private property in land; the S.R. ministers in the Provisional Government sent punitive expeditions against the peasants who had seized landed estates. On the eve of the October armed uprising this party openly sided with the counter-revolutionary bourgeoisie in defence of the capitalist system and found itself isolated from the mass of the revolutionary people.

At the end of November 1917 the Left wing of the party founded a separate Left Socialist-Revolutionary Party. In an endeavour to maintain their influence among the peasant masses, the Left S.R.s formally recognised the Soviet Government and entered into an agreement with the Bolsheviks, but very soon turned against the Soviet power.

During the years of foreign military intervention and civil war the S.R.s engaged in counter-revolutionary subversive activities, zealously supported the interventionists and whiteguard generals, took part in counter-revolutionary plots, and organised terrorist acts against leaders of the Soviet state and Communist Party. After the Civil War they continued their anti-Soviet activities within the country and as whiteguard émigrés abroad.

Popular Socialists—members of the petty-bourgeois Labour Popular Socialist Party, which separated from the Right wing of the Socialist-Revolutionary Party in 1906. The P.S.s stood for a bloc with the Cadets. Lenin called them "Social-Cadets", "petty-bourgeois opportunists", and "Socialist-Revolutionary Mensheviks" who vacillated between the Cadets and the S.R.s, and he emphasised that this party "differs very little from the Cadets, for it deletes from its programme both the republicanism and the demand for all the land" (see *LCW*, Vol. 11, 1972, p. 228). The party's leaders were A. V. Peshekhonov, N. F. Annensky, V. A. Myakotin, and others. During the First World War the P.S.s took a social-chauvinist stand. After the bourgeois-democratic revolution of February 1917 the Popular Socialist Party merged with the Trudoviks and actively supported the bourgeois Provisional Government, in which it was represented. After the October Socialist yielded to the influence of the bourgeoisie and spread that influence among the proletariat.

The masses must be made to see that the Soviets of Workers' Deputies are the *only possible* form of revolutionary government, and that therefore our task is, as long as *this* government yields to the influence of the bourgeoisie, to present a patient, systematic, and persistent *explanation* of the errors of their tactics, an explanation especially adapted to the practical needs of the masses.

As long as we are in the minority we carry on the work of criticising and exposing errors and at the same time we preach the necessity of transferring the entire state power to the Soviets of Workers' Deputies, so that the people may overcome their mistakes by experience.

5) Not a parliamentary republic—to return to a parliamentary republic from the Soviets of Workers' Deputies would be a retrograde step—but a republic of Soviets of Workers', Agricultural Labourers' and Peasants' Deputies throughout the country, from top to bottom.

Abolition of the police, the army and the bureaucracy.[3]

The salaries of all officials, all of whom are elective and displaceable at any time, not to exceed the average wage of a competent worker.

6) The weight of emphasis in the agrarian programme to be shifted to the Soviets of Agricultural Labourers' Deputies.

Confiscation of all landed estates.

Nationalisation of *all* lands in the country, the land to be disposed of by the local Soviets of Agricultural Labourers' and Peasants' Deputies. The organisation of separate Soviets of Deputies of Poor Peasants. The setting up of a model farm on each of the large estates

....

Revolution the P.S.s participated in plots and armed acts against the Soviet government. The party went out of existence during the period of foreign military intervention and civil war.

The *Organising Committee* (O.C.) was set up in 1912 at the August conference of the liquidators. During the First World War the O.C. justified the war on the part of tsarism and advocated the ideas of nationalism and chauvinism. The O.C. published the journal *Nasha Zarya*, and when this was closed down, *Nashe Dyelo*, then *Dyelo*, and the newspapers *Rabocheye Utro*, then *Utro*. The O.C. functioned up to the time of the election of the Central Committee of the Menshevik party in August 1917.

[3] I.e., the standing army to be replaced by the arming of the whole people. —*Au.*

(ranging in size from 100 to 300 dessiatines, according to local and other conditions, and to the decisions of the local bodies) under the control of the Soviets of Agricultural Labourers' Deputies and for the public account.

7) The immediate amalgamation of all banks in the country into a single national bank, and the institution of control over it by the Soviet of Workers' Deputies.

8) It is not our *immediate* task to "introduce" socialism, but only to bring social production and the distribution of products at once under the *control* of the Soviets of Workers' Deputies.

9) Party tasks:

(a) Immediate convocation of a Party congress;

(b) Alteration of the Party Programme, mainly:

(1) On the question of imperialism and the imperialist war;

(2) On our attitude towards the state and *our* demand for a "commune state"[4];

(3) Amendment of our out-of-date minimum programme;

(c) Change of the Party's name.[5]

10) A new International.

We must take the initiative in creating a revolutionary International, an International against the *social-chauvinists* and against the "Centre".[6]

In order that the reader may understand why I had especially to emphasise as a rare exception the "case" of honest opponents, I invite him to compare the above theses with the following objection by Mr. Goldenberg: Lenin, he said, "has planted the banner of civil war in the midst of revolutionary democracy" (quoted in No. 5 of Mr. Plekhanov's *Yedinstvo*[7]).

[4] I.e., a state of which the Paris Commune was the prototype.—*Au.*

[5] Instead of "Social-Democracy", whose official leaders *throughout* the world have betrayed socialism and deserted to the bourgeoisie (the "defencists" and the vacillating "Kautskyites"), we must call ourselves the *Communist Party.—Au.*

[6] The "Centre" in the international Social-Democratic movement is the trend which vacillates between the chauvinists (="defencists") and internationalists, i.e., Kautsky and Co. in Germany, Longuet and Co. in France, Chkheidze and Co. in Russia, Turati and Co. in Italy, MacDonald and Co. in Britain, etc.—*Au.*

[7] *Yedinstvo* (Unity)—a daily published in Petrograd from March to November

Isn't it a gem?

I write, announce and elaborately explain: "In view of the undoubted honesty of those *broad* sections of the *mass* believers in revolutionary defencism . . . in view of the fact that they are being deceived by the bourgeoisie, it is necessary with *particular* thoroughness, persistence and *patience* to explain their error to them . . . ."

Yet the bourgeois gentlemen who call themselves Social-Democrats, who *do not* belong either to the *broad* sections or to the *mass* believers in defencism, with serene brow present my views thus: "The banner [!][8] of civil war" (of which there is not a word in the theses and not a word in my speech!) has been planted (!) "in the midst [!!] of revolutionary democracy . . .".

What does this mean? In what way does this differ from riot-inciting agitation, from *Russkaya Volya*[9]?

I write, announce and elaborately explain: "The Soviets of Workers' Deputies are the *only possible* form of revolutionary government, and therefore our task is to present a patient, systematic, and persistent *explanation* of the errors of their tactics, an explanation especially adapted to the practical needs of the masses."

Yet opponents of a certain brand present my views as a call to "civil war in the midst of revolutionary democracy"!

I attacked the Provisional Government for *not* having appointed an early date, or any date at all, for the convocation of the Constituent Assembly, and for confining itself to promises. I argued that *without* the Soviets of Workers' and Soldiers' Deputies the convocation of the Constituent Assembly is not guaranteed and its success is impossible.

And the view is attributed to me that I am opposed to the speedy convocation of the Constituent Assembly!

....

1917, and then under another name from December 1917 to January 1918. Edited by G. V. Plekhanov. United the extreme Right of the Menshevik defencists and gave unqualified support to the bourgeois Provisional Government. Carried on a fierce struggle against the Bolshevik Party.

8 Interpolations in square brackets (within passages quoted by Lenin) have been introduced by Lenin, unless otherwise indicated.

9 *Russkaya Volya* (Russian Freedom)—a bourgeois daily founded and run by the big banks. Carried on a riot-provoking campaign against the Bolsheviks. Lenin called it one of the most disreputable bourgeois newspapers. Appeared in Petrograd from December 1916 to October 1917.

I would call this "raving", had not decades of political struggle taught me to regard honesty in opponents as a rare exception.

Mr. Plekhanov in his paper called my speech "raving". Very good, Mr. Plekhanov! But look how awkward, uncouth, and slow-witted you are in your polemics. If I delivered a raving speech for two hours, how is it that an audience of hundreds tolerated this "raving"? Further, why does your paper devote a whole column to an account of the "raving"? Inconsistent, highly inconsistent!

It is, of course, much easier to shout, abuse, and howl than to attempt to relate, to explain, to recall *what* Marx and Engels said in 1871, 1872 and 1875 about the experience of the Paris Commune[10] and about the *kind* of state the proletariat needs.

Ex-Marxist Mr. Plekhanov evidently does not care to recall Marxism.

I quoted the words of Rosa Luxemburg, who on August 4, 1914,[11] called *German* Social-Democracy a "stinking corpse". And the Plekhanovs, Goldenbergs and Co. feel "offended". On whose behalf? On behalf of the *German* chauvinists, because they were called chauvinists!

They have got themselves in a mess, these poor Russian social-chauvinists—socialists in word and chauvinists in deed.

N. Lenin

Published April 7, 1917 in *Pravda,* No. 26
Published according to the newspaper text

[10] See Marx and Engels, *Selected Works,* Vol. I, Moscow, 1962, pp. 21-22, 516-30, Vol. II, Moscow, 1962, pp. 42, 463-64.

[11] On August 4, 1914, the Social-Democrats in the Reichstag voted together with the bourgeois M.P.s in favour of a 5,000 million war loan for the Kaiser government, thereby approving the imperialist policy of Wilhelm II. As it afterwards emerged, the Left Social-Democrats, during the discussion of this question by the Social-Democratic group previous to the Reichstag session, were against granting the government war loans, but they bowed to the decision of the opportunist majority and voted in favour.

THE TASKS OF THE PROLETARIAT IN OUR REVOLUTION

Draft Platform for the Proletarian Party

The moment of history through which Russia is now passing is marked by the following main characteristics:

THE CLASS CHARACTER OF THE REVOLUTION THAT HAS TAKEN PLACE

1. The old tsarist power, which represented only a handful of feudalist landowners who commanded the entire state machinery (the army, the police, and the bureaucracy), has been overthrown and removed, but not completely destroyed. The monarchy has not been formally abolished; the Romanov gang continues to hatch monarchist intrigues. The vast landed possessions of the feudalist squirearchy have not been abolished.

2. State power in Russia has passed into the hands of a new *class*, namely, the bourgeoisie and landowners who had become bourgeois. *To this extent* the bourgeois-democratic revolution in Russia is completed.

Having come to power, the bourgeoisie has formed a bloc (an alliance) with the overt monarchists, who are notorious for their exceptionally ardent support of Nicholas the Bloody and Stolypin the Hangman in 1906-14 (Guchkov and other politicians to the right of the Cadets[1]). The new bourgeois government of Lvov and Co. has

[1] *Cadets*—(abbreviated) members of the Constitutional-Democratic Party, the chief party of the liberal monarchist bourgeoisie in Russia. Founded in October 1905, its membership was made up of representatives of the bourgeoisie, Zemstvo leaders of the landowning class and bourgeois intellectuals. Among the leading personalities of the party were P. N. Milyukov, S. A. Muromtsev, V. A. Maklakov, A. I. Shingaryov, P. B. Struve and F. I. Rodichev. Eventually, the Cadets became a party of the imperialist bourgeoisie. During the First World War they fully supported the tsarist government's aggressive foreign policy. During the bourgeois-democratic revolution of February 1917 they tried their hardest to save the monarchy. They used their key positions in the bourgeois Provisional Government to

attempted and has begun to negotiate with the Romanovs for the restoration of the monarchy in Russia. Behind a screen of revolutionary phrases, this government is appointing partisans of the old regime to key positions. It is striving to reform the whole machinery of state (the army, the police, and the bureaucracy) as little as possible, and has turned it over to the bourgeoisie. The new government has already begun to hinder in every way the revolutionary initiative of mass action and the seizure of power by the people *from below*, which is the *sole* guarantee of the real success of the revolution.

Up to now this government has not even fixed a date for the convocation of the Constituent Assembly. It is not laying a finger on the landed estates, which form the material foundation of feudal tsarism. This government does not even contemplate starting an investigation into, and making public, the activities of the monopolist financial organisations, the big banks, the syndicates and cartels of the capitalists, etc., or instituting control over them.

The key positions, the decisive ministerial posts in the new government (the Ministry of the Interior and the War Ministry, i.e., the command over the army, the police, the bureaucracy—the entire apparatus for oppressing the people) are held by outright monarchists and supporters of the system of big landed estates. The Cadets, those day-old republicans, republicans against their own will, have been assigned minor posts, having no direct relation to the *command* over the people or to the apparatus of state power. A. Kerensky, a Trudovik[2]

....

pursue a counter-revolutionary policy opposed to the interests of the people, but favouring the U.S., British and French imperialists. After the victory of the October Revolution the Cadets came out as implacable enemies of the Soviet power. They took part in all the counter-revolutionary armed actions and campaigns of the interventionists. Living abroad as émigrés after the defeat of the interventionists and whiteguards, the Cadets did not cease their anti-Soviet counter-revolutionary activities.

[2] *Trudoviks* (the Trudovik group)—a group of petty-bourgeois democrats in the Russian Duma consisting of peasants and intellectuals of the Narodnik trend. The Trudovik group was formed in April 1906 by peasant deputies to the First Duma. In the Duma the Trudoviks vacillated between the Cadets and the revolutionary Social-Democrats. During the First World War most of the Trudoviks took a social-chauvinist stand.

After the bourgeois-democratic revolution of February 1917 the Trudoviks, representing the interests of the kulaks, actively supported the and "would-be socialist", has no function whatsoever, except to lull the vigilance and attention of the people with sonorous phrases.

For all these reasons, the new bourgeois government does not deserve the confidence of the proletariat even in the sphere of internal policy, and no support of this government by the proletariat is admissible.

THE FOREIGN POLICY OF THE NEW GOVERNMENT

3. In the field of foreign policy, which has now been brought to the forefront by objective circumstances, the new government is a government for the continuation of the imperialist war, a war that is being waged in alliance with the imperialist powers—Britain, France, and others—for division of the capitalist spoils and for subjugating small and weak nations.

Subordinated to the interests of Russian capitalism and its powerful protector and master—Anglo-French imperialist capitalism, the wealthiest in the world, the new government, notwithstanding the wishes expressed in no uncertain fashion on behalf of the obvious majority of the peoples of Russia through the Soviet of Soldiers' and Workers' Deputies, has taken no real steps to put an end to the slaughter of peoples for the interests of the capitalists. It has not even published the secret treaties of an obviously predatory character (for the partition of Persia, the plunder of China, the plunder of Turkey, the partition of Austria, the annexation of Eastern Prussia, the annexation of the German colonies, etc.), which, as everybody knows, bind Russia to Anglo-French predatory imperialist capital. It has *confirmed* these treaties concluded by tsarism, which for centuries robbed and oppressed more nations than other tyrants and despots, and which not only oppressed, but also disgraced and demoralised the Great-Russian nation by making it an executioner of other nations.

The new government has confirmed these shameful depredatory

....

Provisional Government. The Trudovik Zarudny, who became Minister of Justice after the July events, persecuted the Bolshevik Party. The Trudoviks were enemies of the October Revolution and sided with the bourgeois counter-revolution.

treaties and has not proposed an immediate armistice to all the belligerent nations, in spite of the clearly expressed demand of the majority of the peoples of Russia, voiced through the Soviets of Workers' and Soldiers' Deputies. It has evaded the issue with the help of solemn, sonorous, bombastic, but absolutely empty declarations and phrases, which, in the mouths of bourgeois diplomats, have always served, and still serve, to deceive the trustful and naïve masses of the oppressed people.

4. Not only, therefore, is the new government unworthy of the slightest confidence in the field of foreign policy, but to go on demanding that it should proclaim the will of the peoples of Russia for peace, that it should renounce annexations, and so on and so forth, is in practice merely to deceive the people, to inspire them with false hopes and to retard the clarification of their minds. It is indirectly to reconcile them to the continuation of a war the true social character of which is determined not by pious wishes, but by the class character of the government that wages the war, by the connection between the class represented by this government and the imperialist finance capital of Russia, Britain, France, etc., by *the real and actual policy* which that class is pursuing.

THE PECULIAR NATURE OF THE DUAL POWER AND ITS CLASS SIGNIFICANCE

5. The main feature of our revolution, a feature that most imperatively demands thoughtful consideration, is the *dual power* which arose in the very first days after the triumph of the revolution.

This dual power is evident in the existence of *two* governments: one is the main, the real, the actual government of the bourgeoisie, the "Provisional Government" of Lvov and Co., which holds in its hands all the organs of power; the other is a supplementary and parallel government, a "controlling" government in the shape of the Petrograd Soviet of Workers' and Soldiers' Deputies, which holds no organs of state power, but directly rests on the support of an obvious and indisputable majority of the people, on the armed workers and soldiers.

The class origin and the class significance of this dual power is the following: the Russian revolution of March 1917 not only swept away the whole tsarist monarchy, not only transferred the entire power to the bourgeoisie, but also *moved close towards* a revolutionary-democratic dictatorship of the proletariat and the peasantry. The Petrograd and the other, the local, Soviets constitute precisely such a dictatorship (that is, a power resting not on the law but directly on the force of armed masses of the population), a dictatorship precisely of the above-mentioned classes.

6. The second highly important feature of the Russian revolution is the fact that the Petrograd Soviet of Soldiers' and Workers' Deputies, which, as everything goes to show, enjoys the confidence of most of the local Soviets, is *voluntarily* transferring state power to the bourgeoisie and *its* Provisional Government, is voluntarily *ceding* supremacy to the latter, having entered into an agreement to support it, and is limiting its own role to that of an observer, a supervisor of the convocation of the Constituent Assembly (the date for which has not even been announced as yet by the Provisional Government).

This remarkable feature, unparalleled in history in such a form, has led to the *interlocking of two* dictatorships: the dictatorship of the bourgeoisie (for the government of Lvov and Co. is a dictatorship, i.e., a power based not on the law, not on the previously expressed will of the people, but on seizure by force, accomplished by a definite class, namely, the bourgeoisie) and the dictatorship of the proletariat and the peasantry (the Soviet of Workers' and Soldiers' Deputies).

There is not the slightest doubt that such an "interlocking" *cannot* last long. Two powers *cannot exist* in a state. One of them is bound to pass away; and the entire Russian bourgeoisie is already trying its hardest everywhere and in every way to keep out and weaken the Soviets, to reduce them to nought, and to establish the undivided power of the bourgeoisie.

The dual power merely expresses a *transitional* phase in the revolution's development, when it has gone farther than the ordinary bourgeois-democratic revolution, *but has not yet reached* a "pure" dictatorship of the proletariat and the peasantry.

The class significance (and the class explanation) of this

transitional and unstable situation is this: like all revolutions, our revolution required the greatest heroism and self-sacrifice on the part of the people for the struggle against tsarism; it also immediately *drew* unprecedentedly vast numbers of ordinary citizens *into the movement*.

From the point of view of science and practical politics, one of the chief symptoms of *every* real revolution is the unusually rapid, sudden, and abrupt increase in the number of "ordinary citizens" who begin to participate actively, independently and effectively in political life and in the *organisation of the state*.

Such is the case in Russia. Russia at present is seething. Millions and tens of millions of people, who had been politically dormant for ten years and politically crushed by the terrible oppression of tsarism and by inhuman toil for the landowners and capitalists, have *awakened and taken eagerly* to politics. And who are these millions and tens of millions? For the most part small proprietors, petty bourgeois, people standing midway between the capitalists and the wage-workers. Russia is the most petty-bourgeois of all European countries.

A gigantic petty-bourgeois wave has swept over everything and overwhelmed the class-conscious proletariat, not only by force of numbers but also ideologically; that is, it has infected and imbued very wide circles of workers with the petty-bourgeois political outlook.

The petty bourgeoisie are in real life dependent upon the bourgeoisie, for they live like masters and not like proletarians (from the point of view of their *place* in social *production*) and follow the bourgeoisie in their outlook.

An attitude of unreasoning trust in the capitalists—the worst foes of peace and socialism—characterises the politics of the *popular masses* in Russia at the present moment; this is the fruit that has *grown* with revolutionary rapidity on the social and economic soil of the most petty-bourgeois of all European countries. This is the *class* basis for the "*agreement*" between the Provisional Government and the Soviet of Workers' and Soldiers' Deputies (I emphasise that I am referring not so much to the formal agreement as to *actual* support, a tacit agreement, the surrender of power inspired by unreasoning trust), an agreement which has given the Guchkovs a fat piece—real power—and the Soviet merely promises and honours (for the time being), flattery, phrases, assurances, and the bowings and scrapings of the Kerenskys.

On the other side we have the inadequate numerical strength of the proletariat in Russia and its insufficient class-consciousness and organisation.

All the Narodnik parties, including the Socialist-Revolutionaries, have always been petty-bourgeois. This is also true of the party of the Organising Committee (Chkheidze, Tsereteli, etc.). The non-party revolutionaries (Steklov and others) have similarly yielded to the tide, or have not been able to stand up to it, have not had the time to do it.

THE PECULIAR NATURE OF THE TACTICS WHICH FOLLOW FROM THE ABOVE

7. For the Marxist, who must reckon with objective facts, with the masses and classes, and not with individuals and so on, the peculiar nature of the actual situation as described above must determine the peculiar nature of the tactics for the *present* moment.

This peculiarity of the situation calls, in the first place, for the "pouring of vinegar and bile into the sweet water of revolutionary-democratic phraseology" (as my fellow member on the Central Committee of our Party, Teodorovich, so aptly put it at yesterday's session of the All-Russia Congress of Railwaymen in Petrograd). Our work must be one of criticism, of *explaining* the mistakes of the petty-bourgeois Socialist-Revolutionary and Social-Democratic parties, of preparing and welding the elements of a *consciously* proletarian, Communist Party, and of *curing* the proletariat of the "general" petty-bourgeois intoxication.

This *seems* to be "nothing more" than propaganda work, but in reality it is most *practical revolutionary* work; for there is no advancing a revolution that has come to a standstill, that has choked itself with phrases, and that keeps "marking time", *not because* of external obstacles, *not because of the violence* of the bourgeoisie (Guchkov is still only threatening to employ violence against the soldier mass), but *because* of the unreasoning trust of the people.

Only by overcoming this unreasoning trust (and we can and should overcome it only ideologically, by comradely persuasion, by pointing to the *lessons of experience*) can we set ourselves free from the prevailing *orgy of revolutionary phrase-mongering* and really stimulate the consciousness both of the proletariat and of the mass in general, as well as their bold and determined initiative *in the localities*—the independent realisation, development and consolidation of liberties, democracy, and the principle of people's ownership of all the land.

8. The world-wide experience of bourgeois and landowner governments has evolved *two* methods of keeping the people in subjection. The first is violence. Nicholas Romanov I, nicknamed Nicholas of the Big Stick, and Nicholas II, the Bloody, demonstrated to the Russian people the maximum of what can and cannot be done in the way of these hangmen's practices. But there is another method, best developed by the British and French bourgeoisie, who "learned their lesson" in a series of great revolutions and revolutionary movements of the masses. It is the method of deception, flattery, fine phrases, promises by the million, petty sops, and concessions of the unessential while retaining the essential.

The peculiar feature of the present situation in Russia is the transition at a dizzy speed from the first method to the second, from violent oppression of the people to *flattering* and deceiving the people by promises. Vaska the Cat listens, but goes on eating.[3] Milyukov and Guchkov are holding power, they are protecting the profits of the capitalists, conducting an imperialist war in the interests of Russian and Anglo-French capital, and trying to get away with promises, declamation and bombastic statements in reply to the speeches of "cooks" like Chkheidze, Tsereteli and Steklov, who threaten, exhort, conjure, beseech, demand and proclaim . . . . Vaska the Cat listens, but goes on eating.

But from day to day trustful lack of reasoning and unreasoning trust will be falling away, especially among the proletarians and *poor* peasants, who are being taught by experience (by their social and economic position) to distrust the capitalists.

The leaders of the petty bourgeoisie "must" teach the people

[3] A quotation from Krylov's fable "The Cat and the Cook".

to trust the bourgeoisie. The proletarians must teach the people to distrust the bourgeoisie.

REVOLUTIONARY DEFENCISM AND ITS CLASS SIGNIFICANCE

9. *Revolutionary defencism* must be regarded as the most important, the most striking manifestation of the petty-bourgeois wave that has swept over "nearly everything". It is the worst enemy of the further progress and success of the Russian revolution.

Those who have yielded on this point and have been unable to extricate themselves are lost to the revolution. But the masses yield in a different way from the leaders, and they extricate themselves *differently*, by a different course of development, by different means.

Revolutionary defencism is, on the one hand, a result of the deception of the masses by the bourgeoisie, a result of the trustful lack of reasoning on the part of the peasants and a section of the workers; it is, on the other, an expression of the interests and point of view of the small proprietor, who is to some extent interested in annexations and bank profits, and who "sacredly" guards the traditions of tsarism, which demoralised the Great Russians by making them do a hangman's work against the other peoples.

The bourgeoisie deceives the people by working on their noble pride in the revolution and by pretending that the *social and political* character of the war, as far as Russia is concerned, underwent a change because of this stage of the revolution, because of the substitution of the near-republic of Guchkov and Milyukov for the tsarist monarchy. And the people believed it—for a time—largely owing to age-old prejudices, which made them look upon the other peoples of Russia, i.e., the non-Great Russians, as something in the nature of a property and private estate of the Great Russians. This vile demoralisation of the Great Russian people by tsarism which taught them to regard the other peoples as something inferior, something belonging "by right" to Great Russia, could not disappear *instantly*.

What is required of us is the *ability* to explain to the masses that the social and political character of the war is determined not by the "good will" of individuals or groups, or even of nations, but by the position of the *class* which conducts the war, by the class *policy* of which the war is a continuation, by the *ties* of capital, which is the dominant economic force in modern society, by the *imperialist character* of international capital, by Russia's dependence in finance, banking and diplomacy upon Britain, France, and so on. To explain this skilfully in a way the people would understand *is not easy*; none of us would be able to do it at once without committing errors.

But this, and only this, must be the aim or, rather, the message of our propaganda. The slightest concession to revolutionary defencism is a *betrayal of socialism*, a complete renunciation of *internationalism*, no matter by what fine phrases and "practical" considerations it may be justified.

The slogan "Down with the War!" is, of course, correct. But it fails to take into account the specific nature of the tasks of the present moment and the necessity of *approaching* the broad mass of the people *in a different way*. It reminds me of the slogan "Down with the Tsar!" with which the inexperienced agitator of the "good old days" went simply and directly to the countryside—and got a beating for his pains. The mass believers in revolutionary defencism are *honest*, not in the personal, but in the class sense, i.e., they belong to *classes* (workers and the peasant poor) which *in actual fact* have nothing to gain from annexations and the subjugation of other peoples. This is nothing like the bourgeois and the "intellectual" fraternity, who know very well that you *cannot* renounce annexations without renouncing the rule of capital, and who unscrupulously deceive the people with fine phrases, with unlimited promises and endless assurances.

The rank-and-file believer in defencism regards the matter in the simple way of the man in the street: "I don't want annexations, but the Germans are 'going for' *me*, therefore I'm defending a just cause and not any kind of imperialist interests at all." To a man like this it must be explained again and again that it is not a question of his personal wishes, but of mass, *class*, political relations and conditions, of the connection between the war and the interests of capital and the international network of banks, and so forth. Only such a struggle against defencism will be serious and will promise success—perhaps not a very rapid success, but one that will be real and enduring.

HOW CAN THE WAR BE ENDED?

10. The war cannot be ended "at will". It cannot be ended by the decision of one of the belligerents. It cannot be ended by "sticking your bayonet into the ground", as one soldier, a defencist, expressed it.

The war cannot be ended by an "agreement" among the socialists of the various countries, by the "action" of the proletarians of all countries, by the "will" of the peoples, and so forth. All the phrases of this kind, which fill the articles of the defencist, semi-defencist, and semi-internationalist papers as well as innumerable resolutions, appeals, manifestos, and the resolutions of the Soviet of Soldiers' and Workers' Deputies—all such phrases are nothing but idle, innocent and pious wishes of the petty bourgeois. There is nothing more harmful than phrases like "ascertaining the will of the peoples for peace", like the *sequence* of revolutionary actions of the proletariat (after the Russian proletariat comes the turn of the German), etc. All this is Blancism, fond dreams, a playing at "political campaigning", and in reality just a repetition of the fable of Vaska the Cat.

The war is not a product of the evil will of rapacious capitalists, although it is undoubtedly being fought *only* in their interests and they alone are being enriched by it. The war is a product of half a century of development of world capitalism and of its billions of threads and connections. It is *impossible* to slip out of the imperialist war and achieve a democratic, non-coercive peace without overthrowing the power of capital and transferring state power to *another* class, the proletariat.

The Russian revolution of February-March 1917 was the beginning of the transformation of the imperialist war into a civil war. This revolution took the *first* step towards ending the war; but it requires a *second* step, namely, the transfer of state power to the proletariat, to make the end of the war a *certainty*. This will be the beginning of a "break-through" on a world-wide scale, a break-through in the front of capitalist interests; and only by breaking through *this* front *can* the proletariat save mankind from the horrors of war and endow it with the blessings of peace.

It is directly to such a "break-through" in the front of capitalism that the Russian revolution has *already* brought the Russian proletariat by creating the Soviets of Workers' Deputies.

A NEW TYPE OF STATE EMERGING FROM OUR REVOLUTION

11. The Soviets of Workers', Soldiers', Peasants' and other Deputies are not understood, not only in the sense that their class significance, their role in the *Russian* revolution, is not clear to the majority. They are not understood also in the sense that they constitute a new form or rather a new *type of state*.

The most perfect, the most advanced type of bourgeois state is the *parliamentary democratic republic*: power is vested in parliament; the state machine, the apparatus and organ of administration, is of the customary kind: the standing army, the police, and the bureaucracy—which in practice is undisplaceable, is privileged and stands *above* the people.

Since the end of the nineteenth century, however, revolutionary epochs have advanced a *higher* type of democratic state, a state which in certain respects, as Engels put it, ceases to be a state, is "no longer a state in the proper sense of the word".[4] This is a state of the Paris Commune type, one in which a standing army and police divorced from the people are *replaced* by the direct arming of the people themselves. It is *this feature* that constitutes the very essence of the Commune, which has been so misrepresented and slandered by the bourgeois writers, and to which has been erroneously ascribed, among other things, the intention of immediately "introducing" socialism.

This is the type of state which the Russian revolution *began* to create in 1905 and in 1917. A Republic of Soviets of Workers', Soldiers', Peasants', and other Deputies, united in an All-Russia Constituent

[4] See Marx and Engels, *Selected Works*, Vol. II, Moscow, 1962, p. 42.

Assembly of people's representatives or in a Council of Soviets, etc., is what is *already being realised* in our country now, at this juncture. It is being realised by the initiative of the nation's millions, who are creating a democracy on their own, *in their own way*, without waiting until the Cadet professors draft their legislative bills for a parliamentary bourgeois republic, or until the pedants and routine-worshippers of petty-bourgeois "Social-Democracy", like Mr. Plekhanov or Kautsky, stop distorting the Marxist teaching on the state.

Marxism differs from anarchism in that it recognises the *need* for a state and for state power in the period of revolution in general, and in the period of transition from capitalism to socialism in particular.

Marxism differs from the petty-bourgeois, opportunist "Social-Democratism" of Plekhanov, Kautsky and Co. in that it recognises that what is required during these two periods is *not* a state of the usual parliamentary bourgeois republican type, but a state of the Paris Commune type.

The main distinctions between a state of the latter type and the old state are as follows.

It is quite easy (as history proves) to revert from a parliamentary bourgeois republic to a monarchy, for all the machinery of oppression—the army, the police, and the bureaucracy—is left intact. The Commune and the Soviets *smash* that machinery and do away with it.

The parliamentary bourgeois republic hampers and stifles the independent political life of the *masses*, their direct participation in the *democratic* organisation of the life of the state from the bottom up. The opposite is the case with the Soviets.

The latter reproduce the type of state which was being evolved by the Paris Commune and which Marx described as "the political form at last discovered under which to work out the economic emancipation of labour".[5]

We are usually told that the Russian people are not yet prepared for the "introduction" of the Commune. This was the argument of the serf-owners when they claimed that the peasants were not prepared for emancipation. The Commune, i.e., the Soviets, does not "introduce",

[5] See Marx and Engels, *Selected Works*, Vol. I, Moscow, 1962, pp. 522-23.

does not intend to "introduce", and must not introduce *any* reforms which have not absolutely matured both in economic reality and in the minds of the overwhelming majority of the people. The deeper the economic collapse and the crisis produced by the war, the more urgent becomes the need for the most perfect political form, which will *facilitate* the healing of the terrible wounds inflicted on mankind by the war. The less the organisational experience of the Russian people, the more resolutely must we *proceed* to organisational development by the *people themselves*, and not merely by the bourgeois politicians and "well-placed" bureaucrats.

The sooner we shed the old prejudices of pseudo-Marxism, a Marxism falsified by Plekhanov, Kautsky and Co., the more actively we set about helping the people to organise Soviets of Workers' and Peasants' Deputies everywhere and immediately, and helping the latter to take life *in its entirety* under their control, and the longer Lvov and Co. delay the convocation of the Constituent Assembly, the easier will it be for the people (through the medium of the Constituent Assembly, or independently of it, if Lvov delays its convocation too long) to cast their decision in favour of a republic of Soviets of Workers' and Peasants' Deputies. Errors in the new work of organisational development by the people themselves are at first inevitable; but it is better to make mistakes and go forward than to *wait* until the professors of law summoned by Mr. Lvov draft their laws for the convocation of the Constituent Assembly, for the perpetuation of the parliamentary bourgeois republic and for the strangling of the Soviets of Workers' and Peasants' Deputies.

If we organise ourselves and conduct our propaganda skilfully, not only the proletarians, but nine-tenths of the peasants will be opposed to the restoration of the police, will be opposed to an undisplaceable and privileged bureaucracy and to an army divorced from the people. And that is all the new type of state stands for.

12. The substitution of a people's militia for the police is a reform that follows from the entire course of the revolution and that is now being introduced in most parts of Russia. We must explain to the people that in most of the bourgeois revolutions of the usual type, this

reform was always extremely short-lived, and that the bourgeoisie—even the most democratic and republican—restored the police of the old, tsarist type, a police divorced from the people, commanded by the bourgeoisie and capable of oppressing the people in every way.

There is only one way to *prevent* the restoration of the police, and that is to create a people's militia and to fuse it with the army (the standing army to be replaced by the arming of the entire people). Service in this militia should extend to all citizens of both sexes between the ages of fifteen and sixty-five without exception, if these tentatively suggested age limits may be taken as indicating the participation of adolescents and old people. Capitalists must pay their workers, servants, etc., for days devoted to public service in the militia. Unless women are brought to take an independent part not only in political life generally, but also in daily and universal public service, it is no use talking about full and stable democracy, let alone socialism. And such "police" functions as care of the sick and of homeless children, food inspection, etc., will never be satisfactorily discharged until women are on an equal footing with men, not merely nominally but in reality.

The tasks which the proletariat must put before the people in order to safeguard, consolidate and develop the revolution are prevention of the restoration of the police and enlistment of the organisational forces of the entire people in forming a people's militia.

THE AGRARIAN AND NATIONAL PROGRAMMES

13. At the present moment we cannot say for certain whether a mighty agrarian revolution will develop in the Russian countryside in the near future. We cannot say exactly how profound the class cleavage is among the peasants, which has undoubtedly grown more profound of late as a division into agricultural labourers, wage-workers and poor peasants ("semi-proletarians"), on the one hand, and wealthy and middle peasants (capitalists and petty capitalists), on the other. Such questions will be, and can be, decided only by experience.

Being the party of the proletariat, however, we are unquestionably in duty bound not only immediately to advance an agrarian (land) programme but also to advocate practical measures which can be immediately realised *in the interests* of the peasant agrarian revolution in Russia.

We must demand the nationalisation of *all* the land, i.e., that all the land in the state should become the property of the central state power. This power must fix the size, etc., of the resettlement land fund, pass legislation for the conservation of forests, for land improvement, etc., and absolutely prohibit any middlemen to interpose themselves between the owner of the land, i.e., the state, and the tenant, i.e., the tiller (prohibit all subletting of land). However, the *disposal* of the land, the determination of the *local regulations* governing ownership and tenure of land, must in no case be placed in the hands of bureaucrats and officials, but wholly and exclusively in the hands of the regional and local *Soviets of Peasants' Deputies.*

In order to improve grain production techniques and increase output, and in order to develop rational cultivation on a large scale under public control, we must strive within the peasants' committees to secure the transformation of every confiscated landed estate into a large model farm controlled by the *Soviet of Agricultural Labourers' Deputies.*

In order to counteract the petty-bourgeois phrase-mongering and the policy prevailing among the Socialist-Revolutionaries, particularly the idle talk about "subsistence" standards or "labour" standards, "socialisation of the land", etc., the party of the proletariat must make it clear that small-scale farming under commodity production *cannot* save mankind from poverty and oppression.

Without necessarily splitting the Soviets of Peasants' Deputies at once, the party of the proletariat must explain the need for organising separate Soviets of Agricultural Labourers' Deputies and separate Soviets of deputies from the poor (semi-proletarian) peasants, or, at least, for holding regular separate conferences of deputies of *this class status* in the shape of separate groups or parties within the general Soviets of Peasants' Deputies. Otherwise all the honeyed petty-bourgeois talk of the Narodniks[6] regarding the peasants in general

[6] The term *Narodniks* is here used to denote the three petty-bourgeois parties of the Narodnik trend, namely, the Trudoviks, the Socialist-Revolutionaries,

will serve as a shield for the deception of the propertyless mass by the wealthy peasants, who are merely a variety of *capitalists*.

To counteract the bourgeois-liberal or purely bureaucratic sermons preached by many Socialist-Revolutionaries and Soviets of Workers' and Soldiers' Deputies, who advise the peasants not to seize the landed estates and not to start the agrarian reform pending the convocation of the Constituent Assembly, the party of the proletariat must urge the peasants to carry out the agrarian reform at once on their own, and to confiscate the landed estates immediately, upon the decisions of the peasants' deputies in the localities.

At the same time, it is most important to insist on the necessity of *increasing* food production for the soldiers at the front and for the towns, and on the absolute inadmissibility of causing any damage or injury to livestock, implements, machinery, buildings, etc.

14. As regards the national question, the proletarian party first of all must advocate the proclamation and immediate realisation of complete freedom of secession from Russia for all the nations and peoples who were oppressed by tsarism, or who were forcibly joined to, or forcibly kept within the boundaries of, the state, i.e., annexed.

All statements, declarations and manifestos concerning renunciation of annexations that are not accompanied by the realisation of the right of secession in practice, are nothing but bourgeois deception of the people, or else pious petty-bourgeois wishes.

The proletarian party strives to create as large a state as possible, for this is to the advantage of the working people; it strives to *draw* nations *closer together*, and bring about their *further fusion*; but it desires to achieve this aim not by violence, but exclusively through a free fraternal union of the workers and the working people of all nations.

The more democratic the Russian republic, and the more successfully it organises itself into a Republic of Soviets of Workers' and Peasants' Deputies, the more powerful will be the force of *voluntary* attraction to such a republic on the part of the working people of *all* nations.

Complete freedom of secession, the broadest local (and national)

....

and the Popular Socialists.

autonomy, and elaborate guarantees of the rights of national minorities—this is the programme of the revolutionary proletariat.

NATIONALISATION OF THE BANKS AND CAPITALIST SYNDICATES

15. Under no circumstances can the party of the proletariat set itself the aim of "introducing" socialism in a country of small peasants so long as the overwhelming majority of the population has not come to realise the need for a socialist revolution.

But only bourgeois sophists, hiding behind "near-Marxist" catchwords, can deduce from this truth a justification of the policy of postponing immediate revolutionary measures, the time for which is fully ripe; measures which *have been* frequently *resorted to during the war by a number of bourgeois states*, and which are absolutely indispensable in order to combat impending total economic disorganisation and famine.

Such measures as the nationalisation of the land, of all the banks and capitalist syndicates, or, at least, the *immediate* establishment of the *control* of the Soviets of Workers' Deputies, etc., over them—measures which do not in any way constitute the "introduction" of socialism—must be absolutely insisted on, and, whenever possible, carried out in a revolutionary way. Without such measures, which are only steps towards socialism, and which are perfectly feasible economically, it will be impossible to heal the wounds caused by the war and to avert the impending collapse; and the party of the revolutionary proletariat will never hesitate to lay hands on the fabulous profits of the capitalists and bankers, who are enriching themselves on the war in a particularly scandalous manner.

THE SITUATION WITHIN THE SOCIALIST INTERNATIONAL

16. The international obligations of the working class of Russia are precisely now coming to the forefront with particular force.

Only lazy people do not swear by internationalism these days. Even the chauvinist defencists, even Plekhanov and Potresov, even Kerensky, call themselves internationalists. It becomes the duty of the proletarian party all the more urgently, therefore, to clearly, precisely and definitely counterpose internationalism in deed to internationalism in word.

Mere appeals to the workers of all countries, empty assurances of devotion to internationalism, direct or indirect attempts to fix a "sequence" of action by the revolutionary proletariat in the various belligerent countries, laborious efforts to conclude "agreements" between the socialists of the belligerent countries *on the question* of the revolutionary struggle, all the fuss over the summoning of socialist congresses *for the purpose* of a peace campaign, etc., etc.—no matter how sincere the authors of such ideas, attempts, and plans may be—amount, as far as their *objective*-significance is concerned, to mere phrase-mongering, and at *best* are innocent and pious wishes, fit only to conceal the *deception* of the people by the chauvinists. The *French* social-chauvinists, who are the most adroit and accomplished in methods of parliamentary hocus-pocus, have long since broken the record for ranting and resonant pacifist and internationalist phrases *coupled with* the incredibly brazen betrayal of socialism and the International, the acceptance of posts in governments which conduct the imperialist war, the voting of credits *or loans* (as Chkheidze, Skobelev, Tsereteli and Steklov have been doing recently in Russia), opposition to the revolutionary struggle in *their own country*, etc., etc.

Good people often forget the brutal and savage setting of the imperialist world war. This setting does not tolerate phrases, and mocks at innocent and pious wishes.

There is one, and only one, kind of real internationalism, and that is—working whole-heartedly for the development of the revolutionary movement and the revolutionary struggle in *one's own* country, and supporting (by propaganda, sympathy, and material aid) *this struggle*, this, *and only this*, line, in *every* country without exception.

Everything else is deception and Manilovism.[7]

During the two odd years of the war the international socialist and

[7] *Manilovism*—from the name Manilov, a character in Gogol's *Dead Souls*, represented as a type of easy-going sentimental landowner, whose name has become a synonym for an idle weak-willed dreamer and gas-bag.

working-class movement in *every* country has evolved three trends. Whoever ignores *reality* and refuses to recognise the existence of these three trends, to analyse them, to fight consistently for the trend that is really internationalist, is doomed to impotence, helplessness and errors.

The three trends are:

1). The social-chauvinists, i.e., socialists in word and chauvinists in deed, people who recognise "defence of the fatherland" in an imperialist war (and above all in the present imperialist war).

These people are our *class* enemies. They have gone over to the bourgeoisie.

They are the majority of the official leaders of the official Social-Democratic parties in *all* countries—Plekhanov and Co. in Russia, the Scheidemanns in Germany, Renaudel, Guesde and Sembat in France, Bissolati and Co. in Italy, Hyndman, the Fabians[8] and the Labourites (the leaders of the "Labour Party") in Britain, Branting and Co. in Sweden, Troelstra and his party in Holland, Stauning and his party in Denmark, Victor Berger and the other "defenders of the fatherland" in America, and so forth.

2) The second trend, known as the "Centre", consists of people who vacillate between the social-chauvinists and the true internationalists.

The "Centre" all vow and declare that they are Marxists and internationalists, that they are for peace, for bringing every kind of "pressure" to bear upon the governments, for "demanding" in every way that their own government should "ascertain the will of the

[8] Lenin refers to the *Fabian Society*, an English reformist organisation, founded in 1884, so called after the Roman General Quintus Fabius Maximus (III century B.C.) surnamed Cunctator (Procrastinator) for his mark-time tactics and evasion of decisive battles in the war with Hannibal. The membership of the Fabian Society consisted chiefly of bourgeois intellectuals—scholars, writers and politicians (the Webbs, Ramsay MacDonald, Bernard Shaw and others). They denied the need for the proletariat's class struggle and a socialist revolution, and maintained that the transition from capitalism to socialism could be brought about by means of minor and gradual reforms. Lenin described Fabianism as "an *extremely opportunist* trend" (see *LCW*, Vol. 13, 1972, p. 358). In 1900 the Fabian Society joined the Labour Party. Fabian socialism is one of the sources of Labour Party ideology.

During the First World War (1914-18) the Fabians took a social-chauvinist stand.

people for peace", that they are for all sorts of peace campaigns, for peace without annexations, etc., etc.—*and for peace with the social-chauvinists*. The "Centre" is for "unity", the Centre is opposed to a split.

The "Centre" is a realm of honeyed petty-bourgeois phrases, of internationalism in word and cowardly opportunism and fawning on the social-chauvinists in deed.

The crux of the matter is that the "Centre" is not convinced of the necessity for a revolution against one's own government; it does not preach revolution; it does not carry on a whole-hearted revolutionary struggle; and in order to evade such a struggle it resorts to the tritest ultra-"Marxist"-sounding *excuses*.

The social-chauvinists are our *class enemies*, they are *bourgeois* within the working-class movement. They represent a stratum, or groups, or sections of the working class which *objectively* have been bribed by the bourgeoisie (by better wages, positions of honour, etc.), and which help *their own* bourgeoisie to plunder and oppress small and weak peoples and to fight *for* the division of the capitalist spoils.

The "Centre" consists of routine-worshippers, eroded by the canker of legality, corrupted by the parliamentary atmosphere, etc., bureaucrats accustomed to snug positions and soft jobs. Historically and economically speaking, they are not a *separate* stratum but represent only a *transition* from a past phase of the working-class movement—the phase between 1871 and 1914, which gave much that is valuable to the proletariat, particularly in the indispensable art of slow, sustained and systematic organisational work on a large and very large scale—to a new *phase* that became *objectively* essential with the outbreak of the first imperialist world war, which inaugurated the *era of social revolution*.

The chief leader and spokesman of the "Centre" is Karl Kautsky, the most outstanding authority in the Second International (1889-1914), since August 1914 a model of utter bankruptcy as a Marxist, the embodiment of unheard-of spinelessness, and the most wretched vacillations and betrayals. This "Centrist" trend includes Kautsky, Haase, Ledebour and the so-called workers' or labour group[9] in the

[9] *Workers' or labour group*—Arbeitsgemeinschaft (Social-Democratic Labour Group)—an organisation of the German Centrists formed in March 1916 by

Reichstag; in France it includes Longuet, Pressemane and the so-called minoritaires[10] (Mensheviks) in general; in Britain, Philip Snowden, Ramsay MacDonald and many other leaders of the Independent Labour Party,[11] and some leaders of the British Socialist Party[12]; Morris Hillquit

....

breakaway members of the official Social-Democratic group in the Reichstag. Eventually, in 1917, it formed the core of the Centrist Independent Social-Democratic Party of Germany, which sought to justify the overt social-chauvinists and stood for preserving unity with them.

10 *Minoritaires* or *Longuetists*—the minority of the French Socialist Party formed in 1915. The minoritaires were the followers of the social-reformist Longuet; they held Centrist views and pursued a conciliatory policy towards the social-chauvinists. During the First World War they took a social-pacifist stand. After the victory of the October Revolution in Russia they declared themselves adherents of the dictatorship of the proletariat, but in reality they were against it. They continued the policy of co-operation with the social-chauvinists and supported the annexationist Treaty of Versailles. Finding themselves in a minority at the congress of the French Socialist Party held in Tours in December 1920, where the Left wing won ascendancy, the Longuetists together with the open reformists split away from the party and joined the Two-and-a-Half International, and after its break-down returned to the Second International.

11 The *Independent Labour Party*—a reformist organisation founded by the leaders of the "new trade unions" in 1893 during the active strike movement and the mounting drive for independence of the British working class from the bourgeois parties. The membership of the I.L.P. consisted of the "new trade unionists" and members of some of the old trade unions, as well as intellectuals and petty bourgeois holding Fabian views. The leaders of the Party were James Keir Hardie and Ramsay MacDonald. From the day it was founded the I.L.P. took a bourgeois-reformist stand, devoting its chief attention to parliamentary forms of struggle and parliamentary deals with the Liberal Party. In the words of Lenin, the Independent Labour Party was "actually an opportunist party that has always been dependent on the bourgeoisie" (see V. I. Lenin, *On Britain*, Moscow, p. 401).

On the outbreak of the imperialist world war the I.L.P. issued a manifesto against the war, but shortly afterwards adopted a social-chauvinist stand.

12 The *British Socialist Party* was founded in 1911 in Manchester, as a result of the amalgamation of the Social-Democratic Party with other socialist groups. The B.S.P. carried on propaganda in the spirit of Marxist ideas, it was "not opportunist and was *really* independent of the Liberals" (see *LCW*, Vol. 19, 1980, p. 273). Owing to its small membership and poor contact with the masses, however, it was somewhat sectarian in character. During the First World War a sharp struggle developed in the party between the internationalist trend (William Gallacher, Albert Inkpin, John MacLean, Theodore Rothstein and others) and the social-chauvinist trend headed by

and many others in the United States; Turati, Tréves, Modigliani and others in Italy; Robert Grimm and others in Switzerland; Victor Adler and Co. in Austria; the party of the Organising Committee, Axelrod, Martov, Chkheidze, Tsereteli and others in Russia, and so forth.

Naturally, at times individuals unconsciously drift from the social-chauvinist to the "Centrist" position, and vice versa. Every Marxist knows that classes are distinct, even though individuals may move freely from one class to another; similarly, *trends* in political life are distinct in spite of the fact that individuals may change freely from one trend to another, and in spite of all attempts and efforts to *amalgamate* trends.

3) The third trend, that of the true internationalists, is best represented by the "Zimmerwald Left".[13] (We reprint as a supplement

....

Hyndman. There were inconsistent elements within the internationalist trend who took a Centrist stand on a number of issues. In February 1916 a group of the party's active members founded a newspaper *The Call*, which played an important part in uniting the internationalists. The annual conference of the B.S.P. held at Salford in April 1916 condemned the social-chauvinist stand taken by Hyndman and his adherents, and they left the party.

The British Socialist Party hailed the October Revolution, and its members played a great part in the British working people's movement in defence of Soviet Russia against foreign intervention.

In 1919 the majority of the party organisations (98 against 4) declared in favour of joining the Communist International. The B.S.P., together with the Communist Unity Group, played a leading role in the formation of the Communist Party of Great Britain. At the First (Unity) Congress held in 1920 the overwhelming majority of the B.S.P. locals joined the Communist Party.

[13] The *Zimmerwald Left group* was founded on Lenin's initiative at the International Socialist Conference held in Zimmerwald in September 1915. It consisted of delegates from the Central Committee of the R.S.D.L.P., the Left Social-Democrats in Sweden, Norway, Switzerland and Germany, the Polish Social-Democratic opposition and the Social-Democrats of the Latvian area. The Zimmerwald Left group, headed by Lenin, waged a struggle against the Centrist majority of the Conference and moved resolutions condemning the imperialist war, exposing the betrayal by the social-chauvinists, and urging the necessity of active struggle against the war. These draft resolutions were rejected by the Centrist majority. The Zimmerwald Left succeeded, however, in getting a number of points from its own draft resolution included in the manifesto adopted by the Conference. Regarding this manifesto as a first step in the fight against the war, the Zimmerwald Left voted for it, and in a special statement pointed out the inadequacy and inconsistency of the manifesto and their reasons for voting for it. They declared that while remaining within

its manifesto of September 1915, to enable the reader to learn of the inception of this trend at first hand.)

Its distinctive feature is its complete break with both social-chauvinism and "Centrism", and its gallant revolutionary struggle against *its own* imperialist government and *its own* imperialist bourgeoisie. Its principle is: "Our chief enemy is at home." It wages a ruthless struggle against honeyed social-pacifist phrases (a social-pacifist is a socialist in word and a bourgeois pacifist in deed; bourgeois pacifists dream of an everlasting peace *without* the overthrow of the yoke and domination of capital) and against all *subterfuges* employed to deny the possibility, or the appropriateness, or the timeliness of a proletarian revolutionary struggle and of a proletarian socialist revolution in *connection* with the present war.

The most outstanding representative of this trend in Germany is the Spartacus group or the *Internationale* group,[14] to which Karl

....

the Zimmerwald organisation they would disseminate their views and work independently on an international scale. The group elected an executive body—a Bureau, consisting of Lenin, Zinoviev and Radek. The Zimmerwald Left published a journal *Vorbote* (Herald) in German, which carried a number of articles by Lenin.

The Bolsheviks, the only group to take a consistent internationalist stand, were the guiding force in the Zimmerwald Left. Lenin opposed Radek's opportunist waverings and criticised the mistakes of other Leftists. The Zimmerwald Left soon became the rallying point for internationalist elements of world Social-Democracy. At the Second International Socialist Conference in April 1916 in Kienthal, Switzerland, the Zimmerwald Left had 12 out of the 43 delegates to the Conference, and on a number of issues obtained nearly half of the total votes. The Social-Democrats of various countries who belonged to the Zimmerwald Left group carried on active revolutionary work and played an important role in the establishment of Communist parties in their countries.

On the Zimmerwald Left see Lenin's articles: "The First Step", "Revolutionary Marxists at the International Socialist Conference, September 5-8, 1915" (see *LCW*, Vol. 21, 1977, pp. 383-93).

[14] The *Internationale* group, later called the Spartacus League, was formed by the Germen Left Social-Democrats Karl Leibknecht, Rosa Luxemburg, Franz Mehring, Clara Zetkin and others at the beginning of the First World War. The group played an important part in the history of the German Labour movement. At the national conference of the Left Social-Democrats held in January 1916 the group adopted the thesis concerning the tasks of international Social-Democracy drafted and proposed by Rosa Luxemburg.

Liebknecht belongs. Karl Liebknecht is a most celebrated representative of this trend and of the *new*, and genuine, proletarian International.

Karl Liebknecht called upon the workers and soldiers of Germany to *turn their guns* against *their own* government. Karl Liebknecht did that openly from the rostrum of parliament (the Reichstag). He then went to a demonstration in Potsdamer Platz, one of the largest public squares in Berlin, with illegally printed leaflets proclaiming the slogan "Down with the Government!" He was arrested and sentenced to *hard labour*. He is now serving his term in a German convict prison, like *hundreds*, if not thousands, of other *true* German socialists who have been imprisoned for their anti-war activities.

Karl Liebknecht in his speeches and letters mercilessly attacked not only *his own* Plekhanovs and Potresovs (Scheidemanns, Legiens, Davids and Co.), *but also his own Centrists*, his own Chkheidzes and Tseretelis (Kautsky, Haase, Ledebour and Co.).

Karl Liebknecht and his friend Otto Rühle, two out of one hundred and ten deputies, violated discipline, destroyed the "unity" with the "Centre" and the chauvinists, and *went against all of them*. Liebknecht *alone* represents socialism, the proletarian cause, the proletarian revolution. *All* the rest of German Social Democracy, to quote the apt words of Rosa Luxemburg (also a member and one of the leaders of the Spartacus group), is a "*stinking corpse*".

Another group of true internationalists in Germany is that of the Bremen paper *Arbeiterpolitik*.

....

The *Internationale* group carried on revolutionary propaganda among the masses against the imperialist war, exposing the aggressive policy of German imperialism and the treachery of the leaders of Social-Democracy. The group was not free, however, from serious errors on the most important questions of theory and policies: it rejected the principle of self-determination of nations in its Marxist interpretation (that is, including the right of secession and the formation of a separate state), denied the possibility of national liberation wars in the epoch of imperialism, and underestimated the role of the revolutionary party, so on. Lenin criticised the errors of the German Lefts in his articles: "The Junius Pamphlet", "The War Programme of the Proletarian Revolution" and others (see *LCW*, Vols. 22 and 23). In 1917 the *Internationale* group became affiliated to the Centrist Independent Social-Democratic Party of Germany preserving its organisational independence. After the revolution in Germany in 1918 it broke with the "Independents", and in December of the same year founded the Communist Party of Germany.

Closest to the internationalists in deed are: in France, Loriot and his friends (Bourderon and Merrheim have slid down to social-pacifism), as well as the Frenchman Henri Guilbeaux, who publishes in Geneva the journal *Demain*; in Britain, the newspaper *The Trade Unionist*, and *some* of the members of the British Socialist Party and of the Independent Labour Party (for instance, Russel Williams, who openly called for a break with the leaders who have *betrayed* socialism), the Scottish socialist school teacher *MacLean*, who was sentenced to *hard labour* by the bourgeois government of Britain for his revolutionary fight against the war, and hundreds of British socialists who are in jail for the same offence. They, and they alone, are internationalists *in deed*. In the United States, the Socialist Labour Party[15] and those within the opportunist Socialist Party[16] who in January 1917 began

[15] The *Socialist Labour Party of America* was founded in 1876 at the unity congress held in Philadelphia as a result of the amalgamation of the American sections of the First International and other socialist organisations. A leading part at the congress was played by F. A. Sorge, and associate of Marx and Engels. The overwhelming majority of the party were immigrants who had poor contacts with the American working class. During the early years the party was controlled by the Lassalleans who made mistakes of a sectarian and dogmatic nature. Some of the party's leaders considered parliamentary activity to be the chief task of the party and underestimated the importance of leadership of the economic struggle of the mass; others slid down to trade-unionism and anarchism. The ideological and tactical waverings of the leaders weakened the party and led to a number of groups dropping away from it. Marx and Engels sharply criticised the sectarianism of the American socialists.

In the nineties the leadership of the party was assumed by the Left wing, headed by D. De Leon, but this group, too, committed errors of an anarcho-syndicalist nature. The S.L.P. withdrew from the struggle for satisfaction of partial demands of the working class, withdrew from work in the reformist trade unions and gradually lost its already weakened contacts with the mass labour movement. During the First World War (1914-18) the S.L.P. leaned towards internationalism. Under the impact of the October Revoultion in Russia the more revolutionary section of the S.L.P. took an active part in organising the Communist Party of America. Today the S.L.P. is a small organisation having no influence on the labour movement in the U.S.A.

[16] The *Socialist Party of America* was formed in July 1901 at the congress in Indianapoils as a result of the amalgamation of groups that had split away from the Socialist Labour Party and the Social-Democratic Party of the U.S.A., one of whose organisers was Eugene Debs, a popular leader of the American workers, immigrant workers, as well as small farmers and petty

publication of the paper, *The Internationalist*; in Holland, the Party of the "Tribunists"[17] which publishes the paper *De Tribune* (Pannekoek, Herman Gorter, Wijnkoop, and Henriette Roland-Holst, who, although Centrist at Zimmerwald, has now joined our ranks); in Sweden, the Party of the Young, or the Left,[18] led by Lindhagen, Ture Nerman, Carleson, Strölm and Z. Höglund, who at Zimmerwald was personally

....

bourgeois. The Centrist and Right opportunist leadership of the party (Victor L. Berger, Morris Hillquit and others) denied the need for a dictatorship of the proletariat, rejecting revolutionary methods of struggle, and reduced the activities of the party mainly to participation in the election campaigns. During the First World War three trends appeared in the S.P.—the social chauvinists, who supported the government's imperialist policy, the Centrists, who paid only lip-service to the cause of anti-imperialism, and the revolutionary minority, who took an internationalist stand and were actively anti-war.

The Left wing of the Socialist Party headed by Charles Ruthenberg, William Foster, William Haywood and others, and backed by the proletarian membership, waged a struggle against the party's opportunist leadership and for independent political action by the proletariat, for the creation of industrial trade unions based on the principles of the class struggle. In 1919 a split occurred in the Socialist Party. The breakaway Left wing took the lead in forming the Communist Party of America, of which it was the core.

At the present time the Socialist Party is a small sectarian organisation.

17 *Tribunsits*—members of the Social-Democratic Party of Holland, whose mouthpiece was the newspaper *De Tribune*. The leaders of the Tribunists were David Wijnkoop, Herman Gorter, Anton Pannekoek, and Henriette Roland-Holst. The Tribunists were not a consistently revolutionary party, but they represented the Left wing of the Dutch labour movement, and during the First World War (1914-18) they adopted, in the main, an internationalist stand.

In 1918 the Tribunists formed the Communist Party of Holland.

De Tribune—a newspaper founded in 1907 by the Left wing of the Social-Democratic Labour Party of Holland. In 1909, after the expulsion of the Leftists, who formed the Social-Democratic Party of Holland, the paper became the official organ of this party; in 1918 it became the organ of the Dutch Communist Party, and appeared under this name until 1940.

18 *Party of the Young*, or *the Left*—the name given by Lenin to the first Left wing of the Swedish Social-Democrats. During the First World War (1914-18) they took an internationalist stand and aligned themselves with the Zimmerwald Left. In May 1917 they formed the Left Social-Democratic Party of Sweden. At the party's congress in 1919 a resolution was adopted in favour of joining the Communist International. The revolutionary wing of the party formed the Communist Party of Sweden in 1921.

active in the organisation of the "Zimmerwald Left", and who is now in prison for his revolutionary fight against the war; in Denmark, Trier and his friends who have left the now purely *bourgeois* "Social-Democratic" Party of Denmark, headed by the *Minister* Stauning; in Bulgaria, the "Tesnyaki"[19]; in Italy, the nearest are Constantino Lazzari, secretary of the party, and Serrati, editor of the central organ, *Avanti!*[20]; in Poland, Radek, Hanecki and other leaders of the Social-Democrats united under the "Regional Executive", and Rosa Luxemburg, Tyszka and other leaders of the Social-Democrats united under the "Chief Executive"[21]; in Switzerland, those of the Left who drew up the argument for the "referendum" (January 1917) in order to fight the social-chauvinists and the "Centre" in *their own* country and who at the Zürich Cantonal Socialist Convention, held at Töss on February 11, 1917, moved a consistently revolutionary resolution against the war; in Austria, the young Left-wing friends of Friedrich Adler, who acted partly through the Karl Marx Club in Vienna, now closed by the arch-reactionary Austrian Government, which is ruining Adler's life for his heroic though ill-considered shooting at a minister, and so on.

It is not a question of shades of opinion, which certainly exist even among the Lefts. It is a question of *trend*. The thing is that it is not easy to be an internationalist in deed during a terrible imperialist war. Such people are few; but it is on such people *alone* that the future

[19] *Tesnyaki*—the revolutionary Social-Democratic Labour Party of Bulgaria, founded in 1903 after the split in the Social-Democratic Party. The founder and leader of the Party was D. Blagoev; subsequent leaders, Blagoev's disciples, were G. Dimitrov, V. Kolarov and others. In 1914-18 the Tesnyaki came out against the imperialist war. In 1919 they joined the Communist International and formed the Communist Party of Bulgaria, later reorganised into the Bulgarian Workers' Party (Communists).

[20] *Avanti!*—a daily, central organ of the Italian Socialist Party, founded in December 1896 in Rome. During the First World War (1914-18) the paper took an inconsistent internationalist stand without breaking with the reformists. In 1926 it was closed down by Mussolini's fascist government, but continued to appear irregularly outside the country. In 1943 it resumed publication in Italy. At present *Avanti!* Is the central organ of the Italian Socialist Party.

[21] *Regional Executive* and *Chief Executive*—executive bodies of the Social-Democrats of the Kingdom of Poland and Lithuania.

of socialism depends; they *alone are the leaders of the people*, and not their corrupters.

The distinction between the reformists and the revolutionaries, among the Social-Democrats, and socialists generally, was objectively bound to undergo a change under the conditions of the imperialist war. Those who confine themselves to "demanding" that the bourgeois governments should conclude peace or "ascertain the will of the peoples for peace", etc., are *actually* slipping into reforms. For, objectively, the *problem of the war* can be solved only in a *revolutionary way*.

There is no possibility of this war ending in a democratic, non-coercive peace or of the people being relieved of the burden of *billions* paid in interest to the capitalists, who have made fortunes out of the war, except through a revolution of the proletariat.

The most varied reforms can and must be demanded of the bourgeois governments, but one cannot, without sinking to Manilovism and reformism, demand that people and classes entangled by the thousands of threads of imperialist capital should *tear* those threads. And unless they are torn, all talk of a war against war is idle and deceitful prattle.

The "Kautskyites", the "Centre", are revolutionaries in word and reformists in deed, they are internationalists in word and accomplices of the social-chauvinists in deed.

THE COLLAPSE OF THE ZIMMERWALD INTERNATIONAL.— THE NEED FOR FOUNDING A THIRD INTERNATIONAL

17. From the very outset, the Zimmerwald International adopted a vacillating, "Kautskyite", "Centrist" position, which immediately compelled the *Zimmerwald Left* to dissociate itself, to separate itself from the rest, and to issue *its own* manifesto (published in Switzerland in Russian, German and French).

The chief shortcoming of the Zimmerwald International, and the cause of its *collapse* (for politically and ideologically it has already collapsed), was its vacillation and indecision on such a momentous issue of *crucial* practical significance as that of breaking completely with social-chauvinism and the old social-chauvinist International, headed by Vandervelde and Huysmans at The Hague (Holland), etc.

It is not as yet known in Russia that the Zinmerwald majority are *nothing but Kautskyites*. Yet this is the fundamental fact, one which cannot be ignored, and which is now generally known in Western Europe. Even that chauvinist, that extreme German chauvinist, Heilmann, editor of the ultra-chauvinistic *Chemnitzer Volksstimme* and contributor to Parvus's ultra-chauvinistic *Glocke*[22] (a "Social-Democrat", of course, and an ardent partisan of Social-Democratic "unity"), was compelled to acknowledge in the press that the Centre, or "Kautkyism", and the *Zimmerwald majority* were one and the same thing.

This fact was definitely established at the end of 1916 and the beginning of 1917. Although social-pacifism was condemned by the Kienthal Manifesto,[23] the *whole* Zimmerwald Right, the entire Zimmerwald majority, sank to social-pacifism: Kautsky and Co. in a series of utterances in January and February 1917; Bourderon and Merrheim in France, who cast their votes *in unanimity* with the social-chauvinists for the pacifist resolutions of the Socialist Party (December 1916) and of the Confédération Générale du Travail (the national organisation of the French trade unions, also in December 1916); Turati and Co. in Italy, where the entire party took up a social-pacifist position, while Turati himself, in a speech delivered on December 17, 1916, "slipped" (not by accident, of course) into *nationalist* phrases whitewashing the imperialist war.

In January 1917, the chairman of the Zimmerwald and Kienthal conferences, Robert Grimm, joined the social-chauvinists in *his own* party (Greulich, Pflüger, Gustav Müller and others) *against* the internationalists in deed.

[22] *Volksstimme*—organ of the German Social-Democratic Party, published in Chemnitz from January 1891 to February 1933.

Die Glocke—a fortnightly journal published in Munich and subsequently in Berlin between 1915-25 by the social-chauvinist Parvus (A. L. Gelfand), member of the German Social-Democratic Party.

[23] This refers to the appeal "To the Peoples Suffering Ruination and Death" adopted at the Second International Conference of the "Zimmerwaldists" held on April 24-30, 1916 in Kienthal (Switzerland).

At two conferences of *Zimmerwaldists* from various countries in January and February 1917, this equivocal, double-faced behaviour of the Zimmerwald majority was formally stigmatised by the Left internationalists of several countries: by Munzenberg, secretary of the international youth organisation and editor of the excellent internationalist publication *Die Jugendinternationale*;[24] by Zinoviev, representative of the Central Committee of our Party; by K. Radek of the Polish Social-Democratic Party (the "Regional Executive"), and by Hartstein, a German Social-Democrat and member of the Spartacus group.

Much is given to the Russian proletariat; nowhere in the world has the working class yet succeeded in developing so much revolutionary energy as in Russia. But to whom much is given, of him much is required.

The Zimmerwald bog can no longer be tolerated. We must not, for the sake of the Zimmerwald "Kautskyites", continue the semi-alliance with the chauvinist International of the Plekhanovs and Scheidemanns. We must break with this International immediately. We must remain in Zimmerwald *only* for purposes of information.

It is we who must found, and right now, without delay, a *new*, revolutionary, proletarian International, or rather, we must not fear to acknowledge publicly that this new International is *already established* and operating.

This is the International of those "internationalists in deed" whom I precisely listed above. They and they alone are representatives of the revolutionary, internationalist mass, and not their corrupters.

And if socialists *of that type* are few, let every Russian worker ask himself whether there were many really class-conscious revolutionaries in Russia *on the eve* of the February-March revolution of 1917.

It is not a question of numbers, but of giving correct expression to the ideas and policies of the truly revolutionary proletariat. The thing is not to "proclaim" internationalism, but to be able to be an internationalist in deed, even when times are most trying.

[24] *Die Jugendinternationale* (Youth International)—organ of the International Union of Socialist Youth Organisations associated with the Zimmerwald Left. Published in Zürich from September 1915 to May 1918.

Let us not deceive ourselves with hopes of agreements and international congresses. As long as the imperialist war is on, international intercourse is held in the iron vise of the military dictatorship of the imperialist bourgeoisie. If even the "republican" Milyukov, who is obliged to tolerate the parallel government of the Soviet of Workers' Deputies, *did not allow Fritz Platten*, the Swiss socialist, secretary of the party, an internationalist and participant in the Zimmerwald and Kienthal conferences, to enter Russia in April 1917, in spite of the fact that Platten has a Russian wife and was on his way to visit his wife's relatives, and in spite of the fact that he had taken part in the revolution of 1905 in Riga, for which he had been confined in a Russian prison, had given bail to the tsarist government for his release and wished to recover that bail—if the "republican" Milyukov could *do* such a thing in April 1917 in Russia, one can judge what value can be put on the promises and assurances, the phrases and declarations of the bourgeoisie on the subject of peace without annexations, and soon.

And the arrest of Trotsky by the British Government? And the refusal to allow Martov to leave Switzerland, and the attempt to lure him to Britain, where Trotsky's fate awaits him?

Let us harbour no illusions. We must not deceive ourselves.

To "wait" for international congresses or conferences is simply to *betray* internationalism, since it has been shown that even from Stockholm neither socialists loyal to internationalism *nor even their letters* are allowed to come here, although this is quite possible and although a ferocious military censorship exists.

Our Party must not "wait", but must immediately *found* a Third International. Hundreds of socialists imprisoned in Germany and Britain will then heave a sigh of relief, thousands and thousands of German workers who are now holding strikes and demonstrations that are frightening that scoundrel and brigand, Wilhelm, will learn from *illegal* leaflets of our decision, of our fraternal confidence in Karl Liebknecht, and in him alone, of *our* decision to fight "revolutionary defencism" *even now*; they will read this and be strengthened in their revolutionary internationalism.

To whom much is given, of him much is required. No other

country in the world is as free as Russia is *now*. Let us make use of this freedom, not to advocate support for the bourgeoisie, or bourgeois "revolutionary defencism", but in a bold, honest, proletarian, Liebknecht way *to found the Third International*, an International uncompromisingly hostile both to the social-chauvinist traitors and to the vacillating "Centrists".

18. After what has been said, there is no need to waste many words explaining that the amalgamation of Social-Democrats in Russia is out of the question.

It is better to remain with one friend only, like Liebknecht, and *that means remaining with the revolutionary proletariat*, than to entertain even for a moment any thought of amalgamation with the party of the Organising Committee, with Chkheidze and Tsereteli, who can tolerate a bloc with Potresov in *Rabochaya Gazeta*, who voted for the loan in the Executive Committee of the Soviet of Workers' Deputies,[25] and who have sunk to "defencism".

Let the dead bury their dead.

Whoever wants to *help* the waverers must first stop wavering himself.

WHAT SHOULD BE THE NAME OF OUR PARTY—ONE THAT WILL BE CORRECT SCIENTIFICALLY AND HELP TO CLARIFY THE MIND OF THE PROLETARIAT POLITICALLY?

19. I now come to the final point, the name of our Party. We must call ourselves the *Communist Party*—just as Marx and Engels called themselves.

[25] On April 7 (20), 1917, the Executive Committee of the Petrograd Soviet, by a majority of 21 votes against 14, adopted a resolution in favour of supporting the so-called "Liberty Loan" issued by the Provisional Government to finance the continuing imperialist war. The Bolshevik members of the Executive Committee opposed this loan, declaring that support of it was "the worst form of 'civil truce'" and moved a resolution containing a detailed statement of their position. Several members of the E.C. not belonging to the Bolshevik group voted with the Bolsheviks. The question was put before the plenary meeting of the Soviet after a preliminary discussion in the groups.

We must repeat that we are Marxists and that we take as our basis the *Communist Manifesto*, which has been distorted and betrayed by the Social-Democrats on its two main points: (1) the working men have no country: "defence of the fatherland" in an imperialist war is a betrayal of socialism; and (2) the Marxist doctrine of the state has been distorted by the Second International.

The name "Social-Democracy" is *scientifically* incorrect, as Marx frequently pointed out, in particular, in the *Critique of the Gotha Programme* in 1875, and as Engels re-affirmed in a more popular form in 1894.[26] From capitalism mankind can pass directly only to socialism, i.e., to the social ownership of the means of production and the distribution of products according to the amount of work performed by each individual. Our Party looks farther ahead: socialism must inevitably evolve gradually into communism, upon the banner of which is inscribed the motto, "From each according to his ability, to each according to his needs".

That is my first argument.

Here is the second: the second part of the name of our Party (Social-*Democrats*) is also scientifically incorrect. Democracy is a form of *state*, whereas we Marxists are opposed to *every kind* of state.

The leaders of the Second International (1889-1914), Plekhanov, Kautsky and their like, have vulgarised and distorted Marxism.

Marxism differs from anarchism in that it recognises *the need for a state* for the purpose of the transition to socialism; but (and here is where we differ from Kautsky and Co.) *not a state of the type* of the usual parliamentary bourgeois-democratic republic, but a state like the Paris Commune of 1871 and the Soviets of Workers' Deputies of 1905 and 1917.

My third argument: *living reality*, the revolution, has *already actually* established in our colmtry, albeit in a weak and embryonic form, precisely this new type of "state", which is not a state in the proper sense of the word.

This is *already* a matter of the practical action of the people, and not merely a theory of the leaders.

[26] See Engels, Preface to *Internationales aus dem Volkstaat (1871-1875).*

The state in the proper sense of the term is domination over the people by contingents of armed men divorced from the people.

Our *emergent*, new state is also a state, for we too need contingents of armed men, we too need the *strictest* order, and must *ruthlessly* crush by force all attempts at either a tsarist or a Guchkov-bourgeois counter-revolution.

But our *emergent*, new state is *no longer* a state in the proper sense of the term, for in some parts of Russia these contingents of armed men are *the masses themselves*, the entire people, and not certain privileged persons placed over the people, and divorced from the people, and for all practical purposes undisplaceable.

We must look forward, and not backward to the usual bourgeois type of democracy, which consolidated the rule of the bourgeoisie with the aid of the old, *monarchist* organs of administration, the police, the army and the bureaucracy.

We must look forward to the emergent new democracy, which is already ceasing to be a democracy, for democracy means the domination of the people, and the armed people cannot dominate themselves.

The term democracy is not only scientifically incorrect when applied to a Communist Party; it has now, since March 1917, simply become *blinkers* put on the eyes of the revolutionary people and *preventing* them from boldly and freely, on their own initiative, building up the new: the Soviets of Workers', Peasants', and all other Deputies, as *the sole power* in the "state" and as the harbinger of the "withering away" of the state *in every form*.

My fourth argument: we must reckon with the actual situation in which socialism finds itself internationally.

It is not what it was during the years 1871 to 1914, when Marx and Engels knowingly put up with the inaccurate, opportunist term "Social-Democracy". For *in those days*, after the defeat of the Paris Commune, history made slow organisational and educational work the task of the day. Nothing else was possible. The anarchists were then (as they are now) fundamentally wrong not only theoretically, but also economically and politically. The anarchists misjudged the character of the times, for they failed to understand the world situation: the worker of Britain corrupted by imperialist profits, the Commune defeated in Paris, the recent (1871) triumph of the bourgeois national movement in Germany, the age-long sleep of semi-feudal Russia.

Marx and Engels gauged the times accurately; they understood the international situation; they understood that the approach to the beginning of the social revolution must be *slow*.

We, in our turn, must also understand the specific features and tasks of the new era. Let us not imitate those sorry Marxists of whom Marx said: "I have sown dragon's teeth and harvested fleas."[27]

The objective inevitability of capitalism which grew into imperialism brought about the imperialist war. The war has brought mankind to the *brink of a precipice*, to the brink of the destruction of civilisation, of the brutalisation and destruction of more millions, countless millions, of human beings.

The *only* way out is through a proletarian revolution.

At the very moment when such a revolution is beginning, when it is taking its first hesitant, groping steps, steps betraying too great a confidence in the bourgeoisie, at such a moment the majority (that is the truth, that is a fact) of the "Social-Democratic" leaders, of the "Social-Democratic" parliamentarians, of the "Social-Democratic" newspapers—and these are precisely the *organs* that influence the people—have *deserted* socialism, have *betrayed* socialism and have gone over to the side of "their own" national bourgeoisie.

The people have been confused, led astray and deceived by *these* leaders.

And we shall aid and abet that deception if we retain the old and out-of-date Party name, which is as decayed as the Second International!

Granted that "many" workers *understand* Social-Democracy in an honest way; but it is time to learn how to distinguish the subjective from the objective.

Subjectively, such Social-Democratic workers are most loyal leaders of the proletarians.

[27] This expression from Heine was quoted by Marx and Engels in their *German Ideology*.

Objectively, however, the world situation is such that the old name of our Party *makes it easier* to fool the people and *impedes* the onward march; for at every step, in every paper, in every parliamentary group, the masses see *leaders*, i.e., people whose voices carry farthest and whose actions are most conspicuous; yet they are all "would-be Social-Democrats", they are all "for unity" with the betrayers of socialism, with the social-chauvinists; and they are all presenting for payment the old bills issued by "Social-Democracy". . . .

And what are the arguments against? . . . We'll be confused with the Anarchist-Communists, they say . . . .

Why are we not afraid of being confused with the Social-Nationalists, the Social-Liberals, or the Radical-Socialists, the foremost bourgeois party in the French Republic and the most adroit in the bourgeois deception of the people? . . . We are told: The people are used to it, the workers have come to "love" *their* Social-Democratic Party.

That is the only argument. But it is an argument that dismisses the science of Marxism, the tasks of the morrow in the revolution, the objective position of world socialism, the shameful collapse of the Second International, and the harm done to the practical cause by the packs of "would-be Social-Democrats" who surround the proletarians.

It is an argument of routinism, an argument of inertia, an argument of stagnation.

But we are out to rebuild the world. We are out to put an end to the imperialist world war into which hundreds of millions of people have been drawn and in which the interests of billions and billions of capital are involved, a war which cannot end in a truly democratic peace without the greatest proletarian revolution in the history of mankind.

Yet we are afraid of our own selves. We are loth to cast off the "dear old" soiled shirt . . . .

But it is time to cast off the soiled shirt and to put on clean linen.

Petrograd, April 10, 1917

POSTSCRIPT

My pamphlet has become out of date owing to the general

economic disorganisation and the inefficiency of the St. Petersburg presses. The pamphlet was written on April 10, 1917, today is May 28, and it has not come out yet!

It was written as a *draft* platform to propagandise my views *before* the All-Russia Conference of our Party, the Russian Social-Democratic Labour Party of Bolsheviks. The pamphlet was typed in several copies and handed out to Party members before and during the Conference so that it did its job in part. But the Conference took place from April 24 to April 29, 1917, its resolutions have long since been published (see supplement to *Soldatskaya Pravda*[28] No. 13) and the attentive reader will have noticed that my pamphlet often served as the original draft of those resolutions.

It is left for me to express the hope that the pamphlet will still be of some value because of its connection with those resolutions and because it explains them, and to deal here with two points.

I suggested on page 27 that we remain in Zimmerwald only for purposes of information.[29] The Conference did not agree with me on this point, and I had to vote against the resolution on the International. It is now becoming obvious that the Conference made a mistake and that the course taken by events will soon correct it. By remaining in Zimmerwald we (even against our will) are helping delay the creation of the Third International; we are indirectly hampering its foundation, being burdened with the dead ballast of the ideologically and politically dead Zimmerwald.

In the eyes of the working-class parties of the whole world, our Party's position is now such that it is our *duty to found* a Third International without delay. *Today* there is nobody but us to do it, and procrastination can only do harm. If we remain in Zimmerwald for

[28] *Soldatskaya Pravda* (Soldiers' Truth)—a Bolshevik daily, began to appear on April 15 (28), 1917 as the organ of the Military Organisation of the Petrograd Committee, R.S.D.L.P.(B.); from May 19 (June 1), 1917 it became the organ of the Military Organisation of the Central Committee, R.S.D.L.P.(B.); during the July events of 1917 the paper was closed down by the Provisional Government; from July to October 1917 it came out under the names of *Rabochy i Soldat* (Worker and Soldier) and *Soldat* (Soldier). After the October Revolution publication was resumed under the old name and continued up to March 1918.

[29] See p. 113 of the present volume.

information only, we shall have our hands freed to establish the new International (and at the same time be able to *use* Zimmerwald should circumstances make it possible).

Because of the mistake made by the Conference, we must now wait passively, at least until July 5, 1917 (the date set for the Zimmerwald Conference, provided it is not postponed *again*! It has already been postponed once . . .).

The decision unanimously adopted by the Central Committee of our Party after the Conference and published in *Pravda* No. 55, on May 12, has, however, gone half-way towards correcting the mistake; it has been resolved that we shall walk out of Zimmerwald if they decide to confer with ministers.[30] I express the hope that the other half of the mistake will be speedily remedied, as soon as we convene the first international conference of Lefts (the "third trend", the "internationalists in deed", see above, pp. 23-25[31]).

The second point I must deal with is the formation of the "coalition cabinet" on May 6, 1917.[32] On this point the pamphlet may *seem* to be

[30] See *LCW*, Vol. 24, 1977, p. 388.

[31] See pp. 105-111 of the present volume.

[32] The coalition Provisional Government was formed as a result of the crisis caused by the Note which Milyukov, the Minister of Foreign Affairs, had sent to the Allied governments on April 18 (May 1), 1917, confirming the Provisional Government's readiness to honour all the treaties which the tsarist government had concluded with the imperialist powers—Britain and France. Owing to the spontaneous demonstrations of protest, which reached a head on April 20 and 21 (May 3 and 4) in a powerful movement of the workers and soldiers, the Provisional Government, to create the appearance of a change in policy, accepted the resignation of Foreign Minister Milyukov, the War Minister Guchkov, and made a proposal to the Petrograd Soviet to form a coalition government.

Despite its decision of March 1 (14) forbidding members of the Soviet to join the Provisional Government, the Executive Committee, at a special meeting held on the night of May 1 (14), accepted the proposal of the Provisional Government. At the preliminary meetings of the party groups the Bolsheviks were the only group to come out against it. The decision to have representatives of the Soviet join the government was carried by 44 votes to 19 with two abstentions. A commission authorised to negotiate the terms for forming a coalition government was elected, consisting of Chkheidze, Tsereteli, Dan, Bogdanov (Mensheviks), Stankevich, Bramson (Trudoviks), Gots, Chernov (S.R.s), Kamenev (Bolshevik), Yurenev (member of the Inter-District group), and Sukhanov (independent Social-Democratic). On particularly out of date.

But actually on this of all points it is not out of date at all. It is based *wholly* on the *class* analysis, a thing that the Mensheviks and Narodniks, who have provided six ministers as hostages to the ten capitalist ministers, stand in deadly fear of. And it is because the pamphlet is based wholly on a class analysis that it is not out of date—the only change made by Tsereteli, Chernov and Co . joining the cabinet was an *insignificant one* in the *form* of the agreement between the Petrograd Soviet and the capitalist government, and I deliberately stressed in my pamphlet (on page 8) that "I am referring not so much to the formal agreement as to actual support".[33]

With each passing day it is becoming clearer that Tsereteli, Chernov and Co. are nothing more than hostages to the capitalists, that the "renewed" government is neither willing nor able to carry out any of its abundant promises either in foreign or domestic policies. Chernov, Tsereteli and Co. have committed political suicide by turning into assistants of the capitalists, into people who are actually strangling the revolution; Kerensky has come so low as to use force against the masses (cf. p. 9 of the pamphlet: "Guchkov is still only threatening to employ violence against the mass"[34] but Kerensky *had* to carry out those

....

the evening of May 2 (15) an emergency meeting of the Petrograd Soviet was called at which the action of the Executive Committee was approved by a majority vote. After the negotiations an agreement was reached on May 5 (18) for the distribution of posts in the new government as a result of which 6 socialist ministers were to join the cabinet, namely: Kerensky—War and Naval Minister, Skobelev—Labour Minister, Chernov—Minister of Agriculture, Peshekhonov—Minister of Food Supply, Tsereteli—Minister of Post and Telegraph, Pereverzev—Minister of Justice. On the evening of May 5 (18) the Petrograd Soviet, after hearing Skobelev's report on the results of the negotiations with the Provisional Government, decided to have its representatives join the government on condition that they were answerable and accountable to the Soviet, and expressed full confidence in the new government.

Lenin wrote afterwards that by joining the bourgeois government, the Socialist-Revolutionaries and the Mensheviks "saved it from collapse and allowed themselves to be made its servants and defenders" (see *LCW*, Vol. 25, 1980, p. 241).

33 See p. 88 of the present volume.

34 See p. 89 of the present volume.

threats[35]). Chernov, Tsereteli and Co. have killed themselves and their parties—the Mensheviks and Socialist-Revolutionaries—politically. The people will realise this more and more clearly as the days go by.

The coalition cabinet is only a passing moment in the development of the fundamental class contradictions of our revolution briefly analysed in the pamphlet. This situation cannot last long—we must either go backward to counter-revolution all along the line or forward to the transfer of state power to other classes. At a time of revolution, when the imperialist world war is in progress, we cannot stand still.

N. Lenin
St. Petersburg, May 28, 1917

First published September 1917 as a pamphlet by Priboi Publishers
Published according to the pamphlet text

[35] Lenin is referring to the order by War Minister Kerensky published on May 11 (24), 1917, containing a "Declaration of the Rights of the Soldier", in which there was a point allowing a superior officer to use military force in cases of insubordination in the field. This point was aimed against soldiers and officers who refused to go into the attack. Simultaneously with the promulgation of this order Kerensky started to disband regiments and prosecute officers and soldiers guilty of "inciting to insubordination".

LESSONS OF THE CRISIS

Petrograd and the whole of Russia have passed through a serious political crisis, the first political crisis since the revolution.

On April 18 the Provisional Government issued its unhappily notorious Note, which confirmed the predatory aims of the war clearly enough to arouse the indignation of the masses, who had honestly believed in the desire (and ability) of the capitalists to "renounce annexations". On April 20-21 Petrograd was in a turmoil. The streets were crowded; day and night knots and groups of people stood about, and meetings of various sizes sprang up everywhere; big street processions and demonstrations went on without a break. Yesterday evening, April 21, the crisis, or, at any rate, the first stage of the crisis, apparently came to an end with the Executive Committee of the Soviet of Workers' and Soldiers' Deputies, and later the Soviet itself, declaring themselves satisfied with the "explanations", the amendments to the Note and the "elucidations" made by the government (which in fact boil down to empty phrases, saying absolutely nothing, changing nothing and committing the government to nothing). They considered the "incident settled".

Whether the masses consider the "incident settled", the future will show. Our task now is to make a careful study of the *forces*, the classes, that revealed themselves in the crisis, and to draw the relevant lessons for our proletarian party. For it is the great significance of all crises that they make manifest what has been hidden; they cast aside all that is relative, superficial, and trivial; they sweep away the political litter and reveal the real mainsprings of the *class struggle.*

Strictly speaking, the capitalist government on April 18 merely reiterated its previous notes, in which the imperialist war was invested with diplomatic equivocations. The soldiers were angry because they had honestly believed in the sincerity and peaceful intentions of the capitalists. The demonstrations began as *soldiers'* demonstrations, under the contradictory, misguided and ineffectual slogan: "Down with Milyukov" (as though a change of persons or groups could change the *substance* of policy!).

This means that the broad, unstable, and vacillating mass, which is closest to the peasantry and which by its scientific class definition is petty-bourgeois, swung *away from* the capitalists *towards* the revolutionary workers. It was the swing or movement of this mass, strong enough to be a *decisive* factor, that caused the crisis.

It was at this point that other sections began to stir: *not* the middle but the extreme elements, *not* the intermediary petty bourgeoisie but the bourgeoisie and the proletariat, started to come out on to the streets and organise.

The bourgeoisie seized Nevsky Prospekt—or "Milyukov" Prospekt as one paper called it—and the adjacent quarters of prosperous Petrograd, the Petrograd of the capitalists and the government officials. Officers, students, and "the middle classes" demonstrated *in favour of* the Provisional Government. Among the slogans, "Down with Lenin" frequently appeared on the banners.

The proletariat rallied in *its own* centres, the working-class suburbs, around the slogans and appeals of our Party's Central Committee. On April 20-21 the Central Committee adopted resolutions, which were immediately passed on to the proletariat through the Party organisations. The workers poured through the *poor*, less central districts, and then in groups got through to Nevsky. By their mass character and solidarity, these demonstrations were very different from those of the bourgeoisie. Many banners carried the inscription "All Power to the Soviet of Workers' and Soldiers' Deputies".

On Nevsky there were clashes. The "hostile" demonstrations tore down each other's banners. The Executive Committee received news by telephone from various places that there was shooting on both sides, that there were killed and wounded; but the information was extremely contradictory and unconfirmed.

The bourgeoisie shouted about the "spectre of civil war", thus expressing its fear that the real masses, the actual majority of the nation, might seize power. The petty-bourgeois leaders of the Soviet, the Mensheviks and Narodniks—who since the revolution in general, and during the crisis in particular, have had no definite party policy—allowed themselves to be intimidated. In the Executive Committee almost half the votes were cast against the Provisional Government on the eve of the crisis, but now thirty-four votes (with nineteen against) are cast *in favour* of returning to a policy of confidence in and agreement with the capitalists.

And the "incident" was considered "settled".

What is the *essence* of the class struggle? The capitalists are *for* dragging out the war under cover of empty phrases and false promises. They are caught in the meshes of Russian, Anglo-French and *American* banking capital. The proletariat, as represented by its class-conscious vanguard, stands *for* the transfer of power to the revolutionary class, the working class and the semi-proletarians, *for* the development of a world workers' revolution, a revolution which is clearly developing also in Germany, and *for* terminating the war by means of *such* a revolution.

The vast mass of people, chiefly the petty bourgeoisie, who still believe the Menshevik and Narodnik leaders and who have been absolutely intimidated by the bourgeoisie and are carrying out *its* policy, although with reservations, are swinging now to the right, now to the left.

The war is terrible; it has hit the vast mass of the people hardest of all; it is these people who are becoming aware, albeit still very vaguely, that the war is criminal, that it is being carried on through the rivalry and scramble of the capitalists, for the division of *their* spoils. The world situation is growing more and more involved. The *only way out* is a world workers' revolution, a revolution which is *now* more advanced in Russia than in any other country, but which is clearly mounting (strikes, fraternisation) in Germany too. And the people are wavering: wavering between confidence in their old masters, the capitalists, and bitterness towards them; between confidence in the new class, the only consistently revolutionary class, which opens up the prospect of a bright future for all the working people—the proletariat—and a vague awareness of its role in world history.

This is not the first time the petty bourgeoisie and semi-proletarians have wavered and *it will not be the last*!

The lesson is clear, comrade workers! There is no time to be lost. The first crisis will be followed by others. You must devote *all* your efforts to enlightening the backward, to making extensive, comradely and direct contact (not only by meetings) with every regiment and with every group of working people who have not had their eyes opened yet! *All* your efforts must be devoted to consolidating your own ranks, to organising the workers from the bottom upwards, including every district, every factory, every quarter of the capital and its suburbs! Do *not* be misled by those of the petty bourgeoisie who "compromise" with the capitalists, by the defencists and by the "supporters", nor by individuals who are inclined to be in a hurry and to shout "Down with the Provisional Government!" before the majority of the people are solidly united. The crisis cannot be overcome by violence practised by individuals against individuals, by the local action of small groups of armed people, by Blanquist attempts to "seize power", to "arrest" the Provisional Government, etc.

Today's task is to explain more precisely, more clearly, more widely the proletariat's policy, *its* way of terminating the war. Rally more resolutely, more widely, wherever you can, to the ranks and columns of the proletariat! Rally round your Soviets; and within them endeavour to rally behind you a majority by comradely persuasion and by re-election of individual members!

Written April 22 (May 5), 1917
Published May 6 (April 23), 1917 in *Pravda* No. 39
Published according to the newspaper text

WAR AND REVOLUTION

A Lecture Delivered May 14 (27), 1917

The question of war and revolution has been dealt with so often lately in the press and at every public meeting that probably many of you are not only familiar with many aspects of the question but have come to find them tedious. I have not yet had a single opportunity to address or even attend any Party or for that matter any public meetings in this district, and therefore I run the risk, perhaps, of repetition or of not dealing in sufficient detail with those aspects of the question that interest you most.

It seems to me that the most important thing that is usually overlooked in the question of the war, a key issue to which insufficient attention is paid and over which there is so much dispute—useless, hopeless, idle dispute, I should say—is the question of the class character of the war: what caused that war, what classes are waging it, and what historical and historico-economic conditions gave rise to it. As far as I have been able to follow the way the question of the war is dealt with at public and Party meetings, I have come to the conclusion that the reason why there is so much misunderstanding on the subject is because, all too often, when dealing with the question of the war, we speak in entirely different languages.

From the point of view of Marxism, that is, of modern scientific socialism, the main issue in any discussion by socialists on how to assess the war and what attitude to adopt towards it is this: what is the war being waged for, and what classes staged and directed it. We Marxists do not belong to that category of people who are unqualified opponents of all war. We say: our aim is to achieve a socialist system of society, which, by eliminating the division of mankind into classes, by eliminating all exploitation of man by man and nation by nation, will inevitably eliminate the very possibility of war. But in the war to win that socialist system of society we are bound to encounter conditions under which the class struggle within each given nation may come up against a war between the different nations, a war conditioned by this very class struggle. Therefore, we cannot rule out the possibility of revolutionary wars, i.e., wars arising from the class struggle, wars waged by revolutionary classes, wars which are of direct and immediate revolutionary significance. Still less can we rule this out when we remember that though the history of European revolutions during the last century, in the course of 125-135 years, say, gave us wars which were mostly reactionary, it also gave us revolutionary wars, such as the war of the French revolutionary masses against a united monarchist, backward, feudal and semi-feudal Europe. No deception of the masses is more widespread today in Western Europe, and latterly here in Russia, too, than that which is practised by citing the example of revolutionary wars. There are wars and wars. We must be clear as to what historical conditions have given rise to the war, what classes are waging it, and for what ends. Unless we grasp this, all our talk about the war will necessarily be utterly futile, engendering more heat than light. That is why I take the liberty, seeing that you have chosen war and revolution as the subject of today's talk, to deal with this aspect of the matter at greater length.

We all know the dictum of Clausewitz, one of the most famous writers on the philosophy and history of war, which says: "War is a continuation of policy by other means."[1] This dictum comes from a writer who reviewed the history of wars and drew philosophic lessons from it shortly after the period of the Napoleonic wars. This writer, whose basic views are now undoubtedly familiar to every thinking person, nearly eighty years ago challenged the ignorant man-in-the-street conception of war as being a thing apart from the policies of the governments and classes concerned, as being a simple attack that disturbs the peace, and is then followed by restoration of the peace thus disturbed, as much as to say: "They had a fight, then they made up!" This is a grossly ignorant view, one that was repudiated scores of years ago and is repudiated by any more or less careful analysis of any historical epoch of wars.

War is a continuation of policy by other means. All wars are inseparable from the political systems that engender them. The policy which a given state, a given class within that state, pursued for a long

[1] See Clausewitz, *On War*, Vol. 1.

time before the war is inevitably continued by that same class during the war, the form of action alone being changed.

War is a continuation of policy by other means. When the French revolutionary townspeople and revolutionary peasants overthrew the monarchy at the close of the eighteenth century by revolutionary means and established a democratic republic—when they made short work of their monarch, and short work of their landowners, too, in a revolutionary fashion—that policy of the revolutionary class was bound to shake all the rest of autocratic, tsarist, imperial, and semi-feudal Europe to its foundations. And the inevitable continuation of this policy of the victorious revolutionary class in France was the wars in which all the monarchist nations of Europe, forming their famous coalition, lined up against revolutionary France in a counter-revolutionary war. Just as within the country the revolutionary people of France had then, for the first time, displayed revolutionary energy on a scale it had never shown for centuries, so in the war at the close of the eighteenth century it revealed a similar gigantic revolutionary creativeness when it remodelled its whole system of strategy, broke with all the old rules and traditions of warfare, replaced the old troops with a new revolutionary people's army, and created new methods of warfare. This example, to my mind, is noteworthy in that it clearly demonstrates to us things which the bourgeois journalists are now always forgetting when they pander to the philistine prejudices and ignorance of the backward masses who do not understand this intimate economic and historical connection between every kind of war and the preceding policy of every country, every class that ruled before the war and achieved its ends by so-called "peaceful" means. So-called, because the brute force required to ensure "peaceful" rule in the colonies, for example, can hardly be called peaceful.

Peace reigned in Europe, but this was because domination over hundreds of millions of people in the colonies by the European nations was sustained only through constant, incessant, interminable wars, which we Europeans do not regard as wars at all, since all too often they resembled, not wars, but brutal massacres, the wholesale slaughter of unarmed peoples. The thing is that if we want to know what the present war is about we must first of all make a general survey of the policies of the European powers as a whole. We must not take this or that example, this or that particular case, which can easily be wrenched out of the context of social phenomena and which is worthless, because an opposite example can just as easily be cited. We must take the whole policy of the entire system of European states in their economic and political interrelations if we are to understand how the present war steadily and inevitably grew out of this system.

We are constantly witnessing attempts, especially on the part of the capitalist press—whether monarchist or republican—to read into the present war an historical meaning which it does not possess. For example, no device is more frequently resorted to in the French Republic than that of presenting this war on France's part as a continuation and counterpart of the wars of the Great French Revolution of 1792. No device for hoodwinking the French masses, the French workers and the workers of all countries is more widespread than that of applying to our epoch the "jargon" of that other epoch and some of its watchwords, or the attempt to present matters as though now, too, republican France is defending her liberty against the monarchy. One "minor" fact overlooked is that then, in 1792, war was waged in France by a revolutionary class, which had carried out an unparalleled revolution and displayed unmatched heroism in utterly destroying the French monarchy and rising against a united monarchist Europe with the sole and single aim of carrying on its revolutionary struggle.

The war in France was a continuation of the policy of the revolutionary class which had carried out the revolution, won the republic, settled accounts with the French capitalists and landowners with unprecedented vigour, and was waging a revolutionary war against a united monarchist Europe in continuation of that policy.

What we have at present is primarily two leagues, two groups of capitalist powers. We have before us all the world's greatest capitalist powers—Britain, France, America, and Germany—who for decades have doggedly pursued a policy of incessant economic rivalry aimed at achieving world suprermacy, subjugating the small nations, and making threefold and tenfold profits on banking capital, which has caught the whole world in the net of its influence. That is what Britain's and Germany's policies really amount to. I stress this fact. This fact can never be emphasised strongly enough, because if we forget this we shall never understand what this war is about, and we shall then be easy game for any bourgeois publicist who tries to foist lying phrases on us.

The real policies of the two groups of capitalist giants—Britain and Germany, who, with their respective allies, have taken the field against each other—policies which they were pursuing for decades before the war, should be studied and grasped in their entirety. If we did not do this we should not only be neglecting an essential requirement of scientific socialism and of all social science in general, but we should be unable to understand anything whatever about the present war. We should be putting ourselves in the power of Milyukov, that deceiver, who is stirring up chauvinism and hatred of one nation for another by methods which are applied everywhere without exception, methods which Clausewitz wrote about eighty years ago when he ridiculed the very view some people are holding today, namely, that the nations lived in peace and then they started fighting. As if this were true! How can a war be accounted for without considering its bearing on the preceding policy of the given state, of the given system of states, the given classes? I repeat: this is a basic point which is constantly overlooked. Failure to understand it makes nine-tenths of all war discussions mere wrangling, so much verbiage. We say: if you have not studied the policies of both belligerent groups over a period of decades—so as to avoid accidental factors and the quoting of random examples—if you have not shown what bearing this war has on preceding policies, then you don't understand what this war is all about.

These policies show us just one thing—continuous economic rivalry between the world's two greatest giants, capitalist economies. On the one hand we have Britain, a country which owns the greater part of the globe, a country which ranks first in wealth, which has created this wealth not so much by the labour of its workers as by the exploitation of innumerable colonies, by the vast power of its banks which have developed at the head of all the others into an insignificantly small group of some four or five super-banks handling billions of rubles, and handling them in such a way that it can be said without exaggeration that there is not a patch of land in the world today on which this capital has not laid its heavy hand, not a patch of land which British capital has not enmeshed by a thousand threads. This capital grew to such dimensions by the turn of the century that its activities extended far beyond the borders of individual states and formed a group of giant banks possessed of fabulous wealth. Having begotten this tiny group of banks, it has caught the whole world in the net of its billions. This is the sum and substance of Britain's economic policy and of the economic policy of France, of which even French writers, some of them contributors to *L'Humanité*,[2] a paper now controlled by ex-socialists (in fact, no less a man than Lysis, the well-known financial writer), stated several years before the war: "France is a financial monarchy, France is a financial oligarchy, France is the world's money-lender."

On the other hand, opposed to this, mainly Anglo-French group, we have another group of capitalists, an even more rapacious, even more predatory one, a group who came to the capitalist banqueting table when all the seats were occupied, but who introduced into the struggle new methods for developing capitalist production, improved techniques, and superior organisation, which turned the old capitalism, the capitalism of the free-competition age, into the capitalism of giant trusts, syndicates, and cartels. This group introduced the beginnings of state-controlled capitalist production, combining the colossal power of capitalism with the colossal power of the state into a single mechanism and bringing tens of millions of people within the single organisation of state capitalism. Here is economic history, here is diplomatic history, covering several decades, from which no one can get away. It is the one and only guide-post to a proper solution of the problem of war; it leads you to the conclusion that the present war, too,

[2] *L'Humanité*—a daily founded by Jean Jaurès in 1904 as the organ of the French Socialist Party. During the First World War (1914-18) it was controlled by the extreme Right wing of the party and took a social-chauvinist stand.

In 1918, Marcel Cachin, a prominent leader of the French and international labour movement, became political director and head of the newspaper. In 1918-20 the paper came out against the imperialist policy of the French Government, which had sent its armed forces against the Soviet Republic. In December 1920, after the split in the French Socialist Party and the formation of the Communist Party of France, the newspaper became the latter's central organ.

is the outcome of the policies of the classes who have come to grips in it, of the two supreme giants, who, long before the war, had caught the whole world, all countries, in the net of financial exploitation and economically divided the globe up among themselves. They were bound to clash, because a redivision of this supremacy, from the point of view of capitalism, had become inevitable.

The old division was based on the fact that Britain, in the course of several centuries, had ruined her former competitors. A former competitor was Holland, which had dominated the whole world. Another was France, which had fought for supremacy for nearly a hundred years. After a series of protracted wars Britain was able, by virtue of her economic power, her merchant capital, to establish her unchallenged sway over the world. In 1871 a new predator appeared, a new capitalist power arose, which developed at an incomparably faster pace than Britain. That is a basic fact. You will not find a book on economic history that does not acknowledge this indisputable fact—the fact of Germany's faster development. This rapid development of capitalism in Germany was the development of a young strong predator, who appeared in the concert of European powers and said: "You ruined Holland, you defeated France, you have helped yourself to half the world—now be good enough to let us have our fair share." What does "a fair share" mean? How is it to be determined in the capitalist world, in the world of banks? There power is determined by the number of banks, there power is determined in the way described by a mouthpiece of the American multimillionaires, which declared with typically American frankness and typically American cynicism: "The war in Europe is being waged for world domination. To dominate the world two things are needed: dollars and banks. We have the dollars, we shall make the banks and we shall dominate the world." This statement was made by a leading newspaper of the American multimillionaires. I must say, there is a thousand times more truth in this cynical statement of a blustering American multimillionaire than in thousands of articles by bourgeois liars who try to make out that this war is being waged for national interests, on national issues, and utter similar glaringly patent lies which dismiss history completely and take an isolated example like the case of the German beast of prey who attacked Belgium. The case is undoubtedly a real one. This group of predators did attack Belgium with brutal ferocity, but it did the same thing the other group did yesterday by other means and is doing today to other nations.

When we argue about annexations—and this bears on the question I have been trying briefly to explain to you as the history of the economic and diplomatic relations which led up to the present war—when we argue about annexations we always forget that these, generally, are what the war is being waged for; it is for the carve-up of conquered territories, or, to put it more popularly, for the division of the plundered spoils by the two robber gangs. When we argue about annexations we constantly meet with methods which, scientifically speaking, do not stand up to criticism, and which, as methods of public journalism, are deliberate humbug. Ask a Russian chauvinist or social-chauvinist what annexation by Germany means, and he will give you an excellent explanation, because he understands that perfectly well. But he will never answer a request for a general definition of annexation that will fit them all—Germany, Britain, and Russia. He will never do that! And when *Rech* (to pass from theory to practice) sneered at *Pravda*, saying, "These Pravdists consider Kurland a case of annexation! How can you talk to such people!" and we answered: "Please give us such a definition of annexation as would apply to the Germans, the English, and the Russians, and we add that either you evade this issue or we shall expose you on the spot"[3]—*Rech* kept silent. We maintain that no newspaper, either of the chauvinists in general, who simply say that the fatherland must be defended, or of the social-chauvinists, has ever given a definition of annexation that would fit both Germany and Russia, that would be applicable to any side. It cannot do this for the simple reason that this war is the continuation of a policy of annexations, that is, a policy of conquest, of capitalist robbery on the part of both groups involved in the war. Obviously, the question of which of these two robbers was the first to draw the knife is of small account to us. Take the history of the naval and military expenditures of these two groups over a period of decades, take the history of the little wars they waged before the big war—"little" because

[3] See *LCW*, Vol. 24, 1977, pp. 35-36.

few Europeans died in those wars, whereas hundreds of thousands of people belonging to the nations they were subjugating died in them, nations which from their point of view could not be regarded as nations at all (you couldn't very well call those Asians and Africans nations!); the wars waged against these nations were wars against unarmed people, who were simply shot down, machine-gunned. Can you call them wars? Strictly speaking, they were not wars at all, and you could forget about them. That is their attitude to this downright deception of the masses.

The present war is a continuation of the policy of conquest, of the shooting down of whole nationalities, of unbelievable atrocities committed by the Germans and the British in Africa, and by the British and the Russians in Persia—which of them committed most it is difficult to say. It was for this reason that the German capitalists looked upon them as their enemies. Ah, they said, you are strong because you are rich? But we are stronger, therefore we have the same "sacred" right to plunder. That is what the real history of British and German finance capital in the course of several decades preceding the war amounts to. That is what the history of Russo-German, Russo-British, and German-British relations amounts to. There you have the clue to an understanding of what the war is about. That is why the story that is current about the cause of the war is sheer duplicity and humbug. Forgetting the history of finance capital, the history of how this war had been brewing over the issue of redivision, they present the matter like this: two nations were living at peace, then one attacked the other, and the other fought back. All science, all banks are forgotten, and the peoples are told to take up arms, and so are the peasants, who know nothing about politics. All they have to do is to fight back! The logical thing, following this line of argument, would he to close down all newspapers, burn all books and ban all mention of annexations in the press. In this way such a view of annexations could be justified. They can't tell the truth about annexations because the whole history of Russia, Britain, and Germany has been one of continuous, ruthless and sanguinary war over annexations. Ruthless wars were waged in Persia and Africa by the Liberals, who flogged political offenders in India for daring to put forward demands which were being fought for here in

Russia. The French colonial troops oppressed peoples too. There you have the pre-history, the real history of unprecedented plunder! Such is the policy of these classes, of which the present war is a continuation. That is why, on the question of annexations, they cannot give the reply that we give, when we say that any nation joined to another one, not by the voluntary choice of its majority but by a decision of a king or government, is an annexed nation. To renounce annexation is to give each nation the right to form a separate state or to live in union with whomsoever it chooses. An answer like that is perfectly clear to every worker who is at all class-conscious.

In every resolution, of which dozens are passed, and published even in such a paper as *Zemlya i Volya*,[4] you will find the answer, poorly expressed: We don't want a war for supremacy over other nations, we are fighting for our freedom. That is what all the workers and peasants say, that is how they express the view of the workingman, his understanding of the war. They imply by this that if the war were in the interests of the working people against the exploiters they would be for such a war. So would we, and there is not a revolutionary party that could be against it. Where they go wrong, these movers of numerous resolutions, is when they believe that the war is being waged by them. We soldiers, we workers, we peasants are fighting for our freedom. I shall never forget the question one of them asked me after a meeting. "Why do you speak against the capitalists all the time?" he said. "I'm not a capitalist, am I? We're workers, we're defending our freedom." You're wrong, you are fighting because you are obeying your capitalist government; it's the governments, not the peoples, who are carrying on this war. I am not surprised at a worker or peasant, who doesn't know his politics, who has not had the good or bad fortune of being initiated into the secrets of diplomacy or the picture of this finance plunder (this oppression of Persia by Russia and Britain, say)—I am not surprised at him forgetting this history and saying naïvely: Who cares about the capitalists, when it's me who's fighting! He doesn't understand the connection between the war and the government, he

[4] *Zemlya i Volya* (Land and Freedom)—a daily published by the Regional Committee of the Socialist-Revolutionary Party in Petrograd from March 21 (April 3) to October 13 (26), 1917.

doesn't understand that the war is being waged by the government, and that he is just a tool in the hands of that government. He can call himself a revolutionary people and write eloquent resolutions—to Russians this means a lot, because this has come into their lives only recently. There has recently appeared a "revolutionary" declaration by the Provisional Government. This doesn't mean anything. Other nations, more experienced than we are in the capitalist art of hoodwinking the masses by penning "revolutionary" manifestos, have long since broken all the world's records in this respect. If you take the parliamentary history of the French Republic since it became a republic supporting tsarism, you will find dozens of examples during the decades of this history when manifestos full of the most eloquent phrases served to mask a policy of the most outrageous colonial and financial plunder. The whole history of the Third Republic in France is a history of this plunder. Such are the origins of the present war. It is not due to malice on the part of capitalists or the mistaken policy of some monarch. To think so would be incorrect. No, this war is an inevitable outgrowth of super-capitalism, especially banking capital, which resulted in some four banks in Berlin and five or six in London dominating the whole world, appropriating the world's funds, reinforcing their financial policy by armed force, and finally clashing in a savage armed conflict because they had come to the end of their free tether in the matter of conquests. One or the other side had to relinquish its colonies. Such questions are not settled voluntarily in this world of capitalists. This issue could only be settled by war. That is why it is absurd to blame one or another crowned brigand. They are all the same, these crowned brigands. That is why it is equally absurd to blame the capitalists of one or another country. All they are to blame for is for having introduced such a system. But this has been done in full keeping with the law, which is safeguarded by all the forces of a civilised state. "I am fully within my rights, I am a buyer of shares. All the law courts, all the police, the whole standing army and all the navies in the world are safeguarding my sacred right to these shares." Who's to blame for banks being set up which handle hundreds of millions of rubles, for these banks casting their nets of plunder over the whole world, and for their being locked in mortal combat? Find the culprit if you can!

The blame lies with half a century of capitalist development, and the only way out of this is by the overthrow of the rule of the capitalists and by a workers' revolution. That is the answer our Party has arrived at from an analysis of the war, and that is why we say: the very simple question of annexations has been so muddled up and the spokesmen of the bourgeois parties have uttered so many lies that they are able to make out that Kurland is not annexation by Russia. They have shared Kurland and Poland between them, those three crowned brigands. They have been doing this for a hundred years, carving up the living flesh. And the Russian brigand snatched most because he was then the strongest. And now that the young beast of prey, Germany, who was then a party to the carve-up, has grown into a strong capitalist power, she demands a redivision. You want things to stay as they were? she says. You think you are stronger? Let's try conclusions!

That is what the war boils down to. Of course, the challenge "let's try conclusions" is merely an expression of the decade-long policy of plunder, the policy of the big banks. That is why no one but we can tell this truth about annexations, a simple truth that every worker and peasant will understand. That is why the question of treaties, such a simple question, is deliberately and disgracefully confused by the whole press. You say that we have a revolutionary government, that there are ministers in that government who are well-nigh socialists—Narodniks and Mensheviks. But when they make declarations about peace without annexations, on condition that this term is not defined (because it means taking away German annexations and keeping our own), then we say: Of what value are your "revolutionary" cabinet, your declarations, your statements that you are not out for a war of conquest, if at the same time you tell the army to take the offensive? Don't you know that we have treaties, that these treaties were concluded by Nicholas the Bloody in the most predatory fashion? You don't know it? It is pardonable for the workers or peasants not to know that. They did not plunder, they read no clever books. But when educated Cadets preach this sort of stuff they know perfectly well what these treaties are about. Although they are "secret" treaties, the whole diplomatic press in all countries talks about them, saying: "You'll get the Straits, you'll get Armenia, you'll get Galicia, you'll get Alsace-Lorraine, you'll get

Trieste, and we'll make a final carve-up of Persia." And the German capitalist says: "I'll seize Egypt, I'll subjugate the European nations unless you return my colonies to me with interest." Shares are things that can't do without interest. That is why the question of treaties, itself a clear, simple question, has touched off such a torrent of barefaced outrageous lies as those that are now pouring from the pages of all the capitalist newspapers.

Take today's paper *Dyen*. Vodovozov, a man absolutely innocent of Bolshevism, but who is an honest democrat, states in it: I am opposed to secret treaties; let me say this about the treaty with Rumania. There *is* a secret treaty with Rumania and it says that Rumania will receive a number of foreign peoples if she fights on the side of the Allies. The treaties which the other Allies have are all the same. They wouldn't have started to subjugate nations if they had not had these treaties. To know their contents you do not have to burrow in special journals. It is sufficient to recollect the basic facts of economic and diplomatic history. For decades Austria has been after the Balkans with an eye to subjugation. And if they have clashed it is because they couldn't help clashing. That is why, when the masses demand that these treaties should be published, a demand that is growing more insistent every day, ex-Minister Milyukov and the present Minister Tereshchenko (one in a government without socialist ministers, the other in a government with a number of near-socialist ministers) declare that publication of the treaties would mean a break with the Allies.

Obviously, you can't publish the treaties because you are all participants in the same gang of robbers. We agree with Milyukov and Tereshchenko that the treaties cannot be published. Two different conclusions can be drawn from this. If we agree with Milyukov and Tereshchenko that the treaties cannot be published—what follows from this? If the treaties cannot be published, then we've got to help the capitalist ministers continue the war. The other conclusion is this: since the capitalists cannot publish the treaties themselves, then the capitalists have got to be overthrown. Which of these two conclusions you consider to be correct, I leave it to you to decide, but be sure to consider the consequences. If we reason the way the Narodnik and Menshevik ministers reason, we come to this: once the government says that the treaties cannot be published, then we must issue a new manifesto. Paper is not so dear yet that we cannot write new manifestos. We shall write a new manifesto and start an offensive. What for? With what aims? Who is to set these aims? The soldiers are called upon to carry out the predatory treaties with Rumania and France. Send Vodovozov's article to the front and then complain that this is all the Bolsheviks' doing, the Bolsheviks must have invented this treaty-with-Rumania business. In that case you would not only have to make life a hell for *Pravda*, but even kick Vodovozov out for having studied history. You would have to make a bonfire of all Milyukov's books—terribly dangerous books those. Just open any book by the leader of the party of "people's freedom", by this ex-Minister of Foreign Affairs. They are good books. What do they say? They say that Russia has "a right" to the Straits, to Armenia, to Galicia, to Eastern Prussia. He has carved them all up, and even appends a map. Not only the Bolsheviks and Vodovozov will have to be sent to Siberia for writing such revolutionary articles, but Milyukov's books will have to be burnt too, because if you collected simple quotations from these books today and sent them to the front, no inflammatory leaflet would have such an inflammatory effect as this would have.

It remains for me now, according to the brief plan of this talk I have sketched for myself, to touch on the question of "revolutionary defencism". I believe, after what I have had the honour of reporting to you, that I may now be allowed to touch only briefly on this question.

By "revolutionary defencism" we mean vindication of the war on the plea that, after all, we have made the revolution, after all, we are a revolutionary people, a revolutionary democracy. But what answer do we give to that? What revolution did we make? We overthrew Nicholas. The revolution was not so very difficult compared with one that would have overthrown the whole class of landowners and capitalists. Who did the revolution put in power? The landowners and capitalists—the very same classes who have long been in power in Europe. Revolutions like this occurred there a hundred years ago. The Tereshchenkos, Milyukovs, and Konovalovs have been in power there for a long time, and it doesn't matter a bit whether they have a civil list to pay their tsars or whether they do without this luxury.

A bank remains a bank, whether capital is invested in concessions by the hundred or not; profits remain profits, be it in a republic or in a monarchy. If any savage country dares to disobey our civilised Capital, which sets up such splendid banks in the colonies, in Africa and Persia—if any savage nation should disobey our civilised bank, we send troops out who restore culture, order, and civilisation, as Lyakhov did in Persia,[5] and the French "republican" troops did in Africa, where they exterminated peoples with equal ferocity. What difference does it make? We have here the same "revolutionary defencism", displayed only by the unenlightened masses, who see no connection between war and the government, who do not know that this policy is sanctioned by treaties. The treaties have remained, the banks have remained, the concessions have remained. In Russia the best men of their class are in the government, but the nature of the war has not changed a bit because of this. The new "revolutionary defencism" uses the great concept of revolution merely as a cloak to cover up the dirty and bloody war waged for the sake of dirty and outrageous treaties.

The Russian revolution has not altered the war, but it has created organisations which exist in no other country and were seldom found in revolutions in the West. Most of the revolutions were confined to the emergence of governments of our Tereshchenko and Konovalov type, while the country remained passive and disorganised. The Russian revolution has gone further than that. In this we have the germ of hope that it may overcome the war. Besides the government of "near-socialist" ministers, the government of imperialist war, the government of offensive, a government tied up with Anglo-French capital—besides this government and independent of it we have all over Russia a network of Soviets of Workers', Soldiers', and Peasants' Deputies. Here is a revolution which has not said its last word yet. Here is a revolution which Western Europe, under similar conditions, has not known. Here are organisations of those classes which really have no need for annexations, which have not put millions in the banks, and which are probably not interested in whether the Russian Colonel

[5] *Lyakhov, V. P.* (1869-1919)—a colonel of the tsarist army who made a name for himself as a result of the suppression of the national-revolutionary movement in the Caucasus and Persia.

Lyakhov and the British Liberal ambassador divided Persia properly or not. Here is the pledge of this revolution being carried further, i.e., that the classes which have no interest in annexations, and despite the fact that they put too much trust in the capitalist government, despite the appalling muddle and appalling deception contained in the very concept "revolutionary defencism", despite the fact that they support the war loan, support the government of imperialist war—despite all this—have succeeded in creating organisations in which the mass of the oppressed classes are represented. These are the Soviets of Workers', Soldiers', and Peasants' Deputies, which, in very many local areas in Russia, have gone much further than the Petrograd Soviet in their revolutionary work. It is only natural, because in Petrograd we have the central authority of the capitalists.

And when Skobelev in his speech yesterday said: "We'll take all the profits, we'll take 100 per cent," he was just letting himself go with ministerial *élan*. If you take today's *Rech* you will see what the response is to this passage in Skobelev's speech. They write there: "Why, this means starvation, death! One hundred per cent means all!" Minister Skobelev goes farther than the most extreme Bolshevik. It's slandering the Bolsheviks to say that they are the extreme Left. Minister Skobelev is much more "Left". They called me all the ugly names they could think of, saying that I wanted to take their last shirt from the capitalists. At any rate, it was Shulgin who said: "Let them take our last shirt!" Imagine a Bolshevik going up to Citizen Shulgin and wanting to take his shirt from him. He could just as well and with greater justification accuse Minister Skobelev of this. We never went as far as that. We never suggested taking 100 per cent of profits. Nevertheless, it is a valuable promise. If you take the resolution of our Party you will see that we propose there, only in a more closely reasoned form, exactly what I have been proposing. Control must be established over the banks, followed by a fair tax on incomes.[6] And nothing more! Skobelev suggests taking a hundred kopeks in the ruble. We proposed and propose nothing of the sort. Skobelev doesn't really mean it, and if he does he would not be able to do it for the simple reason that to promise such things while making friends with Tereshchenko and

[6] See *LCW*, Vol. 24, 1977, pp. 311.

Konovalov is somewhat ludicrous. You could take 80 or 90 per cent of a millionaire's income, but not arm in arm with such ministers. If the Soviets had the power they would really take it, but not all of it—they have no need to. They would take the bulk of the income. No other state authority could do that. Minister Skobelev may have the best of intentions. I have known those parties for several decades—I have been in the revolutionary movement for thirty years. I am the last person, therefore, to question their good intentions. But that is not the point. It is not a question of good intentions. Good intentions pave the road to hell. All the government offices are full of papers signed by our ministers, but nothing has changed as a result of it. If you want to introduce control, start it! Our programme is such that in reading Skobelev's speech we can say: we do not demand more. We are much more moderate than Minister Skobelev. He proposes both control and 100 per cent. We don't want to take 100 per cent, but we say: "Until you start doing things we don't believe you!" Here lies the difference between us: we don't believe words and promises and don't advise others to believe them. The lessons of parliamentary republics teach us not to believe in paper utterances. If you want control, you've got to start it. One day is enough to have a law on such control issued. The employees' council at every bank, the workers' council at every factory, and all the parties receive the right of control. But you can't do that, we shall be told. This is a commercial secret, this is sacred private property. Well, just as you like, make your choice. If you want to safeguard all those ledgers and accounts, all the transactions of the trusts, then don't chatter about control, about the country going to ruin.

In Germany the situation is still worse. In Russia you can get grain but in Germany you can't. You can do a lot in Russia through organisation, but you can do nothing more in Germany. There is no more grain left, and the whole nation is faced with disaster. People today write that Russia is on the brink of ruin. If that is so, then it is a crime to safeguard "sacred" private property. Therefore, what do the words about control mean? Surely you haven't forgotten that Nicholas Romanov, too, wrote a good deal about control. You will find him repeating a thousand times the words "state control", "public control", "appointment of senators". In the two months following the revolution the industrialists have robbed the whole of Russia. Capitalists have made staggering profits; every financial report tells you that. And when the workers, two months after the revolution, had the "audacity" to say they wanted to live like human beings, the whole capitalist press throughout the country set up a howl. Every number of *Rech* is a wild howl about the workers wanting to rob the country, but all we promise is merely control over the capitalists. Can't we have less promises and more deeds? If what you want is bureaucratic control, control through the same organs as before, our Party declares its profound conviction that you cannot be given support in this, even if there were a dozen Narodnik and Menshevik ministers in your government instead of half a dozen. Control can only be exercised by the people. You must arrange control by bank employees' councils, engineers' councils, and workers' councils, and start that control right away, tomorrow. Every official should be made responsible, on pain of criminal persecution, for any wrong information he may give in any of these institutions. It is a matter of life and death to the country. We want to know how much grain there is, how much raw material, how many work hands there are and where they are to be placed.

This brings me to the last question—that of how to end the war. The ridiculous view is ascribed to us that we are out for a separate peace. The German robber capitalists are making peace overtures, saying: "We'll give you a piece of Turkey and Armenia if you give us ore-bearing lands. That is what the diplomats are talking about in every neutral city! Everybody knows it. Only it is veiled with conventional diplomatic phrases. That's what diplomats are for—to speak in diplomatic language. What nonsense it is to allege that we are for ending the war by a separate peace! To end the war which is being waged by the capitalists of all the wealthiest powers, a war stemming from the decade-long history of economic development, by one-sided withdrawal from military operations is such a stupid idea that it would be absurd even to refute it. The fact that we specially drew up a resolution to refute it is because we wanted to explain things to the broad masses before whom we were being slandered. It is not a matter that can be seriously discussed. The war which the capitalists of all countries are waging cannot be ended without a workers' revolution against these capitalists. So long as control remains a mere phrase instead of deed, so long as the government of the capitalists has not been replaced by a government of the revolutionary proletariat, the government is doomed merely to reiterate: We are heading for disaster, disaster, disaster. Socialists are now being jailed in "free" Britain for saying what I am saying. In Germany Liebknecht has been imprisoned for saying what I am saying, and in Austria Friedrich Adler is in jail for saying the same thing with the help of a revolver (he may have been executed by now). The sympathy of the mass of workers in all countries is with these socialists and not with those who have sided with their capitalists. The workers' revolution is mounting throughout the world. In other countries it is a more difficult matter, of course. They have no half-wits there like Nicholas and Rasputin. There the best men of their class are at the head of the government. They lack conditions there for a revolution against autocracy. They have there a government of the capitalist class. The most talented representatives of that class have been governing there for a long time. That is why the revolution there, though it has not come yet, is bound to come, no matter how many revolutionaries, men like Friedrich Adler and Karl Liebknecht, may die in the attempt. The future belongs to them, and the workers of all countries follow their lead. The workers in all countries are bound to win.

On the question of America entering the war I shall say this. People argue that America is a democracy, America has the White House. I say: Slavery was abolished there half a century ago. The anti-slave war ended in 1865. Since then multimillionaires have mushroomed. They have the whole of America in their financial grip. They are making ready to subdue Mexico and will inevitably come to war with Japan over a carve-up of the Pacific. This war has been brewing for several decades. All literature speaks about it. America's real aim in entering the war is to prepare for this future war with Japan. The American people do enjoy considerable freedom and it is difficult to conceive them standing for compulsory military service, for the setting up of an army pursuing any aims of conquest—a struggle with Japan, for instance. The Americans have the example of Europe to show them what this leads to. The American capitalists have stepped into this war in order to have an excuse, behind a smoke-screen of lofty ideals championing the rights of small nations, for building up a strong standing army.

The peasants refuse to give up their grain for money and demand implements, boots, and clothes. There is a great measure of profound truth in this decision. Indeed, the country has reached a stage of ruin when it now faces the same situation, although to a less intensive degree, that other countries have long been facing, a situation in which money has lost its value. The rule of capitalism is being so strongly undermined by the whole course of events that the peasants, for instance, refuse to accept money. They say: "What do we want money for?" And they are right. The rule of capitalism is being undermined not because somebody is out to seize power. "Seizure" of power would be senseless. It would be impossible to put an end to the rule of capitalism if the whole course of economic development in the capitalist countries did not lead up to it. The war has speeded up this process, and this has made capitalism impossible. No power could destroy capitalism if it were not sapped and undermined by history.

And now we see this clearly demonstrated. The peasant expresses what everybody sees that the power of money has been undermined. The only way out is for the Soviets to agree to give implements, boots, and clothes in exchange for grain. This is what we are coming to, this is the answer that life dictates. Without this, tens of millions of people will go hungry, without clothes and boots. Tens of millions of people are facing disaster and death; safeguarding the interests of the capitalists is the last thing that should bother us. The only way out is for all power to be transferred to the Soviets, which represent the majority of the population. Possibly mistakes may be made in the process. No one claims that such a difficult task can be disposed of offhand. We do not say anything of the sort. We are told that we want the power to be in the hands of the Soviets, but they don't want it. We say that life's experience will suggest this solution to them, and the whole nation will see that there is no other way out. We do not want a "seizure" of power, because the entire experience of past revolutions teaches us that the only stable power is the one that has the backing of the majority of the population. "Seizure" of power, therefore, would be adventurism, and our Party will not have it. If the government will be a government of the majority, it may perhaps embark on a policy that will prove, at first, to be erroneous, but there is no other way out. We shall then have a peaceful policy shift within the same organisations. No other organisations can be invented. That is why we say that no other solution of the question is conceivable.

How can the war be ended? If the Soviet were to assume power and the Germans continued the war—what would we do then? Anyone interested in the views of our Party could have read in *Pravda* the other day an exact quotation of what we said abroad as far back as 1915, namely, that if the revolutionary class in Russia, the working class, comes to power, it will have to offer peace. And if our terms are rejected by the German capitalists or by the capitalists of any other country, then that class will stand wholly for war.[7] We are not suggesting that the war be ended at one blow. We do not promise that. We preach no such impossible and impracticable thing as that the war can be ended by the will of one side alone. Such promises are easy to give but impossible to fulfill. There is no easy way out of this terrible war. It has been going on for three years. You will go on fighting for ten years unless you accept the idea of a difficult and painful revolution. There is no other way out. We say: The war which the capitalist governments have started can only be ended by a workers' revolution. Those interested in the socialist movement should read the Basle Manifesto of 1912 adopted unanimously by all the socialist parties of the world, a manifesto that was published in our newspaper *Pravda*, a manifesto that can be published now in none of the belligerent countries, neither in "free" Britain nor in republican France, because it said the truth about war before the war. It said that there would be war between Britain and Germany as a result of capitalist competition. It said that so much powder had accumulated that the guns would start shooting of their own accord. It told us what the war would be fought for, and said that the war would lead to a proletarian revolution. Therefore, we tell those socialists who signed this Manifesto and then went over to the side of their capitalist governments that they have betrayed socialism. There has been a split among the socialists all

[7] See *LCW*, Vol. 24, 1977, p. 394.

over the world. Some are in ministerial cabinets, others in prison. All over the world some socialists are preaching a war build-up, while others, like Eugene Debs, the American Bebel, who enjoys immense popularity among the American workers, say: "I'd rather be shot than give a cent towards the war. I'm willing to fight only the proletariat's war against the capitalists all over the world." That is how the socialists have split throughout the world. The world's social-patriots think they are defending their country. They are mistaken—they are defending the interests of one band of capitalists against another. We preach proletarian revolution—the only true cause, for which scores of people have gone to the scaffold, and hundreds and thousands have been thrown into prison. These imprisoned socialists are a minority, but the working class is for them, the whole course of economic development is for them. All this tells us that there is no other way out. The only way to end this war is by a workers' revolution in several countries. In the meantime we should make preparations for that revolution, we should assist it. For all its hatred of war and desire for peace, the Russian people could do nothing against the war, so long as it was being waged by the tsar, except work for a revolution against the tsar and for the tsar's overthrow. And that is what happened. History proved this to you yesterday and will prove it to you tomorrow. We said long ago that the mounting Russian revolution must be assisted. We said that at the end of 1914. Our Duma deputies were deported to Siberia for this, and we were told: "You are giving no answer. You talk about revolution when the strikes are off, when the deputies are doing hard labour, and when you haven't a single newspaper!" And we were accused of evading an answer. We heard those accusations for a number of years. We answered: You can be indignant about it, but so long as the tsar has not been overthrown we can do nothing against the war. And our prediction was justified. It is not fully justified yet, but it has already begun to receive justification. The revolution is beginning to change the war on Russia's part. The capitalists are still continuing the war, and we say: Until there is a workers' revolution in several countries the war cannot be stopped, because the people who want that war are still in power. We are told: "In a number of countries everything seems to be asleep. In Germany all the socialists to a man are for the war, and Liebknecht is the only one against it." To this I say: This only one, Liebknecht, represents the working class. The hopes of all are in him alone, in his supporters, in the German proletariat. You don't believe this? Carry on with the war then! There is no other way. If you don't believe in Liebknecht, if you don't believe in the workers' revolution, a revolution that is coming to a head—if you don't believe this, then believe the capitalists!

Nothing but a workers' revolution in several countries can defeat this war. The war is not a game, it is an appalling thing taking toll of millions of lives, and it is not to be ended easily.

The soldiers at the front cannot tear the front away from the rest of the state and settle things their own way. The soldiers at the front are a part of the country. So long as the country is at war the front will suffer along with the rest. Nothing can be done about it. The war has been brought about by the ruling classes and only a revolution of the working class can end it. Whether you will get a speedy peace or not depends on how the revolution will develop. Whatever sentimental things may be said, however much we may be told: Let us end the war immediately—this cannot be done without the development of the revolution. When power passes to the Soviets the capitalists will come out against us. Japan, France, Britain—the governments of all countries will be against us. The capitalists will be against, but the workers will be for us. That will be the end of the war which the capitalists started. There you have the answer to the question of how to end the war.

First published April 23, 1929 in *Pravda* No. 23
Published according to the shorthand report

THE FOREIGN POLICY OF THE RUSSIAN REVOLUTION

No idea could be more erroneous or harmful than to separate foreign from home policy. The monstrous falsity of this separation becomes even more monstrous in war-time. Yet the bourgeoisie are doing everything possible and impossible to suggest and promote this idea. Popular ignorance of foreign policy is incomparably greater than of home policy. The "secrecy" of diplomatic relations is sacredly observed in the freest of capitalist countries, in the most democratic republics.

Popular deception has become a real art in foreign "affairs", and our revolution suffers very badly from this deception. The poison of deception is spread far and wide by the millions of copies of bourgeois newspapers.

You must side with one of the two immensely wealthy and immensely powerful groups of imperialist predators—that is how capitalist reality poses the basic issue of present-day foreign policy. That is how this issue is posed by the capitalist class. And that, it goes without saying, is how it is posed by the broad mass of the petty bourgeoisie who have retained their old, capitalist views and prejudices.

Those whose thinking does not go beyond capitalist relations cannot understand why the workers, if they are politically conscious, cannot side with *either* group of imperialist plunderers. Conversely, the worker cannot understand why socialists who remain true to the fraternal alliance of the workers of the world against the capitalists of the world are accused of being inclined towards a separate peace treaty with the Germans, or of virtually serving such a peace treaty. Under no circumstances can these socialists (and hence the Bolsheviks) agree to a separate peace treaty between the capitalists. The basis for the foreign policy of the politically-conscious proletariat is no separate peace treaty with the German capitalists and no alliance with the Anglo-French capitalists.

By rising up in arms against that programme because they fear a break with "Britain and France", our Mensheviks and Socialist-

Revolutionaries are virtually carrying out a capitalist foreign policy programme, while embellishing it with florid and innocent phrases about "revision of treaties", declarations in support of "peace without annexations", etc. All these pious wishes are doomed to remain hollow phrases, for *capitalist* reality puts the issue bluntly: either submit to the imperialists of one of the two groups, or wage a revolutionary struggle against all imperialists.

Have we any allies for this struggle? Yes. The oppressed classes of Europe, primarily the proletariat. The peoples oppressed by imperialism, primarily our neighbours in Asia.

The Mensheviks and Socialist-Revolutionaries, who call themselves "revolutionary democrats", are in fact pursuing a counter-revolutionary and anti-democratic foreign policy. Were they revolutionaries, they would advise the workers and peasants of Russia to march at the head of all peoples oppressed by imperialism and of all the oppressed classes.

"But in that event the capitalists of all other countries would rally against Russia," the frightened philistines object. That is not impossible. No "*revolutionary*" democrat has the right to renounce revolutionary war in advance. But the practical likelihood of such a war is not very great. The British and German imperialists will not be able to "come to terms" against revolutionary Russia.

The Russian revolution, which as early as 1905 led to revolutions in Turkey, Persia and China, would have placed the German and British imperialists in a very difficult position if it had begun to establish a truly revolutionary alliance of the workers and peasants of the colonies and semi-colonies against the despots, against the khans, for expulsion of the Germans from Turkey, the British from Turkey, Persia, India, Egypt, etc.

Social-chauvinists, both French and Russian, like to refer to 1793. By this spectacular reference they try to cover up their betrayal of the revolution. But people here refuse to think that the *truly* "revolutionary" democrats in Russia could and should act *in the spirit* of 1793 towards the oppressed and backward nations.

The foreign policy of the capitalists and the petty bourgeoisie is "alliance" with the imperialists, that is, disgraceful dependence on them. The foreign policy of the proletariat is alliance with the revolutionaries of the advanced countries and with all the oppressed nations against all and any imperialists.

Pravda No. 81, June 27 (14), 1917
Published according to the *Pravda* text

THREE CRISES[1]

The more violent the slander and lies against the Bolsheviks these days, the more calmly must we, while refuting the lies and slander, reflect upon the historical interrelation of events and the political, i.e., *class*, significance of the revolution's present course.

To refute the lies and slander, we only have to refer again to *Listok "Pravdy"* of July 6, and to call the reader's attention especially to the article printed below which gives documentary evidence that on July 2 the Bolsheviks campaigned *against* the demonstration (as admitted by the Socialist-Revolutionaries' paper). The article indicates that on July 3 the popular mood exploded into action and the demonstration started against our advice. It shows that on July 4, in a leaflet (reprinted by the Socialist-Revolutionary paper *Dyelo Naroda*), we called for a *peaceful* and *organised* demonstration, that on the night of July 4 we passed a decision to call off the demonstration. Slanderers, continue your slander! You can never refute these facts and their decisive significance in every connection!

[1] The offices of *Pravda* having been wrecked on July 5 (18), 1917, by the Provisional Government, the article "Three Crises" appeared in *Rabotnitsa* No. 7 on July 19 (August 1). The editors of the journal wanted that particular issue to be circulated as widely as possible and therefore published on the cover an appeal to all workers, trade unions, factory committees, and R.S.D.L.P.(B.) cells and district organisations earnestly asking them to take energetic steps for the widest possible dissemination of the issue.

Rabotnitsa (Woman Worker)—a legal periodical published by the C.C. R.S.D.L.P.(B.) on Lenin's initiative in St. Petersburg, with money collected by women workers. It appeared from February 23 (March 8) to June 1914. Seven issues were brought out, of which the police confiscated three. Among the members of its editorial board were I. F. Armand, A. I. Yelizarova, N. K. Krupskaya, P. F. Kudelli, L. R. Menzhinskaya, Y. F. Rozmirovich, K. N. Samoilova and L. N. Stal.

The periodical resumed publication on May 10 (23), 1917, and continued till January 1918.

Rabotnitsa played an important part in the political education of women workers during the Bolshevik Party's preparations for the socialist revolution in Russia.

Let us turn to the question of the historical interrelation of the events. When, as early as the beginning of April, we opposed support for the Provisional Government, we were attacked by both the S.R.s and the Mensheviks. But what has reality proved?

What have the three political crises proved—April 20 and 21, June 10 and 18, July 3 and 4?

They have proved, in the first place, that the masses are becoming increasingly dissatisfied with the bourgeois policy of the Provisional Government's bourgeois majority.

It is rather interesting to note that the ruling Socialist-Revolutionaries' newspaper, *Dyelo Naroda*, despite its marked hostility to the Bolsheviks, is compelled to admit, in its July 6 issue, the deep economic and political causes of the action of July 3 and 4. The stupid, crude, infamous lie that this action was artificially created, that the Bolsheviks campaigned in *favour* of action, will daily be more and more exposed.

The common cause, the common origin, the deep common root of the three above-mentioned political crises is clear, especially if we look at them in their interrelation, as science demands that politics be looked at. It is absurd even to think that three such crises could be produced artificially.

In the second place, it is instructive to grasp what each one of them had in common with the others, and what was its specific features.

What is common to all three is a mass dissatisfaction overflowing all bounds, a mass resentment with the bourgeoisie and *their* government. Whoever forgets, ignores or underestimates *this essence of the matter*, renounces the ABC of socialism concerning the class struggle.

Let those who call themselves socialists, who know something about the character of the class struggle in European revolutions, think about the class struggle in the Russian revolution.

These crises are peculiar in the ways they manifested themselves. The first (April 20-21) was stormy and spontaneous, and completely unorganised. It led to Black Hundreds firing on the demonstrators and to unprecedentedly savage and lying accusations against the Bolsheviks. After the outburst came a political crisis.

In the second case, the demonstration was called by the Bolsheviks, and was cancelled after a stern ultimatum and direct ban by the Congress of Soviets; then, on June 18, came a general demonstration in which the Bolshevik slogans clearly predominated. As the Socialist-Revolutionaries and Mensheviks themselves admitted on the evening of June 18, a political crisis would certainly have broken out had it not been for the offensive at the front.

The third crisis broke out spontaneously on July 3 despite the Bolsheviks' efforts on July 2 to check it. Reaching its climax on July 4, it led to a furious outburst of counter-revolution on July 5 and 6. The vacillation of the S.R.s and Mensheviks expressed itself in Spiridonova and a number of other S.R.s declaring for the transfer of power to the Soviets, and in the Menshevik internationalists, previously opposed to it, voicing the same idea.

The last, and perhaps the most instructive, conclusion to be drawn from considering the events in their interconnection is that *all* three crises manifested some form of demonstration that is new in the history of our revolution, a demonstration of a more complicated type in which the movement proceeds in waves, a sudden drop following a rapid rise, revolution and counter-revolution becoming more acute, and the middle elements being eliminated for a more or less extensive period.

In all three crises, the movement took the form of a *demonstration*. An anti-government demonstration—that would be the most exact, formal description of events. But the fact of the matter is that it was not an ordinary demonstration; it was something considerably more than a demonstration, but less than a revolution. It was an outburst of revolution and counter-revolution *together*, a sharp, sometimes almost sudden elimination of the middle elements, while the proletarian and bourgeois elements made a stormy appearance.

In this respect it is extremely typical that, for *each* of these movements, the middle elements blame *both* of the specific class forces—the proletariat as well as the bourgeoisie. Look at the S.R.s and Mensheviks. They lean over backwards to frantically shout that, by their extremes, the Bolsheviks are helping the counter-revolution.

At the same time, however, they admit again and again that the Cadets (with whom they form a bloc in the government) are counter-revolutionary. "Our urgent task is to draw a line," wrote *Dyelo Naroda* yesterday, "to dig a deep moat between ourselves and all the Right elements, including *Yedinstvo*, which has gone militant" (with which, we may add, the S.R.s formed a bloc during the elections).

Compare that with today's (July 7) issue of *Yedinstvo*, in which Plekhanov's editorial is compelled to state the indisputable fact that the Soviets (i.e., the S.R.s and Mensheviks) will "think over the matter for a fortnight" and that, if power were to pass to the Soviets, "it would be tantamount to victory for Lenin's supporters". "If the Cadets don't stick to the rule—the worse, the better . . . ," says Plekhanov, "they themselves will have to admit that they have made a big mistake [by withdrawing from the Cabinet], making the work of Lenin's supporters easier."

Isn't that typical? The middle elements blame the Cadets for making the Bolsheviks' work easier, and the Bolsheviks for making the Cadets' work easier! Is it so hard to guess that if we substitute class names for political ones we have before us the dreams of the petty bourgeoisie about the disappearance of the class struggle between the proletariat and the bourgeoisie? Isn't the petty bourgeoisie complaining about the class struggle between the proletariat and the bourgeoisie? Is it really so hard to guess that no Bolsheviks in the world could have "created" even a single "popular movement", let alone three movements, if the deepest economic and political causes had not set the proletariat into action? Is it so difficult to guess that no Cadets and monarchists combined could have called forth any movement "from the Right" if it had not been for the equally deep causes that make the bourgeoisie as a class counter-revolutionary?

Both we and the Cadets were blamed for the April 20-21 movement—for intransigence, extremes, and for aggravating the situation. The Bolsheviks were even accused (absurd as it may be) of the firing on Nevsky. When the movement was over, however, those same S.R.s and Mensheviks, in their joint, official organ, *Izvestia*, wrote that the "popular movement" had "swept away the imperialists, Milyukov, etc.", i.e., they *praised* the movement!! Isn't that typical? Doesn't it show very clearly that the petty bourgeoisie do not understand the workings, the meaning, of the class struggle between the proletariat and the bourgeoisie?

The objective situation is this. The vast majority of the country's population is petty-bourgeois by its living conditions and more so by its ideas. But big capital rules the country, primarily through banks and syndicates. There is an urban proletariat in this country, mature enough to go its own way, but not yet able to draw at once the majority of the semi-proletarians to its side. From this fundamental, class fact follows the inevitability of such crises as the three we are now examining, as well as their forms.

In future the forms of crises may, of course, change, but the substance of the issue will remain the same even if, for instance, the S.R. Constituent Assembly meets in October. The S.R.s have promised the peasants: (1) to abolish private landownership; (2) to transfer the land to the working people; (3) to confiscate the landed estates and transfer them to the peasants without compensation. These great reforms can never be realised without the most decisive revolutionary measures against the bourgeoisie, measures that can *only* be taken when the poor peasants join the proletariat, *only* when the banks and the syndicates are nationalised.

The credulous peasants, believing for a time that these beautiful things can be achieved by compromising with the bourgeoisie, will inevitably be disappointed and . . ."dissatisfied" (mildly speaking) with the sharp class struggle of the proletariat against the bourgeoisie for the implementation of the promises of the S.R.s. So it was, and so it will be.

Written on July 7 (20), 1917
Published in the magazine *Rabotnitsa* No. 7, July 19, 1917
Published according to the manuscript

THE POLITICAL SITUATION[1]

FOUR THESES

1. The counter-revolution has become organised and consolidated, and has actually taken state power into its hands.

The complete organisation and consolidation of the counter-revolution consists in a combination of its three main forces, a combination excellently conceived and already put into practice: (1.) The Constitutional-Democratic Party, i.e., the real leader of the organised bourgeoisie, has, by withdrawing from the Cabinet, confronted it with an ultimatum, thus clearing the way for the Cabinet's overthrow by the counter-revolution; (2.) The General Staff and the military leaders, with the deliberate or semi-deliberate assistance of Kerensky, whom even the most prominent Socialist-Revolutionaries now call a Cavaignac, have seized actual state power and have proceeded to shoot down revolutionary units at the front, disarm the revolutionary troops and workers in Petrograd and Moscow, suppress unrest in Nizhni-Novgorod, arrest Bolsheviks and ban their papers, not only without trial, but even without a government order. At present, basic state power in Russia is virtually a military dictatorship. This fact is still obscured by a number of institutions that are revolutionary in words but powerless in deeds. Yet it is so obvious and fundamental a fact that, without understanding it, one cannot understand anything about the political situation. (3.) The Black Hundred-monarchist and bourgeois press, which has switched from hounding Bolsheviks to hounding the Soviets, the "incendiary" Chernov, etc., has indicated with the utmost clarity that the true meaning of the policy of military dictatorship, which now reigns supreme and is supported by the Cadets

[1] The article "*The Political Situation*" was first published in the Kronstadt Bolshevik paper *Proletarskoye Dyelo* No. 6 on August 2 (July 20), 1917, under the heading "Political Mood".

To safeguard the newspaper against suppression by the Provisional Government, the editors substituted "a resolute fight" for "an armed uprising". In this volume, the article appears according to the manuscript.

and monarchists, is preparation for disbanding the Soviets. Many of the leaders of the S.R.s and Mensheviks, i.e., the present majority in the Soviets, have admitted and expressed this during the past few days, but, true to their petty-bourgeois nature, they shrug off this formidable reality with meaningless high-sounding phrases.

2. The leaders of the Soviets and of the Socialist-Revolutionary and Menshevik parties, headed by Tsereteli and Chernov, have completely betrayed the cause of the revolution by putting it in the hands of the counter-revolutionaries and by turning themselves, their parties and the Soviets into mere fig-leaves of the counter-revolution.

Proof of this is that the Socialist-Revolutionaries and Mensheviks have betrayed the Bolsheviks and have tacitly agreed to close down their papers without daring to tell the people plainly and openly that they are doing so and why. By sanctioning the disarming of the workers and the revolutionary regiments, they have deprived themselves of all real power. They have turned into the most loud-mouthed ranters who help the reaction to "divert" the people's attention until it is finally ready to disband the Soviets. It is impossible to understand anything at all about the present political situation without realising this complete and final bankruptcy of the S.R.s and Mensheviks and the present majority in the Soviets and without realising that their "Directory" and other masquerades are an absolute sham.

3. All hopes for a peaceful development of the Russian revolution have vanished for good. This is the objective situation: either complete victory for the military dictatorship, or victory for the workers' armed uprising; the latter victory is only possible when it coincides with a deep mass upheaval against the government and the bourgeoisie caused by economic disruption and the prolongation of the war.

The slogan "All Power to the Soviets!" was a slogan for peaceful development of the revolution which was possible in April, May, June, and up to July 5-9, i.e., up to the time when actual power passed into the hands of the military dictatorship. This slogan is no longer correct, for it does not take into account that power has changed hands and that the revolution has in fact been completely betrayed by the S.R.s and Mensheviks. Reckless actions, revolts, partial resistance, or hopeless hit-and-run attempts to oppose reaction will not help. What will help is a clear understanding of the situation, endurance and determination of the workers' vanguard, preparation of forces for the armed uprising, for the victory of which conditions at present are extremely difficult, but still possible if the facts and trends mentioned in the thesis coincide. Let us have no constitutional or republican illusions of any kind, no more illusions about a peaceful path, no sporadic actions, no yielding *now* to provocation from the Black Hundreds and Cossacks. Let us muster our forces, reorganise them, and resolutely prepare for the armed uprising, if the course of the crisis permits it on a really mass, country-wide scale. The transfer of land to the peasants is impossible at present without an armed uprising, since the counter-revolutionaries, having taken power, have completely united with the landowners as a class.

The aim of the insurrection can only be to transfer power to the proletariat, supported by the poor peasants, with a view to putting our Party programme into effect.

4. The party of the working class, without abandoning legal activity but never for a moment overrating it, must *combine* legal with illegal work, as it did in 1912-14.

Don't let a single hour of legal work slip by. But don't cherish any constitutional or "peaceful" illusions. Form illegal organisations or cells everywhere and at once for the publication of leaflets, etc. Reorganise immediately, consistently, resolutely, all along the line.

Act as we did in 1912-14, when we could speak about overthrowing tsarism by a revolution and an armed uprising, without at the same time losing our legal base in the Duma, the insurance societies, the trade unions, etc.

Written on July 10 (23), 1917
Published on August 2 (July 20), 1917
in *Proletarskoye Dyelo* No. 6
Signed: W
Published according to the manuscript

THE STATE AND REVOLUTION

Chapter 2: The Experience of 1848-51

1. THE EVE OF THE REVOLUTION

The first works of mature Marxism—*The Poverty of Philosophy* and the *Communist Manifesto*—appeared just on the eve of the revolution of 1848. For this reason, in addition to presenting the general principles of Marxism, they reflect to a certain degree the concrete revolutionary situation of the time. It will, therefore, be more expedient, perhaps, to examine what the authors of these works said about the state immediately before they drew conclusions from the experience of the years 1848-51.

In *The Poverty of Philosophy*, Marx wrote:

> "The working class, in the course of development, will substitute for the old bourgeois society an association which will preclude classes and their antagonism, and there will be no more political power proper, since political power is precisely the official expression of class antagonism in bourgeois society." (p. 182, German edition, 1885.)[1]

It is instructive to compare this general exposition of the idea of the state disappearing after the abolition of classes with the exposition contained in the *Communist Manifesto*, written by Marx and Engels a few months later—in November 1847, to be exact:

> ". . . In depicting the most general phases of the development of the proletariat, we traced the more or less veiled civil war, raging within existing society up to the point where that war breaks out into open revolution, and where the violent overthrow of the bourgeoisie lays the foundation for the sway of the proletariat . . . .
>
> ". . . We have seen above that the first step in the revolution by the

[1] See Karl Marx, *The Poverty of Philosophy*, Moscow, 1973, p. 151.

working class is to raise the proletariat to the position of ruling class, to win the battle of democracy.

"The proletariat will use its political supremacy to wrest, by degrees, all capital from the bourgeoisie, to centralise all instruments of production in the hands of the state, i.e., of the proletariat organised as the ruling class; and to increase the total productive forces as rapidly as possible." (pp. 31 and 37, seventh German edition, 1906.)[2]

Here we have a formulation of one of the most remarkable and most important ideas of Marxism on the subject of the state, namely, the idea of the "dictatorship of the proletariat" (as Marx and Engels began to call it after the Paris Commune); and, also, a highly interesting definition of the state, which is also one of the "forgotten words" of Marxism: "*the state, i.e., the proletariat organised as the ruling class*".

This definition of the state has never been explained in the prevailing propaganda and agitation literature of the official Social-Democratic parties. More than that, it has been deliberately ignored, for it is absolutely irreconcilable with reformism, and is a slap in the face for the common opportunist prejudices and philistine illusions about the "peaceful development of democracy".

The proletariat needs the state—this is repeated by all the opportunists, social-chauvinists and Kautskyites, who assure us that this is what Marx taught. But they "*forget*" to add that, in the first place, according to Marx, the proletariat needs only a state which is withering away, i.e., a state so constituted that it begins to wither away immediately, and cannot but wither away. And, secondly, the working people need a "state, i.e., the proletariat organised as the ruling class".

The state is a special organisation of force: it is an organisation of violence for the suppression of some class. What class must the proletariat suppress? Naturally only the exploiting class, i.e., the bourgeoisie. The working people need the state only to suppress the resistance of the exploiters, and only the proletariat can direct this suppression, can carry it out. For the proletariat is the only class that is consistently revolutionary, the only class that can unite all the

[2] See Karl Marx and Frederick Engels, *Selected Works*, Vol. I, Moscow, 1973, pp. 118-19 and 126.

working and exploited people in the struggle against the bourgeoisie, in completely removing it.

The exploiting classes need political rule to maintain exploitation, i.e., in the selfish interests of an insignificant minority against the vast majority of all people. The exploited classes need political rule in order to completely abolish all exploitation, i.e., in the interests of the vast majority of the people, and against the insignificant minority consisting of the modern slave-owners—the landowners and capitalists.

The petty-bourgeois democrats, those sham socialists who replaced the class struggle by dreams of class harmony, even pictured the socialist transformation in a dreamy fashion—not as the overthrow of the rule of the exploiting class, but as the peaceful submission of the minority to the majority which has become aware of its aims. This petty-bourgeois utopia, which is inseparable from the idea of the state being above classes, led in practice to the betrayal of the interests of the working classes, as was shown, for example, by the history of the French revolutions of 1848 and 1871, and by the experience of "socialist" participation in bourgeois Cabinets in Britain, France, Italy and other countries at the turn of the century.

All his life Marx fought against this petty-bourgeois socialism, now revived in Russia by the Socialist-Revolutionary and Menshevik parties. He developed his theory of the class struggle consistently, down to the theory of political power, of the state.

The overthrow of bourgeois rule can be accomplished only by the proletariat, the particular class whose economic conditions of existence prepare it for this task and provide it with the possibility and the power to perform it. While the bourgeoisie break up and disintegrate the peasantry and all the petty-bourgeois groups, they weld together, unite and organise the proletariat. Only the proletariat—by virtue of the economic role it plays in large-scale production—is capable of being the leader of *all* the working and exploited people, whom the bourgeoisie exploit, oppress and crush, often not less but more than they do the proletarians, but who are incapable of waging an *independent* struggle for their emancipation.

The theory of class struggle, applied by Marx to the question of the state and the socialist revolution, leads as a matter of course to the recognition of the *political rule* of the proletariat, of its dictatorship, i.e., of undivided power directly backed by the armed force of the people. The overthrow of the bourgeoisie can be achieved only by the proletariat becoming the *ruling class*, capable of crushing the inevitable and desperate resistance of the bourgeoisie, and of organising *all* the working and exploited people for the new economic system.

The proletariat needs state power, a centralised organisation of force, an organisation of violence, both to crush the resistance of the exploiters and to *lead* the enormous mass of the population—the peasants, the petty bourgeoisie, and semi-proletarians—in the work of organising a socialist economy.

By educating the workers' party, Marxism educates the vanguard of the proletariat, capable of assuming power and *leading the whole people* to socialism, of directing and organising the new system, of being the teacher, the guide, the leader of all the working and exploited people in organising their social life without the bourgeoisie and against the bourgeoisie. By contrast, the opportunism now prevailing trains the members of the workers' party to be the representatives of the better-paid workers, who lose touch with the masses, "get along" fairly well under capitalism, and sell their birthright for a mess of pottage, i.e., renounce their role as revolutionary leaders of the people against the bourgeoisie.

Marx's theory of "the state, i.e., the proletariat organised as the ruling class", is inseparably bound up with the whole of his doctrine of the revolutionary role of the proletariat in history. The culmination of this role is the proletarian dictatorship, the political rule of the proletariat.

But since the proletariat needs the state as a *special* form of organisation of violence *against* the bourgeoisie, the following conclusion suggests itself: is it conceivable that such an organisation can be created without first abolishing, destroying the state machine created by the bourgeoisie *for themselves*? The *Communist Manifesto* leads straight to this conclusion, and it is of this conclusion that Marx speaks when summing up the experience of the revolution of 1848-51.

2. THE REVOLUTION SUMMED UP

Marx sums up his conclusions from the revolution of 1848-51, on the subject of the state we are concerned with, in the following argument contained in *The Eighteenth Brumaire of Louis Bonaparte*:

> "But the revolution is thoroughgoing. It is still journeying through purgatory. It does its work methodically. By December 2, 1851 [the day of Louis Bonaparte's *coup d'état*], it had completed one half of its preparatory work. It is now completing the other half. First it perfected the parliamentary power, in order to be able to overthrow it. Now that it has attained this, it is perfecting the *executive power*, reducing it to its purest expression, isolating it, setting it up against itself as the sole object, *in order to concentrate all its forces of destruction against it* [italics ours]. And when it has done this second half of its preliminary work, Europe will leap from its seat and exultantly exclaim: well grubbed, old mole!
>
> "This executive power with its enormous bureaucratic and military organisation, with its vast and ingenious state machinery, with a host of officials numbering half a million, besides an army of another half million, this appalling parasitic body, which enmeshes the body of French society and chokes all its pores, sprang up in the days of the absolute monarchy, with the decay of the feudal system, which it helped to hasten." The first French Revolution developed centralisation, "but at the same time" it increased "the extent, the attributes and the number of agents of governmental power. Napoleon completed this state machinery". The legitimate monarchy and the July monarchy "added nothing but a greater division of labour".
>
> "... Finally, in its struggle against the revolution, the parliamentary republic found itself compelled to strengthen, along with repressive measures, the resources and centralisation of governmental power. *All revolutions perfected this machine instead of smashing it* [italics ours]. The parties that contended in turn for domination regarded the possession of this huge state edifice as the principal spoils of the victor." (*The Eighteenth Brumaire of Louis Bonaparte*, pp. 98-99,

fourth edition, Hamburg, 1907)[3]

In this remarkable argument, Marxism takes a tremendous step forward compared with the *Communist Manifesto*. In the latter the question of the state is still treated in an extremely abstract manner, in the most general terms and expressions. In the above-quoted passage, the question is treated in a concrete manner, and the conclusion is extremely precise, definite, practical and palpable: all previous revolutions perfected the state machine, whereas it must be broken, smashed.

This conclusion is the chief and fundamental point in the Marxist theory of the state. And it is precisely this fundamental point which has been completely *ignored* by the dominant official Social-Democratic parties and, indeed, *distorted* (as we shall see later) by the foremost theoretician of the Second International, Karl Kautsky.

The *Communist Manifesto* gives a general summary of history, which compels us to regard the state as the organ of class rule and leads us to the inevitable conclusion that the proletariat cannot overthrow the bourgeoisie without first winning political power, without attaining political supremacy, without transforming the state into the "proletariat organised as the ruling class"; and that this proletarian state will begin to wither away immediately after its victory because the state is unnecessary and cannot exist in a society in which there are no class antagonisms. The question as to how, from the point of view of historical development, the replacement of the bourgeois by the proletarian state is to take place is not raised here.

This is the question Marx raises and answers in 1852. True to his philosophy of dialectical materialism, Marx takes as his basis the historical experience of the great years of revolution, 1848 to 1851. Here, as everywhere else, his theory is a *summing up of experience*, illuminated by a profound philosophical conception of the world and a rich knowledge of history.

The problem of the state is put specifically: How did the bourgeois state, the state machine necessary for the rule of the bourgeoisie, come

[3] See Karl Marx, *The Eighteenth Brumaire of Louis Bonaparte* (Karl Marx and Frederick Engels, *Selected Works*, Vol. I, Moscow, 1973, p. 477).

into being historically? What changes did it undergo, what evolution did it perform in the course of bourgeois revolutions and in the face of the independent actions of the oppressed classes? What are the tasks of the proletariat in relation to this state machine?

The centralised state power that is peculiar to bourgeois society came into being in the period of the fall of absolutism. Two institutions most characteristic of this state machine are the bureaucracy and the standing army. In their works, Marx and Engels repeatedly show that the bourgeoisie are connected with these institutions by thousands of threads. Every worker's experience illustrates this connection in an extremely graphic and impressive manner. From its own bitter experience, the working class learns to recognise this connection. That is why it so easily grasps and so firmly learns the doctrine which shows the inevitability of this connection, a doctrine which the petty-bourgeois democrats either ignorantly and flippantly deny, or still more flippantly admit "in general", while forgetting to draw appropriate practical conclusions.

The bureaucracy and the standing army are a "parasite" on the body of bourgeois society—a parasite created by the internal antagonisms which rend that society, but a parasite which "chokes" all its vital pores. The Kautskyite opportunism now prevailing in official Social-Democracy considers the view that the state is a *parasitic organism* to be the peculiar and exclusive attribute of anarchism. It goes without saying that this distortion of Marxism is of vast advantage to those philistines who have reduced socialism to the unheard-of disgrace of justifying and prettifying the imperialist war by applying to it the concept of "defence of the fatherland"; but it is unquestionably a distortion, nevertheless.

The development, perfection, and strengthening of the bureaucratic and military apparatus proceeded during all the numerous bourgeois revolutions which Europe has witnessed since the fall of feudalism. In particular, it is the petty bourgeois who are attracted to the side of the big bourgeoisie and are largely subordinated to them through this apparatus, which provides the upper sections of the peasants, small artisans, tradesmen, and the like with comparatively comfortable, quiet, and respectable jobs raising their holders *above* the people.

Consider what happened in Russia during the six months following February 27, 1917. The official posts which formerly were given by preference to the Black Hundreds have now become the spoils of the Cadets, Mensheviks, and Socialist-Revolutionaries. Nobody has really thought of introducing any serious reforms. Every effort has been made to put them off "until the Constituent Assembly meets", and to steadily put off its convocation until after the war! But there has been no delay, no waiting for the Constituent Assembly, in the matter of dividing the spoils, of getting the lucrative jobs of ministers, deputy ministers, governors-general, etc., etc.! The game of combinations that has been played in forming the government has been, in essence, only an expression of this division and redivision of the "spoils", which has been going on above and below, throughout the country, in every department of central and local government. The six months between February 27 and August 27, 1917, can be summed up, objectively summed up beyond all dispute, as follows: reforms shelved, distribution of official jobs accomplished and "mistakes" in the distribution corrected by a few redistributions.

But the more the bureaucratic apparatus is "redistributed" among the various bourgeois and petty-bourgeois parties (among the Cadets, Socialist-Revolutionaries and Mensheviks in the case of Russia), the more keenly aware the oppressed classes, and the proletariat at their head, become of their irreconcilable hostility to the *whole* of bourgeois society. Hence the need for all bourgeois parties, even for the most democratic and "revolutionary-democratic" among them, to intensify repressive measures against the revolutionary proletariat, to strengthen the apparatus of coercion, i.e., the state machine. This course of events compels the revolution "*to concentrate all its forces of destruction*" against the state power, and to set itself the aim, not of improving the state machine, but of *smashing and destroying* it.

It was not logical reasoning, but actual developments, the actual experience of 1848-51, that led to the matter being presented in this way. The extent to which Marx held strictly to the solid ground of historical experience can be seen from the fact that, in 1852, he did not yet specifically raise the question of *what* was to take the place of the state machine to be destroyed. Experience had not yet provided material for dealing with this question, which history placed on the agenda later on, in 1871. In 1852, all that could be established with the accuracy of scientific observation was that the proletarian revolution *had approached* the task of "concentrating all its forces of destruction" against the state power, of "smashing" the state machine.

Here the question may arise: is it correct to generalise the experience, observations and conclusions of Marx, to apply them to a field that is wider than the history of France during the three years 1848-51? Before proceeding to deal with this question, let us recall a remark made by Engels and then examine the facts. In his introduction to the third edition of *The Eighteenth Brumaire*, Engels wrote:

> "France is the country where, more than anywhere else, the historical class struggles were each time fought out to a finish, and where, consequently, the changing political forms within which they move and in which their results are summarised have been stamped in the sharpest outlines. The centre of feudalism in the Middle Ages, the model country, since the Renaissance, of a unified monarchy based on social estates, France demolished feudalism in the Great Revolution and established the rule of the bourgeoisie in a classical purity unequalled by any other European land. And the struggle of the upward-striving proletariat against the ruling bourgeoisie appeared here in an acute form unknown elsewhere." (p. 4, 1907 edition)

The last remark is out of date insomuch as since 1871 there has been a lull in the revolutionary struggle of the French proletariat, although, long as this lull may be, it does not at all preclude the possibility that in the coming proletarian revolution France may show herself to be the classic country of the class struggle to a finish.

Let us, however, cast a general glance over the history of the advanced countries at the turn of the century. We shall see that the same process went on more slowly, in more varied forms, in a much wider field: on the one hand, the development of "parliamentary power" both in the republican countries (France, America, Switzerland), and in the monarchies (Britain, Germany to a certain extent, Italy, the Scandinavian countries, etc.); on the other hand, a struggle for power among the various bourgeois and petty-bourgeois parties which distributed and redistributed the "spoils" of office, with the foundations of bourgeois society unchanged; and, lastly, the perfection and consolidation of the "executive power", of its bureaucratic and military apparatus.

There is not the slightest doubt that these features are common to the whole of the modern evolution of all capitalist states in general. In the three years 1848-51 France displayed, in a swift, sharp, concentrated form, the very same processes of development which are peculiar to the whole capitalist world.

Imperialism—the era of bank capital, the era of gigantic capitalist monopolies, of the development of monopoly capitalism into state-monopoly capitalism—has clearly shown an extraordinary strengthening of the "state machine" and an unprecedented growth in its bureaucratic and military apparatus in connection with the intensification of repressive measures against the proletariat both in the monarchical and in the freest, republican countries.

World history is now undoubtedly leading, on an incomparably larger scale than in 1852, to the "concentration of all the forces" of the proletarian revolution on the "destruction" of the state machine.

What the proletariat will put in its place is suggested by the highly instructive material furnished by the Paris Commune.

3. THE PRESENTATION OF THE QUESTION BY MARX IN 1852[4]

In 1907, Mehring, in the magazine *Neue Zeit*[5] (Vol. XXV, 2, p.

[4] Added in the second edition.

[5] *Die Neue Zeit* (New Times)—theoretical journal of the German Social-Democratic Party, published in Stuttgart from 1883 to 1923. It was edited by Karl Kautsky till October 1917 and by Heinrich Cunow in the subsequent period. It published some of Marx's and Engels's writings for the first time. Engels offered advice to its editors and often criticised them for departures from Marxism.

In the second half of the nineties, upon Engels's death, the journal began systematically to publish revisionist articles, including a serial by Bernstein entitled "Problems of Socialism", which initiated a revisionist campaign against Marxism. During the First World War the journal adhered to a

164), published extracts from Marx's letter to Weydemeyer dated March 5, 1852. This letter, among other things, contains the following remarkable observation:

> "And now as to myself, no credit is due to me for discovering the existence of classes in modern society or the struggle between them. Long before me bourgeois historians had described the historical development of this class struggle and bourgeois economists, the economic anatomy of classes. What I did that was new was to prove: (1) that the *existence of classes* is only bound up with the *particular, historical phases in the development of production* (historische Entwicklungsphasen der Produktion), (2) that the class struggle necessarily leads to the *dictatorship of the proletariat*, (3) that this dictatorship itself only constitutes the transition to the *abolition of all classes* and to a *classless society*."[6]

In these words, Marx succeeded in expressing with striking clarity, first, the chief and radical difference between his theory and that of the foremost and most profound thinkers of the bourgeoisie; and, secondly, the essence of his theory of the state.

It is often said and written that the main point in Marx's theory is the class struggle. But this is wrong. And this wrong notion very often results in an opportunist distortion of Marxism and its falsification in a spirit acceptable to the bourgeoisie. For the theory of the class struggle was created *not* by Marx, *but* by the bourgeoisie *before* Marx, and, generally speaking, it is *acceptable* to the bourgeoisie. Those who recognise *only* the class struggle are not yet Marxists; they may be found to be still within the bounds of bourgeois thinking and bourgeois politics. To confine Marxism to the theory of the class struggle means curtailing Marxism, distorting it, reducing it to something acceptable to the bourgeoisie. Only he is a Marxist who *extends* the recognition of the class struggle to the recognition of the *dictatorship of the proletariat*. That is what constitutes the most profound distinction between the

....

Centrist position, and virtually backed the social-chauvinists.

[6] See Karl Marx and Frederick Engels, *Selected Correspondence*, Moscow, 1965, p. 69

Marxist and the ordinary petty (as well as big) bourgeois. This is the touchstone on which the *real* understanding and recognition of Marxism should be tested. And it is not surprising that when the history of Europe brought the working class face to face with this question as a *practical* issue, not only all the opportunists and reformists, but all the Kautskyites (people who vacillate between reformism and Marxism) proved to be miserable philistines and petty-bourgeois democrats *repudiating* the dictatorship of the proletariat. Kautsky's pamphlet, *The Dictatorship of the Proletariat*, published in August 1918, i.e., long after the first edition of the present book, is a perfect example of petty-bourgeois distortion of Marxism and base renunciation of it *in deeds*, while hypocritically recognising it *in words* (see my pamphlet, *The Proletarian Revolution and the Renegade Kautsky*, Petrograd and Moscow, 1918).

Opportunism today, as represented by its principal spokesman, the ex-Marxist Karl Kautsky, fits in completely with Marx's characterisation of the *bourgeois* position quoted above, for this opportunism limits recognition of the class struggle to the sphere of bourgeois relations. (Within this sphere, within its framework, not a single educated liberal will refuse to recognise the class struggle "in principle"!) Opportunism *does not extend* recognition of the class struggle to the cardinal point, to the period of *transition* from capitalism to communism, of the *overthrow* and the complete *abolition* of the bourgeoisie. In reality, this period inevitably is a period of an unprecedentedly violent class struggle in unprecedentedly acute forms, and, consequently, during this period the state must inevitably be a state that is democratic *in a new way* (for the proletariat and the propertyless in general) and dictatorial *in a new way* (against the bourgeoisie).

Further. The essence of Marx's theory of the state has been mastered only by those who realise that the dictatorship of a *single* class is necessary not only for every class society in general, not only for the *proletariat* which has overthrown the bourgeoisie, but also for the entire *historical period* which separates capitalism from "classless society", from communism. Bourgeois states are most varied in form, but their essence is the same: all these states, whatever their form, in the final analysis are inevitably the *dictatorship of the bourgeoisie*. The transition from capitalism to communism is certainly bound to yield a tremendous abundance and variety of political forms, but the essence will inevitably be the same: *the dictatorship of the proletariat.*

THE STATE AND REVOLUTION

Chapter 3: Experience of the Paris Commune of 1871. Marx's Analysis

1. WHAT MADE THE COMMUNARDS' ATTEMPT HEROIC?

It is well known that in the autumn of 1870, a few months before the Commune, Marx warned the Paris workers that any attempt to overthrow the government would be the folly of despair. But when, in March 1871, a decisive battle was forced upon the workers and they accepted it, when the uprising had become a fact, Marx greeted the proletarian revolution with the greatest enthusiasm, in spite of unfavourable auguries. Marx did not persist in the pedantic attitude of condemning an "untimely" movement as did the ill-famed Russian renegade from Marxism, Plekhanov, who in November 1905 wrote encouragingly about the workers' and peasants' struggle, but after December 1905 cried, liberal fashion: "They should not have taken up arms."

Marx, however, was not only enthusiastic about the heroism of the Communards, who, as he expressed it, "stormed heaven". Although the mass revolutionary movement did not achieve its aim, he regarded it as a historic experience of enormous importance, as a certain advance of the world proletarian revolution, as a practical step that was more important than hundreds of programmes and arguments. Marx endeavored to analyse this experiment, to draw tactical lessons from it and re-examine his theory in the light of it.

The only "correction" Marx thought it necessary to make to the *Communist Manifesto* he made on the basis of the revolutionary experience of the Paris Communards.

The last preface to the new German edition of the *Communist Manifesto*, signed by both its authors, is dated June 24, 1872. In this preface the authors, Karl Marx and Frederick Engels, say that the programme of the *Communist Manifesto* "has in some details become out-of-date", and the go on to say:

> "*. . . One thing especially was proved by the Commune, viz., that 'the working class cannot simply lay hold of the ready-made state machinery and wield it for its own purposes' . . . .*"[1]

The authors took the words that are in single quotation marks in this passage from Marx's book, *The Civil War in France.*

Thus, Marx and Engels regarded one principal and fundamental lesson of the Paris Commune as being of such enormous importance that they introduced it as an important correction into the *Communist Manifesto.*

Most characteristically, it is this important correction that has been distorted by the opportunists, and its meaning probably is not known to nine-tenths, if not ninety-nine-hundredths, of the readers of the *Communist Manifesto*. We shall deal with this distortion more fully farther on, in a chapter devoted specially to distortions. Here it will be sufficient to note that the current, vulgar "interpretation" of Marx's famous statement just quoted is that Marx here allegedly emphasises the idea of slow development in contradistinction to the seizure of power, and so on.

As a matter of fact, *the exact opposite is the case*. Marx's idea is that the working class must *break up, smash* the "ready-made state machinery", and not confine itself merely to laying hold of it.

On April 12, 1871, i.e., just at the time of the Commune, Marx wrote to Kugelmann:

> "If you look up the last chapter of my *Eighteenth Brumaire*, you will find that I declare that the next attempt of the French Revolution will be no longer, as before, to transfer the bureaucratic-military machine from one hand to another, but to *smash* it [Marx's italics—the original is *zerbrechen*], and this is the precondition for every real people's revolution on the Continent. And this is what our heroic Party comrades in Paris are attempting." (*Neue Zeit*, Vol. XX, 1, 1901-02, p. 709.)[2] (The letters of Marx to Kugelmann have appeared in Russian

[1] See Karl Marx and Frederick Engels, *Selected Works*, Vol. I, Moscow, 1973, p. 99.

[2] See Karl Marx and Frederick Engels, *Selected Correspondence*, Moscow, 1965,

in no less than two editions, one of which I edited and supplied with a preface.)[3]

The words, "to smash the bureaucratic-military machine", briefly express the principal lesson of Marxism regarding the tasks of the proletariat during a revolution in relation to the state. And this is the lesson that has been not only completely ignored, but positively distorted by the prevailing, Kautskyite, "interpretation" of Marxism!

As for Marx's reference to *The Eighteenth Brumaire*, we have quoted the relevant passage in full above.

It is interesting to note, in particular, two points in the above-quoted argument of Marx. First, he restricts his conclusion to the Continent. This was understandable in 1871, when Britain was still the model of a purely capitalist country, but without a militarist clique and, to a considerable degree, without a bureaucracy. Marx therefore excluded Britain, where a revolution, even a people's revolution, then seemed possible, and indeed was possible, *without* the precondition of destroying "ready-made state machinery".

Today, in 1917, at the time of the first great imperialist war, this restriction made by Marx is no longer valid. Both Britain and America, the biggest and the last representatives—in the whole world—of Anglo-Saxon "liberty", in the sense that they had no militarist cliques and bureaucracy, have completely sunk into the all-European filthy, bloody morass of bureaucratic-military institutions which subordinate everything to themselves, and suppress everything. Today, in Britain and America, too, "the precondition for every real people's revolution" is the *smashing*, the *destruction* of the "ready-made state machinery" (made and brought up to the "European", general imperialist, perfection in those countries in the years 1914-17).

Secondly, particular attention should be paid to Marx's extremely profound remark that the destruction of the bureaucratic-military state machine is "the precondition for every real *people's* revolution". This idea of a "people's" revolution seems strange coming from Marx, so that the Russian Plekhanovites and Mensheviks, those followers of

....

pp. 262-63.

[3] See *LCW*, Vol. 12, 1980, pp. 104-12.

Struve who wish to be regarded as Marxists, might possibly declare such an expression to be a "slip of the pen" on Marx's part. They have reduced Marxism to such a state of wretchedly liberal distortion that nothing exists for them beyond the antithesis between bourgeois revolution and proletarian revolution, and even this antithesis they interpret in an utterly lifeless way.

If we take the revolutions of the twentieth century as examples we shall, of course, have to admit that the Portuguese and the Turkish revolutions are both bourgeois revolutions. Neither of them, however, is a "people's" revolution, since in neither does the mass of the people, their vast majority, come out actively, independently, with their own economic and political demands to any noticeable degree. By contrast, although the Russian bourgeois revolution of 1905-07 displayed no such "brilliant" successes as at times fell to the Portuguese and Turkish revolutions, it was undoubtedly a "real people's" revolution, since the mass of the people, their majority, the very lowest social groups, crushed by oppression and exploitation, rose independently and stamped on the entire course of the revolution the imprint of *their* own demands, *their* attempts to build in their own way a new society in place of the old society that was being destroyed.

In Europe, in 1871, the proletariat did not constitute the majority of the people in any country on the Continent. A "people's" revolution, one actually sweeping the majority into its stream, could be such only if it embraced both the proletariat and the peasants. These two classes then constituted the "people". These two classes are united by the fact that the "bureaucratic-military state machine" oppresses, crushes, exploits them. To *smash* this machine, *to break it up*, is truly in the interest of the "people", of their majority, of the workers and most of the peasants, is "the precondition" for a free alliance of the poor peasants and the proletarians, whereas without such an alliance democracy is unstable and socialist transformation is impossible.

As is well known, the Paris Commune was actually working its way toward such an alliance, although it did not reach its goal owing to a number of circumstances, internal and external.

Consequently, in speaking of a "real people's revolution", Marx, without in the least discounting the special features of the petty bourgeois (he spoke a great deal about them and often), took strict account of the actual balance of class forces in most of the continental countries of Europe in 1871. On the other hand, he stated that the "smashing" of the state machine was required by the interests of both the workers and the peasants, that it united them, that it placed before them the common task of removing the "parasite" and of replacing it by something new.

By what exactly?

2. WHAT IS TO REPLACE THE SMASHED STATE MACHINE?

In 1847, in the *Communist Manifesto*, Marx's answer to this question was as yet a purely abstract one; to be exact, it was an answer that indicated the tasks, but not the ways of accomplishing them. The answer given in the *Communist Manifesto* was that this machine was to be replaced by "the proletariat organised as the ruling class", by the "winning of the battle of democracy".

Marx did not indulge in utopias; he expected the *experience* of the mass movement to provide the reply to the question as to the specific forms this organisation of the proletariat as the ruling class would assume and as to the exact manner in which this organisation would be combined with the most complete, most consistent "winning of the battle of democracy".

Marx subjected the experience of the Commune, meagre as it was, to the most careful analysis in *The Civil War in France*. Let us quote the most important passages of this work.

> Originating from the Middle Ages, there developed in the 19th century "the centralised state power, with its ubiquitous organs of standing army, police, bureaucracy, clergy, and judicature". With the development of class antagonisms between capital and labour, "state power assumed more and more the character of a public force for the suppression of the working class, of a machine of class rule. After every revolution, which marks an advance in the class struggle, the purely coercive character of the state power stands out in bolder and

bolder relief". After the revolution of 1848-49, state power became "the national war instruments of capital against labour". The Second Empire consolidated this.

"The direct antithesis to the empire was the Commune." It was the "specific form" of "a republic that was not only to remove the monarchical form of class rule, but class rule itself . . . ."

What was this "specific" form of the proletarian, socialist republic? What was the state it began to create?

> ". . . The first decree of the Commune . . . was the suppression of the standing army, and its replacement by the armed people . . . ."

This demand now figures in the programme of every party calling itself socialist. The real worth of their programmes, however, is best shown by the behaviour of our Socialist-Revolutionaries and Mensheviks, who, right after the revolution of February 27, actually refused to carry out this demand!

> "The Commune was formed of the municipal councillors, chosen by universal suffrage in the various wards of Paris, responsible and revocable at any time. The majority of its members were naturally working men, or acknowledged representatives of the working class . . . . The police, which until then had been the instrument of the Government, was at once stripped of its political attributes, and turned into the responsible and at all times revocable instrument of the Commune. So were the officials of all other branches of the administration. From the members of the Commune downwards, the public service had to be done at *workmen's wages*. The privileges and the representation allowances of the high dignitaries of state disappeared along with the high dignitaries themselves . . . . Having once got rid of the standing army and the police, the instruments of physical force of the old Government, the Commune proceeded at once to break the instrument of spiritual suppression, the power of the priests . . . . The judicial functionaries lost that sham independence . . . they were

thenceforward to be elective, responsible, and revocable . . . ."[4]

The Commune, therefore, appears to have replaced the smashed state machine "only" by fuller democracy: abolition of the standing army; all officials to be elected and subject to recall. But as a matter of fact this "only" signifies a gigantic replacement of certain institutions by other institutions of a fundamentally different type. This is exactly a case of "quantity being transformed into quality": democracy, introduced as fully and consistently as is at all conceivable, is transformed from bourgeois into proletarian democracy; from the state (= a special force for the suppression of a particular class) into something which is no longer the state proper.

It is still necessary to suppress the bourgeoisie and crush their resistance. This was particularly necessary for the Commune; and one of the reasons for its defeat was that it did not do this with sufficient determination. The organ of suppression, however, is here the majority of the population, and not a minority, as was always the case under slavery, serfdom, and wage slavery. And since the majority of the people *itself* suppresses its oppressors, a "special force" for suppression *is no longer necessary*! In this sense, the state *begins to wither away*. Instead of the special institutions of a privileged minority (privileged officialdom, the chiefs of the standing army), the majority itself can directly fulfill all these functions, and the more the functions of state power are performed by the people as a whole, the less need there is for the existence of this power.

In this connection, the following measures of the Commune, emphasised by Marx, are particularly noteworthy: the abolition of all representation allowances, and of all monetary privileges to officials, the reduction of the remuneration of *all* servants of the state to the level of "*workmen's wages*". This shows more clearly than anything else the *turn* from bourgeois to proletarian democracy, from the democracy of the oppressors to that of the oppressed classes, from the state as a "*special force*" for the suppression of a particular class to the

[4] See Karl Marx, *The Civil War in France* (Karl Marx and Frederick Engels, *Selected Works*, Vol. II, Moscow, 1973, pp. 217-21).

suppression of the oppressors by the *general force* of the majority of the people—the workers and the peasants. And it is on this particularly striking point, perhaps the most important as far as the problem of the state is concerned, that the ideas of Marx have been most completely ignored! In popular commentaries, the number of which is legion, this is not mentioned. The thing done is to keep silent about it as if it were a piece of old-fashioned "naïveté", just as Christians, after their religion had been given the status of state religion, "forgot" the "naïveté" of primitive Christianity with its democratic revolutionary spirit.

The reduction of the remuneration of high state officials seems to be "simply" a demand of naïve, primitive democracy. One of the "founders" of modern opportunism, the ex-Social-Democrat Eduard Bernstein, has more than once repeated the vulgar bourgeois jeers at "primitive" democracy. Like all opportunists, and like the present Kautskyites, he did not understand at all that, first of all, the transition from capitalism to socialism is *impossible* without a certain "reversion" to "primitive" democracy (for how else can the majority, and then the whole population without exception, proceed to discharge state functions?); and that, secondly, "primitive democracy" based on capitalism and capitalist culture is not the same as primitive democracy in prehistoric or pre-capitalist times. Capitalist culture has *created* large-scale production, factories, railways, the postal service, telephones, etc., and *on this basis* the great majority of the functions of the old "state power" have become so simplified and can be reduced to such exceedingly simple operations of registration, filing, and checking that they can be easily performed by every literate person, can quite easily be performed for ordinary "workmen's wages", and that these functions can (and must) be stripped of every shadow of privilege, of every semblance of "official grandeur".

All officials, without exception, elected and subject to recall *at any time*, their salaries reduced to the level of ordinary "workmen's wages"—these simple and "self-evident" democratic measures, while completely uniting the interests of the workers and the majority of the peasants, at the same time serve as a bridge leading from capitalism to socialism. These measures concern the reorganisation of the state, the purely political reorganisation of society; but, of course, they acquire their full meaning and significance only in connection with the "expropriation of the expropriators" either being accomplished or in preparation, i.e., with the transformation of capitalist private ownership of the means of production into social ownership.

> "The Commune," Marx wrote, "made the catchword of all bourgeois revolutions, cheap government, a reality, by abolishing the two greatest sources of expenditure—the army and the officialdom."

From the peasants, as from other sections of the petty bourgeoisie, only an insignificant few "rise to the top", "get on in the world" in the bourgeois sense, i.e., become either well-to-do, bourgeois, or officials in secure and privileged positions. In every capitalist country where there are peasants (as there are in most capitalist countries), the vast majority of them are oppressed by the government and long for its overthrow, long for "cheap" government. This can be achieved *only* by the proletariat; and by achieving it, the proletariat at the same time takes a step towards the socialist reorganisation of the state.

3. ABOLITION OF PARLIAMENTARISM

> "The Commune," Marx wrote, "was to be a working, not a parliamentary, body, executive and legislative at the same time . . . .
>
> "Instead of deciding once in three or six years which member of the ruling class was to represent and repress [ver- und zertreten] the people in parliament, universal suffrage was to serve the people constituted in communes, as individual suffrage serves every other employer in the search for workers, foremen and accountants for his business."

Owing to the prevalence of social-chauvinism and opportunism, this remarkable criticism of parliamentarism, made in 1871, also belongs now to the "forgotten words" of Marxism. The professional Cabinet Ministers and parliamentarians, the traitors to the proletariat and the "practical" socialists of our day, have left all criticism of parliamentarism to the anarchists, and, on this wonderfully reasonable ground, they denounce *all* criticism of parliamentarism as "anarchism"!! It is not surprising that the proletariat of the "advanced" parliamentary countries, disgusted with such "socialists" as the Scheidemanns, Davids, Legiens, Sembats, Renaudels, Hendersons, Vanderveldes, Staunings, Brantings, Bissolatis and Co., has been with increasing frequency giving its sympathies to anarcho-syndicalism, in spite of the fact that the latter is merely the twin brother of opportunism.

For Marx, however, revolutionary dialectics was never the empty fashionable phrase, the toy rattle, which Plekhanov, Kautsky and others have made of it. Marx knew how to break with anarchism ruthlessly for its inability to make use even of the "pigsty" of bourgeois parliamentarism, especially when the situation was obviously not revolutionary; but at the same time he knew how to subject parliamentarism to genuinely revolutionary proletarian criticism.

To decide once every few years which member of the ruling class is to repress and crush the people through parliament—this is the real essence of bourgeois parliamentarism, not only in parliamentary-constitutional monarchies, but also in the most democratic republics.

But if we deal with the question of the state, and if we consider parliamentarism as one of the institutions of the state, from the point of view of the tasks of the proletariat in *this* field, what is the way out of parliamentarism? How can it be dispensed with?

Once again, we must say: the lessons of Marx, based on the study of the Commune, have been so completely forgotten that the present-day "Social-Democrat" (i.e., present-day traitor to socialism) really cannot understand any criticism of parliamentarism other than anarchist or reactionary criticism.

The way out of parliamentarism is not, of course, the abolition of representative institutions and the elective principle, but the conversion of the representative institutions from talking shops into "working" bodies. "The Commune was to be a working, not a parliamentary, body, executive and legislative at the same time."

"A working, not a parliamentary body"—this is a blow straight from the shoulder at the present-day parliamentarians and parliamentary "lap dogs" of Social-Democracy! Take any parliamentary country, from America to Switzerland, from France to Britain, Norway and so forth—in these countries the real business of "state" is performed behind the scenes and is carried on by the departments, chancelleries, and General Staffs. Parliament is given up to talk for the special purpose of fooling the "common people". This is so true that even in the Russian republic, a bourgeois-democratic republic, all these sins of parliamentarism came out at once, even before it managed to set up a real parliament. The heroes of rotten philistinism, such as the Skobelevs and Tseretelis, the Chernovs and Avksentyevs, have even succeeded in polluting the Soviets after the fashion of the most disgusting bourgeois parliamentarism, in converting them into mere talking shops. In the Soviets, the "socialist" Ministers are fooling the credulous rustics with phrase-mongering and resolutions. In the government itself a sort of permanent shuffle is going on in order that, on the one hand, as many Socialist-Revolutionaries and Mensheviks as possible may in turn get near the "pie", the lucrative and honorable posts, and that, on the other hand, the "attention" of the people may be "engaged". Meanwhile the chancelleries and army staffs "do" the business of "state".

Dyelo Naroda, the organ of the ruling Socialist-Revolutionary Party, recently admitted in a leading article—with the matchless frankness of people of "good society", in which "all" are engaged in political prostitution—that even in the ministries headed by the "socialists" (save the mark!), the whole bureaucratic apparatus is in fact unchanged, is working in the old way and quite "freely" sabotaging revolutionary measures! Even without this admission, does not the actual history of the participation of the Socialist-Revolutionaries and Mensheviks in the government prove this? It is noteworthy, however, that in the ministerial company of the Cadets, the Chernovs, Rusanovs, Zenzinovs, and other editors of *Dyelo Naroda* have so completely lost all sense of shame as to brazenly assert, as if it were a mere bagatelle, that in "their" ministries everything is unchanged!! Revolutionary-democratic phrases to gull the rural Simple Simons, and bureaucracy and red tape to "gladden the hearts" of the capitalists—that is the *essence* of the "honest" coalition.

The Commune substitutes for the venal and rotten parliamentarism of bourgeois society institutions in which freedom of opinion and discussion does not degenerate into deception, for the parliamentarians themselves have to work, have to execute their own laws, have themselves to test the results achieved in reality, and to account directly to their constituents. Representative institutions remain, but there is *no* parliamentarism here as a special system, as the division of labour between the legislative and the executive, as a privileged position for the deputies. We cannot imagine democracy, even proletarian democracy, without representative institutions, but we can and *must* imagine democracy without parliamentarism, if criticism of bourgeois society is not mere words for us, if the desire to overthrow the rule of the bourgeoisie is our earnest and sincere desire, and not a mere "election" cry for catching workers' votes, as it is with the Mensheviks and Socialist-Revolutionaries, and also the Scheidemanns and Legiens, the Sembats and Vanderveldes.

It is extremely instructive to note that, in speaking of the function of *those* officials who are necessary for the Commune and for proletarian democracy, Marx compares them to the workers of "every other employer", that is, of the ordinary capitalist enterprise, with its "workers, foremen, and accountants".

There is no trace of utopianism in Marx, in the sense that he made up or invented a "new" society. No, he studied the *birth* of the new society *out* of the old, and the forms of transition from the latter to the former, as a natural-historical process. He examined the actual experience of a mass proletarian movement and tried to draw practical lessons from it. He "learned" from the Commune, just as all the great revolutionary thinkers learned unhesitatingly from the experience of great movements of the oppressed classes, and never addressed them with pedantic "homilies" (such as Plekhanov's: "They should not have taken up arms" or Tsereteli's: "A class must limit itself").

Abolishing the bureaucracy at once, everywhere and completely, is out of the question. It is a utopia. But to *smash* the old bureaucratic machine at once and to begin immediately to construct a new one that will make possible the gradual abolition of all bureaucracy—this is *not* a utopia, it is the experience of the Commune, the direct and immediate task of the revolutionary proletariat.

Capitalism simplifies the functions of "state" administration; it makes it possible to cast "bossing" aside and to confine the whole matter to the organisation of the proletarians (as the ruling class), which will hire "workers, foremen and accountants" in the name of the whole of society.

We are not utopians, we do not "dream" of dispensing *at once* with all administration, with all subordination. These anarchist dreams, based upon incomprehension of the tasks of the proletarian dictatorship, are totally alien to Marxism, and, as a matter of fact, serve only to postpone the socialist revolution until people are different. No, we want the socialist revolution with people as they are now, with people who cannot dispense with subordination, control, and "foremen and accountants".

The subordination, however, must be to the armed vanguard of all the exploited and working people, i.e., to the proletariat. A beginning can and must be made at once, overnight, to replace the specific "bossing" of state officials by the simple functions of "foremen and accountants", functions which are already fully within the ability of the average town dweller and can well be performed for "workmen's wages".

We, the workers, shall organise large-scale production on the basis of what capitalism has already created, relying on our own experience as workers, establishing strict, iron discipline backed up by the state power of the armed workers. We shall reduce the role of state officials to that of simply carrying out our instructions as responsible, revocable, modestly paid "foremen and accountants" (of course, with the aid of technicians of all sorts, types and degrees). This is *our* proletarian task, this is what we can and must *start* with in accomplishing the proletarian revolution. Such a beginning, on the basis of large-scale production, will of itself lead to the gradual "withering away" of all bureaucracy, to the gradual creation of an order—an order without inverted commas, an order bearing no similarity to wage slavery—an order under which the functions of control and accounting, becoming more and more simple, will be performed by each in turn, will then become a habit and will finally die out as the *special* functions of a special section of the population.

A witty German Social-Democrat of the seventies of the last century called the *postal service* an example of the socialist economic system. This is very true. At the present the postal service is a business organised on the lines of state-*capitalist* monopoly. Imperialism is gradually transforming all trusts into organisations of a similar type, in which, standing over the "common" people, who are overworked and starved, one has the same bourgeois bureaucracy. But the mechanism of social management is here already to hand. Once we have overthrown the capitalists, crushed the resistance of these exploiters with the iron hand of the armed workers, and smashed the bureaucratic machine of the modern state, we shall have a splendidly-equipped mechanism, freed from the "parasite", a mechanism which can very well be set going by the united workers themselves, who will hire technicians, foremen and accountants, and pay them *all*, as indeed *all* "state" officials in general, workmen's wages. Here is a concrete, practical task which can immediately be fulfilled in relation to all trusts, a task whose fulfilment will rid the working people of exploitation, a task which takes account of what the Commune had already begun to practice (particularly in building up the state).

To organise the *whole* economy on the lines of the postal service so that the technicians, foremen and accountants, as well as *all* officials, shall receive salaries no higher than "a workman's wage", all under the control and leadership of the armed proletariat—that is our immediate aim. This is the state and this is the economic foundation we need. This is what will bring about the abolition of parliamentarism and the preservation of representative institutions. This is what will rid the labouring classes of the bourgeoisie's prostitution of these institutions.

4. ORGANISATION OF NATIONAL UNITY

> "In a brief sketch of national organisation which the Commune had no time to develop, it states explicitly that the Commune was to be the political form of even the smallest village . . . ." The communes were to elect the "National Delegation" in Paris.
>
> ". . . The few but important functions which would still remain for a central government were not to be suppressed, as had been deliberately mis-stated, but were to be transferred to communal, i.e., strictly responsible, officials.

"... National unity was not to be broken, but, on the contrary, organised by the communal constitution; it was to become a reality by the destruction of state power which posed as the embodiment of that unity yet wanted to be independent of, and superior to, the nation, on whose body it was but a parasitic excrescence. While the merely repressive organs of the old governmental power were to be amputated, its legitimate functions were to be wrested from an authority claiming the right to stand above society, and restored to the responsible servants of society."

The extent to which the opportunists of present-day Social-Democracy have failed—perhaps it would be more true to say, have refused—to understand these observations of Marx is best shown by that book of Herostratean fame of the renegade Bernstein, *The Premises of Socialism and the Tasks of the Social-Democrats*. It is in connection with the above passage from Marx that Bernstein wrote that "as far as its political content is concerned", this programme "displays, in all its essential features, the greatest similarity to the federalism of Proudhon .... In spite of all the other points of difference between Marx and the 'petty-bourgeois' Proudhon [Bernstein places the word "petty-bourgeois" in inverted commas to make it sound ironical] on these points, their lines of reasoning run as close as could be." Of course, Bernstein continues, the importance of the municipalities is growing, but "it seems doubtful to me whether the first job of democracy would be such a dissolution [Auflösung] of the modern states and such a complete transformation [Umwandlung] of their organisation as is visualised by Marx and Proudhon (the formation of a National Assembly from delegates of the provincial of district assemblies, which, in their turn, would consist of delegates from the communes), so that consequently the previous mode of national representation would disappear." (Bernstein, *Premises*, German edition, 1899, pp. 134 and 136)

To confuse Marx's view on the "destruction of state power, a parasitic excrescence", with Proudhon's federalism is positively monstrous! But it is no accident, for it never occurs to the opportunist that Marx does not speak here at all about federalism as opposed to centralism, but about smashing the old, bourgeois state machine which exists in all bourgeois countries.

The only thing that does occur to the opportunist is what he sees around him, in an environment of petty-bourgeois philistinism and "reformists" stagnation, namely, only "municipalities"! The opportunist has even grown out of the habit of thinking about proletarian revolution.

It is ridiculous. But the remarkable thing is that nobody argued with Bernstein on this point. Bernstein has been refuted by many, especially by Plekhanov in Russian literature and by Kautsky in European literature, but neither of them has said *anything* about *this* distortion of Marx by Bernstein.

The opportunist has so much forgotten how to think in a revolutionary way and to dwell on revolution that he attributes "federalism" to Marx, whom he confuses with the founder of anarchism, Proudhon. As for Kautsky and Plekhanov, who claim to be orthodox Marxists and defenders of the theory of revolutionary Marxism, they are silent on this point! Here is one of the roots of the extreme vulgarisation of the views on the difference between Marxism and anarchism, which is characteristic of both the Kautskyites and the opportunists, and which we shall discuss again later.

There is not a trace of federalism in Marx's above-quoted observation on the experience of the Commune. Marx agreed with Proudhon on the very point that the opportunist Bernstein did not see. Marx disagreed with Proudhon on the very point on which Bernstein found a similarity between them.

Marx agreed with Proudhon in that they both stood for the "smashing" of the modern state machine. Neither the opportunists nor the Kautskyites wish to see the similarity of views on this point between Marxism and anarchism (both Proudhon and Bakunin) because this is where they have departed from Marxism.

Marx disagreed both with Proudhon and Bakunin precisely on the question of federalism (not to mention the dictatorship of the proletariat). Federalism as a principle follows logically from the petty-bourgeois views of anarchism. Marx was a centralist. There is no departure whatever from centralism in his observations just quoted. Only those who are imbued with the philistine "superstitious belief" in the state can mistake the destruction of the bourgeois state machine for the destruction of centralism!

Now if the proletariat and the poor peasants take state power into their own hands, organise themselves quite freely in communes, and *unite* the action of all the communes in striking at capital, in crushing the resistance of the capitalists, and in transferring the privately-owned railways, factories, land and so on to the *entire* nation, to the whole of society, won't that be centralism? Won't that be the most consistent democratic centralism and, moreover, proletarian centralism?

Bernstein simply cannot conceive of the possibility of voluntary centralism, of the voluntary amalgamation of the communes into a nation, of the voluntary fusion of the proletarian communes, for the sole purpose of destroying bourgeois rule and the bourgeois state machine. Like all philistines, Bernstein pictures centralism as something which can be imposed and maintained solely from above, and solely by the bureaucracy and the military clique.

As though foreseeing that his views might be distorted, Marx expressly emphasised that the charge that the Commune had wanted to destroy national unity, to abolish the central authority, was a deliberate fraud. Marx purposely used the words: "National unity was . . . to be organised", so as to oppose conscious, democratic, proletarian centralism to bourgeois, military, bureaucratic centralism.

But there are none so deaf as those who will not hear. And the very thing the opportunists of present-day Social-Democracy do not want to hear about is the destruction of state power, the amputation of the parasitic excrescence.

5. ABOLITION OF THE PARASITE STATE

We have already quoted Marx's words on the subject, and we must now supplement them.

"It is generally the fate of new historical creations," he wrote, "to be mistaken for the counterpart of older and even defunct forms of social life, to which they may bear a certain likeness. Thus, this new Commune, which breaks [*bricht*, smashes] the modern state power, has been regarded as a revival of the medieval communes . . . as a federation of small states (as Montesquieu and the Girondins[5] visualised it) . . . as an exaggerated form of the old struggle against over-centralisation . . . .

". . . The Communal Constitution would have restored to the social body all the forces hitherto absorbed by that parasitic excrescence, the 'state', feeding upon and hampering the free movement of society. By this one act it would have initiated the regeneration of France . . . .

". . . The Communal Constitution would have brought the rural producers under the intellectual lead of the central towns of their districts, and there secured to them, in the town working men, the natural trustees of their interests. The very existence of the Commune involved, as a matter of course, local self-government, but no longer as a counterpoise to state power, now become superfluous."

"Breaking state power", which was a "parasitic excrescence"; its "amputation", its "smashing"; "state power, now become superfluous"—these are the expressions Marx used in regard to the state when appraising and analysing the experience of the Commune.

All this was written a little less than half a century ago; and now one has to engage in excavations, as it were, in order to bring undistorted Marxism to the knowledge of the mass of the people. The conclusions drawn from the observation of the last great revolution which Marx lived through were forgotten just when the time for the next great proletarian revolutions has arrived.

". . . The multiplicity of interpretations to which the Commune has been subjected, and the multiplicity of interests which expressed themselves in it show that it was a thoroughly flexible political

5 *The Girondists*—a political grouping during the French bourgeois revolution of the late eighteenth century, expressed the interests of the moderate bourgeoisie. They wavered between revolution and counter-revolution, and made deals with the monarchy.

form, while all previous forms of government had been essentially repressive. Its true secret was this: it was essentially *a working-class government*, the result of the struggle of the producing against the appropriating class, the political form at last discovered under which the economic emancipation of labour could be accomplished ....

"Except on this last condition, the Communal Constitution would have been an impossibility and a delusion ...."

The utopians busied themselves with "discovering" political forms under which the socialist transformation of society was to take place. The anarchists dismissed the question of political forms altogether. The opportunists of present-day Social-Democracy accepted the bourgeois political forms of the parliamentary democratic state as the limit which should not be overstepped; they battered their foreheads praying before this "model", and denounced as anarchism every desire to *break* these forms.

Marx deduced from the whole history of socialism and the political struggle that the state was bound to disappear, and that the transitional form of its disappearance (the transition from state to non-state) would be the "proletariat organised as the ruling class". Marx, however, did not set out to *discover* the political *forms* of this future stage. He limited himself to carefully observing French history, to analysing it, and to drawing the conclusion to which the year 1851 had led, namely, that matters were moving towards the *destruction* of the bourgeois state machine.

And when the mass revolutionary movement of the proletariat burst forth, Marx, in spite of its failure, in spite of its short life and patent weakness, began to study the forms it had *discovered*.

The Commune is the form "at last discovered" by the proletarian revolution, under which the economic emancipation of labour can take place.

The Commune is the first attempt by a proletarian revolution to *smash* the bourgeois state machine; and it is the political form "at last discovered", by which the smashed state machine can and must be *replaced*.

We shall see further on that the Russian revolutions of 1905 and 1917, in different circumstances and under different conditions, continue the work of the Commune and confirm Marx's brilliant historical analysis.

Written in August-September 1917
Published as a pamphlet in 1918 by Zhizn I Znaniye Publishers
Printed according to the pamphlet text published by
Kommunist Publishers in 1919 and verified with the
manuscript and the 1918 edition

THE IMPENDING CATASTROPHE AND HOW TO COMBAT IT

FAMINE IS APPROACHING

Unavoidable catastrophe is threatening Russia. The railways are incredibly disorganised and the disorganisation is progressing. The railways will come to a standstill. The delivery of raw materials and coal to the factories will cease. The delivery of grain will cease. The capitalists are deliberately and unremittingly sabotaging (damaging, stopping, disrupting, hampering) production, hoping that an unparalleled catastrophe will mean the collapse of the republic and democracy, and of the Soviets and proletarian and peasant associations generally, thus facilitating the return to a monarchy and the restoration of the unlimited power of the bourgeoisie and the landowners.

The danger of a great catastrophe and of famine is imminent. All the newspapers have written about this time and again. A tremendous number of resolutions have been adopted by the parties and by the Soviets of Workers', Soldiers' and Peasants' Deputies—resolutions which admit that a catastrophe is unavoidable, that it is very close, that extreme measures are necessary to combat it, that "heroic efforts" by the people are necessary to avert ruin, and so on.

Everybody says this. Everybody admits it. Everybody has decided it is so.

Yet nothing is being done.

Six months of revolution have elapsed. The catastrophe is even closer. Unemployment has assumed a mass scale. To think that there is a shortage of goods in the country, the country is perishing from a shortage of food and labour, although there is a sufficient quantity of grain and raw materials, and yet in such a country, at so critical a moment, there is mass unemployment! What better evidence is needed to show that after six months of revolution (which some call a great revolution, but which so far it would perhaps be fairer to call a rotten revolution), in a democratic republic, with an abundance of unions, organs and institutions which proudly call themselves "revolutionary-democratic", absolutely *nothing* of any importance has actually been done to avert catastrophe, to avert famine? We are nearing ruin with increasing speed. The war will not wait and is causing increasing dislocation in every sphere of national life.

Yet the slightest attention and thought will suffice to satisfy anyone that the ways of combating catastrophe and famine are available, that the measures required to combat them are quite clear, simple, perfectly feasible, and fully within reach of the people's forces, and that these measures are *not* being adopted *only* because, *exclusively* because, their realisation would affect the fabulous profits of a handful of landowners and capitalists.

And, indeed, it is safe to say that every single speech, every single article in a newspaper of any trend, every single resolution passed by any meeting or institution quite clearly and explicitly recognises the chief and principal measure of combating, of averting, catastrophe and famine. This measure is control, supervision, accounting, regulation by the state, introduction of a proper distribution of labour-power in the production and distribution of goods, husbanding of the people's forces, the elimination of all wasteful effort, economy of effort. Control, supervision and accounting are the prime requisites for combating catastrophe and famine. This is indisputable and universally recognised. And it is just what *is not being done* from fear of encroaching on the supremacy of the landowners and capitalists, on their immense, fantastic and scandalous profits, profits derived from high prices and war contracts (and, directly or indirectly, nearly everybody is now "working" for the war), profits about which everybody knows and which everybody sees, and over which everybody is sighing and groaning.

And absolutely nothing is being done to introduce such control, accounting and supervision by the state as would be in the least effective.

COMPLETE GOVERNMENT INACTIVITY

There is a universal, systematic and persistent sabotage of every kind of control, supervision and accounting and of all state attempts to institute them. And one must be incredibly naïve not to understand, one must be an utter hypocrite to pretend not to understand, where this sabotage comes from and by what means it is being carried on. For this sabotage by the bankers and capitalists, their *frustration* of every kind of control, supervision and accounting, is being adapted to the state forms of a democratic republic, to the existence of "revolutionary-democratic" institutions. The capitalist gentlemen have learnt very well a fact which all supporters of scientific socialism profess to recognise but which the Mensheviks and Socialist-Revolutionaries tried to forget as soon as their friends had secured cushy jobs as ministers, deputy ministers, etc. That fact is that the economic substance of capitalist exploitation is in no wise affected by the substitution of republican-democratic forms of government for monarchist forms, and that, consequently, the reverse is also true—only the *form* of the struggle for the inviolability and sanctity of capitalist profits need be changed in order to uphold them under a democratic republic as effectively as under an absolute monarchy.

The present, modern republican-democratic sabotage of every kind of control, accounting and supervision consists in the capitalists "eagerly" accepting in words the "principle" of control and the necessity for control (as, of course, do all Mensheviks and Socialist-Revolutionaries), insisting only that this control be introduced "gradually", methodically and in a "state-regulated" way. In practice, however, these specious catchwords serve to conceal the *frustration* of control, its nullification, its reduction to a fiction, the mere playing at control, the delay of all business-like and practically effective measures, the creation of extraordinarily complicated, cumbersome and bureaucratically lifeless institutions of control which are hopelessly dependent on the capitalists, and which do absolutely nothing and cannot do anything.

So as not to trot out bald statements, let us cite witnesses from among the Mensheviks and Socialist-Revolutionaries, i.e., the very people who had the majority in the Soviets during the first six months of revolution, who took part in the "coalition government" and who are therefore politically responsible to the Russian workers and peasants for winking at the capitalists and allowing them to frustrate all control.

Izvestia TsIK (i.e., the newspaper of the Central Executive Committee of the All-Russia Congress of Soviets of Workers', Soldiers' and Peasants' Deputies), the official organ of the highest of the so-called "fully authorised" (no joke!) bodies of "revolutionary" democracy, in issue No. 164, of September 7, 1917, printed a resolution by a special control organisation created and run by these very Mensheviks and Socialist-Revolutionaries. This special institution is the Economic Department of the Central Executive Committee. Its resolution officially records as a fact "*the complete inactivity of the central bodies set up under the government for the regulation of economic life*".

Now, how could one imagine any more eloquent testimony to the collapse of the Menshevik and Socialist-Revolutionary policy than this statement signed by the Mensheviks and Socialist-Revolutionaries themselves?

The need for the regulation of economic life was already recognised under tsarism, and certain institutions were set up for the purpose. But under tsarism economic chaos steadily grew and reached monstrous proportions. It was at once recognised that it was the task of the republican, revolutionary government to adopt effective and resolute measures to put an end to the economic chaos. When the "coalition" government was formed with the Mensheviks and Socialist-Revolutionaries participating, it promised and undertook, in its most solemn public declaration of May 6, to introduce state control and regulation. The Tseretelis and Chernovs, like all the Menshevik and Socialist-Revolutionary leaders, vowed and swore that not only were they responsible for the government, but that the "authorised bodies of revolutionary democracy" under their control actually kept an eye on the work of the government and verified its activities.

Four months have passed since May 6, four long months, in which Russia has sacrificed the lives of hundreds of thousands of soldiers for the sake of the absurd imperialist "offensive", in which chaos and disaster have been advancing in seven-league strides, in which the summer season afforded an exceptional opportunity to do a great deal in the matter of water transport, agriculture, prospecting for minerals, and so on and so forth—and after four months the Mensheviks and Socialist-Revolutionaries have been obliged officially to admit the "complete inactivity" of the control institutions set up under the government!!

And these Mensheviks and Socialist-Revolutionaries, with the serious mien of statesmen, now prate (I am writing this on the very eve of the Democratic Conference of September 12[1]) that matters can be furthered by replacing the coalition with the Cadets by a coalition with commercial and industrial Kit Kityches,[2] the Ryabushinskys, Bublikovs, Tereshchenkos and Co.

How, one may ask, are we to explain this astonishing blindness of the Mensheviks and Socialist-Revolutionaries? Are we to regard them as political babes in the wood who in their extreme foolishness and naïveté do not realise what they are doing and err in good faith? Or does the abundance of posts they occupy as ministers, deputy ministers, governors-general, commissars and the like have the property of engendering a special kind of "political" blindness?

[1] *The All-Russia Democratic Conference* was held in Petrograd between September 14 and 22 (September 27-October 5), 1917. It was called by the Mensheviks and Socialist-Revolutionaries to stem the rising tide of the revolution. The delegates represented petty-bourgeois parties, the compromising Soviets, the trade unions, Zemstvos, commercial and industrial circles, and troop units. The Bolsheviks attended with the aim of exposing the designs of the Mensheviks and S.R.s. The conference elected a pre-parliament (Provisional Council of the Republic) through which the Mensheviks and S.R.s hoped to check the revolution and divert the country on to the track of a bourgeois parliamentary system.

On Lenin's proposal, the Central Committee of the Party decided that the Bolsheviks should withdraw from the pre-parliament. Only the capitulators Kamenev, Rykov and Ryazanov, who were against the Party's course for the socialist revolution, insisted on participation in the pre-parliament. The Bolsheviks exposed the treacherous activity of the pre-parliament as they trained the people for an armed uprising.

[2] *Kit Kitych* (literally, Whale Whaleson)—nickname of Tit Titych, a rich merchant in Alexander Ostrovsky's comedy *Shouldering Another's Troubles*. Lenin applies the nickname to capitalist tycoons.

CONTROL MEASURES ARE KNOWN TO ALL AND EASY TO TAKE

One may ask: aren't methods and measures of control extremely complex, difficult, untried and even unknown? Isn't the delay due to the fact that although the statesmen of the Cadet Party, the merchant and industrial class, and the Menshevik and Socialist-Revolutionary parties have for six months been toiling in the sweat of their brow, investigating, studying and discovering measures and methods of control, still the problem is incredibly difficult and has not yet been solved?

Unfortunately, this is how they are trying to present matters to hoodwink the ignorant, illiterate and downtrodden muzhiks and the Simple Simons who believe everything and never look into things. In reality, however, even tsarism, even the "old regime", when it set up the War Industries Committees[3] *knew* the principal measure, the chief method and way to introduce control, namely, by uniting the population according to profession, purpose of work, branch of labour, etc. But tsarism *feared* the union of the population and therefore did its best to restrict and artificially hinder this generally known, very easy and quite practical method and way of control.

All the belligerent countries, suffering as they are from the extreme burdens and hardships of the war, suffering—in one degree or another—from economic chaos and famine, have long ago outlined,

[3] *The War Industries Committees*, which came into being in May 1915, were formed by Russia's big imperialist bourgeoisie to help the tsarist regime with the war. The chairman of the Central War Industries Committee was the Octobrist leader A. I. Guchkov, a big capitalist. Among its members were the manufacturer A. I. Konovalov and the banker and sugar manufacturer M. I. Tereshchenko. In an effort to bring the workers under its sway and inspire them with defencist sentiments, the bourgeoisie decided to form "workers' groups" under the committees and thereby to show that "class peace" had been established between the bourgeoisie and the proletariat of Russia. The Bolsheviks declared a boycott of the committees, and maintained it with support from the majority of the workers.

As a result of the Bolsheviks' explanatory work, elections to the "workers' groups" took place only in 70 out of the 239 regional and local War Industries Committees, workers' representatives being elected to only 36 Committees.

determined, applied and tested a *whole series* of control measures, which consist almost invariably in uniting the population and in setting up or encouraging unions of various kinds, in which state representatives participate, which are under the supervision of the state, etc. All these measures of control are known to all, much has been said and written about them, and the laws passed by the advanced belligerent powers relating to control have been translated into Russian or expounded in detail in the Russian press.

If our state really *wanted* to exercise control in a business like and earnest fashion, if its institutions had not condemned themselves to "complete inactivity" by their servility to the capitalists, all the state would have to do would be to draw freely on the rich store of control measures which are already known and have been used in the past. The only obstacle to this—an obstacle concealed from the eyes of the people by the Cadets, Socialist-Revolutionaries and Mensheviks—was, and still is, that control would bring to light the fabulous profits of the capitalists and would cut the ground from under these profits.

To explain this most important question more clearly (a question which is essentially equivalent to that of the programme of *any* truly revolutionary government that would wish to save Russia from war and famine), let us enumerate these principal measures of control and examine each of them.

We shall see that all a government would have had to do, if its name of revolutionary-democratic government were not merely a joke, would have been to decree, in the very first week of its existence, the adoption of the principal measures of control, to provide for strict and severe punishment to be meted out to capitalists who fraudulently evaded control, and to call upon the population itself to exercise supervision over the capitalists and see to it that they scrupulously observed the regulations on control—and control would have been introduced in Russia long ago.

These principal measures are:

(1) Amalgamation of all banks into a single bank, and state control over its operations, or nationalisation of the banks.

(2) Nationalisation of the syndicates, i.e., the largest, monopolistic

capitalist associations (sugar, oil, coal, iron and steel, and other syndicates).

(3) Abolition of commercial secrecy.

(4) Compulsory syndication (i.e., compulsory amalgamation into associations) of industrialists, merchants and employers generally.

(5) Compulsory organisation of the population into consumers' societies, or encouragement of such organisation, and the exercise of control over it.

Let us see what the significance of each of these measures would be if carried out in a revolutionary-democratic way.

NATIONALISATION OF THE BANKS

The banks, as we know, are centres of modern economic life, the principal nerve centres of the whole capitalist economic system. To talk about "regulating economic life" and yet evade the question of the nationalisation of the banks means either betraying the most profound ignorance or deceiving the "common people" by florid words and grandiloquent promises with the deliberate intention of not fulfilling these promises.

It is absurd to control and regulate deliveries of grain, or the production and distribution of goods generally, without controlling and regulating bank operations. It is like trying to snatch at odd kopeks and closing one's eyes to millions of rubles. Banks nowadays are so closely and intimately bound up with trade (in grain and everything else) and with industry that without "laying hands" on the banks nothing of any value, nothing "revolutionary-democratic", can be accomplished.

But perhaps for the state to "lay hands" on the banks is a very difficult and complicated operation? They usually try to scare philistines with this very idea—that is, the capitalists and their defenders try it, because it is to their advantage to do so.

In reality, however, nationalisation of the banks, which would not deprive any "owner" of a single kopek, presents absolutely no technical or cultural difficulties, and is being delayed *exclusively* because of the vile greed of an insignificant handful of rich people. If nationalisation of the banks is so often confused with the confiscation of private property, it is the bourgeois press, which has an interest in deceiving the public, that is to blame for this widespread confusion.

The ownership of the capital wielded by and concentrated in the banks is certified by printed and written certificates called shares, bonds, bills, receipts, etc. Not a single one of these certificates would be invalidated or altered if the banks were nationalised, i.e., if all the banks were amalgamated into a single state bank. Whoever owned fifteen rubles on a savings account would continue to be the owner of fifteen rubles after the nationalisation of the banks; and whoever had fifteen million rubles would continue after the nationalisation of the banks to have fifteen million rubles in the form of shares, bonds, bills, commercial certificates and so on.

What, then, is the significance of nationalisation of the banks?

It is that no effective control of any kind over the individual banks and their operations is possible (even if commercial secrecy, etc., were abolished) because it is impossible to keep track of the extremely complex, involved and wily tricks that are used in drawing up balance sheets, founding fictitious enterprises and subsidiaries, enlisting the services of figureheads, and so on, and so forth. Only the amalgamation of all banks into one, which in itself would imply no change whatever in respect of ownership, and which, we repeat, would not deprive any owner of a single kopek, would make it *possible* to exercise real control—provided, of course, all the other measures indicated above were carried out. Only by nationalising the banks *can* the state *put itself in a position* to know where and how, whence and when, millions and billions of rubles flow. And only control over the banks, over the centre, over the pivot and chief mechanism of capitalist circulation, would make it possible to organise real and not fictitious control over all economic life, over the production and distribution of staple goods, and organise that "regulation of economic life" which otherwise is inevitably doomed to remain a ministerial phrase designed to fool the common people. Only control over banking operations, provided they were concentrated in a single state bank, would make it possible, if certain other easily-practicable measures were adopted, to organise the effective collection of income tax in such a way as to prevent the concealment of property and incomes; for at present the income tax is very largely a fiction.

Nationalisation of the banks has only to be decreed and it would be carried out by the directors and employees themselves. No special machinery, no special preparatory steps on the part of the state would be required, for this is a measure that can be effected by a single decree, "at a single stroke". It was made economically feasible by capitalism itself once it had developed to the stage of bills, shares, bonds and so on. *All* that is required is to *unify accountancy*. And if the revolutionary-democratic government were to decide that immediately, by telegraph, meetings of managers and employees should be called in every city, and conferences in every region and in the country as a whole, for the immediate amalgamation of all banks into a single state bank, this reform would be carried out in a few weeks. Of course, it would be the managers and the higher bank officials who would offer resistance, who would try to deceive the state, delay matters, and so on, for these gentlemen would lose their highly remunerative posts and the opportunity of performing highly profitable fraudulent operations. *That is the heart of the matter*. But there is not the slightest technical difficulty in the way of the amalgamation of the banks; and if the state power were revolutionary not only in word (i.e., if it did not fear to do away with inertia and routine), if it were democratic not only in word (i.e., if it acted in the interests of the majority of the people and not of a handful of rich men), it would be enough to decree confiscation of property and imprisonment as the penalty for managers, board members and big shareholders for the slightest delay or for attempting to conceal documents and accounts. It would be enough, for example, to organise the poorer employees *separately* and to reward them for detecting fraud and delay on the part of the rich for nationalisation of the banks to be effected as smoothly and rapidly as can be.

The advantages accruing to the whole people from nationalisation of the banks—*not* to the workers especially (for the workers have little to do with banks) but to the mass of peasants and small industrialists—would be enormous. The saving in labour would be gigantic, and, assuming that the state would retain the former number of bank employees, nationalisation would be a highly important step towards making the use of the banks universal, towards increasing the number of their branches, putting their operations within easier reach, etc., etc. The availability of credit on easy terms for the *small* owners, for the peasants, would increase immensely. As to the state, it would for the first time be in a position first to *review* all the chief monetary operations, which would be unconcealed, then to *control* them, then to *regulate* economic life, and finally to *obtain* millions and billions for major state transactions, without paying the capitalist gentlemen sky-high "commissions" for their "services". That is the reason—and the only reason—why all the capitalists, all the bourgeois professors, all the bourgeoisie, and all the Plekhanovs, Potresovs and Co., who serve them, are prepared to fight tooth and nail against nationalisation of the banks and invent thousands of excuses to prevent the adoption of this very easy and very pressing measure, although even from the standpoint of the "defence" of the country, i.e., from the military standpoint, this measure would provide a gigantic advantage and would tremendously enhance the "military might" of the country.

The following objection might be raised: why do such advanced states as Germany and the U.S.A. "regulate economic life" so magnificently without even thinking of nationalising the banks?

Because, we reply, *both* these states are not merely capitalist, but also imperialist states, although one of them is a monarchy and the other a republic. As such, they carry out the reforms they need by reactionary-bureaucratic methods, whereas we are speaking here of revolutionary-democratic methods.

This "little difference" is of major importance. In most cases it is "not the custom" to think of it. The term "revolutionary democracy" has become with us (especially among the Socialist-Revolutionaries and Mensheviks) almost a conventional phrase, like the expression "thank God", which is also used by people who are not so ignorant as to believe in God; or like the expression "honourable citizen", which is sometimes used even in addressing staff members of *Dyen* or *Yedinstvo*, although nearly everybody guesses that these newspapers have been founded and are maintained by the capitalists in the interests of the capitalists, and that there is therefore very little "honourable" about the pseudo-socialists contributing to these newspapers.

If we do not employ the phrase "revolutionary democracy" as a stereotyped ceremonial phrase, as a conventional epithet, but *reflect* on its meaning, we find that to be a democrat means reckoning in reality with the interests of the majority of the people and not the minority, and that to be a revolutionary means destroying everything harmful and obsolete in the most resolute and ruthless manner.

Neither in America nor in Germany, as far as we know, is any claim laid by either the government or the ruling classes to the name "revolutionary democrats", to which our Socialist-Revolutionaries and Mensheviks lay claim (and which they prostitute).

In Germany there are only *four* very large private banks of national importance. In America there are only *two*. It is easier, more convenient, more profitable for the financial magnates of those banks to unite privately, surreptitiously, in a reactionary and not a revolutionary way, in a bureaucratic and not a democratic way, bribing government officials (this is the general rule both in America *and in Germany*), and preserving the private character of the banks in order to preserve secrecy of operations, to milk the state of millions upon millions in "super-profits", and to make financial frauds possible.

Both America and Germany "regulate economic life" in such a way as to create conditions of *war-time penal servitude* for the workers (and partly for the peasants) and a *paradise* for the bankers and capitalists. Their regulation consists in "squeezing" the workers to the point of starvation, while the capitalists are guaranteed (surreptitiously, in a reactionary-bureaucratic fashion) profits *higher* than before the war.

Such a course is quite possible in republican-imperialist Russia too. Indeed, it is the course being followed not only by the Milyukovs and Shingaryovs, but also by Kerensky in partnership with Tereshchenko, Nekrasov, Bernatsky, Prokopovich and Co., who *also uphold*, in a reactionary-bureaucratic manner, the "inviolability" of the banks and their sacred right to fabulous profits. So let us better tell the *truth*, namely, that in republican Russia they want to regulate economic life in a reactionary-bureaucratic manner, but "often" find it difficult to do so owing to the existence of the "Soviets", which Kornilov No. 1 did not manage to disband, but which Kornilov No. 2 will try to disband.

That would be the truth. And this simple if bitter truth is more useful for the enlightenment of the people than the honeyed lies about "our", "great", "revolutionary" democracy.

* * *

Nationalisation of the banks would greatly facilitate the simultaneous nationalisation of the insurance business, i.e., the amalgamation of all the insurance companies into one, the centralisation of their operations, and state control over them. Here, too, congresses of insurance company employees could carry out this amalgamation immediately and without any great effort, provided a revolutionary-democratic government decreed this and ordered directors and big shareholders to effect the amalgamation without the slightest delay and held every one of them strictly accountable for it. The capitalists have invested hundreds of millions of rubles in the insurance business; the work is all done by the employees. The amalgamation of this business would lead to lower insurance premiums, would provide a host of facilities and conveniences for the insured and would make it possible to increase their number without increasing expenditure of effort and funds. Absolutely nothing but the inertia, routine and self-interest of a handful of holders of remunerative jobs are delaying this reform, which, among other things, would enhance the country's defence potential by economising national labour and creating a number of highly important opportunities to "regulate economic life" not in word, but in deed.

NATIONALISATION OF THE SYNDICATES

Capitalism differs from the old, pre-capitalistic systems of economy in having created the closest interconnection and interdependence of the various branches of the economy. Were this not so, incidentally, no steps towards socialism would be technically feasible. Modern capitalism, under which the banks dominate production, has carried this interdependence of the various branches of the economy to the utmost. The banks and the more important branches of industry and commerce have become inseparably merged. This means, on the one hand, that it is impossible to nationalise the banks alone, without proceeding to create a state monopoly of commercial and industrial syndicates (sugar, coal, iron, oil, etc.), and without nationalising them. It means, on the other hand, that if carried out in earnest, the regulation of economic activity would demand the simultaneous nationalisation of the banks and the syndicates.

Let us take the sugar syndicate as an example. It came into being under tsarism, and at that time developed into a huge capitalist combine of splendidly equipped refineries. And, of course, this combine, thoroughly imbued with the most reactionary and bureaucratic spirit, secured scandalously high profits for the capitalists and reduced its employees to the status of humiliated and downtrodden slaves lacking any rights. Even at that time the state controlled and regulated production—in the interests of the rich, the magnates.

All that remains to be done here is to transform reactionary-bureaucratic regulation into revolutionary-democratic regulation by simple decrees providing for the summoning of a congress of employees, engineers, directors and shareholders, for the introduction of uniform accountancy, for control by the workers' unions, etc. This is an exceedingly simple thing, yet it has not been done! Under what is a democratic republic, the regulation of the sugar industry *actually* remains reactionary-bureaucratic; everything remains as of old—the dissipation of national labour, routine and stagnation, and the enrichment of the Bobrinskys and Tereshchenkos. Democrats and not bureaucrats, the workers and other employees and not the "sugar barons", should be called upon to exercise independent initiative—and this could and should be done in a few days, at a single stroke, if only the Socialist-Revolutionaries and Mensheviks did not befog the minds of the people by plans for "association" with these very sugar barons, for the very association with the wealthy from which the "complete inaction" of the government in the matter of regulating economic life follows with absolute inevitability, and of which it is a consequence.[4]

[4] These lines had been written when I learnt from the newspapers that the Kerensky government is introducing a sugar monopoly, and, of course, is introducing it in a reactionary-bureaucratic way, without congresses of workers and other employees, without publicity, and without curbing the capitalists!—*Au.*

Take the oil business. It was to a vast extent "socialised" by the earlier development of capitalism. Just a couple of oil barons wield millions and hundreds of millions of rubles, clipping coupons and raking in fabulous profits from a "business" which is *already* actually, technically and socially organised on a national scale and is *already* being conducted by hundreds and thousands of employees, engineers, etc. Nationalisation of the oil industry could be effected *at once* by, and is imperative for, a revolutionary-democratic state, especially when the latter suffers from an acute crisis and when it is essential to economise national labour and to increase the output of fuel at all costs. It is clear that here bureaucratic control can achieve nothing, can change nothing, for the "oil barons" can cope with the Tereshchenkos, the Kerenskys, the Avksentyevs and the Skobelevs as easily as they coped with the tsar's ministers—by means of delays, excuses and promises, and by bribing the bourgeois press directly or indirectly (this is called "public opinion", and the Kerenskys and Avksentyevs "reckon" with it), by bribing officials (left by the Kerenskys and Avksentyevs in their old jobs in the old state machinery which remains intact).

If anything real is to be done bureaucracy must be abandoned for democracy, and in a truly revolutionary way, i.e., war must be declared on the oil barons and shareholders, the confiscation of their property and punishment by imprisonment must be decreed for delaying nationalisation of the oil business, for concealing incomes or accounts, for sabotaging production, and for failing to take steps to increase production. The initiative of the workers and other employees must be drawn on; *they* must be immediately summoned to conferences and congresses; a certain proportion of the profits must be assigned to *them*, provided they institute overall control and increase production. Had these revolutionary-democratic steps been taken at once, immediately, in April 1917, Russia, which is one of the richest countries in the world in deposits of liquid fuel, could, using water transport, have done a very great deal during this summer to supply the people with the necessary quantities of fuel.

Neither the bourgeois nor the coalition Socialist-Revolutionary-Menshevik-Cadet government has done anything at all. Both have confined themselves to a bureaucratic playing at reforms. They have not dared to take a single revolutionary-democratic step. Everything has remained as it was under the tsars—the oil barons, the stagnation, the hatred of the workers and other employees for their exploiters, the resulting chaos, and the dissipation of national labour—only the *letterheads* on the incoming and outgoing papers in the "republican" offices have been changed!

Take the coal industry. It is technically and culturally no less "ripe" for nationalisation, and is being no less shamelessly managed by the robbers of the people, the coal barons, and there are a number of most striking *facts* of direct sabotage, direct *damage* to and stoppage of production by the industrialists. Even the ministerial *Rabochaya Gazeta* of the Mensheviks has admitted these facts. And what do we find? Absolutely nothing has been done, except to call the old, reactionary-bureaucratic meetings "on a half-and-half basis"—an equal number of workers and bandits from the coal syndicate! Not a single revolutionary-democratic step has been taken, not a shadow of an attempt has been made to establish the only control which is real—control from *below*, through the employees' union, through the workers, and by using terror against the coal industrialists who are ruining the country and bringing production to a standstill! How can this be done when we are "all" in favour of the "coalition"—if not with the Cadets, then with commercial and industrial circles. And coalition means leaving power in the hands of the capitalists, letting them go unpunished, allowing them to hamper affairs, to blame everything on the workers, to intensify the chaos and *thus* pave the way for a new Kornilov revolt!

ABOLITION OF COMMERCIAL SECRECY

Unless commercial secrecy is abolished, either control over production and distribution will remain an empty promise, only needed by the Cadets to fool the Socialist-Revolutionaries and Mensheviks, and by the Socialist-Revolutionaries and Mensheviks to fool the working classes, or control can be exercised only by reactionary-bureaucratic methods and means. Although this is obvious to every unprejudiced person, and although *Pravda* persistently demanded the abolition of commercial secrecy[5] (and was suppressed largely for this reason by the Kerensky government which is subservient to capital), neither our republican government nor the "authorised bodies of revolutionary democracy" have even thought of this *first step* to real control.

This is the very key to all control. Here we have the most sensitive spot of capital, which is robbing the people and sabotaging production. And this is exactly why the Socialist-Revolutionaries and Mensheviks are afraid to do anything about it.

The usual argument of the capitalists, one reiterated by the petty bourgeoisie without reflection, is that in a capitalist economy the abolition of commercial secrecy is in general absolutely impossible, for private ownership of the means of production, and the dependence of the individual undertakings on the market render essential the "sanctity" of commercial books and commercial operations, including, of course, banking operations.

Those who in one form or another repeat this or similar arguments allow themselves to be deceived and themselves deceive the people by shutting their eyes to two fundamental, highly important and generally known facts of modern economic activity. The first fact is the existence of large-scale capitalism, i.e., the peculiar features of the economic system of banks, syndicates, large factories, etc. The second fact is the war.

It is modern large-scale capitalism, which is everywhere becoming monopoly capitalism, that deprives commercial secrecy of every shadow of reasonableness, turns it into hypocrisy and into an instrument exclusively for concealing financial swindles and the fantastically high profits of big capital. Large-scale capitalist economy, by its very technical nature, is socialised economy, that is, it both operates for millions of people and, directly or indirectly, unites by its operations hundreds, thousands and tens of thousands of families. It is not like the economy of the small handicraftsman or the middle peasant who keep no commercial books at all and who would therefore not be affected by the abolition of commercial secrecy!

As it is, the operations conducted in large-scale business are known

[5] See *LCW*, Vol. 24, 1977, pp. 521-22 and Vol. 25, 1980, pp. 140-41.

to hundreds or more persons. Here the law protecting commercial secrecy does not serve the interests of production or exchange, but those of speculation and profit-seeking in their crudest form, and of direct fraud, which, as we know, in the case of joint-stock companies is particularly widespread and very skilfully concealed by reports and balance-sheets, so compiled as to deceive the public.

While commercial secrecy is unavoidable in small commodity production, i.e., among the small peasants and handicraftsmen, where production itself is not socialised but scattered and disunited, in large-scale capitalist production, the protection of commercial secrecy means protection of the privileges and profits of literally a handful of people *against* the interest of the whole people. This has already been recognised by the law, inasmuch as provision is made for the publication of the accounts of joint-stock companies. But *this* control, which has already been introduced in all advanced countries, as well as in Russia, is a reactionary-bureaucratic control which does not open the eyes of the *people* and which *does not allow the whole truth* about the operations of joint-stock companies to become known.

To act in a revolutionary-democratic way, it would be necessary to immediately pass another law abolishing commercial secrecy, compelling the big undertakings and the wealthy to render the fullest possible accounts, and investing every group of citizens of substantial democratic numerical strength (1,000 or 10,000 voters, let us say) with the right to examine *all* the records of any large undertaking. Such a measure could be fully and easily effected by a simple decree. It *alone* would allow full scope for *popular* initiative in control, through the office employees' unions, the workers' unions and all the political parties, and it alone would make control effective and democratic.

Add to this the war. The vast majority of commercial and industrial establishments are now working not for the "free market", but *for the government*, for the war. This is why I have already stated in *Pravda* that people who counter us with the argument that socialism cannot be introduced are liars, and barefaced liars at that, because it is not a question of introducing socialism now, directly, overnight, but of *exposing plunder of the state.*[6]

[6] *LCW*, Vol. 25, 1980, pp. 68-69.

Capitalist "war" economy (i.e., economy directly or indirectly connected with war contracts) is systematic and legalised *plunder*, and the Cadet gentry, who, together with the Mensheviks and Socialist-Revolutionaries, are opposing the abolition of commercial secrecy, are nothing but *aiders and abettors of plunder*.

The war is now costing Russia fifty million rubles *a day*. These fifty million go mostly to army contractors. Of these fifty, at least five million *daily*, and probably ten million or more, constitute the "honest income" of the capitalists, and of the officials who are in one way or another in collusion with them. The very large firms and banks which lend money for war contracts transactions thereby make fantastic profits, and do so by plundering the state, for no other epithet can be applied to this defrauding and plundering of the people "on the occasion of" the hardships of war, "on the occasion of" the deaths of hundreds of thousands and millions of people.

"Everybody" knows about these scandalous profits made on war contracts, about the "letters of guarantee" which are concealed by the banks, about who benefits by the rising cost of living. They are smiled on in "society". Quite a number of precise references are made to them *even* in the bourgeois press, which as a general rule keeps silent about "unpleasant" facts and avoids "ticklish" questions. Everybody knows about them, yet everybody keeps silent, everybody tolerates them, everybody puts up with the government, which prates eloquently about "control" and "regulation"!!

The revolutionary democrats, were they real revolutionaries and democrats, would immediately pass a law abolishing commercial secrecy, compelling contractors and merchants to render accounts public, forbidding them to abandon their field of activity without the permission of the authorities, imposing the penalty of confiscation of property and shooting[7] for concealment and for deceiving the people, organising verification and control *from below*, democratically,

[7] I have already had occasion to point out in the Bolshevik press that it is right to argue against the death penalty only when it is applied by the exploiters against the *mass* of the working people with the purpose of maintaining exploitation. (See *LCW*, Vol. 25, 1980, pp. 265-68.) It is hardly likely that any revolutionary government whatever could do without applying the death penalty to the *exploiters* (i.e., the landowners and capitalists).—*Au.*

by the people themselves, by unions of workers and other employees, consumers, etc.

Our Socialist-Revolutionaries and Mensheviks fully deserve to be called scared democrats, for on this question they repeat what is said by all the scared philistines, namely, that the capitalists will "run away" if "too severe" measures are adopted, that "we" shall be unable to get along without the capitalists, that the British and French millionaires, who are, of course, "supporting" us, will most likely be "offended" in their turn, and so on. It might be thought that the Bolsheviks were proposing something unknown to history, something that has never been tried before, something "utopian", while, as a matter of fact, even 125 years ago, in France, people who were real "revolutionary democrats", who were really convinced of the just and defensive character of the war they were waging, who really had popular support and were sincerely convinced of this, were able to establish *revolutionary* control over the rich and to achieve results which earned the admiration of the world. And in the century and a quarter that have since elapsed, the development of capitalism, which resulted in the creation of banks, syndicates, railways and so forth, has greatly facilitated and simplified the adoption of measures of really democratic control by the workers and peasants over the exploiters, the landowners and capitalists.

In point of fact, the whole question of control boils down to who controls whom, i.e., which class is in control and which is being controlled. In our country, in republican Russia, with the help of the "authorised bodies" of supposedly revolutionary democracy, it is the landowners and capitalists who are still recognised to be, and still are, the controllers. The inevitable result is the capitalist robbery that arouses universal indignation among the people, and the economic chaos that is being artificially kept up by the capitalists. We must resolutely and irrevocably, not fearing to break with the old, not fearing boldly to build the new, pass to control *over* the landowners and capitalists *by* the workers and peasants. And this is what our Socialist-Revolutionaries and Mensheviks fear worse than the plague.

COMPULSORY ASSOCIATION

Compulsory syndication, i.e., compulsory association, of the industrialists, for example, is already being practised in Germany. Nor is there anything new in it. Here, too, through the fault of the Socialist-Revolutionaries and Mensheviks, we see the utter stagnation of republican Russia, whom these none-too-respectable parties "entertain" by dancing a quadrille with the Cadets, or with the Bublikovs, or with Tereshchenko and Kerensky.

Compulsory syndication is, on the one hand, a means whereby the state, as it were, expedites capitalist development, which everywhere leads to the organisation of the class struggle and to a growth in the number, variety and importance of unions. On the other hand, compulsory "unionisation" is an indispensable precondition for any kind of effective control and for all economy of national labour.

The German law, for instance, binds the leather manufacturers of a given locality or of the whole country to form an association, on the board of which there is a representative of the state for the purpose of control. A law of this kind does not directly, i.e., in itself, affect property relations in any way; it does not deprive any owner of a single kopek and does not predetermine whether the control is to be exercised in a reactionary-bureaucratic or a revolutionary-democratic form, direction or spirit.

Such laws can and should be passed in our country immediately, without wasting a single week of precious time; is should be left to *social conditions themselves* to determine the more specific forms of enforcing the law, the speed with which it is to be enforced, the methods of supervision over its enforcement, etc. In this case, the state requires no special machinery, no special investigation, nor preliminary enquiries for the passing of such a law. All that is required is the determination to break with certain private interests of the capitalists, who are "not accustomed" to such interference and have no desire to forfeit the super-profits which are ensured by the old methods of management and the absence of control.

No machinery and no "statistics" (which Chernov wanted to substitute for the revolutionary initiative of the peasants) are required to *pass* such a law, inasmuch as its implementation must be made the duty of the manufacturers or industrialists themselves, of the *available* public forces, under the control of the available public (i.e., non-government, non-bureaucratic) forces too, which, however, must consist by all means of the so-called "lower estates", i.e., of the oppressed and exploited classes, which in history have always proved to be immensely *superior* to the exploiters in their capacity for heroism, self-sacrifice and comradely discipline.

Let us assume that we have a really revolutionary-democratic government and that it decides that the manufacturers and industrialists in every branch of production who employ, let us say, not less than two workers shall immediately amalgamate into uyezd and gubernia associations. Responsibility for the strict observance of the law is laid in the first place on the manufacturers, directors, board members, and big shareholders (for they are the real leaders of modern industry, its real masters). They shall be regarded as deserters from military service, and punished as such, if they do not work for the immediate implementation of the law, and shall bear mutual responsibility, one answering for all, and all for one, with the whole of their property. Responsibility shall next be laid on all office employees, who shall also form *one* union, and on all workers and their trade union. The purpose of "unionisation" is to institute the fullest, strictest and most detailed accountancy, but chiefly to *combine operations* in the purchase of raw materials, the sale of products, and the *economy* of national funds and forces. When the separate establishments are amalgamated into a single syndicate, this economy can attain tremendous proportions, as economic science teaches us and as is shown by the example of all syndicates, cartels and trusts. And it must be repeated that this unionisation will not in itself alter property relations one iota and will not deprive any owner of a single kopek. This circumstance must be strongly stressed, for the bourgeois press constantly "frightens" small and medium proprietors by asserting that socialists in general, and the Bolsheviks in particular, want to "expropriate" them—a deliberately false assertion, as socialists do not intend to, cannot and will not expropriate the small peasant *even if there is a fully socialist revolution*. All the time we are speaking *only* of the immediate and urgent measures, which have already been introduced in Western Europe and which a democracy that is at all consistent ought to introduce immediately in our country to combat the impending and inevitable catastrophe.

Serious difficulties, both technical and cultural, would be encountered in amalgamating the small and very small proprietors into associations, owing to the extremely small proportions and technical primitiveness of their enterprises and the illiteracy or lack of education of the owners. But precisely such enterprises could be exempted from the law (as was pointed out above in our hypothetical example). Their non-amalgamation, let alone their belated amalgamation, could create no serious obstacle, for the part played by the huge number of small enterprises in the sum total of production and their importance to the economy as a whole are *negligible*, and, moreover, they are often in one way or another dependent on the big enterprises.

Only the big enterprises are of decisive importance; and here the technical and cultural means and forces for "unionisation" *do exist*; what is lacking is the firm, determined initiative of a *revolutionary* government which should be ruthlessly severe towards the exploiters to set these forces and means in motion.

The poorer a country is in technically trained forces, and in intellectual forces generally, the more *urgent* it is to decree compulsory association as early and as resolutely as possible and to begin with the bigger and biggest enterprises when putting the decree into effect, for it is association that will *economise* intellectual forces and make it possible to use them *to the full* and to distribute them more correctly. If, after 1905, even the Russian peasants in their out-of-the-way districts, under the tsarist government, in face of the thousands of obstacles raised by that government, were able to make a tremendous forward stride in the creation of all kinds of associations, it is clear that the amalgamation of large- and medium-scale industry and trade could be effected in several months, if not earlier, provided compulsion to this end were exercised by a really revolutionary-democratic government relying on the support, participation, interest and advantage of the "lower ranks", the democracy, the workers and other employees, and calling upon *them* to exercise control.

REGULATION OF CONSUMPTION

The war has compelled all the belligerent and many of the neutral countries to resort to the regulation of consumption. Bread cards have been issued and have become customary, and this has led to the appearance of other ration cards. Russia is no exception and has also introduced bread cards.

Using this as an example, we can draw, perhaps, the most striking comparison of all between reactionary-bureaucratic methods of combating a catastrophe, which are confined to minimum reforms, and revolutionary-democratic methods, which, to justify their name, must directly aim at a violent rupture with the old, obsolete system and at the achievement of the speediest possible progress.

The bread card—this typical example of how consumption is regulated in modern capitalist countries—aims at, and achieves (at best), one thing only, namely, distributing available supplies of grain to give everybody his share. A maximum limit to consumption is established, not for all foodstuffs by far, but only for principal foodstuffs, those of "popular" consumption. And that is all. There is no intention of doing anything else. Available supplies of grain are calculated in a bureaucratic way, then divided on a per capita basis, a ration is fixed and introduced, and there the matter ends. Luxury articles are not affected, for they are "anyway" scarce and "anyway" so dear as to be beyond the reach of the "people". And so, in *all* the belligerent countries without exception, *even* in Germany, which evidently, without fear of contradiction, may be said to be a model of the most careful, pedantic and strict regulation of consumption—*even* in Germany we find that the rich constantly *get around* all "rationing". This, too, "everybody" knows and "everybody" talks about with a smile; and in the German socialist papers, and sometimes even in the bourgeois papers, despite the fierce military stringency of the German censorship, we constantly find items and reports about the "menus" of the rich, saying how the wealthy can obtain white bread in any quantity at a certain health resort (visited, on the plea of illness, by everybody who has plenty of money), and how the wealthy substitute choice and rare articles of luxury for articles of popular consumption.

A reactionary capitalist state which *fears* to undermine the pillars of capitalism, of wage slavery, of the economic supremacy of the rich, which *fears* to encourage the initiative of the workers and the working people generally, which *fears* to provoke them to a more exacting attitude—*such* a state will be quite content with bread cards. Such a state does not for a moment, in any measure it adopts, lose sight of the *reactionary* aim of strengthening capitalism, preventing its being undermined, and confining the "regulation of economic life" in general, and the regulation of consumption in particular, to such measures as are absolutely essential to feed the people, *and makes no attempt* whatsoever at real regulation of consumption by exercising *control over the rich* and laying the *greater part* of the burden in war-time on those who are better off, who are privileged, well fed and overfed in peace-time.

The reactionary-bureaucratic solution to the problem with which the war has confronted the peoples confines itself to bread cards, to the equal distribution of "popular" foodstuffs, of those absolutely essential to feed the people, without retreating one little bit from bureaucratic and reactionary ideas, that is, from the aim of *not* encouraging the initiative of the poor, the proletariat, the mass of the people ("demos"), of *not* allowing *them* to exercise control over the rich, and of leaving *as many* loopholes *as possible* for the rich to compensate themselves with articles of luxury. And a great number of loopholes are left in *all* countries, we repeat, even in Germany—not to speak of Russia; the "common people" starve while the rich visit health resorts, supplement the meagre official ration by all sorts of "extras" obtained on the side, and do *not* allow *themselves* to be controlled.

In Russia, which has only just made a revolution against the tsarist regime in the name of liberty and equality, in Russia, which, as far as its actual political institutions are concerned, has at once become a democratic republic, what particularly strikes the people, what particularly arouses popular discontent, irritation, anger and indignation is that *everybody* sees the easy way in which the wealthy get around the bread cards. They do it very easily indeed. "From under the counter", and for a very high price, especially if one has "*pull*" (which only the rich have), one can obtain anything, and in large quantities, too. It is the people who are starving. The regulation of consumption is confined within the narrowest bureaucratic-reactionary limits. The government has not the slightest intention of putting regulation on a really revolutionary-democratic footing, is not in the least concerned about doing so.

"Everybody" is suffering from the queues but—but the rich send their servants to stand in the queues, and even engage special servants for the purpose! And that is "democracy"!

At a time when the country is suffering untold calamities, a revolutionary-democratic policy would not confine itself to bread cards to combat the impending catastrophe but would add, firstly, the compulsory organisation of the whole population in consumers' societies, for otherwise control over consumption cannot be fully exercised; secondly, labour service for the rich, making them perform without pay secretarial and similar duties for these consumers' societies; thirdly, the equal distribution among the population of absolutely all consumer goods, so as really to distribute the burdens of the war equitably; fourthly, the organisation of control in such a way as to have the poorer classes of the population exercise control over the consumption of the rich.

The establishment of real democracy in this sphere and the display of a real revolutionary spirit in the organisation of control by the most needy classes of the people would be a very great stimulus to the employment of all available intellectual forces and to the development of the truly revolutionary energies of the entire people. Yet now the ministers of republican and revolutionary-democratic Russia, exactly like their colleagues in all other imperialist countries, make pompous speeches about "working in common for the good of the people" and about "exerting every effort", but the people see, feel and sense the hypocrisy of this talk.

The result is that no progress is being made, chaos is spreading irresistibly, and a catastrophe is approaching, for our government cannot introduce war-time penal servitude for the workers in the Kornilov, Hindenburg, general imperialist way—the traditions, memories, vestiges, habits and institutions of the *revolution* are still too much alive among the people; our government does not want to take any really serious steps in a revolutionary-democratic direction, for it is thoroughly infected and thoroughly enmeshed by its dependence on the bourgeoisie, its "coalition" with the bourgeoisie, and its fear to encroach on their real privileges.

GOVERNMENT DISRUPTION OF THE WORK OF THE DEMOCRATIC ORGANISATIONS

We have examined various ways and means of combating catastrophe and famine. We have seen everywhere that the contradictions between the democrats, on the one hand, and the government and the bloc of the Socialist-Revolutionaries and Mensheviks which is supporting it, on the other, are irreconcilable. To prove that these contradictions exist in reality, and not merely in our exposition, and that their irreconcilability is *actually* borne out by conflicts affecting the people as a whole, we have only to recall two very typical "results" and lessons of the six months' history of our revolution.

The history of the "reign" of Palchinsky is one lesson. The history of the "reign" and fall of Peshekhonov is the other.

The measures to combat catastrophe and hunger described above boil down to the all-round encouragement (even to the extent of compulsion) of "unionisation" of the population, and primarily the democrats, i.e., the majority of the population, or, above all, the oppressed classes, the workers and peasants, especially the poor peasants. And this is the path which the population itself spontaneously began to adopt in order to cope with the unparalleled difficulties, burdens and hardships of the war.

Tsarism did everything to hamper the free and independent "unionisation" of the population. But after the fall of the tsarist monarchy, democratic organisations began to spring up and grow rapidly all over Russia. The struggle against the catastrophe began to be waged by spontaneously arising democratic organisations—by all sorts of committees of supply, food committees, fuel councils, and so on and so forth.

And the most remarkable thing in the whole six months' history of our revolution, as far as the question we are examining is concerned, is that a *government* which calls itself republican and revolutionary, and which is *supported* by the Mensheviks and Socialist-Revolutionaries in the name of the "authorised bodies of revolutionary democracy", *fought* the democratic organisations and *defeated them*!!

By this fight, Palchinsky earned extremely wide and very sad notoriety all over Russia. He acted behind the government's back, without coming out publicly (just as the Cadets generally preferred to act, willingly pushing forward Tsereteli "for the people", while they themselves arranged all the important business on the quiet). Palchinsky hampered and thwarted every serious measure taken by the spontaneously created democratic organisations, for no serious measure could be taken without "injuring" the excessive profits and wilfulness of the Kit Kityches. And Palchinsky was in fact a loyal defender and servant of the Kit Kityches. Palchinsky went so far—and this fact was reported in the newspapers—as simply to *annul* the orders, of the spontaneously created democratic organisations!

The whole history of Palchinsky's "reign"—and he "reigned" for many months, and just when Tsereteli, Skobelev and Chernov were "ministers"—was a monstrous scandal from beginning to end; the will of the people and the decisions of the democrats were frustrated to *please* the capitalists and meet their filthy greed. Of course, only a negligible part of Palchinsky's "feats" could find its way into the press, and a full investigation of the manner in which he *hindered* the struggle against famine can be made only by a truly democratic government of the proletariat when it gains power and submits all the actions of Palchinsky and his like, without concealing anything, *to the judgement* of the people.

It will perhaps be argued that Palchinsky was an exception, and that after all he was removed. But the fact is that Palchinsky was not the exception but the *rule*, that the situation has in no way improved with his removal, that his place has been taken by the same kind of Palchinskys with different names, and that all the "*influence*" of the capitalists, and the entire policy of *frustrating the struggle against hunger to please the capitalists*, has remained intact. For Kerensky and Co. are only a screen for defence of the interests of the capitalists.

The most striking proof of this is the resignation of Peshekhonov, the Food Minister. As we know, Peshekhonov is a very, very moderate Narodnik. But in the organisation of food supply he wanted to work honestly, in contact with and supported by the democratic organisations. The *experience* of Peshekhonov's work and his *resignation* are all the more interesting because this extremely moderate Narodnik, this member of the Popular Socialist Party, who was ready to accept any compromise with the bourgeoisie, was nevertheless compelled to resign! For the Kerensky government, to please the capitalists, landowners and kulaks, had *raised* the fixed prices of grain!

This is how M. Smith describes this "step" and its significance in the newspaper *Svobodnaya Zhizn*[8] No. 1, of September 2:

> "Several days before the government decided to raise the fixed prices, the following scene was enacted in the national Food Committee: Rolovich, a Right-winger, a stubborn defender of the interests of private trade and a ruthless opponent of the grain monopoly and state interference in economic affairs, publicly announced with a smug smile that he understood the fixed grain prices would shortly be raised.
>
> "The representative of the Soviet of Workers' and Soldiers' Deputies replied by declaring that he knew nothing of the kind, that as long as the revolution in Russia lasted such an act could not take place, and that at any rate the government could not take such a step without first consulting the authorised democratic bodies—the Economic Council and the national Food Committee. This statement was supported by the representative of the Soviet of Peasants' Deputies.
>
> "But, alas, reality introduced a very harsh amendment to this counter-version! It was the representative of the wealthy elements and not the representatives of the democrats who turned out to be right. He proved to be excellently informed of the preparations for an attack on democratic rights, although the democratic representatives

[8] *Svobodnaya Zhizn* (Free Life)—a newspaper with a Menshevik trend published in Petrograd from September 2-8 (15-21), 1917, instead of the suspended *Novaya Zhizn*.

indignantly denied the very possibility of such an attack."

And so, both the representative of the workers and the representative of the peasants explicitly state their opinion in the name of the vast majority of the people, yet the Kerensky government acts contrary to that opinion, in the interests of the capitalists!

Rolovich, a representative of the capitalists, turned out to be excellently informed behind the backs of the democrats—just as we have always observed, and now observe, that the bourgeois newspapers, *Rech* and *Birzhevka*, are best informed of the doings in the Kerensky government.

What does this possession of excellent information show? Obviously, that the capitalists have their "channels" and *virtually* hold power in their own hands. Kerensky is a figurehead which they use as and when they find necessary. The interests of tens of millions of workers and peasants turn out to have been sacrificed to the profits of a handful of the rich.

And how do our Socialist-Revolutionaries and Mensheviks react to this outrage to the people? Did they address an appeal to the workers and peasants, saying that after this, prison was the only place for Kerensky and his colleagues?

God forbid! The Socialist-Revolutionaries and Mensheviks, through their Economic Department, confined themselves to adopting the impressive resolution to which we have already referred! In this resolution they declare that the raising of grain prices by the Kerensky government is "a *ruinous* measure which deals a *severe blow* both at the food supply and at the whole economic life of the country", and that these ruinous measures have been taken in direct "*violation*" of the law!!

Such are the results of the policy of compromise, of flirting with Kerensky and desiring to "spare" him!

The government violates the law by adopting, in the interests of the rich, the landowners and capitalists, a measure which *ruins* the whole business of control, food supply and the stabilisation of the extremely shaky finances, yet the Socialist-Revolutionaries and Mensheviks continue to talk about an understanding with commercial and industrial circles, continue to attend conferences with Tereshchenko and to spare Kerensky, and confine themselves to a paper resolution of protest, which the government very calmly pigeonholes!!

This reveals with great clarity the fact that the Socialist-Revolutionaries and Mensheviks have betrayed the people and the revolution, and that the Bolsheviks are becoming the real leaders of the masses, *even* of the Socialist-Revolutionary and Menshevik masses.

For only the winning of power by the proletariat, headed by the Bolshevik Party, can put an end to the outrageous actions of Kerensky and Co. and *restore* the work of democratic food distribution, supply and other organisations, which Kerensky and his government are *frustrating*.

The Bolsheviks are acting—and this can be very clearly seen from the above example—as the representatives of the interests of the *whole* people, which are to ensure food distribution and supply and meet the most urgent needs of the workers *and peasants*, despite the vacillating, irresolute and truly treacherous policy of the Socialist-Revolutionaries and Mensheviks, a policy which has brought the country to an act as shameful as this raising of grain prices!

FINANCIAL COLLAPSE AND MEASURES TO COMBAT IT

There is another side to the problem of raising the fixed grain prices. This raising of prices involves a new chaotic increase in the issuing of paper money, a further increase in the cost of living, increased financial disorganisation and the approach of financial collapse. Everybody admits that the issuing of paper money constitutes the worst form of compulsory loan, that it most of all affects the conditions of the workers, of the poorest section of the population, and that it is the chief evil engendered by financial disorder.

And it is to this measure that the Kerensky government, supported by the Socialist-Revolutionaries and Mensheviks, is resorting!

There is no way of effectively combating financial disorganisation and inevitable financial collapse except that of revolutionary rupture with the interests of capital and that of the organisation of really democratic control, i.e., control from "below", control by the workers and the poor peasants *over* the capitalists, a way to which we referred throughout the earlier part of this exposition.

Large issues of paper money encourage profiteering, enable the capitalists to make millions of rubles, and place tremendous difficulties in the way of a very necessary expansion of production, for the already high cost of materials, machinery, etc., is rising further by leaps and bounds. What can be done about it when the wealth acquired by the rich through profiteering is being concealed?

An income tax with progressive and very high rates for larger and very large incomes might be introduced. Our government has introduced one, following the example of other imperialist governments. But it is largely a fiction, a dead letter, for, firstly, the value of money is falling faster and faster, and, secondly, the more incomes are derived from profiteering and the more securely commercial secrecy is maintained, the greater their concealment.

Real and not nominal control is required to make the tax real and not fictitious. But control over the capitalists is impossible if it remains bureaucratic, for the bureaucracy is itself bound to and interwoven with the bourgeoisie by thousands of threads. That is why in the West-European imperialist states, monarchies and republics alike, financial order is obtained solely by the introduction of "labour service", which creates *war-time penal servitude or war-time slavery* for the workers.

Reactionary-bureaucratic control is the only method known to imperialist states—not excluding the democratic republics of France and America—of foisting the burdens of the war on to the proletariat and the working people.

The basic contradiction in the policy of our government is that, in order not to quarrel with the bourgeoisie, not to destroy the "coalition" with them, the government has to introduce reactionary-bureaucratic control, which it calls "revolutionary-democratic" control, deceiving the people at every step and irritating and angering the masses who have just overthrown tsarism.

Yet only revolutionary-democratic measures, only the organisation of the oppressed classes, the workers and peasants, the masses, into unions would make it possible to establish a most effective control *over the rich* and wage a most successful fight against the concealment of incomes.

An attempt is being made to encourage the use of cheques as a means of avoiding excessive issue of paper money. This measure is of no significance as far as the poor are concerned, for anyway they live from hand to mouth, complete their "economic cycle" in one week and return to the capitalists the few meagre coppers they manage to earn. The use of cheques might have great significance as far as the rich are concerned. It would enable the state, especially in conjunction with such measures as nationalisation of the banks and abolition of commercial secrecy, *really to control* the incomes of the capitalists, really to impose taxation on them, and really to "democratise" (and at the same time bring order into) the financial system.

But this is hampered by the fear of infringing the privileges of the bourgeoisie and destroying the "coalition" with them. For unless truly revolutionary measures are adopted and compulsion is very seriously resorted to, the capitalists will not submit to any control, will not make known their budgets, and will not surrender their stocks of paper money for the democratic state to "keep account" of.

The workers and peasants, organised in unions, by nationalising the banks, making the use of cheques legally compulsory for all rich persons, abolishing commercial secrecy, imposing confiscation of property as a penalty for concealment of incomes, etc., might with extreme ease make control both effective and universal—control, that is, over the rich, and such control as would *secure the return* of paper money *from those* who have it, *from those* who conceal it, *to the treasury*, which issues it.

This requires a revolutionary dictatorship of the democracy, headed by the revolutionary proletariat; that is, it requires that the democracy should become revolutionary *in fact*. That is the crux of the matter. But that is just what is not wanted by our Socialist-Revolutionaries and Mensheviks, who are deceiving the people by displaying the *flag* of "revolutionary democracy" while they are in fact supporting the reactionary-bureaucratic policy of the bourgeoisie, who, as always, are guided by the rule: "*Après nous le déluge*"—after us the deluge!

We usually do not even notice how thoroughly we are permeated by anti-democratic habits and prejudices regarding the "sanctity" of bourgeois property. When an engineer or banker publishes the income and expenditure of a worker, information about his wages and the productivity of his labour, this is regarded as absolutely legitimate and fair. Nobody thinks of seeing it as an intrusion into the "private life" of the worker, as "spying or informing" on the part of the engineer. Bourgeois society regards the labour and earnings of a wage-worker as *its* open book, any bourgeois being entitled to peer into it at any moment, and at any moment to expose the "luxurious living" of the worker, his supposed "laziness", etc.

Well, and what about reverse control? What if the unions of employees, clerks and *domestic servants* were invited by a *democratic* state to verify the income and expenditure of capitalists, to publish information on the subject and to assist the government in combating concealment of incomes?

What a furious howl against "spying" and "informing" would be raised by the bourgeoisie! When "masters" control servants, or when capitalists control workers, this is considered to be in the nature of things; the private life of the working and exploited people is *not* considered inviolable. The bourgeoisie are entitled to call to account any "wage slave" and at any time to make public his income and expenditure. But if the oppressed attempt to control the oppressor, to show up *his* income and expenditure, to expose *his* luxurious living even in war-time, when his luxurious living is directly responsible for armies at the front starving and perishing—oh, no, the bourgeoisie will not tolerate "spying" and "informing"!

It all boils down to the same thing: the rule of the bourgeoisie is *irreconcilable* with truly-revolutionary true democracy. We cannot be revolutionary democrats in the twentieth century and in a capitalist country *if we fear* to advance towards socialism.

CAN WE GO FORWARD IF WE FEAR TO ADVANCE TOWARDS SOCIALISM?

What has been said so far may easily arouse the following objection on the part of a reader who has been brought up on the current opportunist ideas of the Socialist-Revolutionaries and Mensheviks. Most measures described here, he may say, are *already* in effect socialist and not democratic measures!

This current objection, one that is usually raised (in one form or another) in the bourgeois, Socialist-Revolutionary and Menshevik press, is a reactionary defence of backward capitalism, a defence decked out in a Struvean garb. It seems to say that we are not ripe for socialism, that it is too early to "introduce" socialism, that our revolution is a bourgeois revolution and therefore we must be the menials of the bourgeoisie (although the great bourgeois revolutionaries in France 125 years ago made their revolution a great revolution by exercising *terror* against all oppressors, landowners and capitalists alike!).

The pseudo-Marxist lackeys of the bourgeoisie, who have been joined by the Socialist-Revolutionaries and who argue in this way, do not understand (as an examination of the theoretical basis of their opinion shows) what imperialism is, what capitalist monopoly is, what the state is, and what revolutionary democracy is. For anyone who understands this is bound to admit that there can be no advance except towards socialism.

Everybody talks about imperialism. But imperialism is merely monopoly capitalism.

That capitalism in Russia has also become monopoly capitalism is sufficiently attested by the examples of the Produgol, the Prodamet, the Sugar Syndicate, etc. This Sugar Syndicate is an object-lesson in the way monopoly capitalism develops into state-monopoly capitalism.

And what is the state? It is an organisation of the ruling class—in Germany, for instance, of the Junkers and capitalists. And therefore what the German Plekhanovs (Scheidemann, Lensch, and others) call "war-time socialism" is in fact war-time state-monopoly capitalism, or, to put it more simply and clearly, war-time penal servitude for the workers and war-time protection for capitalist profits.

Now try to *substitute* for the Junker-capitalist state, for the landowner-capitalist state, a *revolutionary-democratic* state, i.e., a state which in a revolutionary way abolishes *all* privileges and does not fear to introduce the fullest democracy in a revolutionary way. You will find that, given a really revolutionary-democratic state, state-monopoly capitalism inevitably and unavoidably implies a step, and more than one step, towards socialism!

For if a huge capitalist undertaking becomes a monopoly, it means that it serves the whole nation. If it has become a state monopoly, it means that the state (i.e., the armed organisation of the population, the workers and peasants above all, provided there is *revolutionary* democracy) directs the whole undertaking. In whose interest?

Either in the interest of the landowners and capitalists, in which case we have not a revolutionary-democratic, but a reactionary-bureaucratic state, an imperialist republic.

Or in the interest of revolutionary democracy—and then *it is a step towards socialism.*

For socialism is merely the next step forward from state-capitalist monopoly. Or, in other words, socialism is merely state-capitalist monopoly *which is made to serve the interests of the whole people* and has to that extent *ceased* to be capitalist monopoly.

There is no middle course here. The objective process of development is such that it is *impossible* to advance from *monopolies* (and the war has magnified their number, role and importance tenfold) without advancing towards socialism.

Either we have to be revolutionary democrats in fact, in which case we must not fear to take steps towards socialism. Or we fear to take steps towards socialism, condemn them in the Plekhanov, Dan or Chernov way, by arguing that our revolution is a bourgeois revolution, that socialism cannot be "introduced", etc., in which case we inevitably sink to the level of Kerensky, Milyukov and Kornilov, i.e., we in a *reactionary-bureaucratic* way suppress the "revolutionary-democratic" aspirations of the workers and peasants.

There is no middle course.

And therein lies the fundamental contradiction of our revolution.

It is impossible to stand still in history in general, and in war-time in particular. We must either advance or retreat. It is *impossible* in twentieth-century Russia, which has won a republic and democracy in a revolutionary way, to go forward without *advancing* towards socialism, without taking *steps* towards it (steps conditioned and determined by the level of technology and culture: large-scale machine production cannot be "introduced" in peasant agriculture nor abolished in the sugar industry).

But to fear to advance *means* retreating—which the Kerenskys, to the delight of the Milyukovs and Plekhanovs, and with the foolish assistance of the Tseretelis and Chernovs, are actually doing.

The dialectics of history is such that the war, by extraordinarily expediting the transformation of monopoly capitalism into state-monopoly capitalism, has *thereby* extraordinarily advanced mankind towards socialism.

Imperialist war is the eve of socialist revolution. And this not only because the horrors of the war give rise to proletarian revolt—no revolt can bring about socialism unless the economic conditions for socialism are ripe—but because state-monopoly capitalism is a complete *material* preparation for socialism, the *threshold* of socialism, a rung on the ladder of history between which and the rung called socialism *there are no intermediate rungs.*

***

Our Socialist-Revolutionaries and Mensheviks approach the question of socialism in a doctrinaire way, from the standpoint of a doctrine learnt by heart but poorly understood. They picture socialism as some remote, unknown and dim future.

But socialism is now gazing at us from all the windows of modern capitalism; socialism is outlined directly, *practically*, by every important measure that constitutes a forward step on the basis of this modern capitalism.

What is universal labour conscription?

It is a step forward on the basis of modern monopoly capitalism, a step towards the regulation of economic life as a whole, in accordance with a certain general plan, a step towards the economy of national labour and towards the prevention of its senseless wastage by capitalism.

In Germany it is the Junkers (landowners) and capitalists who are introducing universal labour conscription, and therefore it inevitably becomes war-time penal servitude for the workers.

But take the same institution and think over its significance in a revolutionary-democratic state. Universal labour conscription, introduced, regulated and directed by the Soviets of Workers', Soldiers' and Peasants' Deputies, will *still not* be socialism, but it will *no longer* be capitalism. It will be a tremendous *step towards* socialism, a step from which, if complete democracy is preserved, there can no longer be any retreat back to capitalism, without unparalleled violence being committed against the masses.

THE STRUGGLE AGAINST ECONOMIC CHAOS—AND THE WAR

A consideration of the measures to avert the impending catastrophe brings us to another supremely important question, namely, the connection between home and foreign policy, or, in other words, the relation between a war of conquest, an imperialist war, and a revolutionary, proletarian war, between a criminal predatory war and a just democratic war.

All the measures to avert catastrophe we have described would, as we have already stated, greatly enhance the defence potential, or, in other words, the military might of the country. That, on the one hand. On the other hand, these measures cannot be put into effect without turning the war of conquest into a just war, turning the war waged by the capitalists in the interests of the capitalists into a war waged by the proletariat in the interests of all the working and exploited people.

And, indeed, nationalisation of the banks and syndicates, taken in conjunction with the abolition of commercial secrecy and the establishment of workers' control over the capitalists, would not only imply a tremendous saving of national labour, the possibility of economising forces and means, but would also imply an improvement in the conditions of the working *masses*, of the majority of the population. As everybody knows, economic organisation is of decisive importance in modern warfare. Russia has enough grain, coal, oil and iron; in this respect, we are in a better position than any of the belligerent European countries. And given a struggle against economic chaos by the measures indicated above, enlisting popular initiative in this struggle, improving the people's conditions, and nationalising the banks and syndicates, Russia could use her revolution and her democracy to raise the whole country to an incomparably higher level of economic organisation.

If instead of the "coalition" with the bourgeoisie, which is hampering every measure of control and sabotaging production, the Socialist-Revolutionaries and Mensheviks had in April effected the transfer of power to the Soviets and had directed their efforts not to playing at "ministerial leapfrog", not to bureaucratically occupying, side by side with the Cadets, ministerial, deputy-ministerial and similar posts, but to guiding the workers and peasants in *their* control *over* the capitalists, in their *war against* the capitalists, Russia would now be a country completely transformed economically, with the land in the hands of the peasants, and with the banks nationalised, i.e., would *to that extent* (and these are extremely important economic bases of modern life) be *superior* to all other capitalist countries.

The defence potential, the military might, of a country whose banks have been nationalised is *superior* to that of a country whose banks remain in private hands. The military might of a peasant country whose land is in the hands of peasant committees is *superior* to that of a country whose land is in the hands of landowners.

Reference is constantly being made to the heroic patriotism and the miracles of military valour performed by the French in 1792-93. But the material, historical and economic conditions which alone made such miracles possible are forgotten. The suppression of obsolete feudalism in a really revolutionary way, and the introduction throughout the country of a superior mode of production and free peasant land tenure, effected, moreover, with truly revolutionary-democratic speed, determination, energy and devotion—such were the material, economic conditions which with "miraculous" speed saved France by *regenerating* and *renovating* her economic foundation.

The example of France shows one thing, and one thing only, namely, that to render Russia capable of self-defence, to obtain in

Russia, too, "miracles" of mass heroism, all that is obsolete must be swept away with "Jacobin" ruthlessness and Russia renovated and regenerated *economically*. And in the twentieth century this cannot be done merely by sweeping tsarism away (France did not confine herself to this 125 years ago). It cannot be done even by the mere revolutionary abolition of the landed estates (we have not even done that, for the Socialist-Revolutionaries and Mensheviks have betrayed the peasants), by the mere transfer of the land to the peasants. For we are living in the twentieth century, and mastery over the land *without mastery over the banks* cannot regenerate and renovate the life of the people.

The material, industrial renovation of France at the end of the eighteenth century was associated with a political and spiritual renovation, with the dictatorship of revolutionary democrats and the revolutionary proletariat (from which the democrats had not dissociated themselves and with which they were still almost fused), and with a ruthless war declared on everything reactionary. The whole people, and especially the masses, i.e., the *oppressed* classes, were swept up by boundless revolutionary enthusiasm; *everybody* considered the war a just war of defence, as it *actually was*. Revolutionary France was defending herself against reactionary monarchist Europe. It was not in 1792-93, but many years later, *after* the victory of reaction within the country, that the counter-revolutionary dictatorship of Napoleon turned France's wars from defensive wars into wars of conquest.

And what about Russia? We continue to wage an imperialist war in the interests of the capitalists, in alliance with the imperialists and in accordance with the secret treaties the *tsar* concluded with the capitalists of Britain and other countries, promising the Russian capitalists in these treaties the spoliation of foreign lands, of Constantinople, Lvov, Armenia, etc.

The war will remain an unjust, reactionary and predatory war on Russia's part as long as she does not propose a just peace and does not break with imperialism. The social character of the war, its true meaning, is not determined by the position of the enemy troops (as the Socialist-Revolutionaries and Mensheviks think, stooping to the vulgarity of an ignorant yokel). What determines this character is the *policy* of which the war is a continuation ("war is the continuation of politics"), the *class* that is waging the war, and the aims for which it is waging this war.

You cannot lead the people into a predatory war in accordance with secret treaties and expect them to be enthusiastic. The foremost class in revolutionary Russia, the proletariat, is becoming increasingly aware of the criminal character of the war, and not only have the bourgeoisie been unable to shatter this popular conviction, but, on the contrary, awareness of the criminal character of the war is growing. The proletariat of *both metropolitan cities* of Russia has definitely become internationalist!

How, then, can you expect mass enthusiasm for the war!

One is inseparable from the other—home policy is inseparable from foreign policy. The country cannot be made capable of self-defence without the supreme heroism of the people in boldly and resolutely carrying out great economic transformations. And it is impossible to arouse popular heroism without breaking with imperialism, without proposing a democratic peace to all nations, and without thus turning the war from a criminal war of conquest and plunder into a just, revolutionary war of defence.

Only a thorough and consistent break with the capitalists in both home and foreign policy can save our revolution and our country, which is gripped in the iron vice of imperialism.

THE REVOLUTIONARY DEMOCRATS AND THE REVOLUTIONARY PROLETARIAT

To be really revolutionary, the democrats of Russia today must march in very close alliance with the proletariat, supporting it in its struggle as the only thoroughly revolutionary class.

Such is the conclusion prompted by an analysis of the means of combating an impending catastrophe of unparalleled dimensions.

The war has created such an immense crisis, has so strained the material and moral forces of the people, has dealt such blows at the entire modern social organisation that humanity must now choose between perishing or entrusting its fate to the most revolutionary class for the swiftest and most radical transition to a superior mode of production.

Owing to a number of historical causes—the greater backwardness of Russia, the unusual hardships brought upon her by the war, the utter rottenness of tsarism and the extreme tenacity of the traditions of 1905—the revolution broke out in Russia earlier than in other countries. The revolution has resulted in Russia catching up with the advanced countries in a few months, as far as her *political* system is concerned.

But that is not enough. The war is inexorable; it puts the alternative with ruthless severity: either perish or overtake and outstrip the advanced countries *economically as well.*

That is possible, for we have before us the experience of a large number of advanced countries, the fruits of their technology and culture. We are receiving moral support from the war protest that is growing in Europe, from the atmosphere of the mounting world-wide workers' revolution. We are being inspired and encouraged by a revolutionary-democratic freedom which is extremely rare in time of imperialist war.

Perish or forge full steam ahead. That is the alternative put by history.

And the attitude of the proletariat to the peasants in such a situation confirms the old Bolshevik concept, correspondingly modifying it, that the peasants must be wrested from the influence of the bourgeoisie. That is the sole guarantee of salvation for the revolution.

And the peasants are the most numerous section of the entire petty-bourgeois mass.

Our Socialist-Revolutionaries and Mensheviks have assumed the reactionary function of keeping the peasants under the influence of the bourgeoisie and leading them to a coalition with the bourgeoisie, and not with the proletariat.

The masses are learning rapidly from the experience of the revolution. And the reactionary policy of the Socialist-Revolutionaries and Mensheviks is meeting with failure: they have been beaten in the

Soviets of both Petrograd and Moscow.[9] A "Left" opposition is growing in both petty-bourgeois-democratic parties. On September 10, 1917, a city conference of the Socialist-Revolutionaries held in Petrograd gave a two-thirds majority to the *Left* Socialist-Revolutionaries, who incline towards an alliance with the proletariat and reject an alliance (coalition) with the bourgeoisie.

The Socialist-Revolutionaries and Mensheviks repeat a favourite bourgeois comparison—bourgeoisie and democracy. But, in essence, such a comparison is as meaningless as comparing pounds with yards.

There is such a thing as a democratic bourgeoisie, and there is such a thing as bourgeois democracy; one would have to be completely ignorant of both history and political economy to deny this.

The Socialist-Revolutionaries and Mensheviks needed a false comparison to *conceal* the indisputable fact that between the bourgeoisie and the proletariat stand the *petty bourgeoisie*. By virtue of their economic class status, the latter inevitably vacillate between the bourgeoisie and the proletariat.

The Socialist-Revolutionaries and Mensheviks are trying to draw the petty bourgeoisie into an alliance with the bourgeoisie. That is the whole meaning of their "coalition", of the coalition cabinet, and of the whole policy of Kerensky, a typical semi-Cadet. In the six months of the revolution this policy has suffered a complete fiasco.

The Cadets are full of malicious glee. The revolution, they say, has suffered a fiasco; the revolution has been *unable* to cope either with the war or with economic dislocation.

That is not true. It is the *Cadets*, and the *Socialist-Revolutionaries and Mensheviks* who have suffered a fiasco, for this alliance has ruled Russia for six months, only to increase economic dislocation and confuse and aggravate the military situation.

[9] On August 31 (September 13), 1917, the Petrograd Soviet for the first time passed, by a majority of 279 to 115, with 50 abstentions, a motion tabled by the Bolshevik group, emphatically rejecting the policy of compromise with the bourgeoisie. The resolution called for the transfer of all power to the Soviets and outlined a programme for revolutionary changes in the country. A few days later the Bolshevik Party won yet another major victory. On September 5 (18) the Moscow Soviet of Workers' and Soldiers' Deputies carried a similar Bolshevik motion by a majority of 355 votes.

The more complete the fiasco of the *alliance* of the bourgeoisie and the *Socialist-Revolutionaries and Mensheviks*, the sooner the people will *learn their lesson* and the more easily they will find the *correct* way out, namely, the alliance of the peasant poor, i.e., the majority of the peasants, and the proletariat.

September 10-14, 1917

Published at the end of October 1917 in pamphlet form by Priboi Publishers
Published according to manuscript

THE TASKS OF THE REVOLUTION

Russia is a country of the petty bourgeoisie, by far the greater part of the population belonging to this class. Its vacillations between the bourgeoisie and the proletariat are inevitable, and only when it joins the proletariat is the victory of the revolution, of the cause of peace, freedom, and land for the working people assured easily, peacefully, quickly, and smoothly.

The course of our revolution shows us these vacillations in practice. Let us then not harbour any illusions about the Socialist-Revolutionary and Menshevik parties; let us stick firmly to the path of our proletarian class. The poverty of the poor peasants, the horrors of the war, the horrors of hunger—all these are showing the masses more and more clearly the correctness of the proletarian path, the need to support the proletarian revolution.

The "peaceful" hopes of the petty bourgeoisie that there might be a "coalition" with the bourgeoisie and agreements with them, that it will be possible to wait "calmly" for the "speedy" convocation of the Constituent Assembly, etc., have been mercilessly, cruelly, implacably destroyed by the course of the revolution. The Kornilov revolt was the last cruel lesson, a lesson on a grand scale, supplementing thousands upon thousands of small lessons in which workers and peasants were deceived by local capitalists and landowners, in which soldiers were deceived by the officers, etc., etc.

Discontent, indignation and wrath are growing in the army, among the peasantry and among the workers. The "coalition" of the Socialist-Revolutionaries and Mensheviks with the bourgeoisie, promising everything and fulfilling nothing, is irritating the masses, is opening their eyes, is pushing them towards insurrection.

There is a growing Left opposition among the Socialist-Revolutionaries (Spiridonova and others) and among the Mensheviks (Martov and others), and has already reached forty per cent of the Council and Congress of those parties. And down *below*, among the proletariat and the peasantry, particularly the poorest sections, the *majority* of the Socialist-Revolutionaries and Mensheviks belong to the *Lefts*.

The Kornilov revolt is instructive and has proved a good lesson.

It is impossible to know whether the Soviets will be able to go farther than the leaders of the Socialist-Revolutionaries and Mensheviks, and thus ensure a peaceful development of the revolution, or whether they will continue to mark time, thus making a proletarian uprising inevitable.

We cannot know this.

Our business is to help get everything possible done to make sure the "last" chance for a peaceful development of the revolution, to help by the presentation of our programme, by making clear its national character, its absolute accord with the interests and demands of a vast majority of the population.

The following lines are an essay in the presentation of such a programme.

Let us take it more to those down below, to the masses, to the office employees, to the workers, to the peasants, not only to our supporters, but particularly to those who follow the Socialist-Revolutionaries, to the non-party elements, to the ignorant. Let us lift them up so that they can pass an independent judgement, make their own decisions, send *their own* delegations to the Conference, to the Soviets, to the government and our work will not have been in vain, *no matter what* the outcome of the Conference. This will then prove useful for the Conference, for the elections to the Constituent Assembly, and for all other political activity in general.

Experience teaches us that the Bolshevik programme and tactics are correct. So little time passed, so much happened from April 20 to the Kornilov revolt.

The experience of the *masses*, the experience of *oppressed* classes taught them very, very much in that time; the leaders of the Socialist-Revolutionaries and Mensheviks have completely cut adrift from the masses. This will most certainly be revealed in the discussion of our concrete programme insofar as we are able to bring it to the notice of the masses.

AGREEMENTS WITH THE CAPITALISTS ARE DISASTROUS

1.To leave in power the representatives of the bourgeoisie, even a small number of them, to leave in power such notorious Kornilovites as Generals Alexeyev, Klembovsky, Bagration, Gagarin, and others, or such as have proved their complete powerlessness in face of the bourgeoisie, and their ability of acting Bonaparte-fashion like Kerensky, is, on the one hand, merely opening the door wide to famine and the inevitable economic catastrophe which the capitalists are purposely accelerating and intensifying; on the other hand, it will lead to a military catastrophe, since the army hates the General Staff and cannot enthusiastically participate in the imperialist war. Besides, there is no doubt that Kornilovite generals and officers remaining in power will *deliberately open the front to the Germans*, as they have done in Galicia and Riga. This can be prevented only by the formation of a new government on a new basis, as expounded below. To continue any kind of agreements with the bourgeoisie after all that we have gone through since April 20 would be, on the part of the Socialist-Revolutionaries and Mensheviks, not only an error but a direct betrayal of the people and of the revolution.

POWER TO THE SOVIETS

2. All power in the country must pass exclusively to the representatives of the Soviets of Workers', Soldiers' and Peasants' Deputies on the basis of a definite programme and under the condition of the government being fully responsible to the Soviets. New elections to the Soviets must be held immediately, both to record the experience of the people during the recent weeks of the revolution, which have been particularly eventful, and to eliminate crying injustices (lack of proportional representation, unequal elections, etc.) which in some cases still remain.

All power locally, wherever there are not yet any democratically elected institutions, and also in the army, must be taken over exclusively by the local Soviets and by commissars and other institutions elected by them, but only those that have been properly elected.

Workers and revolutionary troops, i.e., those who have in practice shown their ability to suppress the Kornilovites, must everywhere be armed, and this must be done with the full support of the state.

PEACE TO THE PEOPLES

3. The Soviet Government must *straight away* offer to *all* the belligerent peoples (i.e., simultaneously both to their governments and to the worker and peasant masses) to conclude an immediate general peace on democratic terms, and also to conclude an immediate armistice (even if only for three months).

The main condition for a democratic peace is the renunciation of annexations (seizures)—not in the incorrect sense that all powers get back what they have lost, but in the only correct sense that *every* nationality without any exception, both in Europe and in the colonies, shall obtain its freedom and the possibility to decide for itself whether it is to form a *separate* state or whether it is to enter into the composition of some other state.

In offering the peace terms, the Soviet Government must itself immediately take steps towards their fulfilment, i.e., it must publish and repudiate the secret treaties by which we have been bound up to the present time, those which were concluded by the tsar and which give Russian capitalists the promise of the pillaging of Turkey, Austria, etc. Then we must immediately satisfy the demands of the Ukrainians and the Finns, ensure them, as well as all other non-Russian nationalities in Russia, full freedom, including freedom of secession, applying the same *to all* Armenia, undertaking to evacuate that country as well as the Turkish lands occupied by us, etc.

Such peace terms will not meet with the approval of the capitalists, but they will meet with such tremendous sympathy on the part of all the peoples and will cause such a great world-wide outburst of enthusiasm and of general indignation against the continuation of the predatory war that it is extremely probable that we shall at once obtain a truce and a consent to open peace negotiations. For the workers' revolution against the war is irresistibly growing everywhere, and it can be spurred on, not by phrases about peace (with which the workers and peasants have been deceived by *all* the imperialist governments including our own Kerensky government), but by a break with the capitalists and by the offer of peace.

If the least probable thing happens, i.e., if not a single belligerent state accepts even a truce, then as far as we are concerned the war becomes truly forced upon us, it becomes a truly just war of defence. If this is understood by the proletariat and the poor peasantry Russia will become many times stronger even in the military sense, especially after a complete break with the capitalists who are robbing the people; furthermore, under such conditions it would, as far as we are concerned, be a war in league with the oppressed classes of all countries, a war in league with the oppressed peoples of the whole world, not in word, but in deed.

The people must be particularly cautioned against the capitalists' assertion which sometimes influences the petty bourgeoisie and others who are frightened, namely, that the British and other capitalists are capable of doing serious damage to the Russian revolution if we break the present predatory alliance with them. Such an assertion is false through and through, for "Allied financial aid" enriches the bankers and "supports" the Russian workers and peasants in exactly the same way as a rope supports a man who has been hanged. There is plenty of bread, coal, oil and iron in Russia; for these products to be properly distributed it is only necessary for us to rid ourselves of the landowners and capitalists who are robbing the people. As to the possibility of the Russian people being threatened with war by their present Allies, it is obviously absurd to assume that the French and Italians could unite their armies with those of the Germans and move them against Russia who offers a just peace. As to Britain, America, and Japan, even if they were to declare war against Russia (which for them is extremely difficult, both because of the extreme unpopularity of such a war among the masses and because of the divergence of material interests of the capitalists of those countries over the partitioning of Asia, especially over the plunder of China), they could not cause Russia one-hundredth part of the damage and misery which the war with Germany, Austria, and Turkey is causing her.

LAND TO THOSE WHO TILL IT

4. The Soviet Government must immediately declare the abolition of private landed estates without compensation and place all these estates under the management of the peasant committees pending the solution of the problem by the Constituent Assembly. These peasant committees are also to take over all the landowners' stock and implements, with the proviso that they be placed primarily at the disposal of the poor peasants for their use free of charge.

Such measures, which have long been demanded by an immense majority of the peasantry, both in the resolutions of congresses and in hundreds of mandates from local peasants (as may be seen, for instance, from a summary of 242 mandates published by *Izvestia Soveta Krestyanskikh Deputatov*[1]), are absolutely and urgently necessary. There must be no further procrastination like that from which the peasantry suffered so much at the time of the "coalition" government.

Any government that hesitates to introduce these measures should be regarded as a government *hostile to the people* that should be overthrown and crushed by an uprising of the workers and peasants. On the other hand, only a government that realises these measures will be a government of all the people.

STRUGGLE AGAINST FAMINE AND ECONOMIC RUIN

5. The Soviet Government must immediately introduce workers' control of production and distribution on a nation-wide scale. Experience since May 6 has shown that in the absence of such control all the promises of reforms and attempts to introduce them are powerless, and famine, accompanied by unprecedented catastrophe is becoming a greater menace to the whole country week by week.

[1] *Izvestia Vserossiiskogo Soveta Krestyanskikh Deputatov* (News of the All-Russia Soviet of Peasants' Deputies)—a daily, the official organ of the All-Russia Soviet of Peasants' Deputies, published in Petrograd from May 9 (22) to December 1917. It expressed the views of the Right wing of the Socialist-Revolutionary Party. It met the October Socialist Revolution with hostility and was closed down for counter-revolutionary propaganda.

It is necessary to nationalise the banks and the insurance business immediately, and also the most important branches of industry (oil, coal, metallurgy, sugar, etc.), and at the same time, to abolish commercial secrets and to establish unrelaxing supervision by the workers and peasants over the negligible minority of capitalists who wax rich on government contracts and evade accounting and just taxation of their profits and property.

Such measures, which do not deprive either the middle peasants, the Cossacks or the small handicraftsmen of a single kopek, are urgently needed for the struggle against famine and are absolutely just because they distribute the burdens of the war equitably. Only after capitalist plunder has been curbed and the deliberate sabotage of production has been stopped will it be possible to work for an improvement in labour productivity, introduce universal labour conscription and the proper exchange of grain for manufactured goods, and return to the Treasury thousands of millions in paper money now being hoarded by the rich.

Without such measures, the abolition of the landed estates without compensation is also impossible, for the major part of the estates is mortgaged to the banks, so that the interests of the landowners and capitalists are inseparably linked up.

The latest resolution of the Economic Department of the All-Russia Central Executive Committee of Soviets of Workers' and Soldiers' Deputies (*Rabochaya Gazeta* No. 152) recognises not only the "*harm*" caused by the government's measures (like the raising of grain prices for the enrichment of the landowners and kulaks), not only "the fact of the *complete inactivity* on the part of the central organs set up by the government for the regulation of economic life", but even the "*contravention of the laws*" by this government. This admission on the part of the ruling parties, the Socialist-Revolutionaries and Mensheviks, proves once more the criminal nature of the policy of conciliation with the bourgeoisie.

STRUGGLE AGAINST THE COUNTER-REVOLUTION OF THE LANDOWNERS AND CAPITALISTS

6. The Kornilov and Kaledin revolt was supported by the entire class of the landowners and capitalists, with the party of the Cadets ("people's freedom" party) at their head. This has already been fully proved by the facts published in *Izvestia* of the Central Executive Committee.

However, nothing has been done either to suppress this counter-revolution completely or even to investigate it, and nothing serious can be done without the transfer of power to the Soviets. No commission can conduct a full investigation, or arrest the guilty, etc., unless it holds state power. Only a Soviet government can do this, and must do it. Only a Soviet government can make Russia secure against the otherwise inevitable repetition of "Kornilov" attempts by arresting the Kornilovite generals and the ringleaders of the bourgeois counter-revolution (Guchkov, Milyukov, Ryabushinsky, Maklakov and Co.), by disbanding the counter-revolutionary associations (the State Duma, the officers' unions, etc.), by placing their members under the surveillance of the local Soviets and by disbanding counter-revolutionary armed units.

This government alone can set up a commission to make a full and public investigation of the Kornilov case and all the other cases, even those started by the bourgeoisie; and the party of the Bolsheviks, in its turn, would appeal to the workers to give full co-operation and to submit only to such a commission.

Only a Soviet government could successfully combat such a flagrant injustice as the capitalists' seizure of the largest printing presses and most of the papers with the aid of millions squeezed out of the people. It is necessary to suppress the bourgeois counter-revolutionary papers (*Rech*, *Russkoye Slovo*,[2] etc.), to confiscate their printing presses,

[2] *Russkoye Slovo* (Russian Word)—a daily published in Moscow from 1895 (a pilot issue was published in 1894). Ostensibly independent, it took a moderately liberal attitude in the interests of the Russian bourgeoisie. In 1917, the paper sided with the bourgeois Provisional Government and bitterly attacked Lenin and the Bolshevik Party.

In November 1917, it was closed down for carrying slanderous antito declare private advertisements in the papers a state monopoly, to transfer them to the paper published by the Soviets, the paper that tells the peasants the truth. Only in this way can and must the bourgeoisie be deprived of its powerful weapon of lying and slandering, deceiving the people with impunity, misleading the peasantry, and preparing a counter-revolution.

PEACEFUL DEVELOPMENT OF THE REVOLUTION

7. A possibility very seldom to be met with in the history of revolutions now faces the democracy of Russia, the Soviets and the Socialist-Revolutionary and Menshevik parties—the possibility of convening the Constituent Assembly at the appointed date without further delays, of making the country secure against a military and economic catastrophe, and of ensuring the peaceful development of the revolution.

If the Soviets now take full state power exclusively into their own hands for the purpose of carrying out the programme set forth above, they will not only obtain the support of nine-tenths of the population of Russia, the working class and an overwhelming majority of the peasantry; they will also be assured of the greatest revolutionary enthusiasm on the part of the army and the majority of the people, an enthusiasm without which victory over famine and war is impossible.

There could be no question of any resistance to the Soviets if the Soviets themselves did not waver. No class will dare start an uprising against the Soviets, and the landowners and capitalists, taught a lesson by the experience of the Kornilov revolt, will give up their power peacefully and yield to the ultimatum of the Soviets. To overcome the capitalists' resistance to the programme of the Soviets, supervision over the exploiters by workers and peasants and such measures of punishing the recalcitrants as confiscation of their entire property coupled with a short term of arrest will be sufficient.

By seizing full power, the Soviets could still today—and this is

....

Soviet reports. From January 1918, it appeared for a time under the name of *Novoye Slovo* (New Word) and *Nashe Slovo* (Our Word). It was finally closed down in July 1918.

probably their last chance—ensure the peaceful development of the revolution, peaceful elections of deputies by the people, and a peaceful struggle of parties inside the Soviets; they could test the programmes of the various parties in practice and power could pass peacefully from one party to another.

The entire course of development of the revolution, from the movement of April 20 to the Kornilov revolt, shows that there is bound to be the bitterest civil war between the bourgeoisie and the proletariat if this opportunity is missed. Inevitable catastrophe will bring this war nearer. It must end, as all data and considerations accessible to human reason go to prove, in the full victory of the working class, in that class, supported by the poor peasantry, carrying out the above programme; it may, however, prove very difficult and bloody, and may cost the lives of tens of thousands of landowners, capitalists, and officers who sympathise with them. The proletariat will not hesitate to make every sacrifice to save the revolution, which is possible only by implementing the programme set forth above. On the other hand, the proletariat would support the Soviets in every way if they were to make use of their last chance to secure a peaceful development of the revolution.

Signed: *N.K.*
Rabochy Put Nos. 20-21, October 9 and 10
(September 26 and 27), 1917
Published according to the newspaper text

THE CRISIS HAS MATURED[1]

I

The end of September undoubtedly marked a great turning-point in the history of the Russian revolution and, to all appearances, of the world revolution as well.

The world working-class revolution began with the action of individuals, whose boundless courage represented everything honest that remained of that decayed official "socialism" which is in reality social-chauvinism. Liebknecht in Germany, Adler in Austria, MacLean in Britain—these are the best-known names of the isolated heroes who have taken upon themselves the arduous role of forerunners of the world revolution.

The second stage in the historical preparation for this revolution was a widespread mass discontent, expressing itself in the split of the official parties, in illegal publications and in street demonstrations. The protest against the war became stronger, and the number of victims of government persecution increased. The prisons of countries famed for their observance of law and even for their freedom—Germany, France, Italy and Britain—became filled with tens and hundreds of internationalists, opponents of the war and advocates of a working-class revolution.

The third stage has now begun. This stage may be called the eve of revolution. Mass arrests of party leaders in free Italy, and particularly the beginning of *mutinies* in the German army,[2] are indisputable

[1] Written in Vyborg. It consisted of six chapters, the last not being intended for publication but for circulation among members of the Central Committee, the Petrograd and Moscow Committees and the Soviets. Only the manuscript of the last two chapters has come down to us. The article was first published in four chapters in *Rabochy Put* No. 30 of October 20 (7), 1917; a comparison of the newspaper text and the manuscript shows that one of the chapters was omitted and Chapter V was headed as Chapter IV.

The article was widely carried by Bolshevik periodicals.

[2] The reference is to the revolutionary action by German sailors in August 1917, who were led by a revolutionary sailors' organisation numbering 4,000

symptoms that a great turning-point is at hand, that we are *on the eve of a worldwide revolution.*

Even before this there were, no doubt, individual cases of mutiny among the troops in Germany, but they were so small, so weak and isolated that it was possible to hush them up—and that was the chief way of checking the *mass contagion* of seditious action. Finally, there developed such a movement in the navy that it was *impossible* to hush it up, despite all the severity of the German regime of military servitude, severity elaborated with amazing minuteness of detail and observed with incredible pedantry.

Doubt is out of the question. We are on the threshold of a world proletarian revolution. And since of all the proletarian internationalists in all countries only we Russian Bolsheviks enjoy a measure of freedom—we have a legal party and a score or so of papers, we have the Soviets of Workers' and Soldiers' Deputies of both capitals on our side, and we have the support of a *majority* of the people in a time of revolution—to us the saying, "To whom much has been given, of him much shall be required" in all justice can and must be applied.

II

The crucial point of the revolution in Russia has undoubtedly arrived.

In a peasant country, and under a revolutionary, republican government which enjoys the support of the Socialist-Revolutionary

....

members (late July 1917). It was led by seamen Max Reichpietsch and Albin Köbis of the *Friedrich der Grosse*. The organisation decided to fight for a democratic peace and prepare for an uprising. Manifestations broke out in the navy in early August. Sailors of the warship *Prinzeregent Luitpold*, which was at Wilhelmshaven, took absence without leave to fight for the release of their comrades who had earlier been arrested for staging a strike; on August 16, the firemen of the *Westphali*a refused to work; at the same time the crew of the cruiser *Nürnberg*, which was out at sea, staged an uprising. The sailors' movement spread to the ships of several squadrons at Wilhelmshaven. These manifestations were put down with great savagery. Reichpietsch and Köbis were shot and other active participants were sentenced to long terms of hard labour.

and Menshevik parties that only yesterday dominated petty-bourgeois democracy, a *peasant revolt* is developing.

Incredible as this is, it is a fact.

We Bolsheviks are not surprised by this fact. We have always said that the government of the notorious "coalition" with the bourgeoisie is a government that *betrays* democracy and the revolution, that it is a government of *imperialist* slaughter, a government that *protects* the capitalists and landowners *from* the people.

Owing to the deception practised by the Socialist-Revolutionaries and the Mensheviks, there still exists in Russia, under a republic and in a time of revolution, a government of capitalists and landowners side by side with the Soviets. This is the bitter and sinister reality. Is it then surprising, in view of the incredible hardship inflicted on the people by prolonging the imperialist war and by its consequences, that a peasant revolt has begun and is spreading in Russia?

Is it then surprising that the enemies of the Bolsheviks, the leaders of the *official* Socialist-Revolutionary Party, the very party that supported the "coalition" all along, the party that until the last few days or weeks had the majority of the people on its side, the party that continues to harry and abuse the "new" Socialist-Revolutionaries, who have realised that the policy of coalition is a betrayal of the interests of the peasants—is it surprising that these leaders of the official Socialist-Revolutionary Party wrote the following in an editorial in their official organ, *Dyelo Naroda* of September 29:

> "So far practically nothing has been done to put an end to the relations of bondage that still prevail in the villages of central Russia . . . . The bill for the regulation of land relations in the countryside, which was introduced in the Provisional Government long ago, and which has even passed through such a purgatory as the Judicial Conference, has got hopelessly stuck in some office . . . . Are we not right in asserting that our republican government is still a long way from having rid itself of the old habits of the tsarist administration, and that the dead hand of Stolypin is still making itself strongly felt in the methods of the revolutionary ministers?"

This is written by the official Socialist-Revolutionaries! Just think: the supporters of the coalition are *forced* to admit that in a peasant country, after seven months of revolution, "practically nothing has been done to put an end to the bondage" of the peasants, to their enslavement by the landowners! These Socialist-Revolutionaries are *forced* to give the name of *Stolypins* to their colleague, Kerensky, and his gang of ministers.

Could we get more eloquent testimony than this from the camp of our opponents, not only to the effect that the coalition has collapsed and that the official Socialist-Revolutionaries who tolerate Kerensky have become an *anti-popular, anti-peasant and counter-revolutionary* party, but also that the whole Russian revolution has reached a turning-point?

A peasant revolt in a peasant country against the government of the Socialist-Revolutionary Kerensky, the Mensheviks Nikitin and Gvozdyov, and other ministers who represent capital and the interests of the landowners! The crushing of this revolt by *military measures* by a republican government!

In the face of such facts, can one remain a conscientious champion of the proletariat and yet deny that a crisis has matured, that the revolution is passing through an extremely critical moment, that the government's victory over the peasant revolt would now sound the death knell of the revolution, would be the final triumph of the Kornilov revolt?

III

It is obvious that if in a peasant country, after seven months of a democratic republic, matters could come to a peasant revolt, it irrefutably proves that the revolution is suffering nation-wide collapse, that it is experiencing a crisis of unprecedented severity, and that the forces of counter-revolution have gone the *limit.*

That is obvious. In the face of such a fact as a peasant revolt all other political symptoms, even were they to contradict the fact that a nation-wide crisis is maturing, would have no significance whatsoever.

But on the contrary, all the symptoms do indicate that a nation-wide crisis has matured.

Next to the agrarian question, the most important question in Russia's state affairs is the national question, particularly for the petty-bourgeois masses of the population. And at the "Democratic" Conference, which was fixed by Mr. Tsereteli and Co., we find that the "national" curia takes second place for radicalism, yielding only to the trade unions, and *exceeding* the curia of the Soviets of Workers' and Soldiers' Deputies in the percentage of votes cast *against* the coalition (40 out of 55). The Kerensky government—a government suppressing the peasant revolt—is withdrawing the revolutionary troops from Finland in order to strengthen the reactionary Finnish bourgeoisie. In the Ukraine, the conflicts of the Ukrainians in general, and of the Ukrainian troops in particular, with the government are becoming more and more frequent.

Furthermore, let us take the army, which in war-time plays an exceptionally big role in all state affairs. We find that the army in Finland and the fleet in the Baltic have completely *parted ways* with the government. We have the testimony of the officer Dubasov, a non-Bolshevik, who speaks in the name of the whole front and declares in a manner more revolutionary than that of any Bolsheviks that the soldiers will not fight any longer.[3] We have governmental reports stating that the soldiers are in a state of "agitation" and that it is impossible to guarantee the maintenance of "order" (i.e., participation of these troops in the suppression of the peasant revolt). We have, finally, the voting in Moscow, where fourteen thousand out of seventeen thousand soldiers voted for the Bolsheviks.

This vote in the elections to the district councils in Moscow is in general one of the most striking symptoms of the profound change which has taken place in the mood of the whole nation. It is generally known that Moscow is more petty-bourgeois than Petrograd. It is a fact frequently corroborated and indisputable that the Moscow

[3] The reference is to what an officer, Dubasov, said at a meeting of the Petrograd Soviet on September 21 (October 4), 1917. He had just returned from the front and declared: "Whatever you may say over here, the soldiers will not fight."

proletariat has an incomparably greater number of connections with the countryside, that it has greater sympathy for the peasant and is closer to the sentiments of the peasant.

In Moscow the vote cast for the Socialist-Revolutionaries and the Mensheviks nevertheless dropped from 70 per cent in June to 18 per cent. There can be no doubt that the petty bourgeoisie and the people have turned away from the coalition. The Cadets have increased their strength from 17 to 30 per cent, but they remain a minority, a hopeless minority, despite the fact that they have obviously been joined by the "Right" Socialist-Revolutionaries, and the "Right" Mensheviks. *Russkiye Vedomosti*[4] states that the *absolute* number of votes cast for the Cadets fell from *67,000 to 62,000*. Only the votes cast for the Bolsheviks increased—from 34,000 to 82,000. They received 47 per cent of the total vote. There can be no shadow of doubt that we, together with the Left Socialist-Revolutionaries, now have a majority in the Soviets, in the army, and *in the country*.

Among the symptoms that have not only a symptomatic, but also a very real significance is the fact that the armies of railway and postal employees, who are of immense importance from the general economic, political and military point of view, continue to be in sharp conflict with the government,[5]even the Menshevik defencists are

[4] *Russkiye Vedomosti* (Russian Recorder)—a daily published in Moscow from 1863, expressing the views of moderate liberal intellectuals. From 1905 the paper was an organ of the Right wing of the Cadet Party. In 1918, it was closed down at the same time as other counter-revolutionary newspapers.

[5] The reference is to the nation-wide strike of railwaymen for higher wages. It started on the night of September 23 (October 6), 1917, and threw the Provisional Government into a panic. The bourgeois press attacked the striking railwaymen.

The strike was discussed by the Central Committee of the R.S.D.L.P.(B.) on September 24 (October 7), 1917. In an appeal, "Let's Help the Railwaymen", which was published in *Rabochy Put* (The Workers' Path), the Central Committee exposed the counter-revolutionary policy of the Provisional Government and called on the proletariat to express full sympathy for the railwaymen, protect them from the provocative attacks of the counter-revolutionaries and do everything to prevent their strike from being isolated and defeated. The strike ended on the night of September 26 (October 9), 1917, when the Provisional Government satisfied some of the railwaymen's demands.

dissatisfied with "their" Minister, Nikitin, and the official Socialist-Revolutionaries call Kerensky and Co. "Stolypins". Is it not clear that if such "support" of the government by the Mensheviks and Socialist-Revolutionaries has any value at all it can be only a negative value?

IV

. . .

V

Yes, the leaders of the Central Executive Committee are pursuing the correct tactics of defending the bourgeoisie and the landowners. And there is not the slightest doubt that if the Bolsheviks allowed themselves to be caught in the trap of constitutional illusions, "faith" in the Congress of Soviets and in the convocation of the Constituent Assembly, "waiting" for the Congress of Soviets, and so forth—these Bolsheviks would most certainly be *miserable traitors* to the proletarian cause.

They would be traitors to the cause, for by their conduct they would be betraying the German revolutionary workers who have started a revolt in the navy. To "wait" for the Congress of Soviets and so forth under such circumstances would be a *betrayal of internationalism*, a betrayal of the cause of the world socialist revolution.

For internationalism consists of deeds and not phrases, not expressions of solidarity, not resolutions.

The Bolsheviks would be traitors to the *peasants*, for to tolerate the suppression of the peasant revolt by a government which *even Dyelo Naroda* compares with the Stolypin government would be to *ruin* the whole revolution, to ruin it for good. An outcry is raised about anarchy and about the increasing indifference of the people, but what else can the people be but indifferent to the elections, when the peasants have been *driven to revolt* while the so-called "revolutionary democrats" are patiently tolerating its suppression by military force!

The Bolsheviks would be traitors to democracy and to freedom, for to tolerate the suppression of the peasant revolt at such a moment would *mean* allowing the elections to the Constituent Assembly to be fixed *in exactly the same way* as the Democratic Conference and the "Pre-parliament" were fixed, only even worse and more crudely.

The crisis has matured. The whole future of the Russian revolution is at stake. The honour of the Bolshevik Party is in question. The whole future of the international workers' revolution for socialism is at stake.

The crisis has matured . . . .

September 29, 1917

* * *

Everything to this point may be published, but what follows is *to be distributed* among the members of the *Central Committee, the Petrograd Committee, the Moscow Committee, and the Soviets.*

VI

What, then, is to be done? We must *aussprechen was ist*, "state the facts", admit the truth that there is a tendency, or an opinion, in our Central Committee and among the leaders of our Party which favours *waiting* for the Congress of Soviets, and is *opposed* to taking power immediately, is *opposed* to an immediate insurrection. That tendency, or opinion, must be *overcome*.[6]

Otherwise, the Bolsheviks will cover themselves with eternal *shame and destroy themselves* as a party.

[6] The reference is to the attitude of Kamenev, Zinoviev, Trotsky and their followers. Kamenev and Zinoviev opposed Lenin's plan for an armed uprising, declaring that the working class of Russia was incapable of carrying out a socialist revolution. They slid down to the Menshevik position of demanding a bourgeois republic. Trotsky insisted on a postponement of the uprising until the Second All-Russia Congress of Soviets, which meant frustrating the insurrection because this gave the Provisional Government a chance to concentrate its forces on the opening day of the Congress and crush the uprising.

For to miss such a moment and to "wait" for the Congress of Soviets would be *utter idiocy*, or *sheer treachery*.

It would be sheer treachery to the German workers. Surely we should not wait until their revolution *begins*. In that case even the Lieberdans would be in favour of "supporting" it. But it *cannot* begin as long as Kerensky, Kishkin and Co. are in power.

It would be sheer treachery to the peasants. To allow the peasant revolt to be suppressed when we control the Soviets of both *capitals* would be to *lose*, and *justly lose*, every ounce of the peasants' confidence. In the eyes of the peasants we would be putting ourselves on a level with the Lieberdans and other scoundrels.

To "wait" for the Congress of Soviets would be utter idiocy, for it would mean losing *weeks* at a time when weeks and even days decide *everything*. It would mean faint-heartedly *renouncing* power, for on November 1-2 it will have become impossible to take power (both politically and technically, since the Cossacks would be mobilised for the day of the insurrection so foolishly "appointed"[7]).

To "wait" for the Congress of Soviets is idiocy, for the Congress will *give nothing, and can give nothing!*

"Moral" importance? Strange indeed, to talk of the "importance" of resolutions and conversations with the Lieberdans when we know that the Soviets *support* the peasants and that the peasant revolt is *being suppressed*! We would be reducing the *Soviets* to the status of wretched debating parlours. First defeat Kerensky, then call the Congress.

The Bolsheviks are now *guaranteed* the success of the insurrection: (1) we can[8] (if we do not "wait" for the Soviet Congress) launch a *surprise* attack from three points—from Petrograd, from Moscow and from the Baltic fleet; (2) we have slogans that guarantee us support—down with the government that is suppressing the revolt of the

[7] To "convene" the Congress of Soviets for October 20 in order to decide upon "taking power"—how does that differ from foolishly "appointing" an insurrection? It is possible to take power now, whereas on October 20-29 you will not be given a chance to.—*Au.*

[8] What has the Party done to *study* the disposition of the troops, etc.? What has it done to conduct the insurrection as an "art"? Mere talk in the Central Executive Committee, and so on!—*Au.*

peasants against the landowners! (3) we have a majority *in the country*; (4) the disorganisation among the Mensheviks and the Socialist-Revolutionaries is complete; (5) we are technically in a position to take power in Moscow (where the start might even be made, so as to catch the enemy unawares); (6) we have *thousands* of armed workers and soldiers in Petrograd who could *at once* seize the Winter Palace, the General Staff building, the telephone exchange and the large printing presses. Nothing will be able to drive us out, while agitational work in the *army* will be such as to make it *impossible* to combat this government of peace, of land for the peasants, and so forth.

If we were to attack at once, suddenly, from three points, Petrograd, Moscow and the Baltic fleet, the chances are a hundred to one that we would succeed with smaller sacrifices than on July 3-5, because *the troops will not advance* against a government of peace. Even though Kerensky *already* has "loyal" cavalry, etc., in Petrograd, if we were to attack from two sides, he would be compelled to *surrender* since *we* enjoy the sympathy of the army. If with such chances as we have at present we do not take power, then all talk of transferring the power to the Soviets becomes a *lie*.

To refrain from taking power now, to "wait", to indulge in talk in the Central Executive Committee, to confine ourselves to "fighting for the organ" (of the Soviet), "fighting for the Congress", is *to doom the revolution to failure*.

In view of the fact that the Central Committee has *even left unanswered* the persistent demands I have been making for such a policy ever since the beginning of the Democratic Conference, in view of the fact that the Central Organ is *deleting* from my articles all references to such glaring errors on the part of the Bolsheviks as the shameful decision to participate in the Pre-parliament, the admission of Mensheviks to the Presidium of the Soviet, etc., etc.—I am compelled to regard this as a "subtle" hint at the unwillingness of the Central Committee even to consider this question, a subtle hint that I should keep my mouth shut, and as a proposal for me to retire.

I am compelled to *tender my resignation from the Central Committee*, which I hereby do, reserving for myself freedom to campaign among the *rank and file* of the Party and at the Party Congress.

For it is my profound conviction that if we "wait" for the Congress of Soviets and let the present moment pass, we shall *ruin* the revolution.

N. Lenin

September 29

P.S. There are a number of facts which serve to prove that *even* the Cossack troops will not go against a government of peace! And how many are there? Where are they? And will not the entire army dispatch units *for our support*?

Sections I-III and V published on October 20 (7), 1917
in the newspaper *Rabochy Put* No. 30;
section VI first published in 1924
Sections I-III published according to the
newspaper text, sections V and VI
according to the manuscript

ADVICE OF AN ONLOOKER

I am writing these lines on October 8 and have little hope that they will reach Petrograd comrades by the 9th. It is possible that they will arrive too late, since the Congress of the Northern Soviets has been fixed for October 10. Nevertheless, I shall try to give my "Advice of an Onlooker" in the event that the probable action of the workers and soldiers of Petrograd and of the whole "region" will take place soon but has not yet taken place.

It is clear that all power must pass to the Soviets. It should be equally indisputable for every Bolshevik that proletarian revolutionary power (or Bolshevik power—which is now one and the same thing) is assured of the utmost sympathy and unreserved support of all the working and exploited people all over the world in general, in the belligerent countries in particular, and among the Russian peasants especially. There is no need to dwell on these all too well known and long established truths.

What must be dealt with is something that is probably not quite clear to all comrades, namely, that in practice the transfer of power to the Soviets now means armed uprising. This would seem obvious, but not everyone has or is giving thought to the point. To repudiate armed uprising now would mean to repudiate the key slogan of Bolshevism (All Power to the Soviets) and proletarian revolutionary internationalism in general.

But armed uprising is a *special* form of political struggle, one subject to special laws to which attentive thought must be given. Karl Marx expressed this truth with remarkable clarity when he wrote that "*insurrection is an art quite as much as war*".

Of the principal rules of this art, Marx noted the following:

(1) *Never play* with insurrection, but when beginning it realise firmly that you must *go all the way.*

(2) Concentrate a *great superiority of forces* at the decisive point and at the decisive moment, otherwise the enemy, who has the advantage of better preparation and organisation, will destroy the insurgents.

(3) Once the insurrection has begun, you must act with the greatest *determination*, and by all means, without fail, take the *offensive*. "The defensive is the death of every armed rising."

(4) You must try to take the enemy by surprise and seize the moment when his forces are scattered.

(5) You must strive for *daily* successes, however small (one might say hourly, if it is the case of one town), and at all costs retain "*moral superiority*".

Marx summed up the lessons of all revolutions in respect to armed uprising in the words of "Danton, the greatest master of revolutionary policy yet known: *de l'audace, de l'audace, encore de l'audace*".[1]

Applied to Russia and to October 1917, this means: a simultaneous offensive on Petrograd, as sudden and as rapid as possible, which must without fail be carried out from within and from without, from the working-class quarters and from Finland, from Revel and from Kronstadt, an offensive of the *entire* navy, the concentration of a *gigantic superiority* of forces over the 15,000 or 20,000 (perhaps more) of our "bourgeois guard" (the officers' schools), our "Vendée troops" (part of the Cossacks), etc.

Our *three* main forces—the fleet, the workers, and the army units—must be so combined as to occupy without fail and to hold *at any cost*: (a) the telephone exchange; (b) the telegraph office; (c) the railway stations; (d) and above all, the bridges.

The *most determined* elements (our "shock forces" and *young workers*, as well as the best of the sailors) must be formed into small detachments to occupy all the more important points and to *take part* everywhere in all important operations, for example:

> to encircle and cut off Petrograd; to seize it by a combined attack of the sailors, the workers, and the troops—a task which requires *art and triple audacity*;

[1] See Engels's *Revolution and Counter-Revolution in Germany* which was published in installments in the *New York Daily Tribune* in 1851 and 1852. It bore Marx's signature, who had intended to write the work but was too busy with his economic studies and asked Engels to do it. Engels consulted Marx on various points and submitted the articles for his perusal before dispatching them to the paper. The fact that the work was written by Engels came out later with the publication of their correspondence.

to form detachments from the best workers, armed with rifles and bombs, for the purpose of attacking and surrounding the enemy's "centres" (the officers' schools, the telegraph office, the telephone exchange, etc.). Their watchword must be: "*Better die to a man than let the enemy pass!*"

Let us hope that if action is decided on, the leaders will successfully apply the great precepts of Danton and Marx.

The success of both the Russian and the world revolution depends on two or three days' fighting.

Signed: *An Onlooker*
Written on October 8 (21), 1917
First Published on November 7, 1920
in the newspaper *Pravda* No. 250
Published according to the *Pravda* text

LETTER TO CENTRAL COMMITTEE MEMBERS[1]

Comrades,

I am writing these lines on the evening of the 24th. The situation is critical in the extreme. In fact it is now absolutely clear that to delay the uprising would be fatal.

With all my might I urge comrades to realise that everything now hangs by a thread; that we are confronted by problems which are not to be solved by conferences or congresses (even congresses of Soviets), but exclusively by peoples, by the masses, by the struggle of the armed people.

The bourgeois onslaught of the Kornilovites and the removal of Verkhovsky[2] show that we must not wait. We must at all costs, this very evening, this very night, arrest the government, having first disarmed the officer cadets (defeating them, if they resist), and so on.

We must not wait! We may lose everything!

The value of the immediate seizure of power will be the defence of the *people* (not of the congress, but of the people, the army and the peasants in the first place) from the Kornilovite government, which has driven out Verkhovsky and has hatched a second Kornilov plot.

Who must take power?

That is not important at present. Let the Revolutionary Military Committee do it, or "some other institution" which will declare that it will relinquish power only to the true representatives of the interests of the people, the interests of the army (the immediate proposal of peace), the interests of the peasants (the land to be taken immediately and private property abolished), the interests of the starving.

All districts, all regiments, all forces must be mobilised at once and must immediately send their delegations to the Revolutionary

[1] Written on the night of October 24 (November 6). That same day Lenin secretly arrived at Smolny and took over the leadership of the uprising.

[2] *Verkhovsky, A. I.* (1886-1941)—Minister of War in the last bourgeois Provisional Government. On October 19 (November 1), 1917, he resigned over the Pre-parliament's rejection of his proposal for demobilising a considerable part of the army, and other measures.

Military Committee[3] and to the Central Committee of the Bolsheviks with the insistent demand that under no circumstances should power be left in the hands of Kerensky and Co. until the 25th—not under any circumstances; the matter must be decided without fail this very evening, or this very night.

History will not forgive revolutionaries for procrastinating when they could be victorious today (and they certainly will be victorious today), while they risk losing much tomorrow, in fact, they risk losing everything.

If we seize power today, we seize it not in opposition to the Soviets but on their behalf.

The seizure of power is the business of the uprising; its political purpose will become clear after the seizure.

It would be a disaster, or a sheer formality, to await the wavering vote of October 25. The people have the right and are in duty bound to decide such questions not by a vote, but by force; in critical moments of revolution, the people have the right and are in duty bound to give directions to their representatives, even their best representatives, and not to wait for them.

This is proved by the history of all revolutions; and it would be an infinite crime on the part of the revolutionaries were they to let the chance slip, knowing that the *salvation of the revolution*, the offer of

[3] *The Revolutionary Military Committee of the Petrograd Soviet* was set up on October 12 (25), 1917, on the instructions from the Central Committee of the Bolshevik Party. Its members were drawn from the Central Committee, the Petersburg Committee, the Petrograd Soviet, factory committees, trade unions and military organisations. It operated under the leadership of the Central Committee and was closely bound up with the Bolshevik Military Organisation in forming the Red Guard detachments and arming the workers. Its main task was to prepare the armed uprising in accordance with the Central Committee directives. It carried on diverse activity in organising the combat forces for victory in the October Revolution. Its leading core, the Revolutionary Military Centre, was formed by the Central Committee on October 16 (29), 1917, and received daily directions from Lenin. After the victory of the October Revolution and the election of the Soviet Government at the Second Congress of Soviets, the main task of the Revolutionary Military Committee was to fight the counter-revolution and safeguard the revolutionary order. It handed over its functions to various People's Commissariats as they arose. It was dissolved on December 5 (18), 1917.

peace, the salvation of Petrograd, salvation from famine, the transfer of the land to the peasants depend upon them.

The government is tottering. It must be *given the death blow* at all costs.

To delay action is fatal.

Written on October 24 (November 6), 1917
First published in 1924
Published according to a typewritten copy

LETTER TO COMRADES

Comrades,

We are living in a time that is so critical, events are moving at such incredible speed that a publicist, placed by the will of fate somewhat aside from the mainstream of history, constantly runs the risk either of being late or proving uninformed, especially if some time elapses before his writings appear in print. Although I fully realise this, I must nevertheless address this letter to the Bolsheviks, even at the risk of its not being published at all, for the vacillations against which I deem it my duty to warn in the most decisive manner are of an unprecedented nature and may have a disastrous effect on the Party, the movement of the international proletariat, and the revolution. As for the danger of being too late, I will prevent it by indicating the nature and date of the information I possess.

It was not until Monday morning, October 16, that I saw a comrade who had on the previous day participated in a very important Bolshevik gathering in Petrograd, and who informed me in detail of the discussion.[1] The subject of discussion was that same question of the uprising discussed by the Sunday papers of all political trends. The gathering represented all that is most influential in all branches of Bolshevik work in the capital. Only a most insignificant minority of the gathering, namely, all in all two comrades, took a negative stand. The arguments which those comrades advanced are so weak, they are a manifestation of such an astounding confusion, timidity, and collapse of all the fundamental ideas of Bolshevism and proletarian revolutionary internationalism that it is not easy to discover an explanation for such shameful vacillations. The fact, however, remains, and since the revolutionary party has no right to tolerate vacillations on such a serious question, and since this pair of comrades, who have

[1] A reference to the enlarged Central Committee meeting on October 16 (29), 1917. Lenin remained in hiding in Petrograd and changed the date of the meeting to October 15 (28) in order to conceal his presence at the meeting; for reasons of secrecy he referred to a comrade who had allegedly informed him of the meeting.

scattered their principles to the winds, might cause some confusion, it is necessary to analyse their arguments, to expose their vacillations, and to show how shameful they are. The following lines are an attempt to do this.

* * *

> "We have no majority among the people, and without this condition the uprising is hopeless . . . ."

People who can say this are either distorters of the truth or pedants who want an advance guarantee that throughout the whole country the Bolshevik Party has received exactly one-half of the votes plus one, this they want at all events, without taking the least account of the real circumstances of the revolution. History has never given such a guarantee, and is quite unable to give it in any revolution. To make such a demand is jeering at the audience, and is nothing but a cover to hide one's own *flight* from reality.

For reality shows us clearly that it was after the July days that the majority of the people began quickly to go over to the side of the Bolsheviks. This was demonstrated first by the August 20 elections in Petrograd, even before the Kornilov revolt, when the Bolshevik vote rose from 20 to 33 per cent in the city not including the suburbs, and then by the district council elections in Moscow in September, when the Bolshevik vote rose from 11 to 49.3 per cent (one Moscow comrade, whom I saw recently, told me that the correct figure is 51 per cent). This was proved by the new elections to the Soviets. It was proved by the fact that a majority of the peasant Soviets, their "Avksentyev" central Soviet notwithstanding, has expressed itself *against* the coalition. To be against the coalition means in *practice* to follow the Bolsheviks. Furthermore, reports from the front prove more frequently and more definitely that the soldiers are passing *en masse* over to the side or the Bolsheviks with ever greater determination, in spite of the malicious slanders and attacks by the Socialist-Revolutionary and Menshevik leaders, officers, deputies, etc., etc.

Last, but not least, the most outstanding fact of present-day

Russian life is *the revolt of the peasantry*. This shows objectively, not by words but by deeds, that the people are going over to the side of the Bolsheviks. But the fact remains, notwithstanding the lies of the bourgeois press and its miserable yes-men of the "vacillating" *Novaya Zhizn* crowd, who shout about riots and anarchy. The peasant movement in Tambov Gubernia[2] was an uprising both in the physical and political sense, an uprising that has yielded such splendid political results as, in the first place, agreement to transfer the land to the peasants. It is not for nothing that the Socialist-Revolutionary rabble, including *Dyelo Naroda,* who are frightened by the uprising, now *scream* about the need to transfer the land to the peasants. Here is a *practical* demonstration of the correctness of Bolshevism and of its success. It proved to be impossible to "teach" the Bonapartists and their lackeys in the Pre-parliament otherwise than by an uprising.

This is a fact and facts are stubborn things. And such a factual "argument" *in favour* of an uprising is stronger than thousands of "pessimistic" evasions on the part of confused and frightened politicians.

If the peasant uprising were not an event of nation-wide political import, the Socialist-Revolutionary lackeys from the Pre-parliament would not be shouting about the need to hand over the land to the peasants.

Another splendid political and revolutionary consequence of the peasant uprising, as already noted in *Rabochy Put*, is the delivery of grain to the railway stations in Tambov Gubernia. Here is another "argument" for you, confused gentlemen, an argument in favour of the

[2] The peasant movement in Tambov Gubernia in September 1917 assumed great proportions: the peasants seized tracts of landed estates, destroyed and burned landowners' mansions and confiscated grain stocks. In September, 82 landowners' estates were destroyed in 68 gubernias and regions, including 32 in Tambov Gubernia. Altogether there is a record of 166 peasant manifestations in the gubernia, especially in Kozlov Uyezd. The frightened landowners took their grain to the railway stations in an effort to sell it, so that the railway junctures were literally swamped with grain. The commanding officer of the Moscow Military District sent military units to Tambov Gubernia to crush the peasant uprising, and imposed martial law, but the peasants' revolutionary struggle for land continued to grow in scope.

uprising as the only means to save the country from the famine that is knocking at our door and from a crisis of unheard-of dimensions. While the Socialist-Revolutionary and Menshevik betrayers of the people are grumbling, threatening, writing resolutions, promising to feed the hungry by convening the Constituent Assembly, the people are beginning to solve the bread problem *Bolshevik-fashion*, *by rebelling* against the landowners, capitalists, and speculators.

Even the *bourgeois* press, even *Russkaya Volya*, was compelled to admit the wonderful results of *such* a solution (the only real solution) of the bread problem, by publishing information to the effect that the railway stations in Tambov Gubernia were swamped with grain . . . . *And this after the peasants had revolted!*

To doubt now that the majority of the people are following and will follow the Bolsheviks is shameful vacillation and in practice is the abandoning of *all* the principles of proletarian revolutionism, the complete renunciation of Bolshevism.

* * *

> "We are not strong enough to seize power, and the bourgeoisie is not strong enough to hinder the convening of the Constituent Assembly."

The first part of this argument is a simple paraphrase of the preceding one. It does not gain in strength or power of conviction, when the confusion of its authors and their fear of the bourgeoisie are expressed in terms of pessimism in respect of the workers and optimism in respect of the bourgeoisie. If the officer cadets and the Cossacks say that they will fight against the Bolsheviks to the last drop of blood, this deserves full credence; if, however, the workers and soldiers at hundreds of meetings express full confidence in the Bolsheviks and affirm their readiness to defend the transfer of power to the Soviets, then it is "timely" to recall that voting is one thing and fighting another!

If you argue like that, of course, you "refute" the possibility of an uprising. But, we may ask, in what way does this peculiarly orientated "pessimism" with its peculiar urge differ from a political shift to the side of the bourgeoisie?

Look at the facts. Remember the Bolshevik declarations, repeated thousands of times and now "forgotten" by our pessimists. We have said thousands of times that the Soviets of Workers' and Soldiers' Deputies are a force, that they are the vanguard of the revolution, that they *can* take power. Thousands of times have we upbraided the Mensheviks and Socialist-Revolutionaries for phrase-mongering about the "plenipotentiary organs of democracy" accompanied by *fear* to transfer power to the Soviets.

And what has the Kornilov revolt proved? It has proved that the Soviets are a real force.

And, now, after this has been proved by experience, by facts, we are expected to repudiate Bolshevism, deny ourselves, and say that we are not strong enough (although the Soviets of Petrograd and Moscow and a majority of the provincial Soviets are on the side of the Bolsheviks)! Are these not shameful vacillations? As a matter of fact, our "pessimists" are abandoning the slogan of "All Power to the Soviets", though they *are afraid* to admit it.

How can it be proved that the bourgeoisie are not strong enough to hinder the calling of the Constituent Assembly?

If the Soviets *have not the strength* to overthrow the bourgeoisie, this *means* the latter are strong enough to prevent the convocation of the Constituent Assembly, for there is nobody else to stop them. To trust the promises of Kerensky and Co., to trust the resolutions of the servile Pre-parliament—is this worthy of a member of a proletarian party and a revolutionary?

Not only has the bourgeoisie *strength enough* to hinder the convocation of the Constituent Assembly if the present government is not overthrown, but it can also achieve this result *indirectly* by surrendering Petrograd to the Germans, laying open the front, increasing lockouts, and sabotaging deliveries of foodstuffs. It has been proved by facts that the bourgeoisie have already been partly doing this, which means that they are capable of doing it *to the full extent*, if the workers and soldiers do not overthrow them.

"The Soviets must be a revolver pointed at the head of the government with the demand to convene the Constituent Assembly and stop all Kornilovite plots."

This is how far one of the two sad pessimists has gone.

He had to go that far, for to reject the uprising is *the same* as rejecting the slogan "All Power to the Soviets".

Of course, a slogan is "not sacred"; we all agree to that. But then why has *no one* raised the question of changing this slogan (in the same way as I raised the question after the July days[3])? Why be *afraid* to say it openly, when the Party, since September, has been discussing the question of the uprising, which is now *the only way* to realise the slogan "All Power to the Soviets".

There is no way for our sad pessimists to turn. A renunciation of the uprising is a renunciation of the transfer of power to the Soviets and implies a "transfer" of all hopes and expectations to the kind bourgeoisie, which has "promised" to convoke the Constituent Assembly.

Is it so difficult to understand that once *power* is in the hands of the Soviets, the Constituent Assembly and its success are *guaranteed*? The Bolsheviks have said so thousands of times and no one has ever attempted to refute it. Everybody has recognised this "combined type", but to smuggle in a *renunciation* of the transfer of power to the Soviets under cover of the words "combined type", to smuggle it in *secretly* while *fearing* to renounce our slogan openly is a matter for wonder. Is there any parliamentary term to describe it?

Someone has very pointedly retorted to our pessimist: "Is it a revolver with no cartridges?" If so, it means going over directly to the Lieberdans, who have declared the Soviets a "revolver" thousands of times and have deceived the people thousands of times. For *while they were in control* the Soviets proved to be worthless.

If, however, it is to be a revolver "with cartridges", this cannot mean anything but *technical* preparation for an uprising; the cartridges

[3] See *LCW*, Vol. 25, 1980, pp. 185-92.

have to be procured, the revolver has to be loaded—and cartridges alone will not be enough.

Either go over to the side of the Lieberdans and *openly* renounce the slogan "All Power to the Soviets", or start the uprising.

There is no middle course.

* * *

> "The bourgeoisie cannot surrender Petrograd to the Germans, although Rodzyanko wants to, for the fighting is done not by the bourgeoisie, but by our heroic sailors."

This argument again reduces itself to the same "optimism" *in respect of the bourgeoisie* which is fatally manifested at every step by those who are pessimistic about the revolutionary forces and capabilities of the proletariat.

The fighting is done by the heroic sailors, *but* this did not prevent *two* admirals from *disappearing* before the capture of Esel!

That is a fact and facts are stubborn things. The facts prove that admirals *are capable* of treachery no less than Kornilov. It is an undisputed fact that Field Headquarters has not been reformed, and that the commanding staff is Kornilovite in composition.

If the Kornilovites (with Kerensky at their head, for he is also a Kornilovite) *want* to surrender Petrograd, they can do it in two or even in three ways.

First, they can, through an act of treachery on the part of the Kornilovite officers, open the northern land front.

Second, they can "agree" on freedom of action for the entire German navy, which is *stronger* than we are; they can agree both with the German and the British imperialists. Moreover, the admirals who have disappeared may have delivered the *plans* to the Germans *as well.*

Third, they can, by means of lockouts, and by sabotaging the delivery of food, bring our troops to *complete* desperation and impotence.

Not a single one of these three ways can be denied. The facts have proved that the bourgeois-Cossack party of Russia has already knocked at all three doors and has tried to force open each of them.

What follows? It follows that we have no right to *wait* until the bourgeoisie strangle the revolution.

Experience has proved that Rodzyanko's wishes are no trifle. Rodzyanko is a man of affairs. Rodzyanko is backed by *capital*. This is beyond dispute. Capital is tremendous strength as long as the proletariat do not have power. *For decades*, Rodzyanko has faithfully and truly carried out the policies of capital.

What follows? It follows that to vacillate on the question of an uprising as the only means to save the revolution means to sink into that cowardly credulity in the bourgeoisie which is half-Lieberdan, Socialist-Revolutionary-Menshevik and half "peasant-like" unquestioning credulity, against which the Bolsheviks have been battling most of all.

Either fold your idle arms on your empty chest, wait and swear "faith" in the Constituent Assembly until Rodzyanko and Co. have surrendered Petrograd and strangled the revolution or start an uprising. There is no middle course.

Even the convocation of the Constituent Assembly does not, in itself, change anything, for no "constituting", no voting by any arch-sovereign assembly will have any effect on the famine, or on Wilhelm. Both the convocation and the *success* of the Constituent Assembly depend upon the transfer of power to the Soviets. This old Bolshevik truth is being proved by reality ever more strikingly and ever more *cruelly*.

* * *

> "We are becoming stronger every day. We can enter the Constituent Assembly as a strong opposition; why should we stake everything? . . ."

This is the argument of a philistine who has "read" that the Constituent Assembly is being called, and who trustingly acquiesces in the most legal, most loyal, most constitutional course.

It is a pity, however, that *waiting* for the Constituent Assembly does not solve either the question of famine or the question of surrendering Petrograd. This "trifle" is forgotten by the naïve or the confused or those who have allowed themselves to be frightened.

The famine will not wait. The peasant uprising did not wait. The war will not wait. The admirals who have disappeared did not wait.

Will the famine agree to wait, because we Bolsheviks *proclaim* faith in the convocation of the Constituent Assembly? Will the admirals who have disappeared agree to wait? Will the Maklakovs and Rodzyankos agree to stop the lockouts and the sabotaging of grain deliveries, or to denounce the secret treaties with the British and the German imperialists?

This is what the arguments of the heroes of "constitutional illusions" and parliamentary cretinism amount to. The living reality disappears, and what remains is only a *paper* dealing with the convocation of the Constituent Assembly; there is nothing left but to hold elections.

And blind people are still wondering why hungry people and soldiers betrayed by generals and admirals are indifferent to the elections! Oh, wiseacres!

* * *

> "Were the Kornilovites to start again, we would show them! But why should we take risks and start?"

This is extraordinarily convincing and revolutionary. History does not repeat itself, but if we turn our *backs* on it, contemplate the first Kornilov revolt and repeat: "If only the Kornilovites would start"—if we do that, what excellent revolutionary strategy it would be. How much like a waiting game it is! Maybe the Kornilovites will start again at an inopportune time. Isn't this a "weighty" argument? What kind of an earnest foundation for a proletarian policy is this?

And what if the Kornilovites of the second draft will have learned a thing or two? What if they *wait* for the hunger riots to begin, for the front to be broken through, for Petrograd to be surrendered, *before they begin*? What then?

It is proposed that we build the tactics of the proletarian party on the possibility of the Kornilovites' repeating one of their old errors!

Let us forget all that was being and *has been demonstrated* by the Bolsheviks a hundred times, all that the six months' history of our revolution has proved, namely, that there is no way out, that there is no objective way out and can be none *except* a dictatorship of the Kornilovites or a dictatorship of the proletariat. Let us forget this, let us renounce all this and wait! Wait for what? Wait for a miracle, for the tempestuous and catastrophic course of events from April 20 to August 29 to be succeeded (due to the prolongation of the war and the spread of famine) by a peaceful, quiet, smooth, legal convocation of the Constituent Assembly and by a fulfilment of its most lawful decisions. Here you have the "Marxist" tactics! Wait, ye hungry! Kerensky has promised to convene the Constituent Assembly.

* * *

> "There is really nothing in the international situation that makes it obligatory for us to act immediately, we would be more likely to damage the cause of a socialist revolution in the West, if we were to allow ourselves to be shot . . . ."

This argument is truly magnificent: Scheidemann "himself", Renaudel[4] "himself" would not be able to "manipulate" more cleverly the workers' sympathies for the international socialist revolution!

Just think of it: under devilishly difficult conditions, having but *one* Liebknecht (and he in prison) with no newspapers, with no freedom of assembly, with no Soviets, with *all* classes of the population, including every well-to-do peasant, incredibly hostile to the idea of internationalism, with the imperialist big, middle, and petty bourgeoisie splendidly organised—the Germans, i.e., the German

[4] *Scheidemann, Philip* (1865-1939)—a leader of the extreme Right-wing opportunist section of German Social-Democracy, and an organiser of the bloody suppression of the German working-class movement in 1918-21.

Renaudel, Pierre (1871-1935)—a reformist leader of the French Socialist Party.

revolutionary internationalists, the German workers dressed in sailors' jackets, started a mutiny in the navy with one chance in a hundred of winning.

But we, with dozens of papers at our disposal, freedom of assembly, a *majority* in the Soviets, we, the best situated proletarian internationalists in the world, should refuse to support the German revolutionaries by our uprising. We ought to reason like the Scheidemanns and Renaudels, that it is most prudent not to revolt, for if we are shot, then the world will lose such excellent, reasonable, ideal internationalists!

Let us prove how reasonable we are. Let us pass a resolution of sympathy with the *German insurrectionists*, and let us renounce the *insurrection* in Russia. This would be genuine, reasonable internationalism. Imagine how fast world internationalism would blossom forth, if the same wise policy were to triumph *everywhere*!

The war has fatigued and tormented the workers of all countries to the utmost. Outbursts are becoming frequent in Italy, Germany and Austria. We *alone* have Soviets of Workers' and Soldiers' Deputies. Let us then *keep on waiting*. Let us betray the German internationalists as we are betraying the Russian peasants, who, not by words but by deeds, by their uprising against the landowners, appeal to us to rise against Kerensky's government . . . .

Let the clouds of the imperialist conspiracy of the capitalists of all countries who are ready to strangle the Russian revolution gather—we shall wait patiently until we are strangled *by the ruble*! Instead of attacking the conspirators and breaking their ranks by a victory of the Soviets of Workers' and Soldiers' Deputies, let us wait for the Constituent Assembly, where all international plots will be vanquished by *voting*, provided Kerensky and Rodzyanko conscientiously convene the Constituent Assembly. Have we any right to doubt the honesty of Kerensky and Rodzyanko?

* * *

"But 'everyone' is against us! We are isolated; the Central Executive

> Committee, the Menshevik internationalists, the *Novaya Zhizn* people, and the Left Socialist-Revolutionaries have been issuing and will continue to issue appeals against us!"

A crushing argument. Up to now we have been mercilessly scourging the vacillators for their vacillations. *By so doing*, we have won the sympathies of the people. *By so doing*, we have won over the Soviets, without which the uprising could not be safe, quick, and sure. Now let us use the Soviets which we have won over in order *to move into the camp of the vacillators*. What a splendid career for Bolshevism!

The whole essence of the policy of the Lieberdans and Chernovs, and also of the Left Socialist-Revolutionaries and Mensheviks, consists in *vacillations*. The Left Socialist- Revolutionaries and Menshevik internationalists have *tremendous* political importance as an *indication* of the fact that the *masses are moving to the left*. Two such facts as the passing of some 40 per cent of both Mensheviks and Socialist-Revolutionaries into the camp of the Left, on the one hand, and the peasant uprising, on the other, are clearly and obviously interconnected.

But it is the very character of this connection that reveals the abysmal spinelessness of those who have now undertaken to whimper over the fact that the Central Executive Committee, which has rotted away, or the vacillating Left Socialist-Revolutionaries and Co., have come out against us. For *these* vacillations of the petty-bourgeois leaders—the Martovs, Kamkovs, Sukhanovs and Co.—have to be compared to the *uprising* of the peasants. Here is a *realistic* political comparison. With whom shall we go? Should it be with the vacillating handfuls of Petrograd leaders, who have expressed *indirectly* the *leftward swing* of the masses, but who, at every political turn, have shamefully whimpered, vacillated, run to ask forgiveness of the Lieberdans, Avksentyevs and Co., *or with those masses that have moved to the left*?

Thus, and only thus, can the question be presented.

Because the peasant uprising has been betrayed by the Martovs, Kamkovs, and Sukhanovs, we, the workers' party of revolutionary internationalists, are asked to betray it, too. This is what the policy of blaming the Left Socialist-Revolutionaries and Menshevik internationalists reduces itself to.

But we have said that to help the vacillating, we must stop vacillating ourselves. Have those "nice" Left petty-bourgeois democrats not "vacillated" in favour of the coalition? In the long run we succeeded in making them follow us because we ourselves did not vacillate. Events have shown we are right.

These gentlemen by their vacillations have always held back the revolution. We alone have saved it. Shall we now give up, when the famine is knocking at the gates of Petrograd and Rodzyanko and Co. are preparing to surrender the city?!

* * *

> "But we have not even firm connections with the railwaymen and the postal employees. Their official representatives are the Plansons.[5] And can we win without the post office and without railways?"

Yes, yes, the Plansons here, the Lieberdans there. What confidence have the *masses* shown them? Have we not always shown that those leaders betrayed the *masses*? Did the masses not turn away from those leaders *towards us*, both at the elections in Moscow and at the elections to the Soviets? Or perhaps the mass of railway and postal employees are not starving! Or do not strike against Kerensky and Co.?

"Did we have connections with these unions before February 28?" one comrade asked a pessimist. The latter replied by pointing out that the two revolutions could not be compared. But this reply only *strengthens* the position of the one who asked the question. For it is the Bolsheviks who have spoken thousands of times about prolonged preparation for the *proletarian* revolution *against the bourgeoisie* (and they have not spoken about it in order to forget their words when the decisive moment is at hand). The political and economic life of

[5] *Planson, A. A.*—a Popular Socialist, and member of the Central Executive Committee (First Convocation). A leader of Vikzhel—the All-Russia Executive Committee of the Railwaymen's Trade Union, an organisation run by the compromisers.

the unions of postal and telegraph employees and railwaymen is characterised by the very *separation* of the proletarian elements of the masses from the petty-bourgeois and bourgeois upper layer. It is not absolutely necessary to secure "connections" with one or the other union beforehand; what matters is that only a victory of a proletarian and peasant uprising *can* satisfy the *masses* both of the army of railwaymen and of postal and telegraph employees.

* * *

> "There is only enough bread in Petrograd for two or three days. Can we give bread to the insurrectionists?"

This is one of a thousand sceptical remarks (the sceptics can *always* "doubt" and cannot be refuted by anything but experience), one of those remarks that put the blame on the wrong shoulders.

It is Rodzyanko and Co., it is the bourgeoisie that are preparing the famine and speculating on strangling the revolution by famine. There is no escaping the famine and *there can be none* except by an uprising of the peasants against the landowners in the countryside and by a victory of the workers over the capitalists in the cities and Petrograd and Moscow. There is *no other way* to get grain from the rich, or to transport it despite their sabotage, or to break the resistance of the corrupt employees and the capitalist profiteers, or to establish strict accounting. The history of the supply organisations and of the food difficulties of the "democracy" with its millions of *complaints* against the sabotage of the capitalists, with its *whimpering* and *supplication* is proof of this.

There is no power on earth apart from the power of a victorious proletarian revolution that would advance from complaints and begging and tears to *revolutionary action*. And the longer the proletarian revolution is delayed, the longer it is put off by events or by the vacillations of the wavering and confused, the more victims it will claim and the more difficult it will be to *organise* the transportation and distribution of food.

"In insurrection delay is fatal" this is our answer to those having the sad "courage" to look at the growing economic ruin, at the approaching famine, and still *dissuade* the workers from the uprising (*that is, persuade them to wait and place confidence in the bourgeoisie for some further time*).

* * *

> "There is not yet any danger at the front either. Even if the soldiers conclude an armistice themselves, it is still not a calamity."

But the soldiers will not conclude an armistice. For this state power is necessary and that cannot be obtained without an uprising. The soldiers will simply *desert*. Reports from the front tell that. We must not wait because of the risk of aiding collusion between Rodzyanko and Wilhelm and the risk of *complete* economic ruin, with the soldiers deserting in masses, once they (*being already close to desperation*) sink into absolute despair and leave everything to the mercy of fate.

* * *

> "But if we take power, and obtain neither an armistice nor a democratic peace, the soldiers may not be willing to fight a revolutionary war. What then?"

An argument which brings to mind the saying: one fool can ask ten times more questions than ten wise men can answer.

We have never denied the difficulties of *those in power* during an imperialist war. Nevertheless, we have always *preached* the dictatorship of the proletariat and the poor peasantry. Shall we renounce this, when the moment to act has arrived?

We have always said that the dictatorship of the proletariat in one country creates gigantic changes in the international situation, in the economic life of the country, in the condition of the army and in its mood—shall we now "forget" all this, and allow ourselves to be frightened by the "difficulties" of the revolution?

* * *

> "As everybody reports, the masses are not in a mood that would drive them into the streets. Among the signs justifying pessimism may be mentioned the greatly increasing circulation of the pogromist and Black-Hundred press."

When people allow themselves to be frightened by the bourgeoisie, all objects and phenomena naturally appear yellow to them. First, they substitute an impressionist, intellectualist criterion for the Marxist criterion of the movement; they *substitute* subjective impressions of moods *for* a political analysis of the development of the class struggle and of the course of events in the entire country against the entire international background. They "conveniently" forget, of course, that a firm party line, its unyielding resolve, is *also* a mood-creating *factor*, particularly at the sharpest revolutionary moments. It is sometimes very "convenient" for people to forget that the responsible leaders, by their vacillations and by their readiness to burn their yesterday's idols, cause the most unbecoming vacillations in the mood of certain strata of the masses.

Secondly—and this is at present the main thing—in speaking about the mood of the masses, the spineless people forget to add:

> that "everybody" reports it as a tense and expectant mood;
> that "everybody" agrees that, called upon by the Soviets for the defence of the Soviets, the workers will rise to a man;
> that "everybody" agrees that the workers are greatly dissatisfied with the indecision of the centres concerning the "last decisive struggle", the inevitability of which they clearly recognise;
> that "everybody" unanimously characterises the mood of the broadest masses as close to desperation and points to the anarchy developing therefrom;
> that "everybody" also recognises that there is among the class-conscious workers a definite unwillingness to go out into the streets *only* for demonstrations, *only* for partial struggles, since a general and not a partial struggle is in the air, while the hopelessness of individual

strikes, demonstrations and acts to influence the authorities has been seen and is fully realised.

And so forth.

If we approach this characterisation of the mass mood from the point of view of the entire development of the class and political struggle and of the entire course of events during the six months of our revolution, it will become clear to us how people frightened by the bourgeoisie are distorting the question. Things are not as they were before April 20-21, June 9, July 3, for then it was a matter of *spontaneous excitement* which we, as a party, either failed to comprehend (April 20) or held back and shaped into a peaceful demonstration (June 9 and July 3), for we knew very well at that time that the Soviets were *not yet* ours, that the peasants *still* trusted the Lieberdan-Chernov and not the Bolshevik course (uprising), that consequently we could not have the majority of the people behind us, and that consequently the uprising would be premature.

At that time the majority of the class-conscious workers did *not* raise the question of the last decisive struggle at all; not one of all our Party units would have raised it at that time. As for the unenlightened and very broad masses, there was neither a concerted effort nor the resolve born out of despair; there was only a spontaneous *excitement* with the naïve hope of "influencing" Kerensky and the bourgeoisie by "action", by a demonstration pure and simple.

What is needed for an uprising is not this, but, on the one hand, a conscious, firm and unswerving resolve on the part of the class-conscious elements to fight to the end; and on the other, a mood of despair among the broad masses who *feel* that nothing can now be saved by half-measures; that you cannot "influence" anybody; that the hungry will "smash everything, destroy everything, even anarchically", *if* the Bolsheviks are not able to lead them in a decisive battle.

The development of the revolution has in practice brought *both* the workers *and* the peasantry to precisely this combination of a tense mood resulting from experience among the class-conscious and a mood of hatred towards those using the lockout weapon and the capitalists that is close to despair among the broadest masses.

We can also understand the "success" on this very soil of the scoundrels of the reactionary press who imitate Bolshevism. The malicious glee of the reactionaries at the approach of a decisive battle between the bourgeoisie and the proletariat has been observed in all revolutions without exception; it has always been so, and it is absolutely unavoidable. And if you allow yourselves to be frightened by *this* circumstance, then you have to renounce not only the uprising but the proletarian revolution in general. For in a capitalist society this revolution *cannot* mature *without* being accompanied by malicious glee on the part of the reactionaries and by hopes that they would be able to feather their nest in this way.

The class-conscious workers know perfectly well that the Black Hundreds work hand in hand with the bourgeoisie, and that a decisive victory of the workers (in which the petty bourgeoisie do not believe, which the capitalists are afraid of, which the Black Hundreds sometimes wish for out of sheer malice, convinced as they are that the Bolsheviks cannot retain power)—that this victory will completely *crush* the Black Hundreds, that the Bolsheviks *will be able* to retain power firmly and to the greatest advantage of all humanity tortured and tormented by the war.

Indeed, is there anybody in his senses who can doubt that the *Rodzyankos* and Suvorins are acting in concert, that the roles have been distributed among them?

Has it not been proved by facts that Kerensky acts on Rodzyanko's orders, while the State Printing Press of the Russian Republic (don't laugh!) prints the Black-Hundred speeches of reactionaries in the "Duma" at the expense of the state. Has not this fact been exposed *even* by the lackeys from *Dyelo Naroda*, who serve "their own mannikin"? Has not the experience of *all* elections proved that the Cadet lists were fully supported by *Novoye Vremya*, which is a venal paper controlled by the "interests" of the tsarist landowners?[6]

[6] *Novoye Vremya* (New Times)—a daily published in Petersburg from 1868 to 1917, by various publishers. It changed political colours a number of times, and from 1905 became the organ of the Black Hundreds. After the bourgeois-democratic revolution of February 1917, it took a counter-revolutionary attitude and conducted a rabid campaign against the Bolsheviks. Closed down by the Revolutionary Military Committee of the Petrograd Soviet on

Did we not read yesterday that commercial and industrial capitalists (non-partisan capitalists, of course; oh, non-partisan capitalists, to be sure, for the Vikhlayevs and Rakitnikovs, the Gvozdyovs and Nikitins are not in coalition with the Cadets—God forbid—but with *non-partisan* commercial and industrial circles!) have donated the goodly sum of 300,000 rubles to the Cadets?

The whole Black-Hundred press, if we look at things from a class and not a sentimental point of view, is a *branch* of the firm "Ryabushinsky, Milyukov, and Co.". Capitalists buy, on the one hand, the Milyukovs, Zaslavskys, Potresovs, and so on; on the other, the Black Hundreds.

The *victory of the proletariat* is the only means of putting an end to this most hideous poisoning of the people by the cheap Black-Hundred venom.

Is it any wonder that the crowd, tired out and made wretched by hunger and the prolongation of the war, clutches at the Black-Hundred poison? Can one imagine a capitalist society on the eve of collapse in which the oppressed masses are *not* desperate? Is there any doubt that the desperation of the masses, a large part of whom are still ignorant, *will* express itself in the increased consumption of all sorts of poison?

Those who, in arguing about the mood of the masses, blame the masses for their own personal spinelessness, are in a hopeless position. The masses are divided into those who are consciously biding their time and those who unconsciously are ready to sink into despair; but the masses of the oppressed and the hungry are *not* spineless.

***

> "On the other hand, the Marxist party cannot reduce the question of an uprising to that of a military conspiracy . . . ."

Marxism is an extremely profound and many-sided doctrine. It is, therefore, no wonder that *scraps* of quotations from Marx—especially when the quotations are made *inappropriately*—can always be found

....

October 26 (November 8), 1917. Lenin said it was an example of corrupt press.

among the "arguments" of those who break with Marxism. Military conspiracy is Blanquism, *if* it is organised not by a party of a definite class, *if* its organisers have not analysed the political moment in general and the international situation in particular, *if* the party has not on its side the sympathy of the majority of the people, as proved by objective facts, *if* the development of revolutionary events has not brought about a practical refutation of the conciliatory illusions of the petty bourgeoisie, *if* the majority of the Soviet-type organs of revolutionary struggle that have been recognised as authoritative or have shown themselves to be such in practice have not been won over, *if* there has not matured a sentiment in the army (if in war-time) against the government that protracts the unjust war against the will of the whole people, *if* the slogans of the uprising (like "All power to the Soviets", "Land to the peasants", or "Immediate offer of a democratic peace to all the belligerent nations, with an immediate abrogation of all secret treaties and secret diplomacy", etc.) have not become widely known and popular, *if* the advanced workers are not sure of the desperate situation of the masses and of the support of the countryside, a support proved by a serious peasant movement or by an uprising against the landowners and the government that defends the landowners, *if* the country's economic situation inspires earnest hopes for a favourable solution of the crisis by peaceable and parliamentary means.

This is probably enough.

In my pamphlet entitled: *Can the Bolsheviks Retain State Power?* (I hope it will appear in a day or two), there is a quotation from Marx which really bears upon the question of insurrection and which enumerates the features of insurrection as an "art".[7]

I am ready to wager that if we were to propose to all those chatterers in Russia who are now shouting against a military conspiracy, to open their mouths and explain the difference between the "art" of an insurrection and a military conspiracy that deserves condemnation, they would either repeat what was quoted above or would cover themselves with shame and would call forth the general ridicule of the workers. Why not try, my dear would-be Marxists! Sing us a song *against* "military conspiracy"!

[7] See *LCW*, Vol. 26, 1972, pp. 131-32.

POSTSCRIPT

The above lines had been written when I received, at eight o'clock Tuesday evening, the morning Petrograd papers; there was an article by Mr. V. Bazarov in *Novaya Zhizn*. Mr. V. Bazarov asserts that "a handwritten manifesto was distributed in the city, in which arguments were presented in the name of two eminent Bolsheviks, against immediate action".

If this is true, I beg the comrades, whom this letter cannot reach earlier than Wednesday noon, to *publish it* as quickly as possible.

I did not write it for the press; I wanted to talk to the members of our Party by letter. But we cannot remain silent when the heroes of *Novaya Zhizn*, who do not belong to the Party and who have been ridiculed by it a thousand times for their contemptible spinelessness (they voted for the Bolsheviks the day before yesterday, for the Mensheviks yesterday, and who *almost* united them at the world-famous unity congress)—when such individuals receive a *manifesto* from members of our Party in which they carry on propaganda against an uprising. We must agitate also *in favour* of an uprising. Let the anonymous individuals come right out into the light of day, and let them bear the punishment they deserve for their shameful vacillations, even if it be only the ridicule of all class-conscious workers. I have at my disposal only one hour before I send the present letter to Petrograd, and I therefore can say only a word or two about one of the "methods" of the sad heroes of the brainless *Novaya Zhizn* trend. Mr. V. Bazarov attempts to polemise against Comrade Ryazanov, who has said, and who is a thousand times correct in saying, that "all those who create in the masses a mood of despair and indifference are preparing an uprising".

The sad hero of a sad cause "rejoins" as follows:

"Have despair and indifference ever conquered?"

O contemptible fools from *Novaya Zhizn*! Do they know such examples of uprising in history, in which the masses of the oppressed classes were victorious in a desperate battle without having been reduced to despair by long sufferings and by an extreme sharpening of all sorts of crises, in which those masses had not been seized by indifference towards various lackey-like pre-parliaments, towards idle playing at revolution, towards the Lieberdans' reduction of the Soviets from organs of power and uprising to empty talking shops?

Or have the contemptible little fools from *Novaya Zhizn* perhaps discovered among the masses an indifference—to the question of bread, to the prolongation of the war, to and for the peasants?

Signed *N. Lenin*
Written on October 17 (30), 1917
Published in *Rabochy Put*, Nos. 40, 41 and 42,
November 1, 2 and 3 (October 19, 20 and 21)
Published according to newspaper text

MEETING OF THE PETROGRAD SOVIET OF WORKERS' AND SOLDIERS' DEPUTIES

October 25 (November 7), 1917[1]

1

REPORT ON THE TASKS OF THE SOVIET POWER

NEWSPAPER REPORT

Comrades, the workers' and peasants' revolution, about the necessity of which the Bolsheviks have always spoken, has been accomplished.

What is the significance of this workers' and peasants' revolution? Its significance is, first of all, that we shall have a Soviet government, our own organ of power, in which the bourgeoisie will have no share whatsoever. The oppressed masses will themselves create a power. The old state apparatus will be shattered to its foundations and a new administrative apparatus set up in the form of the Soviet organisations.

From now on, a new phase in the history of Russia begins, and this, the third Russian revolution, should in the end lead to the victory of socialism.

One of our urgent tasks is to put an immediate end to the war. It is clear to everybody that in order to end this war, which is closely bound up with the present capitalist system, capital itself must be fought.

We shall be helped in this by the world working-class movement, which is already beginning to develop in Italy, Britain and Germany.

The proposal we make to international democracy for a just and immediate peace will everywhere awaken an ardent response among the international proletarian masses. All the secret treaties[2] must be

[1] The meeting opened at 2.35 p.m. on October 25 (November 7), and heard a report of the Revolutionary Military Committee on the overthrow of the Provisional Government and the triumph of the revolution. Lenin gave a report on the tasks facing Soviet power. The resolution motioned by Lenin (see p. 241) was adopted by an overwhelming majority.

[2] The reference is to secret diplomatic documents, such as the secret treaties

immediately published in order to strengthen the confidence of the proletariat.

Within Russia a huge section of the peasantry have said that they have played long enough with the capitalists, and will now march with the workers. A single decree putting an end to landed proprietorship will win us the confidence of the peasants. The peasants will understand that the salvation of the peasantry lies only in an alliance with the workers. We shall institute genuine workers' control over production.

We have now learned to make a concerted effort. The revolution that has just been accomplished is evidence of this. We possess the strength of mass organisation, which will overcome everything and lead the proletariat to the world revolution.

We must now set about building a proletarian socialist state in Russia.

Long live the world socialist revolution! (*Stormy applause.*)

2
RESOLUTION

The Petrograd Soviet of Workers' and Soldiers' Deputies hails the victorious revolution of the proletariat and the garrison of Petrograd. The Soviet particularly emphasises the solidarity, organisation, discipline and complete unanimity displayed by the masses in this unusually bloodless and unusually successful uprising.

It is the unshakable conviction of the Soviet that the workers' and peasants' government which will be created by the revolution, as a Soviet government, and which will ensure the urban proletariat the

....

concluded by the tsarist and later by the bourgeois Provisional Government of Russia with the governments of Britain, France, Germany, Japan and other imperialist powers. From November 10 (23), 1917, these documents were published in *Pravda* and *Izvestia*, and in December were put out in a series entitled *Collection of Secret Documents from the Archives of the Former Ministry of Foreign Affairs.* Seven volumes were published from December 1917 to February 1918. By publishing the secret treaties, the Soviet Government's revolutionary propaganda struck a great blow for a general democratic peace, without annexations and indemnities, and exposed the imperialist nature of the First World War.

support of the whole mass of the poor peasantry, will firmly advance towards socialism, the only means of saving the country from the untold miseries and horrors of war.

The new workers' and peasants' government will immediately propose a just and democratic peace to all belligerent nations.

It will immediately abolish landed proprietorship and hand over the land to the peasants. It will institute workers' control over the production and distribution of goods and establish national control over the banks, at the same time transforming them into a single state enterprise.

The Petrograd Soviet of Workers' and Soldiers' Deputies calls on all workers and all peasants to support the workers' and peasants' revolution devotedly and with all their energy. The Soviet expresses the conviction that the urban workers, in alliance with the poor peasants, will display strict, comradely discipline and establish the strictest revolutionary order, which is essential for the victory of socialism.

The Soviet is convinced that the proletariat of the West-European countries will help us to achieve a complete and lasting victory for the cause of socialism.

Izvestia No. 207, October 26, 1917
Published according to *Izvestia* text